Praise for the Lust in the Tudor Court series:

"Descriptive, sensuous, and romantic."

—*RT Book Reviews*

"Sensuous and seductive… Sizzles with red-hot passion."

—*The Good, The Bad, and the Unread*

"Brings yesteryear to life while heating up the pages and fascinating readers."

—*Romance Junkies*

"Fifty Shades of Tudor sex!"

—*The Sunday Times*

"The most inevitable literary mash-up of the twenty-first century."

—*The Independent*

"Will sweep you breathlessly along."

—*Star* magazine

"Passionate, compelling, and hot."

—*Victoria Loves Books*

ROSE BRIDE

ELIZABETH MOSS

sourcebooks
casablanca

Published by Sourcebooks Casablanca, an imprint of Sourcebooks, Inc.
P.O. Box 4410, Naperville, Illinois 60567-4410
(630) 961-3900
Fax: (630) 961-2168
www.sourcebooks.com

Originally published in 2014 in Great Britain by Hodder & Stoughton, an
imprint of Hachette UK.

Library of Congress Cataloging-in-Publication Data
Names: Moss, Elizabeth (Novelist), author.
Title: Rose bride / Elizabeth Moss.
Description: First edition. | Naperville, Illinois : Sourcebooks Casablanca, 2016.
   | ©2014 | Series: Lust in the Tudor court ; 3
Identifiers: LCCN 2016006489 (print) | LCCN 2016010163 (ebook)
Subjects: LCSH: England—Court and courtiers—History—16th century—Fiction.
   | Great Britain—History—Henry VIII, 1509-1547—Fiction. | GSAFD:
   Historical fiction. | Erotic fiction.
Classification: LCC PR6112.A497 R67 2016 (print) | LCC PR6112.A497 (ebook)
   | DC 823/.92—dc23
LC record available at http://lccn.loc.gov/2016006489

Printed and bound in the United States of America.
VP 10 9 8 7 6 5 4 3 2 1

est mollis flamma medullas
interea et tacitum vivit sub pectore vulnus.

Meanwhile she burns with love
even in the tender marrow of her bones,
an unspoken hurt
beating beneath her breast.

Virgil, Aeneid, Book IV, lines 66–67

est mollis flamma medullas
interea et tacitum vivit sub pectore vulnus.

Meanwhile she burns with love
even in the tender marrow of her bones,
an unspoken hurt
beating beneath her breast.

Virgil, Aeneid, Book IV, lines 66–67

One

THE KING'S ATTENDANTS MEANT to rape her. And no man at the court of Henry Tudor would dare call them to account for it. For she had offended the king himself, and this was to be her punishment.

As soon as King Henry had drunkenly bellowed, "Out of my sight, vixen!" Margerie had picked up her skirts and run from the Royal Presence.

She had foolishly refused to lie with the king, disgusted by his reeking breath in her face, and her first thought was of escape. If she could only reach the safety of the women's quarters and conceal herself there…

But his men had followed, swift as hounds on her scent, cornering her in one of the royal antechambers. She counted five attackers, fury in their eyes, with a sixth lurking a few feet away, perhaps less eager than the others for a rape.

She did not waste her breath on pleas for mercy. There was little hope of reasoning with them. Nor would a single gentleman among them step forward to save her. The place was hushed, the hour late. Even if she screamed, none would come running. For these were the king's privy quarters, and it was the king's own gentlemen who had come after her.

The king's gentlemen!

Contempt lit her eyes as she glared round at the ring of leering, drunken faces, smelled the wine on their breath, and could not help seeing how one lewd youth had already unfastened his hose in readiness.

"Fie, sirs!" she exclaimed. "Have you no shame, six men to attack one woman?"

"Perhaps you should have considered the consequences before you insulted His Majesty," one of the older noblemen growled.

"I did not mean to insult the king." Her face grew hot with shame. "His Majesty tried to… That is, the king wanted me to… I may be flame-haired but I am no whore, my lord."

But the lord stepped closer, his look threatening. "A whore is precisely what you are, Margerie Croft, and not because of your red hair." He pointed to the floor. "Now lie down for us, Mistress Croft, or we shall drag you down."

She pressed herself against the wall, suddenly terrified. The vast tapestry behind her swayed precariously, the torchlight dazzling her as she searched for some way of escape.

Dear God, do not let them take me by force.

Sir Christopher, who had pursued her in the past to be his mistress, reached out to stroke her cheek, his own voice slurred with drink like the king's. She shrank from his touch.

"Before you lament this punishment, Margerie, remember you have no one to blame but yourself. You refused the king tonight. And for that insult, you must be chastised."

"It was a misunderstanding, that is all," she told him. "His Majesty thinks me a harlot because of my…my error with Lord Wolf. But that was years ago when I was but a girl. I am a respectable woman now."

"And an ungrateful one. Was it not at the king's pleasure that you were allowed to return after your disgrace?" Sir Christopher clicked his tongue disapprovingly. "Yet you will not grant His Majesty a little pleasure in return."

She shivered, knowing nothing she could say would sway these

men from their purpose. They were king's men, and this secret punishment was to be meted out to her on his behalf so His Majesty's honor might be satisfied.

"Look how she stares, how she pants... Those green eyes bright as a cat's. Oh, she is wanton indeed," one of the younger ones whispered over the nobleman's shoulder, his hand cupping a swollen groin. "Hold her down for me. I want to go first, teach her a lesson."

"Now, Marcus," drawled the older man, turning to clap him on the shoulder, "have a little patience, boy. There is plenty to go 'round."

A slender man in a handsome gold-and-silver doublet, still youthful enough to have no beard, stirred at the back of their group. He was the only one frowning with distaste. "Sirs, I must protest. A rape is no good sport. Let us leave this ugly business, gentlemen. The lady is not willing."

"She'll be willing for a shilling!" one cried out in a jest, and several laughed, gazing hotly at her breasts where they spilled over her bodice.

Sir Christopher turned to the young man, his expression venomous. "What is your objection, Lord Munro? The king bade us use this wench as we would, did he not?"

The young lord muttered, "She should be taught to respect the king's bidding. But not in such a way that the court will be enraged."

"Margerie Croft is no virgin," the older man told him impatiently. "All our pricks together will break nothing but her pride. If such sport is not to your taste, Munro, leave us to our man's work and go find some young stag for your bed."

They all turned then, hooting and mocking the young lord, who slunk away into the darkness with a sullen look. While they were busy laughing at the youth, Margerie picked up her skirts and ran out of the antechamber into an unfamiliar side corridor.

"Ho there, the whore has slipped her leash!" one of them exclaimed.

A shout went up and the men pursued her, laughing and whooping drunkenly, pouring out of the antechamber after her like hounds on the trail of a fox.

Her heart was thumping. She had to get away from them. But the corridor was dimly lit and narrow, and she did not know the way. She glanced back and did not see that the ground was about to slope abruptly upward. Tripping over her own feet, Margerie fell heavily to her knees on the stone floor. She hissed, wincing. The men were almost upon her. Her head swung, searching for some way of escape. There was a darkened doorway to her left, its door partially open.

She clambered through the narrow doorway on hands and knees, hampered by her gown. She could see nothing in the darkness, but the floor was dusty and she knocked over a stack of empty wooden crates in her hurry.

"Oh, sweet Lord, I beg of you, no," Margerie cried in horror as the king's men found her again.

They pushed into the chamber, surrounding her with lusty delight.

"But this place is perfect for a rape," one said, holding his flaming torch aloft to reveal some kind of storeroom. "We will not be disturbed here. Shut the door, let us be about it."

She was dragged unceremoniously to her knees, her arms pulled tight behind her back. One of the younger men tumbled the velvet hood from her head so that her mass of red hair burst out, unrestrained.

"By Christ, she's a beauty!" he exclaimed thickly.

Then Sir Christopher was there again, towering above her. He dragged her head back cruelly, and Margerie found herself blinded by the flaming torch held above their heads. She stared up at avid, jeering faces, on her knees in the center of a tight-pressed ring of male bodies, some unlaced, their stiff members jutting toward her.

"Pray let me go," she moaned, but Sir Christopher pressed a

heavy hand over her mouth, silencing her. She felt sick and dizzy. She could smell sweat and horses, his leather glove, the acrid stink of unwashed flesh. There would be no escape from this rape, she realized, and began to tremble.

Suddenly a door creaked open behind them. She could not see the man, but heard a male voice, deep and quiet.

"My lords? May I be of some assistance?"

There was a sudden silence among them. Sir Christopher's hand lifted from her mouth, shifting to his sword hilt instead. Her other attackers fell back, a few glancing at each other over her head, abashed. Nonetheless they did not seem deterred by his presence, only a little embarrassed at having been caught.

"Who are you, sirrah?" the boy demanded arrogantly, his hand falling to his dagger.

"I am Master Elton, court physician," the man replied calmly. "I treated you recently, my lord Shelby, if you recall."

The boy flushed hard. But his hand dropped away from his dagger. "Oh yes, I remember. Well, go about your business, man. This is no affair of yours."

Her heart sank. She had hoped to be saved by this newcomer. But he was no great lord as she had at first thought, only a doctor. He could not stop this rutting pack of dogs.

But to her surprise, Master Elton did not leave. "What have you there, my lords?" he asked, almost idly. "Some dangerous beast you have cornered, perhaps?"

He came forward. His physician's robe did nothing to disguise the long, lean grace of this man's body, his roped belt accentuating narrow hips beneath a muscular chest. Court physician or not, he did not seem afraid of the company and their cruel purpose. He came toward her without hesitation, stepping between the nobles as though oblivious to any threat they might pose.

"A *woman*?"

Sir Christopher swore under his breath. "Leave us. This is the king's business we are about."

The doctor ignored him. His eyebrows rose as he studied her face, then he glanced about at them. "His Majesty ordered you to attack this defenseless female?"

Nobody replied. His hand reached for hers, and they did not stop him.

"Madam?"

Dazed by this unexpected change in her fortune, Margerie did not stop to think. She looked up at him gratefully, setting her hand in his. She came to her feet in response to his pull, then tried to draw back her hand.

His fingers tightened on hers, refusing to let go.

Her startled gaze shot to his face. She found herself staring into dark eyes that met hers intently. There was a shadow in his face that called to her, as though this man understood hurt and despair for he had known them himself. His hair was dark too, curled at his temples, thick locks falling almost to his shoulders.

Master Elton spoke as though they were alone together, his voice deep and rich, stirring her in some unfathomable way. "I must lock up the storage room," he told her, "but then I beg you will permit me to escort you back to your chamber. The hour is late and a lady should not be wandering the palace corridors unaccompanied."

There was a growl of dissent from the watching nobles. Yet to her astonishment none of them challenged the doctor's right to remove her. Margerie gazed round at them. At any moment she feared to be seized again, and this upstart doctor be dismissed with the threat of a whipping.

Slowly she groped after the truth, though it seemed impossible. These lords were wary of him. Yet how was it that a mere physician could have power over men as influential and highborn as these?

Master Elton was still holding her hand, his strong fingers locked intimately with hers. When she did not reply, he raised his eyebrows, watching her with those dark, intelligent eyes that seemed to know precisely what she was thinking—and feeling.

She found her courage again, and with it her voice. "I…I thank you, sir."

"My lords, I must beg your pardon for interrupting your sport," he said, turning to her attackers. "But this lady seems uncomfortable in your company."

Master Elton drew her out from their silent circle, a look of irony on his face. He bowed to Sir Christopher as the knight shifted to block his way.

"You look *well*, Sir Christopher. I am glad."

Sir Christopher's mouth tightened, as though that soft emphasis had conveyed some special meaning to him. He glared at the doctor sourly. They were about the same height and build, she realized, though the knight was perhaps a shade taller. For a moment the atmosphere was tense in the narrow space, and she feared for her savior.

Then the knight shrugged and stepped aside, letting them pass.

"You may go on your way, physician, and take this creature with you," Sir Christopher said. His gaze flicked over her with contempt. "No man wants soiled goods anyway. Not even for sport."

Without another word, the physician led her away into the small gloomy chamber from which he had emerged, taking a moment to bar the door behind him in case the king's men changed their minds.

She looked about the room. There was a high table crowded with bottles and physicians' instruments, and a small leather-bound volume lying open beside a candle as though he had been reading before he was disturbed. A doctor's workshop, Margerie thought, glancing at more bottles arranged in a shadowy alcove. She found herself breathing more easily, for she had only narrowly escaped harm.

Glancing at the open page of the book, she saw it was not a doctor's journal with a list of medicaments, as she had at first assumed.

It was poetry. In Latin.

Master Elton turned from the door and fixed her with a hard look. His casual air had dropped away. "Do you have a death wish, madam?"

Margerie flushed angrily. "I beg your pardon?"

The physician looked her up and down assessingly, taking in every detail of her flushed cheeks and unbound mass of red hair, then the fine silk gown, her thin-soled leather pumps showing beneath. The bodice sat tight about her breasts, for she had been a girl and narrower in the chest when she last wore it at court, and she saw his gaze linger on the creamy flesh there.

No doubt he was wondering if she was a courtesan. Perhaps even considering if he could afford her services on a physician's wage. She was used to such unpleasant conversations. But for some reason the thought of this man propositioning her left a bitter taste in her mouth.

"I do not recall seeing you at court before," he commented, "so I must assume your foolishness tonight was the result of inexperience rather than a wanton desire to be ravished by those courtiers."

Her lips tightened at this insult. She wanted to speak her mind, tell him exactly what she thought of his misinterpretation of tonight's events. But she kept silent. This man had just saved her from what would undeniably have been a rape.

He raised dark eyebrows at her silence. "Will you give me your name?"

"Margerie Croft."

His eyes narrowed on her face, suddenly fixed and intent. Heat entered her cheeks as she realized her name was known to him. She ought not to be surprised. Everyone at court knew of Margerie Croft, the infamous whore who had taken young Wolf to her bed, then run off to France with another nobleman, an infirm youth who had died without marrying her, leaving Margerie to earn enough for her passage back to England—as a whore, it was whispered by some.

Her eyes met his in sudden anger. Yes, her history was infamous, she thought fiercely. But she was no whore. And never had been one. She had never spoken of those days to anyone, allowing the world to slander her as they wished rather than lower herself to some paltry self-defense. She had her pride.

"Mistress Croft," he said softly, "my name is Master Elton. Do you have any idea how dangerous it was to allow yourself to be alone with those men?"

"You think I *allowed* that to happen, Master Elton? I was summoned by King Henry tonight so he could..." She faltered, seeing the look in his eyes. Caution entered her tone as she finished lamely, "So he could speak with me."

"I see." But his voice had grown cold. She could guess what he was thinking. "And afterward?"

"Afterward," she repeated, shuddering as she remembered what had followed her abortive interview with His Majesty, "they cornered me in one of the royal antechambers. I tried to escape, but they were determined to..."

"Make your better acquaintance?" he suggested.

"Punish me." Margerie lifted her gaze to his, meeting it unflinchingly. "I had displeased the king, you see. So they had little fear of reprisals, whatever they might choose to do to me."

"You seem curiously unmoved by that prospect."

"Merely resigned to my fate. Men rape women. It is the way of the world."

Something flickered in that level stare. Contempt? Her temper rose. "Sir?"

Turning to a nearby shelf, the doctor began to pack away a row of thin-necked bottles into a cloth bag, checking each stopper and label as he did so, his movements careful and precise.

"No doubt you find me impertinent, mistress?"

She could not deny it.

"Forgive me." He glanced over his shoulder at her, his smile thin. "But your story is, you must admit, a little incredible. What was your crime tonight against His Majesty?"

"That is my business."

"Do you remain silent for your own sake or mine? I assure you that I have no intention of becoming embroiled in this affair. But you must know the king's ways, as all the world does. Perhaps if you had taken some respectable female companion with you to His Majesty…"

She glared at him, nettled by the suggestion that she was to blame, and he shrugged, continuing to pack away his bottles.

"I gave you my name, sir," she pointed out. "I am Margerie Croft. Or are you alone at this court in not knowing my reputation?"

"I know your reputation, mistress."

Margerie raised her brows in a delicate question as he turned to face her, but the doctor did not elaborate. His stare moved instead from her face to her breasts, small but made more prominent by the tight silk bodice, then her narrow waist and hips, for her height had kept her figure girlishly slender since childhood.

She felt the touch of his gaze on her body as a physical thing, as though he had stroked her with a long cool finger, and her pulse raced, suddenly wild. Her cheeks began to burn. "You dare to judge me, sir?"

"I have said nothing, madam."

"Your eyes speak for you."

Master Elton came close, still gazing on her body as though imagining how she would look naked. That look made her tremble.

"Do they?"

His voice was curt. She had the impression of tremendous energy held in check, his whole being focused on her in the most disconcerting way. He could not be much older than her, perhaps eight and twenty years of age. Certainly Master Elton was not past thirty. Yet he had the poise and authority of a much older man.

"You are indeed a beautiful woman," Master Elton agreed. "Your form stirs a man to lust, and I am a man like any other. But I am not convinced that men must always act upon their desires, especially when restraint would prove the better course. Man's control over his baser instincts is what separates him from the beasts."

"I thought it was our ability to think that makes us superior to the animal kingdom."

"Oh, not superior." There was a drawl in his voice now, his mouth twisting as the dark gaze lifted to her face. "I cannot allow those men who would have raped you to be superior to a beast in any way."

She was taken aback by his casual insolence toward such powerful men. "They were afraid of you, I think," she said impulsively. "Why?"

He raised his eyebrows. "I saw no fear in them. I am but a doctor. Why should the king's men fear me?"

"I do not know, sir. That is why I asked."

Her height meant they stood as equals, gazing into each other's eyes without speaking. She recalled how her body had responded to the touch of his hand, her heart racing as though in fear for her life, and wondered at it.

Since her girlhood she had been left unmoved by the lustful looks and caresses of men who wished to bed her, and had eventually come to consider herself frigid, a creature without passion. Indeed, Lord Wolf—then an untitled youth—had written as much to her after she fled their illicit night together, blaming her for not responding to his lovemaking.

You must have ice water in your veins, Margerie Croft, not to have been moved by the heat of my desire.

She had not received that letter for several years, until she had returned from France to her grandfather's home. Even now though, she felt again the shame that had risen in her at Wolf's insults.

To be passionless, to be cold at heart… These were crimes against a woman's nature, and she knew it. Yet the merest touch of Master Elton's hand had left her shocked and unsettled. How was this doctor so different from the other men who had tried to seduce her?

She shivered, her gaze dropping.

It was painful to meet those intelligent eyes and guess what Master Elton must be thinking. Her infamous seduction all those years ago meant she was too well known as a wanton for him to hold any other view of her character. And if she continued to look so boldly at this man, he would think she wished to warm his bed tonight, instead of the king's.

"You asked to escort me back to my chamber," she said coolly. "Will you hold to that promise, sir?"

"I have to take these medicaments back to my rooms. I will walk with you to your chamber first."

"Are these not your quarters?"

"No, I lodge in one of the towers. The physicians only use this room when we are summoned to attend His Majesty, as we were earlier tonight."

That surprised her. "You attended the king tonight?"

"Yes."

"For what purpose?"

"I cannot discuss it with you, mistress. I am bound by a sacred oath to keep such matters secret." Master Elton closed his book of Latin poetry, marking the page with a strip of black silk, and placed it in the cloth bag with his medicaments. Then he took up his bag, and gestured her to the door. "It's late, and the courtiers who attacked you should have gone by now. Shall we go?"

She hesitated, studying her rescuer in a moment of indecision. His features were a shade too strong to be classically attractive, his nose aquiline, his mouth straight and unrelenting, like the hard jut of his chin. His dark hair curled under the physician's cap, not cut short like most courtiers' but long enough to brush his broad shoulders. She thought it gave him a very European look, dangerously unconventional. His eyes were impenetrably dark too, deep-set and heavy-lidded, watching her with a hint of the same restless interest she felt for him.

She ought not to find such a man pleasing to look upon. Yet she could not seem to stop staring… There was a sensuality about him that made her heart beat faster, her body aware of his in a way she had never been with any man before. Indeed, she could not help wondering what it would feel like to lie beneath that lean body, to have his mouth on hers, to accept him into her body as she had once accepted Wolf.

A night in Master Elton's bed would be very different from those abortive hours she had spent with Wolf. For she had taken Wolf to her bed on the orders of her mother, whose obsession with her advancement at court had known no limits, and not because she felt any desire for the nobleman.

With Master Elton though, it would be hard to say no if the doctor wished to take his pleasure with her. And this time she would have no virginity to lose.

"Yes," she managed, belatedly realizing that he was still waiting for her response. "Forgive me."

"Mistress Croft, you have done nothing that needs to be forgiven," Master Elton murmured, a faint smile on his lips as he bent to blow out the candle. "The same may not be true for the rest of us, however."

Her breath caught as the room was plunged into smoking,

velvety darkness. And she was glad he could not see her face. For his smile had sent a jolt of heat to her belly and thighs, her whole body suddenly alight with desire.

The darkness brought illumination. He wanted her. And she wanted him. That was what she was feeling.

Lust.

Groping her way into the torchlit corridor afterward, Margerie did not dare look at him again, caught in the grip of some sexual urge so strong she was left breathless and trembling, shocked by the visceral nature of her response.

Don't show him how you feel, she told herself sternly. He was a man, and she was alone with him. Had she no sense of self-preservation whatsoever?

That night, lying in bed in the dark, cramped quarters she shared with the other women of the royal wardrobe, Margerie felt again that sweet, languorous heat burning in her body and secretly wished she had taken advantage of the darkness.

She could have lived up to her reputation for once, grasped the doctor's shoulders and pressed her mouth wantonly against his. Something told her Master Elton would not have pushed her away.

Two

HIS COCK SO HARD it could have been made of stone, Virgil Elton shifted uncomfortably as he woke, then rolled onto his side. His dream had fled before he could fully remember it, but he knew it had concerned a willowy redhead with wicked green eyes and skin pale as alabaster. He stroked himself slowly, staring at the gray strip of light through the shutters that heralded another dawn.

Margerie Croft had done this to him.

She was a courtesan, of course. Everyone knew that. A lady of great beauty, but no virtue. He had heard stories of Margerie Croft's sexual exploits, the gossip circulating for days after her return to court. Not guilty of a single indiscretion, something a man in lust might overlook on his way to her bed, but a towering multitude of sins. Margerie had slept with this lord and that gentleman, she had ridden half the French court, her body was open to any man with enough gold in his purse to satisfy her greed…

And Virgil had been half-inclined to dismiss the gossip as malicious nonsense, until he had met her eyes last night. Slanting green eyes, bright as sin and thrice as inviting. Though with an edge of innocence to belie her wanton reputation, to make him wish to get Margerie Croft alone and show her the private side of his nature, the face that was never revealed to anyone.

She was achingly beautiful. A full-lipped sensual mouth that made a man's cock stiffen with need. High cheekbones, her face pale and elven in its otherworldliness. Those provocative eyes. And a cloud of gathered red hair, so soft and intense in its rich color, begging to be allowed to hang loose to her waist where he could play with it all day, twisting it between his fingers or draping it over her white shoulders while they made love.

Love? Virgil checked himself, smiling grimly as his cock twitched in his fist. Lust, more like.

He could not help this animal response. Her body, so tall and slender, so perfectly female, made the lust rise in him like sap in a fresh-cut branch. It had been all he could do last night, finding himself alone with her in a locked room, not to tear off her silken gown and feast on the immaculate white skin that he knew must lie beneath. But those green eyes searching his face, the way she had bitten her lip with delicacy and a sudden unexpected vulnerability, had given him cause to check.

Why had those courtiers chosen to harry Margerie Croft so cruelly? Had she refused the king's attentions? If so, she was a very brave woman. But foolish too, for His Majesty was not a forgiving man—especially where his bed was concerned.

He could never behave as violently with Margerie as those men who would have raped her. The impulse lay within him to be cruel, to push the woman to her knees and force her to pleasure him. He knew it. Yet he had control of himself. Long might that control remain.

He swung his legs out of bed and stretched, pushing sleep away. It was still early and the air was sharp. He reached for his robe, willing his persistent erection to subside. He had no time to pleasure himself to a climax. The day was already beginning and he had work to do.

Margerie Croft was not a whore. Of that he was sure. He had known plenty of whores, and she lacked their easy ways. But she was no virgin either. A courtesan, then. A sexually available woman, but discreet enough to remain a lady while bedding men of her choice.

"I am going to bed her," he promised the air, then laughed at his own arrogance.

What chance would he, a mere doctor, have with such a delicious and discerning courtesan?

They were afraid of you, she had remarked, and his lie had been swift, for he preferred to deny his power. Of course the king's men were wary of him. Not only did he hold their most embarrassing secrets in his hand, but he held something even more precious. *Influence.* His godfather, Sir John Skelton, had been a poet and one of the king's favorite tutors as a child—and the sole reason Virgil was now a physician at the royal court. Some debts were never forgotten, and His Majesty had a reputation for rewarding his most loyal servants—so long as they were not foolish enough to displease him.

The king had chosen to favor him and advance his career at court. It could not be denied. Where there was kingly favor, there was also power. And it was a fool who did not fear a powerful man.

His power only extended so far though, Virgil thought drily. It was not true power, but an invisible cloak lent him by the king while he was in favor. To lose the king's favor would be the work of a moment, a momentary lapse in judgment, the wrong word in the wrong ear...

A knock at his chamber door surprised him. It could not be his boy, who slept outside, for he would simply have entered without knocking, bringing fresh water for his ablutions or a newly laundered robe for the day's work.

"Come in," Virgil called out, frowning, then shoved a hand through his unruly hair, suddenly aware that he was not yet presentable.

It was Master Greene, one of the king's chief physicians, a heavy-jowled man in his fiftieth year. Soberly suited and booted, the physician seemed irritated to find Virgil still dressing. No doubt he had risen and been dressed before dawn.

"Master Elton, you must dress—and quickly too. We are summoned at once to attend His Majesty." He glanced at Virgil's uncombed hair, then the rumpled bedclothes, his disapproval palpable.

"Call your servant, sir, and make haste to be ready. The king's leg troubles him again and his temper is uneven."

"Then you had best go without me, Master Greene, and not keep His Majesty waiting any longer. I will follow as soon as I am dressed."

"Make sure you do."

Virgil bowed, and Master Greene departed without so much as a nod of his head. So much for courtesy. But no doubt Master Greene feared to be late. Indeed, everyone was afraid of the king these days. And small wonder, for a sovereign who could put his queen on trial for adultery was not a man who would forgive even the slightest flaw in his servants.

Almost at once, his serving boy, Ned, appeared in the doorway, yawning and sleepy-eyed himself, his fair hair tousled. "Forgive me, master. I did not hear Master Greene until he was at the door. Should I fetch fresh water?"

He shook his head. "I'll make do with last night's, Ned. But a clean robe would be good."

"Aye, sir."

The boy scurried away about his business and Virgil threw open the shutters to let the cool daylight in.

As he combed his hair, he noticed the folded and sealed paper lying on his table, addressed to him. It must have arrived yesterday while he was away from his quarters, and he had not seen it on retiring last night. But then he had been both fatigued and aroused when he came to bed, his head confused with thoughts of lust and longing he could not assuage.

Frowning, Virgil picked it up and studied the handwriting.

"Christina," he murmured, then laid the letter down again with an aching heart. Much as he enjoyed hearing from his betrothed, whom he had known since she was a child, his pleasure was always tainted by memories of home.

Later, he thought. *I will read her letter later.*

—᠆ᨆ—

"But what causes this failure?" the king demanded.

His angry gaze roved from Master Greene's apologetic countenance to Master Bellamy's and thence to Virgil's face.

"I was wont to feel these urges every morning as a younger man," he continued, "and act upon them too. Now I can scarcely perform when faced with a comely wench. I feel the pricking of desire when we dance or talk in the court, but once we are alone together, my ardor fails me. What causes this, and how can it be treated?"

"Sire," Master Greene began, carefully not looking at the king, "it is common among men of your age to feel a certain lessening of potency. My belief is that you should be bled. Male impotency is almost always the result of an imbalance of the humors that might respond to—"

"Silence, fool!" Still in his nightshirt, his slippered feet set on a red velvet footrest, King Henry slammed his hand down on the arm of his chair, and the dark wood floorboards of his bedchamber shook. "I will not be bled, you hear me? Little good it did for my leg when I was injured in that fall back in January. The wound still ails me today, though we are well into spring." He almost snarled at them. "Come, you are the best doctors in England, or so one would assume. What else can be done?"

"The herbal remedies we prepared for Your Majesty," Master Bellamy offered. "Are you not still taking them, sire?"

"I still take them on occasion," the king muttered, "but they no longer give me added strength. I drank one last night and felt nothing." His face fell into grim lines. "Though perhaps that was as well, for the wench I had summoned was not to my liking in the end."

Margerie Croft.

"Your Majesty," Virgil murmured, taking advantage of the

silence that had fallen in the Royal Bedchamber, "if you would permit me to present an alternative treatment…"

"Speak."

"I have read of a powerful infusion of exotic herbs and spices, much used in the Orient to combat problems such as these. It might take a while to procure all the ingredients, Your Majesty, but I will work in haste to prepare this infusion for you if you desire it."

Master Bellamy looked horrified. "Ask His Majesty to drink an untried draft of foreign origin? Absolutely not."

The chief physician agreed with this. "It would be unsafe, Your Majesty, to take any infusion we have not previously tested to ensure its safety. What if it was poisonous?"

"Or caused some unpleasant rash or sickness? I have heard these Oriental methods are suspect and highly dangerous if not administered with extreme care," Master Bellamy added, shaking his head at Virgil. "They are not fit for Englishmen."

King Henry sat looking at them, his eyes glacial. "I need an heir to my throne, gentlemen. I must be restored to full health. Is there no other way?"

Virgil thought for a moment. It was true, after all, that he had never used that infusion on a patient before. And though he felt sure it must be safe, else it would not be so widely used in the East, the wisest course would be to test the draft for several weeks before allowing the king to drink it. For even the slightest hint of sickness about the king's person following its prescription could risk his head on the block.

"If I were to prepare and take this Oriental draft myself, Master Greene," he suggested softly, "then observe its effects on my body over the course of several weeks, would that lay your fears to rest?"

The king's eyes flashed in appreciation. "Aye, that would answer. Do it. And bring me frequent reports of your findings, to satisfy these gentlemen that I will survive your exotic draft."

Virgil bowed, and slipped discreetly away before the chief physician could chide him further for suggesting a foreign remedy to the king. It could prove difficult to obtain some of the more unusual ingredients, he thought—but he held great hopes that the Oriental draft would prove efficacious if properly prepared and administered, and bring him into even greater prominence at court.

Nor was his hope groundless. For he had read of miracle cures for ordinary men long impotent, suddenly raised to impressive feats of sexual prowess after only a few drafts of that mixture.

Passing one of the women's day chambers on his way back to his workshop, he glanced inside, hearing female laughter, and saw Margerie Croft herself seated in the sunshine, her sewing forgotten in her lap as she enjoyed a jest with another woman.

Her head turned as he paused in the open doorway, and for an instant their eyes met.

Margerie's laughter died abruptly, and her eyes widened. A slight flush entered her cheeks and her lips parted as though she were breathing more rapidly.

He almost smiled at this show of weakness, then was disconcerted to feel the same physical reaction himself. His eyes were fixed on her, his heart beating more quickly, his cock already stiff under the thick folds of his robe. It was almost animalistic, as though his body could not be near hers without experiencing an urge to mate.

Then she bent over her sewing again, and the woman beside her glanced across at him curiously. Virgil recognized her companion as Mistress Langley, wife to one of the king's clerks, a woman with curves generous enough to please any man—and a smile to match.

Master Langley had a short temper, so men were careful not to call his wife a whore in front of him. But it was whispered that Kate Langley had bedded many of the nobles at court, including the king himself, and most with the tacit permission of her husband. If Margerie did not wish to draw further male attention to herself, spending time with a woman of Kate Langley's reputation was unwise. Though he doubted that Margerie would care for such advice, Virgil thought drily.

He bowed to both women, fighting to regain his composure, then continued through the corridors and stairways of the sprawling palace to his workshop. But soon he fell to remembering the delicate swell of her breasts, the narrow waist and hips that made her almost boyish in form, and began to wonder if Margerie Croft would agree to help with his experiment.

For if he took the Oriental draft, and it worked, he would need to be sure of its effect on a man's stamina as well as his ability to become aroused.

Margerie Croft was no virgin, her reputation already lost, so why not? It would be a dangerous choice though to bed a woman who had refused a chance to be the king's bed partner.

If His Majesty should ever hear of it…

Virgil unlocked his workshop and stood at the open window slit, looking down on the Thames below. The wind blew his hair into disarray, but he smiled, his mind pleasantly engaged in imagining himself in bed with Margerie.

He could hardly ask any other woman at court to bed him, except perhaps her companion, Kate Langley. Any respectable woman would refuse him, and rightly so. Nor did he wish to seek out a common whore to relieve his arousal.

And Margerie was very beautiful.

He stared out at the sun dancing on the river, thinking of her sharp green eyes, and his heart sank.

This train of thought was pure folly. He had seen desire in her face last night when they were together, and observed the flush in her cheeks when she saw him again today. But desire alone did not make a woman wanton, else every lady at court would be a whore. And it might as easily have been a sense of shame that caused her to blush. He had witnessed her humiliation at the hands of those noblemen, after all, and might be afraid he would spread that story too about the court.

He should forget her. Bed a whore if he could not shake this desire. It would take more than an impressive drug-induced erection to get Margerie Croft into bed anyway.

Besides, even if he did succeed in bedding her, heaven help him if news of his debauchery reached Christina's ears.

Lying in bed that evening, he took up the letter from Christina and broke the seal.

His betrothed.

It was a strange and unsettling thought. Yet one he ought to have become used to by now, for the two had been promised to each other for years, having grown up as neighbors.

Odd that he had never questioned it before now.

He sat on his bed, unrolled the parchment, and cast an eye down the familiar slanting scrawl of her hand. The letter was in Latin, like all her letters. It had begun as a game between them, a scholarly exercise as well as a competition. Now it was a habit, but a comfortable one.

He smiled, translating as he read.

Virgilio Christina salutem

Life is so dull here without your company, my dearest Virgil. I miss our time together, reading from the Latin poets and talking of medicine and philosophy. Do you miss me too?

My health is much improved this past year, and I have mentioned our marriage again to my uncle. He is adamant it will never take place while he is alive, of course. He says I am too sick to be a bride, and at eight and twenty years of age you are too old to be my husband. I take comfort then that he is quite old himself, and infirm, and eats rich suppers that give him gout. It would be wicked to pray for his death, but one may hope, surely?

When will you come home to see me, Virgilius? I long for you to kiss my hand as you always do, so gallantly. You see, I am not such a child as you think me. Indeed I shall soon be three and twenty. But I shall be patient. I know your work keeps you at court.

Has the king made a son on his new paramour yet? We are all agog at the news that she is not as comely as Queen Anne. Why choose a woman with a face like a thistle when he could have any virgin in the land for his next bride?

Send me gossip. And your love.
Bene vale

Virgil reread her letter, frowning slightly over the phrases that had disturbed him. Christina must have been in a wild mood when she wrote this. Did she not understand how easily these letters could be intercepted?

He checked the wax seal. Apart from his own clean break, it did not appear to have been tampered with. He would have to respond at once. Yet how to warn her to be more discreet in the future without risking suspicion that he was disloyal to the king? And there was also the question of their marriage, which Christina had not mentioned in several years.

She must be aware of the difficulties that would lie ahead if they set a date for their wedding. Or had Christina chosen to close her eyes to the truth? She was not strong and he did not wish to risk hurting her feelings.

Virgil stood, carefully setting aside her letter. With his belt dagger he cut out a meager rectangle of parchment from the roll on his desk, for the stuff was expensive and he could not spare much for letter-writing.

Then he sharpened his quill, dipped it into his inkwell, and began to write in neat, small letters, composing in Latin as he went. He knew it amused Christina to parse out the more difficult Latin phrases, and the poor girl had little else in her life to entertain her.

Three

MARGERIE HEARD SHOUTS FROM the darkening courtyard below just as the dancing master began instructing the ladies in the latest French dance.

Jane Seymour, circling opposite her and clad lavishly in a heavy foreskirt of yellow silk, an elegant gold net encasing her hair, stopped dancing. Her rounded chin rose, a frown knitting her brows together. She glanced across at the window and shivered.

"Draw those shutters across," Mistress Seymour said to nobody in particular, then snapped her fingers for one of the young maids of honor to fetch her fur-trimmed mantle. "Tomorrow I will request a dancing chamber that does not give onto this courtyard. We should not have our practice disturbed by every new arrival at court."

The older ladies glanced at each other, but said nothing. Since the arrest of Queen Anne, Mistress Seymour's demeanor had changed from that of a timid country mouse to a more confident lady of the court. Nor did anyone dare to question this startling transformation. For the whisper had long since gone about that His Majesty had settled on Jane Seymour for his next bride. Which meant Anne's divorce or death. The latter seemed more likely now, the way the accusations against her had been mounting in vehemence.

Hurrying across the chamber, Margerie reached up to close the wooden shutters. As she did so, she glanced idly down and saw an array of carts and horses drawn up in the torchlit courtyard below. New arrivals, indeed.

Many courtiers long-absent from court had been arriving over the past few days, responding with alacrity to their summons. Everyone knew it was because Henry wished the whole court to be present when he remarried. Yet no one dared discuss it openly, not least because of the king's uncertain temper these days. Besides, as the Greeks would say, why look a gift horse in the mouth?

His Majesty was entertaining his courtiers with the most extravagant masques and plays, with dancing and feasting in the Great Hall, and even wild debauched orgies that it was rumored went on all night in secret rooms, as though to celebrate the king's forthcoming nuptials before Queen Anne was even condemned.

But this was no ordinary arrival, she realized. Margerie stiffened in shock as a man, his cloak thrown back over one shoulder, plainly dressed but with a great ring glittering on one gloved finger, dismounted and limped across to help his lady down from a covered litter. Her breath caught sharp in her throat.

Lord Wolf!

And the woman in the litter must be Eloise, his new bride. The former lady-in-waiting to the queen had been recalled to court for questioning over the recent accusations against Her Majesty.

Her eyes widened.

Suddenly trembling, she steadied herself against the windowsill. She had meant to look away as soon as she recognized him, but instead found herself staring down at Wolf in horrified fascination. A young, golden-haired beauty was descending from the litter, head held high as she took Wolf's hand, turning at once to survey the palace.

Margerie had heard of Eloise Tyrell's beauty—the girl had caught the eye of the king himself, rumor had it, before Wolf claimed her for his own—so she was not surprised by the elegance of this young bride, clad in a dark cloak for traveling, an occasional flash of rich blue skirts beneath, her pale face utterly composed.

So this was Lady Wolf. The woman she might have become. Wolf's bride. His lover and his new baroness.

She did not regret rejecting his offer of marriage. They would never have been happy together. But she did regret throwing away her reputation overnight. Fear of an enforced marriage had led to her wild flight to France, a flight that had brought down ruin on her head. She had spoiled her chance of a respectable marriage by giving herself to Wolf, then abruptly changing her mind. And *that* was a consequence she did regret, with all her heart.

Her hand clenched into a fist against the wooden shutter, Margerie stared down, trying to gauge their happiness as a couple. Wolf hardly took his eyes off his new wife; they might as well have been alone in the courtyard. But Eloise looked calm, her gait steady, giving nothing away as she allowed her husband to lead her inside the palace.

Certainly the young bride did not seem frightened at the prospect of being questioned about the queen. Though Eloise Tyrell had been several years at court before Wolf took her for his wife, so it was possible she had learned how to dissemble and conceal her true feelings.

"What is it?" her friend Kate asked, suddenly close, glancing over her shoulder. The others had started dancing again, the dancing master calling out instructions while the musicians played. "Who are you looking at below?"

She turned to Mistress Langley, willing her heart to be steady, her face not to betray her anxiety. But of course her friend saw at once that something was amiss, and stared past her into the courtyard.

"Oh." A shadow came into Kate's face. "Him."

"Hush, say nothing."

"My dear friend," Kate whispered, squeezing her hand. Her sympathetic gaze searched her face. "You are pale. Pray come away from the window. And do not look so shocked, someone will notice." When Margerie failed to move, she made a sharp tutting noise under her breath. "Dearest, you knew he would come back eventually, for his wife was rumored to be close to the queen."

"I knew, yes," she managed unevenly, and stumbled away from the window as Kate reached up to close the shutters. "But knowing he would come back to court is not the same as being prepared to see him."

The music had stopped again. Mistress Seymour was remonstrating with the dancing instructor over some problem, but mildly, for the king's new paramour was not a woman to raise her voice.

Kate leaned in close, frowning at her. "But it must be ten years since he... You are not still afraid of Wolf, surely?"

Margerie shivered. "No," she insisted, then carefully corrected herself, not wanting to lie to her friend. "I don't know. Maybe. I still dream of him some nights. It was such a terrible error. Though it matters little now: his lordship has married and can trouble me no more."

"That error was your mother's doing, Margerie. You should not blame yourself. You were little better than a child, and she coerced you to lie with him."

"I was old enough to be bedded, and to understand the choice I was making," she reminded Kate sadly. "Wolf was young too. My mother thought...she thought we would suit."

"You mean she wanted to see her daughter marry into the nobility."

"We should not speak ill of the dead." Margerie crossed herself. "Bad enough I lost my mother to the plague when I was still in France. I never saw her face again after I left court. Never had a chance to beg her forgiveness for running away."

"You begged your father's though, and he would not give it," Kate said sharply. "You told me he died of a broken heart after your mother's death, but I have my own thoughts on that. If he had allowed you to come home, your father might still be alive and enjoying the comfort of your company. A man in his middle age soon withers without a female to dote on him. He should have been more forgiving; then God might have forgiven *him* for abandoning his daughter."

Jane Seymour was staring at them across the dancing chamber. Her quiet voice was authoritative, as though she already felt the weight of a crown on her head. "What is the matter you discuss so earnestly, ladies? Is one of you unwell that you cannot join the rest of us in learning this dance?"

"No, Mistress Seymour," Margerie said at once, and hurried to take her place in the row of ladies waiting to dance, holding out her hand to Kate as they both slipped into line.

It was a much-coveted privilege to be allowed to learn these dances alongside the foremost ladies of the land, and she did not want her only friend to get into trouble through her foolish behavior.

"You must forgive me, Mistress Seymour," she added, not quite lifting her eyes to Jane's watchful face, and pinned an apologetic smile to her lips. "It was a moment's dizziness. I am well again now."

Lord Wolf was a man, that was all. He had pursued her once as the Devil would pursue a soul that had been promised to him. But she had shrugged off that madness long ago. Wolf was married now and seemed intent on his new bride. There was no reason to be afraid of him.

There were other men at court she should fear more.

—◦◦◦—

Margerie became aware that it was dark and someone was shaking her violently.

"Wake up!" a voice hissed urgently in her ear. "Margerie, if you love me, wake up!"

A torch came close, dispelling the darkness and with it the dreams that had been haunting her all night. Its flames burned brightly above her head, acrid and smoking.

Slowly, her eyes widened, focusing on the face before her. Where was she? What had happened?

The last thing she remembered was falling asleep in the stuffy warmth of the women's chamber, listening to the snores of those sleeping around her. Now she was on her feet and shivering, yet it was still night and she could not recall having left her bed.

"Kate?"

"Thank God," her friend breathed, a look of relief on her face. Then she turned to the tight huddle of women about them, all clad in nightshifts and caps, staring at Margerie by the light of a flickering torch as though she were mad. "As you can see, Mistress Croft is awake now, so you may all go back to bed. Go, I will tend her."

"We do not answer to you, Mistress Langley," one of the women said sourly, looking her up and down in a contemptuous manner. It was Mistress Lew, one of the chief seamstresses to the royal wardrobe and thrice widowed before she was even forty years of age. "I wish to ask this silly fool what she was thinking, frightening us out of our wits like that."

"And how exactly did she frighten you, Mistress Lew?" Kate demanded.

"Why, screaming so we thought she was murdered, then moaning and stumbling about in the darkness like a soul in torment."

"Aye," said another of the seamstresses, plump Mistress Carew, nudging closer to examine Margerie with round-eyed curiosity, "and refusing to answer to her name, though her eyes were open and she seemed awake. Why would any decent woman do that?"

Margerie frowned at these descriptions, shaking her head. "I was...*what*?" She stared from one woman's face to another. Her voice grew husky. "I pray you forgive me, ladies, I have no memory of these events."

"She lies!" one of the younger exclaimed, then turned back to her bed. "And she ought to be whipped for disturbing our peace at such an hour."

"Come, let us all get back to sleep," said Mistress Lew, her thin lips pursed. "It will be dawn soon."

Margerie tried to explain again that she could not remember what she had done, stuttering a little in her anxiety, but the women were already moving away, back to the warmth of their mattresses. Then someone carried the torch back outside, replacing it in its high sconce in the corridor. The chamber was left in smoky darkness, only a thin and flickering stream of light falling across the women's beds from the open door.

"Come with me," Kate muttered, sounding angry, and led Margerie out of the women's chamber.

Alone together in the smoky corridor, Kate took her by the shoulders and peered closely into her face. "Truly, you remember nothing?"

"Not a moment."

"When they could not rouse you, Mistress Lew sent for me, knowing us to be fast friends. I took it for a jest at first, and was angry myself, for I had only just climbed into bed with my husband. But then I saw you pacing up and down, muttering and wringing your hands, and knew it was no trick. I thought you must be bewitched—or else sick. So I sent one of the guards to fetch a physician."

"*A physician?*"

"I was afraid for you, Margerie. What else could I have done?"

Margerie stared at her friend, beginning to feel sick indeed at the thought of all the fuss she had caused. "The last thing I remember is closing my eyes in bed. Now you say I was wandering in my sleep? Talking to myself? My mother used to say I wandered in my sleep as a child, yet I never had any memory of doing so. What is happening to me?"

"We will wait for the doctor and see what he says." Kate laid a hand on her forehead. "You are not feverish though. Do you feel unwell?"

"Perhaps. I cannot tell." Margerie wrapped her arms about herself, shivering. "Which doctor did you call?"

"Whichever would answer the summons."

She bit her lip. "I am so cold."

"Well, that is no surprise," Kate commented impatiently, rubbing up and down her arms to warm them, "for you are clad in nothing but your shift."

Suddenly aware of her lack of decent covering, Margerie glanced down at the thin material clinging to her breasts and belly. She wore nothing beneath, and could only imagine how she would appear to any respectable gentleman, standing out here in the corridor in such scanty attire, her red hair loose and uncovered.

"Let me fetch a robe," she muttered, turning away, but it was too late.

Torchlight suddenly danced on the walls, long shadows leaping and shifting. She heard brisk footsteps along the corridor, and saw the guard returning with the physician.

Margerie shrank back into the shadows as the men approached, wishing she was as decorously robed and slippered as her friend. Instead she must look like the lewdest of creatures, barefoot and with her shift shamelessly outlining the curves beneath.

It was Doctor Elton, of course.

He came out of the darkness, looking straight at her. The guard was saying something but she could not hear him. The doctor examined her, his dark gaze pausing on her bare feet and ankles before moving up to the swell of her hips and breasts. Oh for a robe to cover them! Worse still, chilled by the cool night air, her nipples had stiffened and were pressing uncomfortably against the simple bodice of her shift.

His eyes narrowed as though noting the response of her body, and the wanton manner in which her loose hair was tumbling over her shoulders and throat, and his mouth tightened.

"Mistress Croft," he murmured, and bowed his head to both women. "Mistress Langley."

When he looked up, she read disapproval in his face and could have screamed in frustration. Though what had she expected? The doctor already thought her a whore. It should not matter to her what he thought, yet it did. Now he had found her out of bed in the middle of the night, her body on show to every passerby, with only the flimsy excuse that she had suffered a nightmare.

Doctor Elton was not in his physician's robe tonight. Instead he wore a dark doublet and hose, his codpiece drawing her eye, his thighs strong and muscular in tight black hose. He had a way of holding himself that told her how confident he was in himself, and how little he feared the dangers of court life. It was rare for a man below the rank of lord to show no fear at the royal court, and she wondered again how he had been so cool and calm in the king's quarters when he had neither wealth nor status to protect him.

"Sir," Margerie began, then met those serious eyes and found herself floundering, her breath suddenly stolen away, "I regret that… that you were roused from your bed for no good reason."

"I would call you an excellent reason to be roused from my bed, Mistress Croft," he countered, watching her.

His words resonated in her head, taunting her with sexual meaning, and for a moment she did not know where to look.

Her mouth became suddenly dry, her breathing short, and Margerie knew herself possessed by lust for this man. *Hot, shameless lust*. Yet while she felt sure the doctor would not resist her advances if she were to offer herself to him, the thought of becoming this man's mistress, a whore by any other name, felt wrong. As though his attentions would shame her more than any other man's.

Kate had been holding her hand, but she dropped it now, curtsying to the doctor. "Sir, my friend was found wandering in her sleep tonight, in a state of some distress, and could not be roused when spoken to. I was able to wake her in the end, but she could not remember anything except going to bed. I fear she has some malady of the brain."

A malady of the brain?

Margerie glared at Kate. "No, I am sure it is nothing of the kind."

She turned to the doctor, wishing fervently that he would go away before he caught the raw desire she was feeling, her voice sharper than she had intended.

"I suffered a nightmare, that is all," Margerie told him firmly. "It seems my nightmares are powerful and fool me into behaving as though I were awake. But now you see me perfectly well, with no ill effects from my bad dreams, so we can all go back to bed."

He was undeterred by this explanation, taking her wrist between finger and thumb, his face unreadable as he felt for her pulse. "You often have these nightmares?"

"No," she admitted.

"Is it a new thing for you to wander while asleep, then?"

Kate answered for her, a knowing smile on her lips as she took in Margerie's nervous reaction to his presence. "It is, sir, and it worries me greatly. Should Mistress Croft take a sleeping draft before retiring each night, do you think? Or perhaps you know of some infusion of herbs that would calm her spirits?"

His gaze flicked to her face, then returned to Margerie's. "Are your spirits upset?"

"No."

"Yet Mistress Langley has described you as being in a state of distress."

"Since I cannot recall what happened, I am not able to confirm that."

"Forgive me," Master Elton said, inclining his head, but she saw an ironic gleam in his eyes. "So you do not recall the dream that caused you to wander from your bed tonight?"

She had been dreaming, yes. But her memories were so confused.

It had been dark in her dream, she remembered that. She had been running down an unlit corridor. Hands had grabbed her from behind, pushing her to the floor. She had struggled, then someone had been kissing and crushing her, suffocating her…

She put her hand to her throat. "No," she managed, then saw that the guard holding the torch aloft was staring at her meager nightgown.

"Might I return to bed now?" she demanded of the doctor. "I am recovered from my nightmare, Master Elton, and have no need of your…services."

Kate stirred at this. "No, you must not be so foolish." She lowered her voice to an urgent whisper as Margerie turned away. "Margerie, you were *screaming* in your sleep. Trust me, you looked half-demented. Let the doctor examine you."

"You have a wise friend there, Mistress Croft," Master Elton murmured, watching her.

"I am perfectly well, thank you, and need no examination."

"Go with him," Kate urged her softly. "He is a doctor, there will be no impropriety."

No, she would not be bullied into betraying herself with this man. To be alone in a room with him would be madness indeed, for she knew how hotly her blood beat for him. It would be but a small step between letting this doctor examine her and slipping into his bed, as willing for his hard body as any wanton.

"You may leave us, Master Elton," she told him steadily, looking him in the eye. "Thank you."

She had expected to see anger in his face, for she had spoken curtly. Yet Master Elton did not seem offended by her dismissal, nor did he protest. His smile was fleeting but she was sure she had not imagined it. The doctor was amused by her refusal, not angered.

He bowed, taking a step backward. "If you do suffer more of this night wandering, Mistress Croft, there is a sleeping draft I could make up for you," he told her calmly. "My workshop and private quarters are on the second floor of the tower above the rose gardens. You can find me there most days, though occasionally I am called away to attend a patient."

"I will bring her to you, sir," Kate promised him, ignoring her stifled gasp.

But Master Elton was already gone, the guard accompanying him back to his rooms with the torch.

Margerie glared at her friend. "Why did you say that? Now he will expect me to visit him."

"You find him handsome," Kate pointed out, her smile broad now, "and he is not married. Why should you not visit him?"

"You are not that naive."

Smiling, Kate kissed her on the cheek. "So what if you end up sleeping with him? You have no virginity to lose, and if you are discreet, no one will chide you for it. Not at this court. And why should you not pursue a little pleasure while you are still young and unwed?"

"I am hardly young, Kate. I am seven and twenty years of age. Nor am I ever likely to be wed. Not with my reputation."

"Reputations can be fixed." Kate shrugged carelessly. "Besides, there is always some wealthy old man willing to accept a less than perfect bride if she will serve him well in bed. Look at me. Who would have believed I could land old Master Langley after bedding so many other men before him? Yet he pretended as well as I did that I was a maid on our wedding night, and rarely grumbles when I take other lovers, so long as I give him what is due a husband. You may be lucky enough to find such a man for yourself. Meanwhile, enjoy yourself with this doctor. He wants you."

Margerie felt her face flood with heat at the mere thought of being in Master Elton's bed. "You think so?"

"I know so. If you had gone with him and not been such a little coward, you could have been riding the good doctor even now. I swear, he lusts after you. That look in his eyes when he saw you waiting here, your hair loose over your shoulders…"

"My wretched shift, more like!" Margerie tugged at her bodice. "It displays more than it conceals."

"Aye, it was a good choice."

Speechless, Margerie stared at her friend. "You think…" Her voice was choked. "You think I did this on purpose? That I pretended to be wandering in my sleep so the doctor would be summoned and I could snare him?"

"Of course not," Kate said soothingly, and pushed Margerie back toward her chamber. "Else you would have gone with him when he asked."

"Oh, but what must he think of me?" Margerie closed her eyes in despair. "Barefoot too."

"He will think you wanton."

"I know it."

Kate laughed at her dismay, embracing her in the doorway to the women's bedchamber. "Come now," she whispered in her ear, "where is the harm in a little lustful dalliance with a physician? Master Elton is not the king, after all. He is not a *dangerous* man."

Four

"It is being whispered about the court that the queen will be found guilty and executed for treason."

Virgil looked up from the medicament he was mixing. "So I understand," he muttered, keeping his voice low in case one of the servants should overhear. It was difficult not to let his disgust show. "Her trial has been undertaken in unseemly haste, so the king may marry Mistress Seymour as soon as possible."

"Careful, Virgil."

He took a slow breath, then expelled it. His master was right. Walls had ears.

"Have Cromwell and the others finished their questioning of the witnesses?"

"Nearly."

"And then Queen Anne will face her accusers directly, I suppose."

"And the executioner soon after, they are saying." Master Greene made a face, not bothering to hide his own distaste. "There has been talk among the chief physicians this morning over who should attend Her Majesty at the Tower if she comes to the stake or the block. At least you are unlikely to be required, for only the most senior will attend. For myself, I have asked to be excused that grim duty. I could never witness such a horror. Yet if the queen is found guilty, we must abide by the law. God save the king!"

Virgil muttered the well-worn phrase too, knowing it would be expected, but in his heart he knew himself sickened by what this monarch was doing. Executing the queen on charges so unlikely they must surely have been falsified, just so His Majesty might marry a fresh young virgin better suited to grant him a son.

"But how goes that exotic potion of yours? The one that will help the king perform his duties as a new husband?" Master Greene smiled, seeming to put aside the queen's impending death without too much trouble. "Is it ready to try yet?"

"Not quite. I am still waiting on a few ingredients, all very difficult to obtain. Indeed, one substance is on its way here from the East. I ordered some from my supplier, but he has none left and is waiting on a new shipment that is nearly a full month late. He fears the merchant ship may have been lost at sea."

Master Greene crossed himself piously. "That is sad news. God rest their souls."

"Yes." Virgil frowned. "If the ship has gone down, you realize, and I am unable to find that ingredient elsewhere, it may severely delay my work."

"The king has been asking about it. You cannot disappoint him."

"But without these Eastern remedies—"

"Oh, there will be no problem with that." His superior shrugged, going to the door with a complacent smile. "So what if it lacks Eastern potency? Our stout English herbs will do the trick as well, I have no doubt, especially if mixed with undiluted wine to confound the king's senses and tickle his need for a woman."

The physician opened the door only to stop, a sudden disapproval in his voice.

"Master Elton, there are two ladies here, waiting outside your workshop to be seen," he said loudly, and stepped aside with only the slightest bow to the women standing cloaked and hooded on the narrow landing near the top of the stairs, their backs against the wall. "Pray attend these ladies quickly, then return to your work. Remember, that infusion must be your priority now."

Master Greene hurried away, leaving Virgil staring out at the two women in surprise. With a jolt of desire, he recognized one as Margerie Croft, the other her smiling friend Kate Langley.

It shook him to feel how swiftly his cock stiffened at the sight of her, his heart beginning to beat faster, his whole body responding to her presence in his modest chamber.

"Ladies," he managed, coming to the door, "pray come inside and let me know how I may help you."

Kate dragged her reluctant friend inside, smiling broadly. "Good day to you, Master Elton."

As Margerie passed him, Virgil caught a hint of her sweet perfume—so redolent of the damask roses he himself used to produce rose oil—and found himself cursing the smallness of the room, knowing it would be impossible to keep his distance from her. But he could at least maintain some control and hide his erection. He was not a brute beast, after all.

Reaching for a leather apron, he stood with his back to the two ladies as he tied it about his waist. Now his arousal would not be so obvious. Though it might help if he were not panting like a dog with the scent of a breeding bitch in his nostrils, he told himself roughly.

"Has your sleep been troubled by bad dreams again, Mistress Croft?" he asked, turning back toward them. He forced himself to breathe more slowly. "Have you come for a sleeping draft as Mistress Langley suggested?"

No, he thought, that was a bad idea, mentioning her night wanderings. Now he was remembering the night he had been roused to attend her and had struggled to soothe her fears while his body was shrieking at him to drag her off into some dark corner.

Margerie looked back at him mutinously, her chin raised. "I need something to help me sleep without fear of wandering, yes." He noticed that her green eyes were too bright, a flushed look to her face, and there were shadows in her face as though she had not slept well for some time. "But only if it will allow me to rise in the morning and attend to my duties."

"Of course."

He frowned, wondering again what nightmares would drive a woman to rise from her bed while still asleep.

"This business with Queen Anne," he said quietly, "has it disturbed your sleep?"

"No," she said, her manner defensive.

"Margerie only came back to court a short while ago. She has been in the country some years, you see, so she missed those first days when all the wild stories were flying about, before the shocking accusations, then the arrests...they were the worst," Kate Langley explained, staring fascinated at the contents of a vast jar on his shelf. "What are these, Master Elton?"

"Pickled sheep bladders."

Kate Langley made a noise of disgust, then moved away to look out of the high tower window as though interested in the view. He had a feeling she wished to give them privacy while he examined her friend more thoroughly.

Margerie Croft remained still during his examination, but he could tell from her rough breathing and the erratic beat of her heart that she was as uncomfortable as he was. He tilted back her chin and gazed into her eyes, checking for bloodshot or yellow whites. He saw nothing there to worry him. There was a dark smudge under her eyes where her sleep had suffered, but otherwise she seemed healthy.

A soft red tendril of hair had escaped her cap. He tucked it back in without thinking, the intimacy of his gesture an outward show of his inward desire. She sucked in her breath and he regretted it instantly. They were, after all, not alone here.

"Forgive me," he murmured.

She had been silent, staring rigidly over his shoulder. But at this, her intelligent green eyes returned to his face. His erection, which had been subsiding, stiffened under that look. What a beauty she was. A red-haired, green-eyed beauty, slender as a wand but so tall for a woman, more than a match for his own height. He cursed her friend Kate's chaperonage and longed to be alone with Margerie Croft, to put quite a different expression on her face.

"What for?"

His mind was clouded with lust. For a moment he could not follow her question. Then he drew a long, careful breath, looking at her intently.

"I should not have touched your hair like that, Mistress Croft. It is not my place."

She lowered her gaze at once, and he saw a faint color enter her cheeks. Triumph swelled in him. There could be no mistake this time. She wanted him too.

It was both a dangerous and a comforting thought. However much he was twisting desperately inside, eager to feel her body against his, he was not alone in this urgency. But to know that only one small step could set light to this dry and very promising tinder was to be tempted beyond human endurance. If she was indifferent to him, it would make his lust easier to bear. Instead, it made it harder, a thousandfold.

He turned away and swiftly made up a mild sleeping draft for her, pouring it into a stoppered flask.

"I can find nothing wrong with you," he managed at last, handing her the flask. "But if you pour five drops of this into a small cup of wine at bedtime, and drain the cup, you should sleep sound enough not to walk in the night. You may also wish to tie yourself to the bed, or sleep in some private place where the door may be barred against your escape until dawn."

Margerie looked embarrassed by his suggestion. "I do not wish to become a...a prisoner."

"I will make sure she takes the proper precautions if your draft does not keep her still at night," Kate said firmly. "Besides, it is only for a short while. Is that not right, Master Elton? My friend will not be wandering in her sleep forever."

"It is unlikely," he agreed, wiping his hands on a clean cloth. "I consulted with the chief physician after your nightmare, Mistress Croft, and he believes most cases of night wandering are due to a temporary imbalance of the humors. What causes such nightmares is less certain, of course. But I cannot imagine they will continue to plague you indefinitely."

She had risen and was rummaging in her belt purse, not looking at him. "I thank you for your pains, Master Elton."

"Please," he insisted, holding up a hand, "I need no recompense."

"But the sleeping draft…"

"Take it."

Her light perfume was breaking his concentration. He was having a hard time not staring at her breasts, and that shadowy cleft between them highlighted by the flattened gold band of her bodice.

Virgil felt like he was going mad. He wanted her to stay so he could ogle her like a lout in the street, but he knew it would be impossible to work for the rest of the day if he did not let her go.

"Come back if the bad dreams continue. Or if the sleeping draft makes you sleep too long."

She curtsied, and Kate Langley did too, mocking him with her knowing smile.

Virgil bowed. "Ladies."

As soon as the door had closed behind the two women, he tore off the leather apron and threw it to the floor. His hand cupped the large aching bulge of his codpiece, and he groaned quietly as he thought ahead to another long day of meticulous, careful toil in his workshop—with no chance of relief.

"If I cannot have that woman soon, I shall run mad," he muttered.

Some nights later, Margerie could almost have wished she were safely tied to her bed. For she would rather face such humiliating imprisonment than endure this meeting Kate had arranged, an encounter she had herself requested yet dreaded with all her soul. Consumed by her own past fears, she shrank into the shadows of the fragrant darkened garden, glad of the soft gray cloak and hood she had chosen to hide herself from prying eyes.

"Must it be now?" she whispered to Kate, her heart beating furiously loud and fast.

"Yes," her friend insisted stubbornly.

"But if we are caught here so late…"

"Then we will claim to have been out whoring, and no man will suspect us of lying, for that is what they all think we do anyway. Now hush," Kate hissed, jerking on her hand, "and remember this was your idea and you are doing this for a friend."

Margerie's face flushed. "Hardly that."

"To make amends, then."

She sighed. "Yes, yes, to make amends. You are right. And it was my idea." Her mouth tightened. "But only because I cannot bear to see another woman falling into the king's hands. Henry's lechery will kill us all."

Kate's eyes flew wide at this. She laid a finger on her lips, shaking her head. "For the love of God, Margerie! Would you be tried for treason too?"

"Quiet, someone is coming!"

Kate turned, staring intently into the misty spring evening. "It is him."

"Oh God."

Kate squeezed her hand reassuringly, though her smile was twisted. "He and I were nearly lovers once," she whispered in her ear. "We were both very young and inexperienced. Did I ever tell you the story of that night? Suffice it to say it was not one of my better seductions. Though I remember he was a very good kisser."

"Kate!"

"Wait here. If his lordship sees you first, it will all be over. You know his temper: it is famous for being easily lost. And don't forget, they were questioning his wife today. He will be on edge."

Kate slipped away across the walled palace garden, surrounded by hushed cloisters, and left Margerie to watch in sudden trepidation as her friend met her former lover, Lord Wolf. She felt a little sick, and kept the gray hood pulled forward, hiding her face. If only she were braver!

The night she had lain with Wolf felt so long ago, another lifetime away, almost as misty in her memory as his face across the palace garden now. Even though still half a boy, he had been an intense lover, his gaze hot and frightening as he pulled up her gown and drew her down into the bed on top of him. She had not wanted him to become her lover, but her mother had insisted, and Margerie had not felt strong enough to resist.

"If he takes your maidenhead, he will be forced to marry you. When his father dies, that boy will be the next Baron Wolf, and you will become a great lady," her mother had explained, eagerly dressing her for a seduction that night. "Never mind if you feel nothing for him, silly girl. Love is not for the nobility. Be quiet and do your duty to our family."

But although Margerie had let him take her virginity, and even agreed afterward in muted tones to be his wife, nonetheless she had changed her mind as soon as Wolf left court to fight for the king. There had been something stark and forbidding in his descriptions of Wolf Hall and the cold northern land she would call home once they were married. And she still shuddered to recall his possessive stare, the way he had insisted on leaving that she look at no other man until his return…

No, she could never have grown to love such a man, not even if they were married for fifty years.

As though he had guessed her identity, and was already angry, she heard Wolf raise his voice to Kate. He grabbed at her wrist, and Margerie knew he had not changed. Older he might be, more politic at court perhaps, but underneath he was still the passionate, hotheaded youth who had courted her so fervently that she had not known how to escape his claws except to run away with another man.

Poor Jack.

If she had not forced her friend Jack to cross the cold swell of the English Channel in such dreadful weather, when he was already suffering from a fever, he might have lived to wed her as he had stoutly promised to do. For Jack had loved her in his own way, without passion but with genuine concern for her well-being, always a friend rather than a lover in her eyes.

But Jack had died within days of arriving at his uncle's home in France, and Margerie had been left to fend for herself among strangers, clearly no longer a maid, nor yet respectably widowed. It had been a desperate time for her.

But that did not mean she could countenance the king's seduction of Wolf's new bride, Eloise. And it was all round the court that Henry intended to bed the former lady-in-waiting now she was safely married to one of his lords. Such arrangements were commonplace these days, for the king was never content with his wife and a mistress. And there were few courtiers who dared confront him openly about such seductions, even though it meant they could not be certain if the child in their wife's womb was theirs or the king's.

Now Lord Wolf was looking over at her, speaking tersely to Kate. She could not delay the moment of their reunion any longer.

Yet fear still held her back.

She could not help staring, remembering how he had tried in vain to pleasure her on the night they spent together. Wolf had changed over the years, but she would have known him anywhere. Strong even as a youth, Wolf had grown broad-chested in manhood, his hips narrow, his thighs long and muscular. He was a man who took what he wanted and did not hide his desires from the world. She had heard he was a born leader of men, a bold commander in battle and a dangerous opponent on the jousting yard. And a man who loved women, but did not always treat them well.

Lord Wolf thrust Kate aside and spun to face her, a hand on his dagger hilt. "Who are you? Speak! Throw back your hood; let me see your face."

His voice struck at her, fierce and commanding. He thought her a man; perhaps an enemy come here to ensnare him in some courtly plot. Instead she had been his lover once. Though to call that night's humiliating embrace *love* was to grant the loss of her virginity more grace than it deserved.

You must have ice water in your veins, Margerie Croft, not to have been moved by the heat of my desire.

She stepped forward, pushing back her hood so Wolf could see her face. His eyes widened as he recognized her, an old agony suddenly raw in his face again, and in that instant she forgave him.

As a youth, this man had frightened her into fleeing England, the king's court, even her own family, and fate had conspired to keep her away for years. But whatever Wolf's intentions toward her, they had not been malicious. And though deep down she had known that, she had still fled to France with the milder Jack. She had feared spending her life with a man whose forceful nature terrified her.

"Margerie!" he cried huskily.

Then his face changed, became more cautious, his eyes shuttered and cold, almost angry again. No, Wolf's passionate attachment to her had been real enough. For the swiftly concealed pain in his eyes was the same pain that was in her heart. And it had a name.

Guilt.

"Wolf," she managed huskily, and saw his face harden at the sound of her voice. "Ah, how you have changed since you were a youth. Your eyes are so cold now."

"As you see."

"Did I do that?" she could not help asking, and saw him flinch.

"What do you want, Margerie?" he demanded, looking from her to Kate Langley, his eyes narrowed. "You must have heard that I am married now. Or perhaps you came because of that. You should know, I have no need of a mistress."

He had grown cruel too. Cruel and unthinking.

But then he did not understand their mission, Margerie reminded herself, and he had a beautiful young bride to protect from the king. Even if that cost him his life. Like a bear tied to the stake, Wolf stood alone in a court of enemies and thought every hand must be turned against him, for he had been given no reason to trust. But she and Kate would help his wife Eloise, if he would only trust them. For if women could not help each other in such dangerous times, their shame was all the greater.

Margerie saw the suspicion and doubt in Wolf's face, and slowly, carefully, began to explain how they could help him keep his wife out of the king's bed.

Perhaps in time they would be able to greet each other as friends, she thought, and found herself almost smiling at such an outlandish idea.

Five

MARGERIE TOOK THE LAST of her sleeping draft the night before Anne Boleyn's execution, not wishing to wake too early. She had made herself almost unwell these past few days, thinking of the beautiful queen, all hope of clemency gone now, preparing herself to meet the horror of the scaffold. Nor could she forget those gentlemen who had been found guilty of treason and already lost their heads to the ax, some for no worse a crime than having thought Her Majesty charming and beautiful, the queen's own brother among them.

The draft of poppy did its task that night. She slept heavily, not even waking when the other women rose and dressed around her, and stirred only at the sound of distant thunder echoing down the river the next morning.

Margerie lay a moment in drowsy confusion, listening to the sound and thinking there must be a storm. Then she turned, blinking across at the bright window. It had been thrown open to air the chamber, dust motes swirling in the thin shafts of May sunshine streaming in.

Slowly her mind groped after the truth. No, it had not been thunder but cannon fire she had heard. From the Tower of London, most likely. There was only one reason why the Tower's defensive cannon would be fired when they were not at war and that was to announce an important event like the execution of a highborn traitor.

Which meant Anne Boleyn was dead.

Margerie buried her face in her pillow and wept, but silently, taking care to muffle her sobs, lest someone hear and claim she did not think the king just in his actions. She had not known Anne Boleyn well, for she had returned to court too late. But the very thought of a wife being condemned to death by her own husband was so terrible, such a shocking crime against nature, it frightened her to know she lived under the power of such a king, and might at any moment lose her own life at his whim…

Later she rose and dressed, fumbling unhappily with the fastenings of her gown, then splashed her face with cold water to hide the fact that she had been weeping.

But it seemed few were at their work that morning anyway, for when she finally stumbled down to the seamstresses' room, she found the sunlit chamber empty, and was told by a surly guardsman that most courtiers were at their prayers.

"Thanking God for His Majesty's release from a wicked adulteress," the guard added sneeringly, looking her up and down as though he thought her cut from the same cloth as the Boleyns.

Margerie turned away from him, sick at heart, wondering where Kate was. She needed her friend more than ever, but no doubt she was with her husband at this difficult time.

Wandering through the empty state rooms in search of Kate, she passed a group of young noblemen at dice, laughing together as though unaware that Anne Boleyn had just knelt for the swordsman.

They glanced at her without interest as she slipped past, then one young man detached himself from the group and took a step in her direction.

"Mistress Croft?"

She turned, surprised to hear her name, then flinched, recognizing him as Lord Munro, one of the courtiers who had tried to rape her the night she rejected the king.

"Might I speak with you in private, mistress?" Lord Munro asked, his blue eyes seeming to admire her figure.

Her gorge rose as she guessed at his thoughts. Another one who wanted her for his mistress, or a few nights of pleasure that might cost him less than a whore's fee. She dropped the nobleman a brief curtsy, then hurried to the door with only a muttered, "Forgive me, my lord. I am late and must attend to my duties."

To her relief, he did not follow.

It was not until she was wearily preparing for bed that evening that she saw Kate again. She had just slipped off her shoes when her name was called, and turned to see Mistress Langley at the door. Kate seemed unusually distressed, her eyes red-rimmed, but then so did many of the women in the aftermath of Anne Boleyn's execution.

No place could have felt closer to Hell than the English court that day, Margerie thought grimly.

Kate took one look at her face and asked quietly, "Are you unwell, Margerie? Or is it just the day's events that have made you so pale?"

"I am well enough, I assure you." Margerie went aside with her so the other women could not overhear their conversation, lowering her voice to add, "Though I will not deny, the queen's death has left me sadly shaken. But how are you, dear Kate?"

"I will survive. I always do."

"I cannot help but think on it constantly. Poor lady. The injustice of it…"

"Hush," Kate warned her, glancing up and down the torchlit corridor. "Listen, my husband will be angry if I do not return to our chamber at once, for I have neglected him sorely these past few weeks. Indeed for several nights now I have not returned to him at all, but shared another's bed."

Margerie stared, not sure whether to be shocked or to congratulate her, for Kate's lack of fidelity to her middle-aged husband was well known. "Have you taken a new lover, then? But what is his name?"

"I will tell you if it becomes serious." Kate smiled at her

expression. "But I have an urgent message for Lord Wolf and find I cannot deliver it without risking my husband's wrath." She met Margerie's eyes intently. "Will you take it to him for me?"

"Speak with Lord Wolf?" She shook her head, feeling sick. "I cannot... Forgive me, Kate. I am not so afraid of him as I once was, but truly I cannot face his lordship again. Not so soon after our reconciliation. Even though I must share some of the blame for what happened between us, the wound is still too raw." She paused. "Why not write a note to him instead?"

Kate bit her lip. "I cannot commit this news to paper, in case it is read by some enemy of his lordship. But if you tell Hugh Beaufort, perhaps he will consent to relay the message to Lord Wolf."

She thought of Hugh Beaufort. A quiet, charming gentleman, and strikingly handsome, she had seen him frequently about the court this year. "Master Beaufort works closely with your husband, is that not so?"

Kate nodded. "And he is a good friend to Wolf. He will not betray us."

"Must it be tonight?"

"I am afraid so." Kate kissed her on the cheek, and Margerie realized that her friend was trembling. "Forgive me, I would not ask but I am desperate. My husband's temper is most uneven at the moment, and I cannot risk his displeasure by not returning at once to bed. I have been told you will find Master Beaufort with Lord Wolf. Merely knock and ask to speak with him outside the chamber. What harm can there be in it?"

"Very well," she agreed, though in truth she was unnerved by the prospect of delivering a secret message on the same day that Anne Boleyn had met her death. The whole court was on edge, everyone watching everyone else. The chances of being followed and accused of some crime—perhaps even treason—were higher than ever. "What is the message I am to deliver?"

Kate whispered it in her ear, and made her repeat it back. "Only be sure not to be overheard when you deliver it to Master Beaufort. Lord Wolf is still closely watched by the king's spies." Kate's smile was bitter. "Those highest in the king's favor are also those he fears the most, it seems."

"I shall be careful."

"You have my thanks." Kate embraced her. "Now I must return to my husband. We'll speak tomorrow."

Margerie bade her farewell, then fetched her shoes and a hooded cloak, for she suspected it would be best not to announce her identity too openly as she wandered the palace that night. Her red hair was too well known at court, she thought ruefully, tucking it away beneath the heavy hood. If her visit to Lord Wolf's quarters was noted, her intimate history with him might mark her out as another to be suspected too.

~~~

There was a terrible hush over the palace. She slipped through long, darkened corridors, the wall torches allowed to burn down as though most courtiers were expected to be abed at this hour. Though in truth it was not so very late at the court; most nights would still see noblemen carousing at this hour.

There was a short man in a cloak leaning against the wall, arms folded, watching Lord Wolf's apartments. She hesitated, then swept past him, her chin high, and knocked at the door. His gaze followed her, then he shrank back into the shadows.

To her relief, it was Hugh who came to the door. "Mistress Croft?" he asked, frowning. No doubt he knew her history with Wolf. He glanced back over his shoulder, then stepped outside into the corridor, pulling the door shut. "How may I help you, mistress?"

"I have an urgent message for his lordship," she whispered, only too aware of the spy watching from the shadows.

His eyes met hers, then he nodded slowly. "Not here," he muttered, then raised his voice. "You are looking for Lord Carlyle, you say? No, his lordship is not here, nor have I seen him. You have mistaken the room perhaps? His quarters are further along here... Come, let me escort you there."

She fell in with his pantomime, pretending to look grateful as they walked past the watching spy. "My thanks, Master Beaufort. I...I admit I mistook the room for Lord Carlyle's apartments."

They came to the corner, passing out of the man's sight, then Hugh Beaufort whisked her more swiftly along the next corridor. He was a tall man, she realized, just a little taller than her, and in truth a very handsome one, green-eyed like herself, with shining fair hair hidden beneath a black velvet cap.

"I see the king's spies are still watching us," he murmured, checking over his shoulder, but the corridor behind them was empty.

"Forgive me, it was not my idea to come. My message is from Mistress Langley. She said it must be delivered tonight."

"I am glad you came then, regardless." He nodded toward a door set into an alcove. "Those are Lord Carlyle's rooms, in case that spy is still watching when I leave."

She raised her eyebrows. "And what reason might I have for visiting a peer at this hour?"

Hugh Beaufort grinned. "A lady of your skills? Come, Mistress Croft, I suspect you could think of a likely reason."

Heat rose in her cheeks, and she felt uncomfortable under his look of frank admiration. He meant no harm by the jest, she was sure. Nonetheless, she could not help wishing she were just a little less notorious at court.

"Now, what is this message?" he asked briskly.

She glanced up and down the corridor, suddenly fearful that she had heard a rustle in the shadows. But there was nobody in sight.

Leaning close, she whispered, "The king knows that Wolf lied about his wife, and intends revenge. His Majesty is looking for some business that will send Wolf away from court, leaving his bride unprotected." Her voice shook, for she knew what danger she stood in simply by delivering such a message. "If any summons should come from the king, Wolf must ensure his bride's safe return to Yorkshire, for His Majesty is unlikely to pursue her there."

Hugh drew a sharp breath, his head close to hers. "I see." His face had hardened as he listened, but now he managed a terse smile. He laid a hand lightly on her arm. "I thank you for coming here tonight, I know it cannot have been easy. But there is a friend I need to consult on this matter. And at once. May I leave you here, Mistress Croft? Or do you require safe escort back to your chambers?"

Suddenly uncertain, Margerie met his earnest gaze. She heard the tower bell chime midnight. If she returned to the women's quarters now, she might lie awake for hours, fearful of what might happen if she let herself fall asleep. For she had run out of her supply of sleeping draft, and without it, she knew her body capable of rising while she was still dreaming and wandering the palace in her nightgown. The shame of what she might do while in that dream-state filled her with horror.

"No," she said, and smiled back at him, her manner equally terse. "I too have someone I must see before I sleep tonight."

"Then I shall bid you good night, mistress."

Hugh Beaufort bowed, raising her hand to his lips, then strode away down the corridor, surprisingly graceful for one so tall.

She watched him go, then wished she had asked for his escort anyway. For now she was alone, Margerie became uncomfortably aware of that rustling sound again in the shadows. She turned, narrowing her eyes as she searched the torchlit corridor, then caught a movement out of the corner of her eye. Someone was watching her!

Startled, and more than a little afraid, Margerie hurried toward the door in the alcove, hoping that Lord Carlyle would not be in his quarters. If she could make it look as though her errand there had indeed been to visit the nobleman, perhaps as his mistress…

But by a happy chance the door was already ajar. Instead of knocking, she opened it, meaning to slip inside and hide until the spy had gone.

The sight that greeted her took her breath away. A fair-haired woman, whom she did not recognize, was bent naked over a daybed, with one naked man entering her vigorously from behind and another—Lord Carlyle, if she was not mistaken—thrusting into her mouth.

She gave a cry, stifling it with her hand, and stumbled back from the door. It swung closed as she hurried away, her cheeks hot. But even while her mind protested, she knew that the sight had aroused her.

Swiftly, she made her way toward the tower where Master Elton lodged, wondering if he would ever indulge in such decadent games. But no, the doctor was too controlled a gentleman. Though if he were ever to lose that control…

She shivered, a chill draft about her feet and ankles as she raised her skirts, climbing the unlit tower stairs to his room. Her footsteps echoed on the stone stairs, and once or twice she paused, frowning as she heard some faint noise below. But the darkness only mocked her and she carried on, keeping one hand cautiously on the wall for balance.

The narrow landing at the top was poorly lit, the one torch almost burnt down to its bracket. She hesitated, still sure someone was following her. It would be foolish to knock at Master Elton's door if she were under scrutiny. Better to wait and see if anyone was coming up the stairs behind her…

She waited, holding her breath. Sure enough, a figure soon emerged from the entrance to the stairs, keeping to the shadows as though trying not to be seen. But it was a woman, not a man.

Margerie stared, almost outraged that she had been scared for nothing. "Who are you?" She frowned, taking a few steps toward her pursuer, whom she was sure she had seen about the court recently. "Wait... You are Lady Wolf's young sister, are you not?"

"Yes." The young woman straightened, her air defiant now she had been discovered. "My name is Susannah Tyrell. My father is Sir John Tyrell. And who are you?"

Margerie looked at her more closely, and could see no malice or ill will in the girl's pretty, heart-shaped face. She pushed back her hood and smiled, wondering why Lady Wolf's sister should have been following her. This was a case of mistaken identity, surely. Margerie decided to proceed cautiously though. Not only was Susannah Tyrell allied to the Wolf family, but there had been rumors about the young maid ever since she arrived at court. She had been a runaway bride, or some such nonsense, dressed as a man! And there had been whispers about the king's interest in her...

She did not wish to be dragged into some foolhardy venture by this girl, not tonight of all nights.

"Me?" she said drily. "Oh, I am nobody."

But Susannah Tyrell was not satisfied. "Do you have a name? And why were you so deep in conversation with Master Hugh Beaufort?"

"My name is Margerie. But as for your other question, I am afraid that I am not at liberty to discuss that matter. You must forgive me, Mistress Tyrell." Margerie curtsied, then very deliberately turned her back on the girl. "I am late for my bed."

"Wait, I must know!"

Margerie glanced back at her, her eyes narrowed at that impulsive command, then suddenly understood. Susannah Tyrell had been watching her with Hugh Beaufort, the gentleman who had brought her back to court after her wild escapade.

"He means something to you, Master Beaufort?"

Susannah's eyes widened. "Not particularly, no. I just wondered if he meant anything to *you*."

It was hard not to smile at such naivety. The girl was so very young and in love. Yet who could blame her?

"Master Beaufort is a handsome gentleman, is he not?" Margerie felt a twinge of sympathy as she tested the girl, noting how her gaze wavered, her cheeks tinged with a most revealing blush. "Those broad shoulders, that narrow waist…"

Susannah's hurt shone out of her face. The girl bit her lip, saying nothing, but there were tears in her eyes.

Margerie looked at her, stung by remorse. Had there not been a recent scandal about Susannah Tyrell and King Henry? She recalled some whispered conversation between the other seamstresses. This girl on the king's lap, and stern Thomas Cromwell interrupting their love play…

Seeing this pretty creature, the story made sense. She was everything the king desired, and perhaps still a virgin, for all the tales about her.

Margerie sighed, and closed the gap between them. "Forgive me, I did not mean to hurt you. May I speak plainly?" She placed a hand on Susannah's arm. "I have heard certain tales about you and His Majesty. No listen, I do not condemn you, for I know what it is to be in a man's power. And an offer from the King of England is not easily refused by any woman, let alone one who has left the safety of her father's protection as you have done. Oh, I can tell by your face that you think yourself free to do whatever you choose and live however you wish. But you must be careful, child. You are so very young."

"I am eighteen," she said proudly, meeting her gaze without flinching. The girl had courage, that was for sure. "That is hardly young."

"So bold, such a firebrand." Margerie smiled, though in truth she felt suddenly sad. "When I was young, I made a terrible mistake over a man because I thought myself in love. It was only a moment's error, but it ruined my life. Do not, I beg you, take any more false steps that might lead you away from your good reputation. Or you may live to regret it, as I have done. Now please stop following me. I have given you my name, and will tell you nothing more." Margerie put up her hood again. "Good night, Mistress Tyrell."

She watched as Susannah Tyrell turned and slowly returned the way she had come. After a moment, she hurried to Master Elton's door and knocked. Her hand faltered, and she found herself wishing she too could run away down the stairs.

What would he think of her, calling on him so late?

Then she lifted her chin and knocked more loudly, three times, and heard movement within.

What did it matter what he thought? It was rather too late to be worrying about her lost reputation now.

The door opened cautiously. It was Master Elton in his somber physician's robe, belted at the waist, but with his dark hair disheveled as though he had been asleep.

His dark eyes met hers, widening slightly, and there was a sudden flare of desire in his face. Then it was gone, hidden behind that shuttered control as he bowed.

"Mistress Croft," he said coolly, almost as though he had been expecting her. He raked down his untidy hair, then stepped aside for her to enter his room. "I take it your supply of my sleeping draft has run out?"

"Forgive me," Margerie said as soon as he had shut the door behind her. "I should not have come. The hour is very late, I know."

His smile was dry as he turned to reach down a bottle from one of his high shelves. "There is not a doctor in the land who has not had his sleep disturbed by a patient. And for far less urgent a cause than yours. Please," he said, indicating a seat, "it will only take a few moments to prepare the medicament you require, then I shall escort you back to your chamber." He hesitated, looking round at her from under his lashes. There was something about his stillness that alarmed her. "If that is what you desire?"

What she desired was to have his mouth against hers, Margerie thought longingly. But although she felt sure he was interested in her as a woman, Master Elton was nonetheless an honorable gentleman and not someone she would ever wish to drag into disgrace.

"Yes," she told him firmly, and tried hard not to look at his mouth. "That is what I *desire*, sir."

Six

THE COURTIERS HAD BEEN gathered in the Great Hall at Greenwich Palace for almost an hour after the feast had finished, still with no sign of the royal couple and their entourage. The courtiers whispered to each other, fanning themselves in the heat, while the musicians stood bored and idle too, for they could not play until the king and his new queen had arrived.

Another feast, Margerie thought wearily, uncomfortably warm in her heavy gown, and yet more festivities to celebrate the king's recent nuptials. When would it end?

The dark-clad seneschal, entering in great pomp and followed by a line of noble young knights and squires in royal livery, banged his staff of office on the ground three times.

The Great Hall hushed with expectation.

The king and queen were formally announced, before their courtly procession through the hall began, the royal company heading for the high dais at the far end.

Dropping to her knees in a rustling whisper of silks and satins, along with the rest of the court, Margerie kept her head lowered as the royal couple approached, her hands clasped before her. She wished hard, prayed to heaven, willed it not to happen…

But it appeared God was not listening.

A pair of shoes stopped in front of her, shining and new-made for the precious feet they shod, richly buckled, undeniably his. Fear possessed her. Her breathing quickened and her nails bit into the flesh of her palms.

Control yourself.

Then he spoke her name and she had no choice but to look up, schooling herself to appear demure and submissive, not to give away by so much as a flicker of her eyelids how much she loathed him.

"Your Majesty," she breathed, and bowed her head again in token of her utter obedience to his will.

"Tell me, how is old Master Croft?" King Henry demanded, staring down at her.

Was he remembering how she had refused his invitation to become his mistress? Or had he forgotten? The king had been very drunk that night. But capable of sending his keenest hounds after her, bent on revenge.

"I was told," he continued in tones of concern, "that he had been taken ill a little after Christmastide."

Heads turned, faces bright with malice and curiosity. One of the king's councilors cleared his throat. A young boy muttered something in the throng of courtiers behind her and was hushed.

Everyone was listening to this exchange. Especially the new queen.

Margerie struggled to keep her voice level. "I thank you for your concern, Your Majesty. My grandfather Thomas is much improved since the spring. Indeed, we have good hope that he may yet make a recovery."

"I am glad to hear it." Henry turned to the fair-haired lady on his arm, his fresh new queen, almost as new as his shoes, and his tone was light and indulgent. For Queen Jane had not yet displeased him, and he was clearly in good spirits. "Do you know Mistress Croft, my lady?"

"I do, Your Majesty," the queen replied in a muted tone. "She serves in the royal wardrobe."

Margerie stared woodenly at the king's legs, stoutly clad in white silk stockings. She resisted the urge to look up at her new queen.

Queen Jane thinks me a whore.

Well, and why should she not think it? Everyone at court had been whispering as much from the moment Margerie returned from the country and took up her new post repairing and caring for the queen's gowns and other royal vestments. Why should the king's new consort be any different from all the rest at court?

"My father, Henry Tudor, owed this throne to men like this woman's grandfather, Jane." The king raised his voice, and it rang about the high rafters of the Great Hall. "Master Croft is no great lord, of course. But he was a fine soldier in his prime and an obedient courtier in old age. I remember him well from my youth."

King Henry looked down at her again; Margerie could feel his eyes boring into her skull.

"I was pleased to agree to your return to court, Mistress Croft, for your grandfather's sake. Let it not be said we forget those who have given the Tudors good service in the past." He lowered his voice and his pale, thick-fingered hand, clustered with gleaming rings. "And those who may serve us well in the future."

Margerie kissed his hand. She bowed her head again. "You are most gracious to your humblest servant, Your Majesty. I shall endeavor to deserve your generosity."

When the king and queen had finally moved on to the high dais, Margerie rose from her knees and reminded herself to breathe properly again.

Glancing down at the reddening half-moons on her palm, where her nails had dug into her flesh, she shuddered. The king's lechery was so present in her mind it had been hard not to let the horror show on her face. She had not forgotten that night…

But at least she was safer as a woman who had roused the king's lust once or twice than as his mistress or—God forbid—his wife.

Margerie watched the king's new consort pass through the crowd of courtiers, and wondered how long it would be before Queen Jane too was cast aside for another woman.

Perhaps never, if she could manage to bear him a son.

At her side, Kate Langley rose from her knees and shook her head. There was a rueful smile on her handsome face. "Margerie, oh my dearest Margerie."

"What?"

Kate took her arm and squeezed it comfortingly, whispering in her ear, "The king himself shows you a great mark of favor before the whole court, yet you tremble and your face turns as white as a ghost's." Her friend sighed. "I will never understand you. Why come back to court when you are so ill at ease here?"

"It makes my grandfather happy to know that I am at court again and in the king's favor," Margerie whispered back, watching with a forced smile as the musicians struck up and dancing began before the royal dais. "He pays no heed to my lost reputation, for he still has hopes that I will make a good marriage."

Margerie thought of how her grandfather had kissed her on the cheek the day she left, pressing a bag of coins into her hand. "Toward your dowry," he had managed hoarsely.

She closed her eyes in pain.

Margerie had told the king that he was much improved, but in truth it was clear now that her grandfather was dying. "A wasting disease," the physician had called it, shrugging as he packed away his instruments, then suggested Master Croft had less than a year to live—as carelessly as though discussing the fate of a sick hound, not a man who had once ridden at the king's side and still commanded a large estate in Devonshire. Then the country doctor had taken his fat fee and ridden away, leaving them with a few grim-smelling drafts and little hope that her grandfather would see another winter.

"I wish you well with that mission." Kate sighed, gathering her skirts. "I must leave you, alas. My husband is suffering from a head cold and refuses to leave his chamber until his strength is restored."

"Give Master Langley my sympathies," Margerie murmured, still watching the courtiers as they danced. She rarely danced these days, for it would only lead to more talk, but she did miss the lifts and turns, the natural sway of her hips to the music. There were few things as exhilarating for a woman as to dance to the beat of the tabor.

"Perhaps I should take him to see the handsome Master Elton." Her friend grinned, pinching her arm as though to mock her, then whispered unrelentingly, "Your condition has troubled you less this past month, has it not? I cannot help but think the courtly physician's ministrations have something to do with that."

Margerie frowned. "My condition?"

"Your nightmares. And your night wanderings, where nothing wakes you and you wander the palace in nothing but your shift."

"Oh, those."

Margerie shrugged, pretending it was nothing, though she felt her insides clench at the thought of another long night ahead. How could she trust herself to sleep when at any moment she might wake in some dark place, not knowing where she was—nor what she might have done in her sleep?

"I told you, I am homesick. And Master Elton knows his business, that is all."

"Aye." Her friend laughed crudely. "And would gladly make you his business, if you would allow it."

"Master Elton is not that kind of man."

"He seems very much that kind to me," Kate remarked. "Or do you have some other view of this miraculous physician?"

Margerie hesitated, but could not find the right words to describe the quiet-spoken court physician who had not laughed at her problem but tried gently and patiently to solve it.

Master Elton was as different from Lord Wolf as any man could be, and she could not hide from either Kate or herself that she found him attractive. He found her desirable too, the way his eyes caught hers whenever they were alone together, his voice husky, and the humming of strange energy between them, her body on fire for his just from being in the same room. And yet he had never laid a finger on her in passion.

"He is a gentleman," she managed in the end, for she could not think of any other reason why he would have held back from seducing her when the flame burned so brightly between them.

"A gentleman?" Kate's lips twitched. She was looking over Margerie's shoulder, a sudden frown on her face. "Best be careful then. If Master Elton is too much of a gentleman, you may fall in love with him. And then where will you be? For you will never make a doctor's wife, Margerie, I can promise you that."

With another quick warning glance over her shoulder, her friend left her, and Margerie stood in silence, her skin prickling, knowing herself to be observed.

"Mistress Croft."

Alarmed, Margerie turned and found herself face-to-face with a fair young man, handsome and well built, his blue eyes sharp with admiration as he looked her up and down.

It was Lord Munro, one of the rowdy pack of young lords fresh come to court from the university at Oxford, who had been carousing the night before and had kept the whole palace awake with their youthful antics.

He was also one of the young nobles who had cornered her in the king's antechamber after she had first arrived at court and refused to become the king's mistress.

This was the second time he had singled her out for attention. What could he want with her?

The answer was clear. And horrifying. He wanted her in his bed.

Her heart thudded painfully. "Lord Munro," she murmured,

curtsying low, wondering how to escape this time without offending him.

The young nobleman seemed surprisingly unsure of himself, given the way he flaunted himself like a peacock, an abundance of jewels on his coat and a prominent red leather codpiece that drew her eye.

Lord Munro hesitated, then held out his hand. "Would you care to dance, mistress?"

She recalled then that this nobleman had slipped away before the other courtiers laid hands on her, protesting that she was unwilling. But refusing to participate did not mean he could be trusted.

One of his friends had turned to watch them, an older nobleman, his eyes narrowed on Munro's face. She sensed some hostility there and at once felt uneasy. What was this? Some kind of trap into which Munro hoped she would tumble unawares? If so, he had mistaken his prey.

"Forgive me, my lord, I…I am not well tonight," she lied, then gave another curtsy and all but ran away, pretending not to hear him call after her.

———

Outside the Great Hall, Margerie stopped and leaned back against the wall to catch her breath, closing her eyes. There would surely come a day when she would have to say yes, and allow one of these noblemen to take her under his protection.

But she prayed God it would not be soon. Not before she had been given a chance to spend more time with Master Elton. There was something about his gentle hands and intent eyes that drew her more than any other man, more even than Lord Wolf; her skin reacted with heat whenever their hands brushed…

But how idiotic she was! What a fool!

Master Elton was a respectable man, a trained physician, and he would wed some equally respectable woman who would not besmirch his good name with a reputation of harlotry.

Indeed she had been careful to avoid visiting Master Elton at times when other patients might be seeking his help, though once she had been seen by Lady Wolf's sister, Susannah. It had been foolish of her to peer out of the door like that, especially after Master Elton had asked her to sit quietly in his privy chamber until his other patient had left the antechamber. But she had heard women's voices and been curious to see who amongst the courtly ladies had sought his advice. A little jealous too, perhaps. For Margerie knew she would never hold his interest like a respectable lady might.

Oh yes, the doctor desired her. She had seen in his eyes that he did.

But Master Elton would never think of her in any terms except those of a passing fancy, a lover to take when he chose and easily discard. He might one day be the king's chief physician, and would not risk his advancement by marrying a wanton. Yet again she regretted her loss of reputation. For despite her grandfather's dearest wish to see her married before he died, she knew herself to be beyond all hope of marriage.

Though if she must be a wanton, she could think of no better man than Master Elton to lie with.

It was warm and dark. Her eyes were still closed. She could smell a beautiful tangle of flowers: roses, lavender, jasmine, thyme, and a hint of her own namesake, the fresh sweet marjoram. Her feet hurt as though she had rubbed them raw, yet they were resting on something soft. Grass, she identified it slowly. Short grass and clover, thick like a lawn, her bare feet sinking into it.

Margerie did not know how long she had been asleep, but she knew, quite suddenly and irrevocably, that she was awake.

Staring upward, her head spun wildly. A dark tower loomed

above her. Margerie gazed up at stone after stone reaching into a black sky. There were stars beyond. Her eyes met and studied them, uncomprehending. Then the clouds drew back to reveal a white shining orb. The moon, almost at its monthly fullness now, brushing everything silver: clouds, tower, stone, trees, flowers, grass.

She was outside. In the queen's gardens. In her night shift. Barefoot.

And she could hear voices. Guards, on the entrance from the palace into the royal rose gardens.

Horrified, Margerie shrank away into the shadows, out of the moon's blank shining. She must be in full view of the guards standing there. Where could she hide from view until she had decided how best to return to her chamber?

There was an ancient yew hedge bordering the rose gardens, broad and stout, with tiny gaps into which a person could creep and be hidden. With shaking hands, she felt along the hedge in the moonlight until she found a likely gap, then crammed herself into it.

"Now what am I to do?" she whispered to herself, covering her face with her hands.

She had walked in her sleep again. That made it three times this month. They had moved back from Whitehall only a short while ago, the king complaining of the city stench. But where her night-time wanderings at Whitehall had been confined to a few narrow corridors, this palace was larger and easier to walk unseen, the entrances on this side not so closely guarded as those along the river. Somehow she must have walked straight out of a side door and into the gardens without being challenged by a sentry. Unless she had been seen and left to walk.

Her cheeks grew hot with shame and helpless fury. The guards were talking quietly amongst themselves in the moonlight. She was out of sight here, at least. But how on earth could she pass them by unnoticed on her return to bed? What possible explanation could she give for being alone and dressed so scantily in the queen's gardens at night?

Desperate, she stared up at the tower as though it might hold the answers to her problem. Her gaze steadied on one dark window slit. Surely that was Master Elton's room there, two stories above her hiding place?

Had she walked here deliberately, to the spot below his tower room, thinking of Master Elton even in her sleep—yet not quite daring to present herself to him again at nighttime?

Last time she had visited the physician after dark, terrified by her nightmares and needing reassurance, the doctor had mixed her a sleeping draft that he swore would keep her safe in bed until dawn. But she had seen how Master Elton had looked at her sideways, his dark eyes narrowed on her face, and how careful he had been to avoid touching her. She guessed that he must be deeply uncomfortable to have her in his room after dark, a known wanton.

Dared she risk offending him again by rousing him to help her?

There were small pebbles near her feet. She picked one up and threw it, on an impulse, up at his tower window. It missed and fell away with a tiny noise. The guards by the entrance did not seem to have heard, for they continued talking.

Emboldened, she picked up two more pebbles, took another few steps forward into the moonlight, and threw both together. One struck wood, and after a long moment, she saw the shutter open and a dark head appear.

Suddenly frozen, Margerie stared up at the doctor.

She could not see his face, for it was in shadow. But it seemed Master Elton had understood her predicament, for he raised a hand, then disappeared. Nothing more happened. Disappointed, she drew back into the shelter of the yew hedge and thanked God for the warm summer night, else she would have been shivering there in the open. The moon shone across the palace, its silvery light finding her even in her hiding place. She stared down at her bare feet and realized that one of her toes had been bleeding; there was dried blood where she must have stubbed it against stone.

After a while, a whisper alerted her and she stiffened. "Mistress Croft, are you there?" A hesitation. "Margerie?"

She knew that voice. She peered out from the gap in the yew hedge and saw Master Elton there in the moonlight, still in his nightclothes but cloaked and capped. A heavy cloak hung over his arm and she smiled in relief, meeting his eyes.

"I am here," she whispered back, letting him see where she was hiding. "Thank you, sir. You are very kind to help me. I cannot thank you enough for your kindness."

Master Elton slid the cloak about her shoulders, his face a mask. Once again, his hands barely touched her, though she felt their warmth near her skin.

"Another walking nightmare? Did you take a sleeping draft tonight?"

Margerie nodded, suddenly ashamed. She could not tell what Master Elton was thinking. But perhaps he thought this a ploy to be alone with him.

"Perhaps I made it too weak, though I would hesitate to make it much stronger," the doctor mused, frowning, "in case it harms you. Though you are tall, you are very slender. You might never wake if I were to make the mixture so powerful that it overwhelms you entirely."

"I do not need another sleeping draft, Master Elton," she muttered. "From now on I...I will tie myself to the bed each night."

"That may help your wanderings, but it will not cure their cause." He was still frowning. "I wish I understood what brings these nightmares on, what troubles your mind so violently that you must leave your bed while sleeping."

"You need not stay, sir," she said, a little clumsily, not wanting him to pry any further. She managed a curtsy, her back against the prickling hedge. "I thank you for the cloak, but I can make my own way back into the palace now."

He raised his eyebrows. "What, past those guards?"

"I must have passed them once already without comment. Perhaps they will leave their post."

"Or perhaps you came out another way."

She had to concede that.

Then suddenly there was no more time to think or speak. For the danger she had feared was upon them. A man's voice, deep and amused, came rolling out of the shadowy gardens under the palace wall, and Margerie realized with a jolt of horror that they were no longer alone.

Seven

"COME HERE, YOU LITTLE minx," the courtier was saying, "for I would not have you slip away before I am satisfied." The girl with him squealed in mock horror as he grabbed her, both of them emerging into bright moonlight only a few yards away from the yew hedge. Then she muttered something that Margerie did not catch. "Oh, I'll make you hop right enough," he told the girl, a hint of laughter in his voice. "Now don't pretend you've never had a man. For I've heard different. And you'll have me too, as soon as I find a good place to lie down where the guards cannot see us."

Margerie inhaled sharply and held her breath, shrinking back against the prickly hedge. If the couple came any closer, they would discover her and the doctor together in the moonlight, and then she would have ruined Master Elton's reputation as well as her own.

"Quick," Master Elton said hoarsely in her ear, bundling her back into the gap in the yew hedge.

Together they squeezed in and stood chest-to-chest in that warm, rustling darkness, hardly daring to breathe. But the amorous pair were more interested in each other and passed by their hiding place without comment, no doubt looking for a way past the yew hedge out of the gardens.

Margerie let out a slow breath, then looked into Master Elton's face. She did not even have to tilt her head, she realized. She was so tall, it was rare to meet a man who could match her height. Then their eyes met, and Margerie suddenly wished she was not so close, for he must surely have seen the tiny shock run through her, and felt how her body trembled as she stared back into his eyes.

"When they have gone, we will look for a way back into the palace that is not guarded," the doctor murmured, watching her.

She nodded, and tried not to look at his mouth. It was so firm though: straight and unsmiling.

Her lips parted and she found it hard to breathe, her fists clenched in the heavy folds of his cloak, struggling to maintain control over her senses.

Surely they would not have to wait long before they were alone again… But to her dismay, the pair did not leave.

"Here is a quieter spot," the courtier suddenly declared, shocking her, his voice close by them on the other side. There was a soft thud as he fell to the grassy lawns behind the yew hedge, presumably taking his lover with him. "We will not be seen or disturbed here. Now pull up your skirts, girl, let's have some good sport before the guards come round again."

The unknown girl squealed again, the lover laughed, then both fell silent.

They must be kissing, Margerie realized, and bit her lip as she watched Master Elton's expression darken.

Abruptly the girl moaned. It was a deep, throaty moan that suggested she had been touched intimately, perhaps even entered. The high-pitched cry that followed, then the man's grunts a moment later, confirmed her horrified suspicions. The shameless pair were fucking on the grass on the other side of the yew hedge, completely unaware of their audience.

Master Elton closed his eyes as though in pain.

She stared at him hungrily in that brief moment when he could not see her. In the faint light from the moon, filtering through the yew branches, she admired the firm chin, the Roman nose, the deep-set eyes, his lashes long where they swept his cheek, the high forehead—a mark of intelligence and great learning, she had once been told—and the dark hair that curled slightly under his cap.

Then his eyes opened and Master Elton looked at her. Dark eyes, heavy-lidded with desire, intent on her face.

"Margerie," he whispered.

She shook her head. "No," she meant to say, but it came out as a kind of strangled gasp.

She had found the physician darkly attractive the first time she saw him, and warned herself not to look too closely. Returning to court had been her grandfather's idea, not hers; he was determined to thrust her back into the world which had forsaken her. A hopeless cause, and she knew it. There was little chance any self-respecting man would court her with an eye to marriage, not when all the world knew she was no virgin.

And Master Elton was no different. Indeed, there was a ruthless-ness behind that quiet intent which she found both fascinating and dangerous. He was a man who knew what he wanted, even if his methods were less coarse than the panting courtier on the grass.

His gaze slid down to her mouth.

"Master Elton," she managed, gathering her strength to resist him.

She had resisted many men's advances since Wolf had seduced her, often with startling ease. A cold look here, a half-promise there, then a hurried flight if those would not prevail. This man would prove as easy to deter, she told herself, but knew part of her wanted him to succeed. Margerie had never felt such desire as this, known the taste of urgent need, felt it tingle through her body…

"Virgil," he corrected her. She stared at him, confused, and the doctor bent his head, whispering in her ear, "My name is Virgil."

His breath was warm on her throat. She drew an unsteady breath. Heat coursed through her and she felt her lips parting, her heart beginning to race.

God in heaven, she wanted him.

Through the yew hedge, the girl moaned again, her voice breathy, and the courtier grunted something incoherent in response. By his gasps, he was nearing his end.

"Call me by my name," Master Elton murmured in her ear, then kissed her throat. "Call me Virgil."

She was so hot, she was shivering. "V—Virgil."

He made a deep satisfied noise under his breath, then abruptly turned his head. Their faces were almost touching now, their lips less than an inch apart, the heat of his body against hers irresistible, a furnace that threatened to consume her own.

"I have tried so hard not to look at you, not to think of you, not to imagine you naked in my bed," he breathed, "but it's no use. I must kiss you or run mad."

His mouth brushed hers and she moaned.

They both stood silent for a moment, breathing hard, lips just touching. His hands came down on her shoulders, holding her close in that narrow space.

Very daringly, unable to prevent herself, she let her tongue slip out and run along his lower lip. His hands tightened and it was his time to groan, holding himself stiffly as she explored his lips with her tongue.

"Margerie," he gasped.

Then his tongue met hers and slipped wetly into her mouth, suddenly thrusting deep, tasting her.

His hands jerked her hard against him and their whole bodies strained together. She could feel the swollen evidence of his arousal through her thin night shift, and moaned in response, helpless to stop or stifle the noise.

He was not alone in his desire. She was hot and wet, ready for him, her core contracting sharply with pleasure at each thrust of his tongue into her mouth. The court had not lied; she must be a wanton if all it took was one kiss to leave her panting and eager, hungry for more.

His hand pushed between their bodies, first cupping her breast, finding and rolling her nipple erect. She arched against him in wordless consent.

The girl on the other side of the hedge began to moan beneath her courtier, crying out, "Harder, yes, harder!"

She heard Virgil's soft laughter, mocking the unseen lovers as they coupled—or perhaps himself, she could not be sure.

His hand slipped lower, cupping her mound. She too moaned. The thin shift was no barrier to his exploration, nor did she care what he did. Her whole body was on fire for him, utterly shameless in her lust. His finger rubbed up and down that damp narrow cleft through the material, until her shift was wet with her own desire. Standing on tiptoe, she directed his fingers higher, toward that sweet bud that seemed to house every pleasure nerve in her body, then gasped as he rolled it between his fingers, still with her night shift between his flesh and hers.

"You want me?" he demanded hoarsely, his face buried in her neck.

"Yes... *Yes!*"

His fingers played her skillfully, taking her higher and higher. She threw back her head, bit down hard on her lip, her hips jerking against his hand, lost in the need for pleasure.

Abruptly, the unknown courtier on the other side of the hedge came to his finish. The man groaned out loud, and under cover of his climax, Margerie cried out too, rubbing herself wantonly against Virgil Elton as her body fractured into thousands of tiny points of light. For a moment she could feel only the driving heat of her flesh, and cared for nothing else, her breasts heaving against him.

It was the same wild pleasure she had taught herself alone in bed, secretly exploring her body, only this time it felt both more intense and more intimate. For a man had brought her to that moment of urgent joy, not her own fingers. A man she barely knew. A man she wished to know better. A man she could fall in love with.

Her scalp tingled, her taut nipples ticked with blood, and her hands slid unbidden up his chest, feeling his heart gallop away beneath her fingers.

"Virgil," she gasped.

Their mouths met and he rocked her aching body against his in the glorious aftermath of her climax, his tongue licking and sliding between her lips. His kiss was hungry, aroused.

She wriggled a hand down and cupped the fullness of his cock, stiff and ready under his night shirt, no codpiece to rein it in. He drew his breath in sharply, and his cock twitched under her hand. Her fingers stroked the swollen head, then played along his impressive length; she was suddenly hot and wet again, imagining how it would feel to take this man inside her. But when she looked into his eyes, seeing the lust there, feeling it hanging in the air between them, thick and heavy, he shook his head.

She drew back, staring, to see his mouth jerk in a strained smile.

"No doubt I will think myself a fool in the morning. But I wish to enjoy you at my leisure, Margerie, both of us naked and between clean sheets. Not take you standing up in a garden in our nightclothes."

He kissed her mouth lightly, but she could sense the doctor drawing back already, his tone cooling. "And now that oaf has finished his sport, mistress, I must escort you back to your quarters."

Unsteady, her body still trembling with the pleasure he had given her, she drew the cloak about herself as they stepped out into the moonlight. The guards on the door had either gone or fallen silent. It was suddenly colder than before, and the dew was wet on her bare feet.

A glint of silver on his finger caught her eye. Her heart froze, barely pumping, and she stopped dead.

"Are you…" Margerie could barely speak; she licked her lips, forced out the cruel words. "Are you married, Master Elton?"

He glanced down at the ring, and his eyes widened, as though shocked by her question, almost as though he had forgotten the ring was there. For a moment there was silence between them. Then he looked back at her, and a hardness came into his face.

"I am betrothed to a lady who does not currently reside at court. We shall be married next year." His cool tone gave her no permission to question him further. "I know a better way back inside than past the guards. Shall we go?"

Eight

"SOMETHING TO IMPROVE A man's performance, you say?" The merchant did not bother to hide his grin, which only faded when he saw Virgil's expression. He rubbed at his beard, then ran an experienced eye over the heaps of sacks and unopened crates in his dockside warehouse. The ship had only arrived in dock two days before and it seemed not everything had been examined and labeled. "We have fresh basil leaves, rocket, garlic, oil of almonds... Oh, and asparagus. My father swears by a goodly bunch of thick asparagus."

"And I wish him well with it, but I have used most of those common aphrodisiacs before, and the results were not spectacular," Virgil explained patiently. "Master Ferney, I'm looking for more exotic herbs and spices, those to be found only in the furthest corners of our globe. Not plants I might come across growing wild by the river here."

"How about the powdered horn of a rhinoceros, then? That is *very* exotic."

Virgil raised his brows in disdain.

"Common aniseed, then. Mixed with garlic oil and mustard seed in a pestle. Very hot and moist, a sanguine mixture that will swiftly cause a man's seed to rise from the testicles." The merchant looked at him speculatively. "I once tried it myself, sir, and the results were impressive. Though it is not...not so pleasant on the tongue."

"I shall bear that in mind. What else do you have?"

"Very well, let me check the new inventory, see what came in on that last shipment. If you would care to wait, Master Elton, it should not take more than a few minutes."

The merchant bowed and made himself scarce. There was probably a cozy back room where he liked to sit, sipping ale and waiting for awkward customers like Virgil Elton to tire of their mission.

Virgil wandered out of the warehouse into the bright sunshine and stood looking down toward the arches of London Bridge, its ambitious span crammed with ancient houses jutting over the water below. The Thames ran broad and deep here, a rolling grayish-brown tide washing against mud banks shored up with steadily rotting wooden struts. The smell was offensive this close to the mud, and Virgil wrinkled his nose. But the stench of the river was no more offensive than the open ditch he had passed on his way into the warehouse, stinking and bejeweled with flies.

The back of his hair lifted in the breeze off the river, the sun beating down on his shoulders. He disliked having to visit the city in summer, as did every sensible man. Indeed the royal court had moved out to the leafy and modest palace at Richmond two days before, fleeing an outbreak of plague close to Greenwich. But Virgil himself had stayed behind on a sennight's leave so he might procure more powerful ingredients for the king's aphrodisiac than he had been able to find so far.

The infusion he had so carefully prepared for the king's wedding night had brought arousal, His Majesty had grudgingly admitted, but not stamina. And the king wished to impress his new bride with his virility, not achieve his end within minutes and have to content himself with one hurried coupling every few days.

"I should have heeded Master Greene and tested that potion properly before giving it to the king," Virgil muttered to himself, then folded his arms, glancing back toward the warehouse. The merchant was still nowhere in sight, just two lads dragging a large brown sack through a doorway. "I shall do so with this batch. And with a woman this time."

He had not found an opportunity to test the finished infusion before the king's marriage to Jane Seymour, other than to drink a few drops himself and observe its effects on his ability to achieve an erection. But in a man of fewer than thirty years, that was no great feat.

No, what he needed was to drink the next infusion before lying with a woman. A woman who was willing for him to perform not once, but several times in a night. A woman who was no virgin, but not a bawdy whore from the streets; he had no wish to infect himself with such inflamed disorders of the groin as he habitually treated in other men who dallied with prostitutes.

Margerie Croft.

He had thought of little else but her firm, pale body since their last heated meeting at Greenwich. Circumstances had kept them apart, but he had to have her. Weeks had gone by and it was becoming a matter of some urgency.

It was possible she was not a wanton. But no lady who wished for a husband would have yielded so readily to such intimacies, surely? Virgil remembered that night in the moonlit rose gardens at Greenwich Palace, and found himself stiffening at the memory of her lips against his, how eagerly she had kissed him back, the feel of her soft red hair under his fingers. He had slid those same fingers inside her later, brought her to climax against him, and she had not protested. What better sign did he need that she was no maid, that her body was available to him sexually?

She was beautiful. More than beautiful. Margerie Croft was captivating. Intoxicating and dangerous to a man's senses, like the nectar of red damask roses. What a heady mistress she would make!

"Master Elton!"

He turned at the sound of his name. It was the merchant, Master Ferney, emerging from the entrance to his warehouse, blinking up at the sunlight as though he rarely saw it. Master Ferney hurried across to him at the water's edge, his rich red doublet strained over a too-rounded belly. As he reached Virgil, his cap came tumbling off as a sudden gust of wind tore along the Thames, making their coats flap violently.

"Master Elton," the merchant exclaimed, racing after his cap like a schoolboy, his thinning hair blown wildly about, his cheeks flushed, "I thought you had gone. I may have found that exotic aphrodisiac you were searching for. Would you care to accompany me back inside, sir?"

———

Margerie had not meant to rise so early. But she had long since finished the flask of sleeping draft that Master Elton had given her, and now slept fitfully, too afraid to allow herself a good night's rest in case she humiliated herself with another nightmare or episode of sleepwalking.

The nights felt too hellishly long now, and as soon as dawn lit the women's chamber with its pale rosy light she was often up and about her business. The other women who woke early would gather for a quiet breakfast, but she could not stomach food at such an hour.

Instead she liked to walk out in the palace grounds, for the pathways were quiet in the soft dawn light and she could be alone there, something next to impossible once the day's duties had begun.

She had heard from Kate, always her willing spy, that Master Elton was due to return to court any day. But her nerve failed her when she thought of visiting him. She was unsure, for a start, of where he would be lodged at Richmond. Perhaps with the other unmarried physicians, a thought which disturbed her, for it would be most unseemly to be seen calling on him in the gentlemen's quarters. There was also the consideration that he must think her a wanton now, after the way she had yielded so readily to his caresses that hot summer night at Greenwich.

Margerie shivered at the memory, drawing her woolen shawl closer about her shoulders. She had shown no shame that night, only an unthinking desire for his body. And she had seen in his face that he felt the same for her.

Pure lust.

If only she had realized how life would change at court before leaping so wantonly into his arms. Since the king's marriage to Jane Seymour, court ladies had been forbidden to wear low-cut bodices, or to cover them discreetly where they had no alternative, and were expected to choose dark or muted colors rather than the bold yellows, golds, and reds that Queen Anne had favored. The wearing of jewelry—apart from a sober cross—was frowned upon, and as for French fashions, they were not to be tolerated. Out went the smart new velvet hoods, so delicately picked out in seed pearls, and back came the old-fashioned gable hoods still popular in the provinces among older women.

Nor was it merely the ladies' fashions which Jane had changed since coming to the throne. Those long hard nights of drinking and debauchery that had so frequently held sway during Anne's reign were no longer mentioned even in whispers, and most courtiers were expected to retire to bed soon after nightfall. Prayer books had replaced Italian poetry among the courtiers close to Her Majesty, and although there was still dancing in the evenings, it was the slow pavane and dignified courtly measures that were played, not the foot-tapping French tunes that required leaps and lifts.

Jane was a modest and sedate queen, and although she frequently pronounced herself the king's servant, it seemed to many that her husband might be brought to heel along with his court. Knowing the king as she did, Margerie did not believe Henry would so easily be changed. Nor would his men. The noblemen still drank deep in the evenings, of course, and continued to debauch maidens. They had not become monks overnight. But such misdeeds were achieved in secret now, behind the closed doors of their privy chambers, not openly in a court of lust and appetite.

She turned down a shady woodland path, keen not only to escape the warmth of the rising sun but also to avoid being seen from the palace. But she had not been walking many minutes into the wood before she heard slight noises behind her and realized that she was being followed.

Slightly alarmed, Margerie hurried her pace. The woodland path would curve round again to join the main walk in a few moments, but here she was out of sight of everyone—and possibly out of earshot too.

Still she heard the footsteps following her, growing closer. Flushed and uncertain of her safety, she picked up her skirts to run, and at that instant felt a hand on her shoulder.

"Mistress Croft?"

Margerie turned at the man's familiar voice, and fell back several steps in surprise when she saw who had been following her.

"Lord M-Munro," she stammered, her eyes fixed on his face, then belatedly remembered to drop him a curtsy.

Sleek fair hair, blue eyes, strong cheekbones, and a hard muscular body clad in fine dark garments as befitted a man of his rank. Munro looked like a younger version of Lord Wolf, she thought, and was at once on her guard against him.

He was looking at her intently, his blue eyes sharp on her face. "Forgive me if I startled you, Mistress Croft. But I must speak to you, and you will not deny me this time."

Fear spiked inside her as she stared back at Lord Munro. What did this lavishly dressed young nobleman want? Had he followed her and seen his chance, finding her alone and unprotected, out of sight of the palace walls?

There was only one thing courtiers sought from a woman of her reputation, and this tall and muscular young man would have no trouble taking it, however hard she fought.

Margerie raised her chin. "My lord?"

"Mistress Croft, I cannot stop thinking about what happened to you on the night when... Well, I am sure you recall the evening to which I refer. I want you to know that none of that was my fault. Nor do I condone what was done to you in the king's name."

"Nothing was done to me," she said coldly. "A gentleman intervened after your departure, and your companions left me alone."

There was a slight flush in his cheeks now. "I am glad to hear it. I wondered when I heard no boasting from them afterward. Well, good." Lord Munro hesitated. "But I would still ask your pardon, for I could have stopped it myself and did not."

"You are pardoned."

"I thank you."

"I must leave you now," she murmured, turning away. "I have walked too far today, I shall be late for my duties."

"Wait."

She looked down at the jeweled hand that restrained her. "My lord?"

"Please," he added, looking embarrassed. "There is something I would ask you, Mistress Croft. It is a question of a somewhat private nature."

A somewhat private nature.

Margerie steeled herself for an unpleasant insult. "Let me hear it then, and quickly, for I must return to the palace before I am missed."

Lord Munro's expression hardened at her lack of courtesy. "Very well, I shall not dress it up in lavish compliments but come straight to the point." His blue gaze met hers directly. "Will you consent to become my mistress?"

~~~

Virgil followed the steward's assistant up the wooden stairs in the east wing of Richmond Palace, bowing to acquaintances as he passed them but not stopping to exchange words, for his traveling bag weighed heavily on his shoulder. He had refused to allow the man to carry his bag though, for it contained his journal and various private papers, and also delicate vials that he could not risk breaking.

So the court had moved again, though not so far as to make the journey arduous. Richmond Palace stood in an idyllic setting, edged by sprawling woodlands on one side and the River Thames on the other, a beautiful and many-turreted building, not quite palatial but perfect for one of the king's favorite pursuits, the hunt.

These shifts of residence were tiresome but necessary, to allow each palace to be cleaned and properly refurbished during the king's absence. And at least Virgil was entitled to bouge of court as one of the king's physicians, enjoying bed and board free of charge along with the rest of the king's entourage. Not all courtiers were so lucky, especially those who wished to bring their wives and children to court, and found the king would not pay their keep too. Another good reason not to marry, he thought drily, unless one could marry a woman already in the king's employ.

"This will be your chamber, sir."

The steward's assistant threw open the door to reveal a bare chamber with two low cots and a straw mattress, one table covered in dust, and an alcove draped across with a threadbare curtain where the chamber pot and washing items were presumably kept.

"Three sleeping spaces?"

The steward's assistant shrugged. "You were to share this chamber with Master Hight and his apprentice. But Master Hight fell sick three days ago and was sent away from court for fear it was the plague, taking his apprentice with him."

"The plague?"

Virgil could not disguise the horror in his voice.

"We have had no word from him as yet, but that means nothing. It may have been some other sickness laid him low. But until Master

Hight returns, you have this chamber to yourself. Unless he dies, in which case the place will be allocated to some other gentleman." The man looked him up and down, then glanced at his bag. "You have an apprentice? Or a servant to see to your needs?"

"I need none," Virgil said shortly, and threw his bag onto one of the cots. "My chests of medicaments and other supplies should follow in a day or two. I put them on a cart and rode ahead. But I have no apprentice, and my servant, Ned, was assigned to Master Greene's service when the court moved. So it is only I who am in need of bouge of court."

The man nodded. "Very good, sir. I will inform the chief steward."

When the door had closed behind him, Virgil went to the generous window and looked down, a smile on his face.

He always enjoyed the court's sojourns at Richmond for, although not as stately as the king's other residences, it had a certain charm with its enclosed privy gardens—the rose garden, in particular, was famed at this season for its fine specimens—and a pretty orchard that took him back to his childhood in Kent. Though the royal apartments along the riverfront were very handsome, the palace had been built as a hunting lodge, less generous in its proportions than Greenwich; sleeping quarters for commoners were often cramped and cold in winter, with many in the king's household forced to share. But now he had been given a chamber on his own, with a view over rolling ground toward woodlands where he might stand and breathe in the clean air of the countryside.

Perhaps his luck was turning.

Virgil turned back to the bed and began to unpack his few possessions, accustomed to seeing to his own needs and not missing his servant. He was itching to begin work on the king's new aphrodisiac, sure now that he could produce something to arouse and maintain a man's performance in bed, even one in middle age and dubious health. But until his chests of medicaments arrived, each bottle and flask wrapped carefully in wool to reduce the chance of breakage between Greenwich and Richmond Palace, that would not be possible.

He drew out his nightclothes, and suddenly remembered walking down to Margerie Croft in the moonlit gardens wearing nothing but these under his cloak. Arousal flooded him at the memory, and Virgil was surprised to feel his breathing quicken. What he would not give to have Mistress Croft naked and spread across his bed right now, her red hair flowing loose over his pillows, her green eyes lusting boldly for his touch…

God's blood! Was she a witch, to move a man to full arousal even when he had not seen her in weeks?

A knock at the door surprised him. "Enter!"

It was Ned, grinning. Virgil smiled back, for he instinctively liked the boy. But he could not hide his surprise on seeing him. "I thought you served Master Greene now," he said, dropping the nightshirt. "Has he dismissed you?"

"Master Greene's chamber is but across the hall, Master Elton, and when he heard you were to be lodged here, he told me to serve you both."

"I see." Virgil laughed, and felt for a penny in his belt pouch. Tossing it to the boy, who caught it with an eager look on his face, he nodded to the clothes laid out on the bed. "In that case, you may start by hanging up my robes, then pack away the rest of my clothes in that chest. And mind you guard against moths."

"Aye, sir," the boy said cheerfully, then paused halfway across the chamber and fished a crumpled paper from within his tunic. "I nearly forgot, sir. This came for you three days ago, and Master Greene bade me keep charge of it until your return to court."

Virgil took the letter and smoothed it out. "Good lad," he said drily, then recognized the hand.

Leaving the child to continue with his work, he took the letter to the window and broke the seal straightaway, holding it to the light as he read. It was from Christina.

Virgilio Christina salutem

I trust this letter finds you well.

My uncle having finally agreed to my leaving this house where I am little better than a prisoner, I shall be presented at court as soon as his physician declares me well enough to travel. Moreover, if I survive the journey, he swears that his objections to our match will be at an end and we may be married.

I know you were planning to visit me this autumn, but it seems I shall be visiting you instead. How does that prospect please you? As much as it pleases me, I trust.

I miss you, my dearest friend, and hold you constantly in my prayers.

vale bene, Christina

Virgil closed his eyes in horror. Christina would surely not contemplate traveling to court? "Jesus Christ," he swore under his breath, then crossed himself to avert bad luck.

Such an arduous journey would kill her, almost certainly. He opened his eyes on a wave of pain and read her letter again, trying to gauge her mood from the words. *Foolish girl*, he thought, and crumpled the paper in his fist. Stubborn as ever, and intent on killing herself to prove that she was alive. Though if Christina died on this ill-advised journey, her death would be on his head. For he had brought her to a state of unruly desperation by giving her hope.

Virgil stared out at the palace grounds, watching trees sway gently in the wind. Yes, this was his fault. But he had given her his word years ago, and now his word must be honored.

When he was still a youth and she little better than a child he had found his young friend Christina in tears, lying on her sickbed and despairing what might happen to her in the future. That day he had asked her to marry him, and she had gladly accepted, knowing it would allow her to reject any other offers as she grew older, and also one day might bring a life beyond those grim four walls she called her "prison."

But in truth he had never believed Christina would live this long. Not to full adulthood. Not to the point where their marriage might become a real possibility.

And nor had she.

Nine

"AND WHAT REPLY DID you give in response to Lord Munro's insolent offer?" Kate demanded, staring at her.

Margerie set another neat stitch in the embroidery frame, then paused, admiring her handiwork.

"I said yes, of course."

Kate's eyes bulged and she gasped, clapping a hand to her mouth. "Margerie Croft, don't you dare lie to me! Tell me you never agreed to be that man's mistress!"

"Hush, for God's sake," she hissed. "Unless you wish the whole court to know my business?"

Margerie glanced cautiously about the narrow chamber, but to her relief the other ladies of the royal wardrobe were also talking amongst themselves. Certainly none seemed to have been listening to their low-voiced conversation. Nonetheless, it would not be wise to discuss Lord Munro's proposal too openly. The court had grown too somber since Jane Seymour's elevation to queen for such loose talk of secret lovers and mistresses to prosper.

Kate's voice dropped to a hoarse whisper. "Forgive me, but Lord Munro of all men… Why, the youth is barely old enough to grow a beard."

"Yet old enough to bed a woman, it seems."

Her friend looked dazed. "Has he…? Did you…? Never say you have already lain with him, Margerie?"

She smiled at that. "I have not."

Kate crossed herself, shaking her head. "Thank God," she

breathed. "Not that I would ever condemn another woman for taking pleasure or advancement from a man's attentions. It is what I have done myself, all my life, and kept my place at court through it. But you are not me, Margerie. Your heart is soft and your bed has stood empty too long. I would not see you hurt by a lover who would call you 'mistress' to your face, but a whore before his friends. For we all know with which pack Lord Munro runs, and those noble dogs have no love for you."

"They are king's men, to be sure."

"So why accept his offer?"

Margerie hesitated, half tempted to admit the truth. But part of her deal with Lord Munro had been a pact of absolute secrecy, and she did not wish to break that agreement. In this court where a promise meant nothing, and an oath was broken easier than a virgin's maidenhead, she was determined to keep her word. Even if it meant her friend thought she was lying with a young nobleman who, in truth, took no interest in womankind but merely wished to keep his reputation as a man intact.

"Will you do this for me, Mistress Croft?" his lordship had asked, cap in hand, standing almost humble before her in the quiet woodlands, and she had seen a pain in his eyes that she understood only too well. "My mother thinks me half a man because I have never lain with a woman. And one day I must marry, and beget an heir, I know it. But that day has not yet come. Meantime, it must seem to the world that I am a man like any other. So if you would consent to pretend to be my mistress, and come to my rooms, then say your time was spent in my bed, I...I would make it worth your while."

She had stared at his lordship, not sure she understood. "Spend time in your *bed*?"

"Alone and unmolested, I swear it," he had explained hurriedly. "I would be occupied in the next room with...with a...a friend."

Her eyes narrowed on his flushed face. By friend, he meant

"man," surely? At once she saw a danger. "But if this friend…is in your rooms too, will not the court believe I have had relations with two men?"

Lord Munro had paused, then nodded abruptly. "It may seem so, yes. Could you countenance such a bold lie?"

Margerie had folded her arms, unsure how to respond. She felt sorry for this young man, but her own reputation was at stake too. Queen Jane had made it clear that unchaste behavior would henceforth be frowned upon, and what if her grandfather heard of such lewd goings-on and wrote to her, shamed by her promiscuity?

"I cannot—" she began, but was interrupted.

"For land," Lord Munro said quickly. "A goodly estate in Sussex, with grazing rights and several orchards, and the deeds to a country manor that stands upon that land, for you and your heirs, in perpetuity. The bond to be completed within one year of this day, and only if I am satisfied that you have spoken to no other person of its terms."

She had stared. "You are offering me land and a manor house in exchange for being your mistress?"

"In exchange for your absolute silence that you are not my mistress," Munro had explained, watching her face eagerly. "I will do my utmost to protect you from censure at court, though we must be discreet. The king will accept discretion in a nobleman's dealings with his mistress, where too open an affair will end in punishment and exile. So in public we shall not acknowledge each other, but it should be believed that you come to my chamber once or twice every sennight to…make love."

Margerie had blushed at his frankness, but said nothing, knowing she should by rights reject him, yet tempted beyond belief by his offer of financial independence.

Lord Munro had drawn off his glove and held out his hand to her. "So what do you say, Margerie? Is it a deal? I give you my word of honor, I shall not touch you, nor allow my friend to touch you."

Not complaining at his intimate use of her name, she had agreed in a daze, only too aware what such payment would mean. It was rare for any woman to be granted land and a home in her own right, to become a landowner was to be a woman of property, an heiress, and no longer reliant on a man for her food and board.

"A twelvemonth pretending to be your mistress," she had agreed, shaking his hand.

Lord Munro had smiled at last, his blue eyes warmer now. "A twelvemonth on my terms, and the land is yours."

Now Kate was looking at her expectantly, and Margerie could not tell her how this business had come about, nor that she was not Lord Munro's mistress, but must lie to her dearest friend. For if she told the truth, and word got out, she would stand to lose the land and property Munro had promised her. And she had never owned anything in her life. Nothing but her reputation.

"I accepted his offer," she told her friend lightly, "because he pleases me."

"Munro pleases you?"

"You sound surprised. Should he not?"

Kate shrugged, lowering her gaze to the embroidery frame they had both been working on that morning. It depicted a hunting scene, with two dogs dragging down a stag, and men in the foreground, carrying knives and sticks, their faces flushed with excitement and exertion.

"I thought him one of those youths who rather prefers the company of other men, that is all." Her friend held a pale green embroidery silk up to the frame, testing the delicate color against the others. "But I must have been mistaken."

"Yes, you must."

Kate looked at her sideways. "And your handsome doctor?"

Her tone was sly. "Master Elton has returned to court, you know. I thought you wished to make his better acquaintance."

Margerie sucked in her breath. Her lip wobbled as she bit it, steadying herself. Master Elton was a dream she could no longer pursue. Not unless she wished the court to think she had the energy and lewd shamelessness to take three men into her bed. Such a scandal would almost certainly bring her behavior to the attention of the queen.

Besides, the good doctor might have wanted her badly at Greenwich, but he would not look at her again once he heard the rumors about her and Munro, which would surely start to circulate after she had spent her first evening in the young lord's company. Virgil Elton was a respectable man, and betrothed to another woman by his own admission. He would not waste his time on Munro's mistress, however desirable he had once thought her.

Her hands trembled as she took up her needle again, but Margerie dismissed the deep sense of loss aching inside her. Better to have the lifetime of independence that Munro had offered her than a few brief nights of pleasure with a man who could never be hers. Though in her heart she knew it would not be easy to set aside all thoughts of Virgil Elton.

———

Virgil Elton had found it impossible to stop thinking of Margerie Croft. Nor was there any reason he should do so, when he was not yet married and she could so easily be his. After all, once he was wedded to Christina—the thought was strange enough to make him uneasy—he would still have physical needs, and Christina was unlikely ever to be well enough to satisfy them. To keep a mistress at court was the obvious solution.

One evening, after three days of waking with a stone-hard cock, Margerie's face and luscious body in his dreams, Virgil made his way with determination to the women's quarters where his resourceful servant, Ned, had discovered she was lodged. He had no very good idea what he would say when he got there. But it would have made little difference if he had prepared some elaborate excuse, for as soon as he made his way up the winding stair and found Mistress Croft standing in the open doorway, he stopped and stared, unable to speak a word.

"Master Elton!"

Her eyes widened at the sight of him, her lips parting, and she half-turned toward him. Her bodice stretched about her breasts, pulled in tight by a belt at her waist, the long draped folds of her gown hiding the delectable beauty of long legs beneath. Virgil gazed at her in the doorway, and was haunted by the memory of her body against his in the rustling darkness of that yew hedge, so sweetly hot and yielding he had been lost in lust as she kissed him.

His cock hardening, Virgil sketched a curt bow that he hoped would conceal his arousal. "Mistress Croft."

She curtsied in response, her expression oddly cautious, considering their last meeting. The bodice gaped as she dipped down, and he caught a tantalizing glimpse of her breasts, pale and rounded.

"How… How may I help you, sir?" she asked, and he could hear her voice trembling.

"Forgive my intrusion, mistress. I merely wish to satisfy myself…that you are not in need of further medicament. I feared you might have run out by now. If so, you are more than welcome to come to my workshop, Mistress Croft, where I will furnish you with a fresh supply."

She had understood his veiled invitation, he was sure of it. There was color in her face now, her green eyes over-bright. But she did not smile in return.

"Sir, I thank you for this kind attention. But I am much improved since…since the court moved from Greenwich."

Virgil stared. Was she rejecting him? An unexpected sensation stole his breath away and for a moment he could not answer. Then he nodded, smiling again to hide his reaction.

"You have no more need of my sleeping draft, in fact?"

"Just so," she murmured.

"Indeed, I am glad to hear that."

Virgil was not glad, but he had at least understood her, that was for certain. She did not wish to repeat the breathless attack of lust they had experienced that night in the gardens at Greenwich, nor had she any plans to consummate the attraction between them. There was no more to be said.

"It seems you are cured of your indisposition. I will bid you a good evening then, Mistress Croft."

Her slight curtsy dismissed him, its brevity almost insolent as she turned away. "Good evening, Master Elton."

So that was that, he thought, and frowned. The meeting had not gone as he had planned. But at least he was left in no doubt of her feelings toward him. He must have been mistaken when he thought Mistress Croft open to his advances. Or perhaps he had left it too late and some other man had laid a claim on her while he was away from court.

Virgil made his way back to his bedchamber, suddenly aware of a need to be alone where no man might see him. He found Ned on his knees lighting the fire, and sent the boy on his way after the exchange of a few idle words. The room was oddly silent after Ned had gone. But then he had hoped to be bringing back a glorious companion for the night, and instead he was alone.

What had he expected? That Margerie Croft would be his for the asking? This was a woman who had refused to lie with the King of England. What would persuade her to accept a humble court physician instead, even one whose godfather had been one of the king's favorite tutors?

The steady glow and crackle of the fire comforted him as he took a book from his bedside, and pulled up his chair to the hearth. But even as he admired the remarkable balance and logic of Sallust's Latin prose, his thoughts were elsewhere, remembering the expression on her face, the way Margerie had avoided looking at him directly, the strange hesitancy of her speech...

Had Margerie Croft lied to him tonight? And if so, why?

———

Five nights later, he had his answer. He had been summoned to the bedside of Sir Christopher late one evening, one of the men he had interrupted during Margerie's attempted rape earlier that year. The knight had been wounded in the leg during a jousting contest before the king and queen, and was feverish. It was clear from his initial examination that the humors were out of balance and the man needed to be bled. Virgil had performed the deed himself, placing the leeches carefully at certain points on his body while Sir Christopher swore and ranted against the opponent who had bested him.

"An idiot who can barely sit a horse," he was telling his friend, who was standing beside the bed with folded arms. "Now I shall hear nothing at court but this failure for the next month at least. And all because my guard was weak. Otherwise the fool could not have got near me."

Virgil's lips twitched. "There," he murmured, beginning to remove the leeches, dropping each one into a small copper bowl. "Your bleeding should bring the fever down. That, along with the cooling draft I will leave you. One drop on your tongue every hour tonight will suffice, sir, and if you are still feverish in the morning send your boy to me and I will attend you again."

"Too full of himself by far, that dolt Munro," his patient told his friend, ignoring Virgil. "On any other day I could have taken him down with one hand tied behind my back, I swear it."

Virgil set the cooling draft beside Sir Christopher's bed, then packed the leeches away one by one in their slimy container, careful not to make any comment. He disliked the man intensely, but one could not pick one's patients at court. Or not without exciting the kind of attention he preferred to avoid.

Sir Christopher continued, "So now my lord Munro has a mistress, and this, we are to believe, has changed him overnight from a boy with two left feet to a champion of the joust. As though all it takes to make a man is a night or two with a skillful whore."

His friend looked askance. "Who is this skilled courtesan that Munro takes to mistress?"

"Margerie Croft, no less. And even the king is displeased now, for she scorned to take His Majesty as a lover, yet accepts this boy into her bed. There will be trouble over this, mark my words."

Virgil stilled, carefully wiping his hands after handling the leeches. *Margerie Croft, no less.* A shaft of pain lanced through him, and it was all he could do to stay silent, slipping his physician's instruments back into his bag. So he had been right. That was why she had rejected him. Because Margerie Croft preferred a nobleman in her bed.

Jealousy buffeted him, violent and unthinking, and he felt a sudden furious urge to find the man who was keeping her bed warm and throttle him. But Virgil kept his face composed, only betraying by the slightest flicker that he had any interest in their conversation.

"Unless there is something else you need, sir," Virgil remarked, "I will leave you."

Sir Christopher waved him away without interest. Then his friend muttered something in his ear, and the knight seemed to change his mind.

"Wait, Master Elton," he called after him. "You will not repeat what you have heard here today. It is a doctor's place to heal the sick, not spread gossip… Even when it concerns a known whore." Sir

Christopher nodded to his friend, who fished a few coins out of his pouch and tossed them onto the bed covers. "Your fee, Master Elton."

Virgil looked at both men coldly, then collected up the scattered coins. "You are sure you have no other complaint that needs my treatment, Sir Christopher?" he asked softly.

A flush came into the knight's face and he said nothing. Virgil bowed, unsmiling, and took himself out of the knight's candlelit chamber. He was bound, under the Hippocratic Oath he had sworn on entering into his profession, not to reveal any secrets he knew about any man, whether told to him as a physician or otherwise. But sometimes he was sorely tempted.

He had treated Sir Christopher in the past for certain embarrassing ailments of the groin, for he was known at court as a doctor who understood the treatment of such disorders better than most. To hear a knight speak about Margerie Croft in those terms had left him furious.

A known whore…

His steps slowing, he deliberately chose to return to his chamber a different way. This route would take him past the women's chambers where he knew Margerie slept. Unless she was in Lord Munro's bed tonight.

Again, the whip of jealousy descended across his shoulders and he ground his teeth. He knew Munro. A wealthy and handsome youth who had come into his title early, while the boy was still a student at Oxford.

"She likes her lords," he muttered to himself.

First Lord Wolf, now Lord Munro. A mere commoner, he should have realized his kisses would compare unfavorably to those of noblemen, however high he might stand in the king's estimation as a physician.

He stopped, listening. Someone was coming along the shadowy corridor ahead. He could hear light footsteps, almost shuffling. Then a dim figure passed beneath the nearest torch and he saw her face, pale, her eyes open but devoid of expression, her lips parted in a string of barely coherent whispers.

He stared. It was Margerie Croft herself, wandering barefoot in her sleep, her unbound hair tumbling in a cloudy red cascade to her waist, clad in nothing but a thin white shift.

Fortuna audaces iuvat, he thought fiercely. Fortune favors the bold. And he would have to be bold if he wished to be favored by this beautiful, elusive creature.

"He will not touch me again. No, I will not allow it." Her voice dwindled to nothing, descending into vague murmurings. Then suddenly, more succinctly, "You must let me go, sir. You cannot keep me here forever…"

So her night wanderings were *not* at an end, as she had tried to pretend. And here was the proof.

Putting down his bag, Virgil stepped into her path and caught her by the shoulders. "Margerie," he said quietly, looking into her face.

But her clear green gaze looked past him, empty and seemingly unaware of her surroundings.

She was asleep.

Virgil stood a moment, thinking, still holding her lightly. He had read of somnambulists in ancient texts, troubled souls who walked in their sleep, and had even prescribed a sleeping draft to keep her nightmares at bay. But he had not truly believed it to be possible until he had seen the phenomenon with his own eyes, thinking she and Kate Langley must have exaggerated her condition.

What was it that stirred her soul so deeply, she must wander the palace at night?

"Are you awake, Margerie? Can you hear me?" His whisper echoed in the narrow corridor. "Do you know where you are?"

She did not respond but stood passive and blank-faced, breathing more deeply now, as though fast asleep. His gaze dropped to her mouth, and a powerful surge of desire moved through his body, surprising him.

She was at once vulnerable and strong, her swaying curves generous, her height imposing, suggesting she was the equal of a man. In any other woman such fiery independence of spirit would have left him cool. Yet something about Margerie threw out a challenge to every male she passed—an instinctive lure as old as time, a dare that he found nigh impossible to resist—to tame and subdue her if he was up to the task. And Virgil knew he was.

His cock hardened, his lust so visceral it was hard to think of anything but burying himself in her body. But not like this. He wanted Margerie to be awake when he took her.

"Margerie, I am going to kiss you," he warned her, but there was no flicker of response in that pale face.

Was she in truth asleep, or just feigning?

There was one way to find out. Grasping her shoulders, Virgil leaned forward and set his lips to hers. The violent shock that ran through him as their mouths touched stole his ability to breathe, to think, to retain control over himself. She was still asleep. He should not be doing this, it was not right. Still he could not draw away.

His kiss deepened, and as her lips parted softly under that pressure, Virgil pushed his tongue inside and tasted her. That was his undoing. His heart sped up at once, heat entering his cheeks, and as his tongue slid against hers he became aware of his cock stiffening with an almost animal instinct to mate.

She tasted like honey, and God's blood, he was drowning in her. Drowning…

Then suddenly Margerie was struggling in his arms, jerking away from him, gasping and shaking. Virgil let her go, not wanting to hurt her by insisting. He was not interested in forcing Margerie into an embrace she did not welcome.

Besides, her eyes held awareness now. She was awake.

Ten

IN HER DREAM, VIRGIL Elton had been kissing her. His mouth had played against hers, gentle at first, then more demanding. Starved for his touch, she had leaned against him in her dream, not ever wishing to wake up if it would mean the end of this kiss. Her whole body had responded to his scent, his hard body against hers, the thrust of his tongue into her mouth.

Then abruptly she was no longer asleep, and upon waking found it was no dream.

She was standing up in her nightgown, her bare feet chilly, a draft making the torchlight flicker on her closed eyelids. Her eyes flew open. Virgil Elton was there in front of her, real and hard and undeniable. And he was kissing her.

"Master Elton!"

Margerie pushed him away and took a few hurried steps backward. Her head was buzzing with shock as she stared wildly about herself, disoriented at waking to find herself not in bed as she had anticipated, but in an unfamiliar place—and with a man kissing her. Her memory flashed back to that night when she had woken to hear her own screams, finding a ring of horrified women about her, and the doctor summoned to help her.

At least there were no leering guards here to witness her shame, nor had she apparently disturbed the ladies this time when she left their palace quarters. But it would still be hard to imagine a more embarrassing awakening. For she was standing in her nightgown in this shadowy corridor, alone with a man she found irresistible.

Slowly, once her countenance was under control, Margerie looked back at him. "Where am I?"

"Not far from the women's chambers."

She shook herself like a dog coming out of water, the tattered remnants of her dream still clinging to her. "Was I walking in my sleep again?" His curt "Yes" made her eyes focus more carefully on his face.

His jaw was set hard, his dark gaze restless as it slipped down her body, and she read frustration in his face. Almost certainly the same frustration she was experiencing too. It was sexual in nature, she could not deny it. She wanted this man. Even in her sleep she had responded unthinkingly to his kiss.

"You kissed me while I was sleeping."

"Forgive me."

He was looking at her, a question in his eyes. She felt as though she could share anything with him, speak the truth straight to him, as she had never spoken to any other man. But instinct warned her to be cautious.

"What is it?" she asked huskily.

His cap had tumbled off when she pushed him away. He bent to pick it up, then shoved a hand through his long dark hair as though to force his tumbled locks into some semblance of order. She looked at the dark curls brushing his shoulder and imagined tangling her fingers in them while they kissed, lying naked together.

"I would ask you something privately, Mistress Croft."

"Are we not private enough here?"

"This is the king's palace," he pointed out drily, glancing about at the flickering darkness before returning his gaze to her. "Walls have ears, as do deserted corridors."

Her mouth was dry. Margerie knew what was coming, and realized she had no intention of trying to stop it. This thing between them felt as inevitable as spring following winter; all she could do was try not to let her need show too badly, for this man could hurt her deeply if he wished.

"Where then?"

Master Elton had been examining her thin and unadorned nightgown, and she was warned by the way his lips had parted, his breathing quickening, that he must be able to see the outline of her naked body through it. The thought both alarmed and aroused her.

His gaze lifted to hers. "My chamber."

"Your *bed*chamber, you mean?"

His slow smile nearly stopped her heart. "The same. You have some objection?"

She ought to have. But she did not. Ever since that night when Virgil Elton had kissed and touched her so intimately in the rose gardens, Margerie had been imagining how it would feel to lie with this man. Now his invitation was clear. Her head said she should refuse him and return to the women's chamber. But her body clamored to lie naked next to his and to discover what pleasure he could bring her.

Yet still she hesitated.

She had only ever lain with one man, Lord Wolf, who had taken her virginity, leaving her hurt and in despair. Margerie knew now that Wolf was a good man, that he had made a mistake as an inexperienced youth and had never intended her harm. But the events of that night still lingered in her mind.

Virgil bent to pick up his bag, then looked at her. "Well?"

His eyebrows rose steeply when Margerie did not reply, and his next words made her blush, wondering if he could read her thoughts.

"I merely wish to speak with you on a matter of some delicacy, Mistress Croft," he said coolly. "I am a physician. There is nothing improper in my suggestion. Many ladies come to visit me at court."

"But not unaccompanied, and not to your *bedchamber*," she replied a little sharply, though in truth she was barely able to raise her eyes to his, half-afraid that this man could tell her fevered imaginings just by studying her face. "You may be a doctor, sir, but if we are discovered alone together in your chamber in the middle of the night, no one will think it an innocent meeting."

"Then let us hope no one either hears or sees us."

He bowed, indicating that she should accompany him, and to her own surprise Margerie found herself walking beside him without argument, as though it was the most natural thing in the world for a man she barely knew to be taking her to his bedchamber.

They walked silently through the darkened palace, passed a few times by patrolling guards with leering expressions, though none of the men dared comment with Master Elton by her side. But she could guess what they were thinking.

"They are jealous, that is all," he said in her ear. "They wish themselves in my shoes."

"They think me a whore."

He looked at her sideways. "Are you a whore?"

"No," she insisted.

"Then what does it matter what such men think?" His smile was dry. "Lift up your head, Mistress Croft, and hold it high. You have done nothing wrong."

Yet, she thought, raising her chin to meet his gaze, but kept the treacherous word to herself.

His bedchamber was warm, a fire still glowing in the hearth. Master Elton locked the door, then set his bag carefully aside. He swung the cloak from his shoulders, and she saw that he was wearing a plain doublet and hose beneath, the clothes of a hard-working man. Even his codpiece was starkly functional, a black leather bulge at the head of long muscular thighs.

The court physician was no wealthy noble like Lord Munro, she thought, a man who donned lavish vestments, gold chains and a glistening red codpiece to draw the eye to his youthful form. Yet there was something equally powerful about Master Elton. A quiet author-ity which excited her in some way she did not entirely understand.

Ridiculously nervous, Margerie stood in the middle of the room and watched while he lit a candle from the fire and set it on the mantel. The bedchamber was empty but neatly swept, and when she stumbled toward the rough cot which clearly served as his bed, she noticed a faint scent of something sweet. Fresh-culled herbs perhaps, strewn under the pillows to improve sleep and ward off bad dreams, just as he had suggested to avert her problem.

The doctor came up behind her, placing his hands on her shoul-ders. Her body tingled with awareness under his touch and she knew he could feel it.

"Margerie," he said quietly. "Are you afraid?"

"Not afraid, no."

Yet she shivered when he bent his head, smoothing her heavy mass of hair to one side, and she felt his lips brush the nape of her neck.

"What then?"

"I am not…" She paused, unwilling to admit that she was not as experienced in the amorous arts as so many at court believed.

He would think she was lying to gain some kind of power over him, perhaps to make him feel guilty for wanting to seduce her. And although her whole being rebelled at the idea of dishonesty between them, part of her also feared that disclosure. For Master Elton might act the gentleman and stop kissing her if she told him her experience in the bedchamber was limited to one night.

"You are not…what?"

She turned in his arms, and found herself locked to the hungry expression in his dark eyes, unable to look away.

"Not sure if this is what you truly want," she lied, wishing she was not so breathless. "I thought you wanted to speak with me privately. That was why you brought me here, after all. Not to seduce me."

"Is that what I'm doing, Margerie? Seducing you?"

His gaze seemed to hold hers for an eternity before she managed to break the spell, looking away.

"Sir, I do not blame you for thinking me a loose woman. The way I behaved last time we were alone together was not customary for me. That is, I do not rightly know what came over me. I must have been out of my senses. But now my head is straight, and we both know this cannot happen. You are one of the king's physicians, Master Elton, and I am a lady whose name is not high in His Majesty's favor at the moment." She ended firmly, "I would not want your reputation to suffer by entertaining me alone in your chamber."

"I have never known a woman to talk more nonsense than you," he said roughly.

Her eyes widened on his face. He was not smiling.

"Sir?"

"I like the way you call me sir," he whispered, then drew a sharp breath. "Your nightmares, your wanderings… What is it that makes you wander the palace in your sleep, Mistress Croft?"

"I do not know."

"I keep thinking of Dido, alone and weeping in Carthage."

Margerie looked at him blankly.

"You do not know the story of Dido and the Trojan Aeneas?" he asked, and she shook her head, bewildered.

"With the help of Venus," he explained softly, "Aeneas escaped from Troy after it burned and voyaged across the seas. It was his destiny to found the city of Rome, you see. Only he came to Carthage first, after his ships were wrecked in a storm. And he fell in love with the queen there, Dido." His smile was almost bitter. "Venus was furious. She was Aeneas's mother, and did not want Dido ruining her son's destiny. So she sent Aeneas away on his travels, and poor weeping Dido was left alone again."

He cupped her face between his hands, then ran a thumb across her mouth, pressing her lips apart. "The poet Virgil wrote of their sad love, *est mollis flamma medullas interea et tacitum vivit sub pectore vulnus*. Which is in Latin, *fire burns in her soft marrow, and a silent wound lives beneath her breast.*" His eyes were intent on her face. "What silent wound do you harbor beneath your breast, Margerie? What hurt makes you wander in your sleep, crying over the past?"

That was too close to the truth, and Margerie shuddered beneath his searching look, thinking of her lost reputation, the stares and whispers of the court, and how her past mistakes had left her achingly empty and afraid of her own shadow.

"Call me sir again," he murmured. "It is strange, but I enjoy hearing that word on your tongue."

The desire in his voice had kindled the long-suppressed fire smoldering in her belly. This was madness, she thought. She was perfectly right to be cautious, she told herself, her senses drugged by the sweet pressure of his thumb against her mouth. What if they were discovered together? No lie in the world could conceal the intimacy between them.

"Obey me, Margerie."

She drew a shaky breath at his arrogance, yet could not seem to deny him. There was something in that authoritative tone that made her melt, all at once his servant.

"Sir," she whispered.

Virgil Elton made a noise under his breath, staring into her eyes, his face suddenly tense. "Now call me master," he commanded her, "and mean it."

Margerie stared back at him, her lips burning where his thumb was stroking back and forth, not quite pushing inside. She knew it was time to pull away, to make him say his piece so she could leave, fleeing back to her own chamber unscathed.

Instead she did a foolish thing.

Unable to resist the tug of his body any longer, Margerie turned her head slightly and brushed her lips against his wrist, just lightly, where the skin showed below the cuff of his sleeve.

She had intended it to be only a momentary caress. Her eyes closed though, and she swayed there, caught in the heady spell cast by his presence, her heartbeat drumming almost painfully.

Everything in her body narrowed to that one inch of warm skin where she could taste him: the veriest salt-tang on her lips, the veins in his wrist begging for her tongue, for the erratic thud of his pulse to be traced to its source. And as Margerie stood there, unable to stop herself from wanting this man, a wave of helpless desire crashed through her body, and she knew it was flooding him too.

"Master," she mumbled against his wrist, her voice thick with lust, unrecognizable. What was the matter with her? she thought. Could she not resist this man even for a moment?

With a groan, he dragged down her lower lip, then bent and kissed her, pushing his tongue deep between her parted lips.

Margerie gasped, her mind and body reeling. She had barely been kissed by Wolf the night they spent together, and she remembered from Greenwich how easily Virgil Elton could arouse her, but the power behind his kiss tonight left her wet and ready for him almost instantly. But perhaps she had secretly been wanting him to kiss her ever since she woke to find herself in his arms, his lips pressed against hers, his tongue exploring her mouth with absolute hunger.

Her head fell back under the force of his kiss. Her arms lifted, locking passionately about his neck, and she kissed him back without reserve.

His hands dropped first to her waist, dragging her close, then slid down her spine to the rounded curve of her buttocks. His touch was urgent, molding her against him in her thin night shift, and she felt the thickening bulge under his codpiece.

"I want you," he muttered against her mouth. "But first I

need to know if it's true you have consented to become Lord Munro's mistress."

She stilled in his arms, her eyes closed tight.

A few days back at court, and he already knew. But of course he knew. Had she thought such an arrangement could be kept quiet at court? Her disgrace would mean little to most courtiers, for she was simply another unmarried woman who had been drawn under a nobleman's protection for a while. And she was no innocent virgin, everyone knew that.

But Virgil Elton might see it in a different way. After all, she had known his intentions toward her since their brief time together at Greenwich, yet she had consented to become Munro's mistress as well. Such promiscuity must be abhorrent to him.

Yet there was nothing she could do to prevent him from thinking her a whore, and perhaps even hating her for it. If she wished to uphold her side of the bargain and receive Munro's generous gift of land, Master Elton must never discover that her relationship with the young lord was a mere convenience, not a true affair. Her future happiness depended upon that arrangement. And that was more important than the fleeting pleasure this man could give her.

A good marriage is out of the question for a woman of my reputation, she reminded herself sternly. Let this man think me a careless wanton; I must do whatever will keep the wolf from the door in years to come.

"Yes, it's true."

Her answer made him hiss under his breath, but to her surprise Master Elton did not push her away. Instead his arms tightened about her.

"You should have told me sooner," he said, his face an unreadable mask. "I dislike the thought of sharing you. But if that is how it must be, so be it."

She stared at him, unsure. "You accept that I am his mistress?"

"I am not happy for you to be his mistress. And I fear his lordship will not wish to share you either. But until he warns me off, I will take whatever is put before me and not ask for more."

It was a convincing speech, but Margerie saw a flicker in his dark eyes as he smoothed a hand over her hip, and guessed the physician was not as forgiving as he was at pains to seem. But at least it seemed he would not leave her cold and frustrated tonight. And for that she must be glad. For her body burned for his in a way she had never experienced before.

"From now on," he said, watching her, "you will keep me informed of any other men you take to your bed. I will have no lies or omissions between us. You understand?"

She nodded, but shivered. For this was a lie in itself.

Virgil must have caught her instinctive response. "Here," he murmured, drawing her closer to the fire, "you are cold. Come sit on my lap before the fire. Trust me, you will soon be warm again."

She had feared he would be angry when he heard about her and Munro. Yet he seemed almost relieved, she realized, struggling to read his expression. Perhaps Virgil had been concerned she might trap him into marriage. With a powerful protector like Munro though, a woman's first thought if she fell pregnant would be to apply to his lordship for help. Not to a court physician.

His smile was wolfish as he pulled forward his chair, sat upon it, then seated her firmly on his lap. His hand gripping the back of her neck, he kissed her again with a fiery possessiveness that bordered on violence.

Margerie gasped, but to her own surprise did not struggle, surrendering with a delicious sensation, part fear, part excitement. He would not hurt her, she knew that. Or if he did, she would surely enjoy it. His mouth played against hers, his tongue stabbing deep, then slipping back out, tracing slowly along her lips as though he found her taste irresistible. She began to breathe more heavily, clinging onto him, her face hot with desire.

"You want me, Margerie?" he asked, bending his head to kiss her throat.

"Yes."

His voice was husky. "Badly?"

She could barely speak, but managed to nod, already busy exploring him, stroking the broad expanse of his shoulders and back. She loved the feel of his strong muscles moving under her fingers, how they stretched and rippled as he shifted. Her mouth became dry as she imagined how he must look naked. He was powerfully built, but lean with it, and she was suddenly impatient to feel his skin against hers.

"Take off your clothes," she whispered.

He gave a short laugh, then stroked a slow hand up her calf under her shift. "Impatient wanton."

She wriggled, biting her lip as his hand moved inexorably higher. Skin on skin now, burning into her. He pushed her shift up, exposing her bare thighs, and she could not stay silent any longer.

"Please."

"Hush, all in good time."

His fingers had found her core, starting to stroke at the apex of her thighs. She gasped as one long finger eased inside her hidden lips, and he gave a twisted smile in response.

"So soft and welcoming." Virgil pushed deeper, using two fingers now, entering and caressing at the same time. He made a guttural noise in the back of his throat, as though aroused by how easily he had penetrated her. "So wet. Is that for me?"

She moaned, staring into his eyes. "Virgil…"

Slowly he withdrew his fingers, then dragged down the bodice of her shift. Not merely content to spill her breasts, he yanked it down to her waist, freeing her arms and leaving her top half naked. Margerie blushed to see him staring at her bare body, his dark eyes intent, but did not move to cover herself. She had known how this would end when she agreed to accompany the doctor to his bed-chamber, and she refused to act the hypocrite or play hard to get when this was what they both wanted.

Her breasts glowed a rosy pink in the firelight, and when he ran a finger, damp with her own juices, across one nipple, she felt the skin harden in expectation.

"Oh," she gasped.

Virgil gave a taut smile. "Oh, indeed." Then he bent his head and took her nipple in his mouth. His hand came round, cupping the other breast, and his thumb stroked back and forth across her nipple until that too was aching and erect.

Margerie found herself whispering, "Oh God," under her breath, and could not stop herself. But it felt so good, his mouth on her breast, suckling like a babe, and yet hot and demanding at the same time, a man's caress that left her in no doubt of his intentions. Her head fell back in abandon, the soft little sounds in her throat urging him on, and her red hair hung loose and heavy against her naked back.

Whatever she had expected, Margerie thought, it was not this. Her breasts ticked with pleasure as his tongue explored them, her head light and dizzy at the onslaught of pleasure. She no longer clung to him in desperation, but let her arms fall to her sides, her body strangely sensual in a way she had never felt before in the company of a man.

She closed her eyes, experiencing a wonderful sense of freedom. "Yes," she whispered, raising herself for his touch. "Yes, please."

How shocking to behave like such a wanton. Yet it seemed to her that she could do whatever she chose in this room and he would not stop her, nor judge her in any way. It was as though they were both free of restraint within the confines of his bedchamber, a place where no other soul could intervene or disturb their peace.

His hand had found her again. He parted her thighs, pushing back inside the soft wet flesh, making her his. Still he sucked on her breast, dragging her erect nipple to the back of his mouth, pressing it deliciously with his tongue until she thought she would die of bliss. She did not struggle, but eagerly opened herself for him, moaning as his fingers scissored inside her, stroking back and forth as he widened her narrow channel to make entry easier.

He lifted his head to stare at her. There was a dark color in his face and he was breathing hard. "You're so tight…"

There had been a question in his voice, but she ignored it, kissing his mouth. Their tongues mated, sliding hotly together, and the heat between them burst into flame.

Suddenly he was on his feet, carrying her swiftly to the table. He swept the books onto the floor and lay her down across the open rolls of paper, dragging her legs apart so that he was standing between them.

Margerie stared up at her seducer, light-headed and unsteady too, her whole body tingling with sexual excitement. She knew that she must look like a whore, thin white shift crumpled about her waist, her breasts carelessly exposed, her pale thighs spread wide for him. But she no longer cared what he thought. Only that he took her.

It seemed right to surrender so completely. Something about Virgil Elton demanded total capitulation from her, would accept nothing less. And it felt natural too. Natural to act the wanton for him, to give what she had given no other man since Wolf.

She was impatient for him to enter her, so arched her back, offering herself to him without reserve. She even slipped her hands between her legs, stroking herself quite shamelessly while he stared.

"Take me," she urged him.

His smile was dark, an air of restraint about him. "Not yet." Bending, Virgil slid both hands warmly down her thighs, forcing them as wide apart as they would go. "First, this."

She gasped in shock when he lowered his head and put his mouth to the slippery flesh between her legs. Surely he did not intend to…?

But he did intend it. Oh dear Lord.

He dragged the sensitive nub into his mouth and suckled on it like a nipple, milking her firmly until she cried out, "Stop!" unable to bear any more of that exquisite torment. Then his tongue stroked further down, tasting her body, slipping firmly inside her, darting back and forth, making her sob with pleasure.

"Please, please," Margerie begged him raggedly, not knowing if she meant "Please stop," or "Please go on," for by then she was almost incoherent with desire.

Whatever she meant, Virgil Elton paid no attention. His mouth returned to the tiny nub of flesh, working it wickedly, rolling and nipping it between his teeth until she was beyond all reason.

She linked both legs behind his head and drew him closer, crying out "Yes!" and thrashing wildly from side to side, her hands gripping the edges of the table in desperation.

Quite suddenly her body stiffened and she came to a high fiery peak, everything in the universe centered in her belly where a brilliant flame had flared up, burning out of control.

Gasping and sobbing, Margerie had no choice but to let the fire consume her, keeping her legs locked tight, his mouth hard against her flesh. "Sweet Lord!" she cried out several times, falling sharply from the heights, deafened by the thundering of her own heart, her skin damp with sweat, limbs trembling.

Finally Virgil relented. He pulled back just as her legs began to weaken about him, and gave a husky laugh.

"My turn," he muttered unsteadily.

Eleven

AFTER HER CRIES HAD died away, Margerie had opened her green eyes, framed by long curling lashes, and was staring up at him through the flickering glow of the firelight. Dear God, she was desirable. And so abandoned in her response to him, he had thought she would wake the whole palace with her cries and moans of passion. Even now she seemed wild-eyed, her cheeks flushed, red hair stuck damply to her forehead, and he could not help smiling when he saw how tightly her hands still gripped the sides of the table.

The hardness of his cock was unbearable. Virgil reared up to release himself from the restraint of his codpiece. He had intended to take her without delay straight after her climax, for it was difficult to resist the way her thighs had fallen open for him again, parting so invitingly, and that red-curled thatch between them, sweet and wet and luscious.

But instead he surprised himself by pausing to strip off more of his clothes, his smile lopsided when he saw how she stared, her green eyes wide, studying his naked form for the first time.

It seemed impossible that Margerie Croft could want him with the same physical urgency he felt for her. Yet he caught the lust shining in her eyes as her gaze moved slowly over him, and knew himself wanted.

What further aphrodisiac could any man want but a woman's desire?

He had removed everything but his shirt, which still hung unfastened, almost slipping from his shoulders. He had intended to shrug it to the floor. But then his cock was in his fist, more rigid than he had ever known it, and a greater need took precedence.

"Virgil," she whispered, and raised her hips for him in willing surrender.

Meeting her gaze, he felt an irrational urge to tear what remained of her creased night shift from about her waist, to see her naked and vulnerable before him, a wondrous green-eyed Eve to his Adam. Yet there was little enough of her body that was still concealed, and he rather enjoyed the reminder that they were both hurrying, neither bothering to undress fully nor to use the more conventional bed behind him.

Virgil examined her body, trying to slow the schoolboyish pounding in his chest at the sight of her nudity. Her breasts were small, but not unpleasingly so, each taut curve tipped with a rosy nipple that begged to be sucked and drawn to a peak. Her waist was narrow, her hips generously feminine, and he almost smiled to recall the pressure of those long lithe thighs about his shoulders and back. At the apex of her thighs lay a riot of soft red curls, the lips beneath still glistening from his tongue.

Besides, he reminded himself, he could hardly tear off her shift like a madman. She would need some kind of garment to wear back to her chamber later.

The need to hurry came back to him with a shock. Virgil stepped forward with sudden purpose, positioning himself between her spread thighs.

"Yes," he muttered as she reached down, guiding him eagerly inside.

Margerie was far tighter than any of the other courtesans he had bedded, and seemed almost agitated in her excitement. Her hands pushed the shirt from his shoulders as he drove inside, her nails digging into his bare skin as though she found it painful.

Certainly it was not easy.

Her damp outer lips gave way to a narrow passage, almost

virginal in its dimensions, and so constrictive he had to adjust his position, then thrust quite powerfully just to enter her. She gave a thin cry beneath him, no doubt in protest at the force he had used, but Virgil did not dare look at her, his head turned away, his eyes shut in sudden fierce concentration.

God's blood!

If he was not careful, he would lose all control and end up looking like a damn virgin. Yet the temptation to thrust straight to a climax was next to unbearable.

Her hot moist walls gripped him like a slippery fist. Every movement, however slight, brought the most delicious—and dangerous—sensation of impending bliss. Virgil felt an intense urge to spend himself and had to pause where he was, panting slightly, embedded deep inside her, until his need became less pressing.

After a moment, the sensation lessened. He risked turning his head, and found her staring up at him, softly flushed, her gaze over-bright.

Were those tears in her eyes?

"Did I hurt you?" he asked, frowning.

Wordlessly, Margerie gave a tiny shake of her head.

"You must forgive me if I was clumsy," he managed with an effort.

"Not clumsy. Not that."

Perhaps he had been too abrupt in his mounting of her. Too certain that it was what she wanted too. Margerie might have the reputation of a courtesan, but she was still a woman, and all women liked to be kissed and caressed during bed play, especially when the play had been rough.

Supporting himself on his hands, not wishing to crush her slender body, Virgil set his mouth to hers. Her lips parted on a groan, admitting his tongue, and he plumbed her mouth luxuriously, her sweetness and submission reminding him of why he had wanted to bed her in the first place.

His eyes closed, and he lost himself in the most sensual kiss he had ever experienced. His cock grew inside her, hardening even more, and as they kissed her thighs relaxed, shifting further apart, almost inviting him to thrust.

Eager to enjoy her body, he took advantage at once, beginning to stroke in and out with a slow, steady rhythm.

He would not hurry, he told himself, but ensure that she took pleasure in their first coupling. There would be plenty of time ahead to teach his new mistress of his tastes in bed, his particular likes and dislikes, how exciting he found a woman's acquiescence…

But when his thrusts increased, Margerie's head fell back, and a strangled moaning noise came from her throat. Her face and throat were flushed, a mottled pink spreading down her breasts, her nipples erect. Her hips rose and fell beneath his in the easy rhythm of fucking, urging him on with every stroke so that he barely needed to thrust, filling her to the hilt each time. It was almost as though they had been coupling for years, that they were in fact man and wife, already familiar with each other's bodies.

His own excitement grew, watching her eager response, feeling how wet and slippery she had become, listening to the sounds they made as they came together at the flux, then seemed to ebb away. They were like two waves of the sea, he thought, powerful and white-crested, crashing onto the shore side by side—and just as inexorable in their drive for completion.

Hunger hollowed him out and left him hot-faced and light-headed, breathing hard, intent on reaching his climax.

"Come with me," he urged her, and slipped a hand between her legs, rubbing at her wetness there.

Her cries grew more piercing and high-pitched, and as the end approached, he leaned forward and covered her mouth with his, muffling the noisy sobs of her pleasure. Then she seemed to shudder, and with a shock of disbelief he felt her contract about him as though *in extremis*, squeezing his flesh in a wave of swift powerful surges until he could bear it no longer.

"Virgil," she moaned against his mouth, "oh please, yes. You are my master. Own me. Possess me."

You are my master.

Own me.

Possess me.

He gathered her legs, bending her knees to her chest and thrusting hard. Margerie gasped, staring up at him, her face flushed, her lips swollen as though he had bruised them with the force of his kisses, her whole body still trembling in the grip of pleasure.

His buttocks clenched hard as he worked toward his own climax, panting as he drove again and again into her gloriously tight channel, his back and shoulders sweating with effort, their lower bodies locked violently together.

The pleasure was so intense it was almost painful, yet he could not stop or rest, he had to finish. And inside her too, though he had intended to pull out before reaching his peak and spill his seed on the floor or her belly. Instead every atom of his being wanted to spend inside her, to fill her womb and consider the consequences later.

Virgil stiffened, groaning, and plunged deep as he came. "Margerie," he gasped at the first release of his seed, surprising himself by experiencing some emotion akin to tenderness.

His mouth sought out her flesh, pressing a kiss against her throat, and the physical relief he had craved at once became sweeter, more intimate…and somehow dangerous.

Virgil struggled against the urge to reach up and kiss her mouth too. What was wrong with him? He had never felt such powerful emotion for a woman before, not even when he was younger and found himself taken with a lady of the court who never so much as glanced in his direction. And this, by her own admission, was no lady but a wanton. To feel tenderly toward her was nothing short of madness.

At last it was over, his body shuddering with passion, and he reluctantly forced himself to withdraw.

His eyes closed, he lay sprawled across her, panting, his heart thundering out of control, uneasily aware that this had been no ordinary coupling. He shifted after another few moments, pushing to his feet. If he remained there much longer, he might give in to that dangerous impulse and kiss her on the mouth.

Her thighs were still parted, damp now, the slender inner curves glimmering in the firelight. His seed, he realized, staring down at the evidence of his weakness. Tenderness fled on a wave of guilt, and suddenly he felt nothing but remorse for having lost control so completely that he had risked engendering a child on a courtesan.

For a second, he wondered if she would be angry with him. He ought to have withdrawn, and he knew it. Then he looked up at her drowsy, hot-cheeked face and guessed that Margerie was perfectly satisfied with what he had done, that she in fact had known the same driving urge as him. To mate and to be mated. Whatever the consequences.

No, that could not be. She was a courtesan. And no courtesan wished to end up with child after an encounter of this nature.

Margerie Croft shifted, sighing luxuriously as she yawned, and her small breasts lifted, her throat and chest still rosy from the pleasure she had experienced. He watched her body stretch, her thighs pulling up provocatively to reveal the beauty of her mons veneris between, and remembered how it had felt to ride there, enjoying the tightness of her body.

Now she was watching him as though remembering too, narrow-eyed and unsmiling, her unbound hair spilling across her shoulders in a soft red cloud.

A second wave of desire possessed him. But it was too soon to act upon it. His body was soft and relaxed, his heart rate slowing.

Or was it?

"Virgil," she whispered, and their eyes locked.

He wanted her again, he realized, and indeed was already hardening. She was the most feminine woman he had ever known. Her soft generous mouth invited him to probe it with his tongue, her emerald eyes spoke of the delights of a few hours alone with her in a bedchamber, and the way she moved…

Small wonder the king had wished to make Margerie his mistress. She was a delicacy few men could pass by untouched. And indeed she had taken other courtiers to her bed since the scandalous affair with a youthful Wolf. Yet here she was, in a mere court physician's chamber, mutely offering herself to him a second time as though he was worth more to her than King Henry himself.

She left him feeling taller just by smiling. More virile, more powerful, more of a man.

Perhaps it was time to test just how much of a man he was.

He moved to the alcove and found two cups. These he partly filled with wine, then turned to his cupboard, his hands still a little unsteady, and hunted through the medicaments for the special preparation he had set aside. Finding it, he unstoppered the bottle and carefully measured out three drops into his wine cup, then replaced the bottle in the cupboard. After a brief hesitation, he drained the cup. The taste was slightly bitter, and he shuddered, dragging a hand across his lips afterward. It was done.

"Here," he murmured, holding out the other cup to her. "Drink deep. It will fortify you."

"Do I need to be fortified?"

His smile was slow as he bent over her. "Put your arms about my neck and let us find out." Lifting her half-naked body against his chest, Virgil carried his new mistress easily to the bed. It was only a few steps, yet he found himself drowning in her heady scent, reminiscent of the damask rose, her body warm and softly feminine in his arms. And she watched him every step of the way, green eyes fixed on his face, her lips already parted as though in anticipation of his kiss.

Unable to resist, he lay her carefully on the bed, then arched over her and took her mouth. His tongue slipped between her lips, teasing and playing, and she responded at once, making a keening noise in her throat when his hands cupped her breasts.

"Why are you called Virgil?" she whispered against his mouth.

"My father's whim." He smiled. "Virgil was a Roman poet whose verses my father much admired. I told you of one of his poems... the story of the Trojan Aeneas, who fell in love with Queen Dido."

A fascinated expression in her eyes, she lifted a hand to his cheek. "You do look Roman. That nose..."

"And you look Celtic," he replied sharply. He tangled his fingers in her disheveled mass of red hair and tugged, dragging her head back so he could kiss her exposed throat. "My very own Boadicea."

"Oh, I am no queen."

Virgil looked up at her bitter tone, searching her face carefully. "My slave girl, then."

Her slow smile made him harden in anticipation. "Yes," she murmured, slipping her hand down to his shoulder, then over his body, stroking him at hip and thigh. "I like that better. I cannot rule but I know well how to serve."

Virgil soon grew rigid again. He stroked the loose strands of hair back from her face, admiring this green-eyed beauty and wishing she was in truth his slave girl. He kissed her deeply while she touched him in return, enjoying the provocative slide of her tongue against his, her hands exploring his body.

A faint scent of roses always hung about her. Yet when he kissed her, she tasted of cherries and wine, rich and sweet, leaving him half-drunk with desire. He was breathing hard when he finally relinquished her lips, his eyes closed, his body tingling with a strange, unfamiliar sensation.

Unfamiliar it might be, yet he knew what it was, and told himself not to be such a green fool. She was a wanton, and a skilled one at that, acting the untouched innocent to perfection, her body tight as any virgin's, her every moan and caress designed to make a man lose his wits over her.

And his wits might already be lost. God's blood, he was in serious danger of falling in love with a courtesan.

—⁓—

Margerie woke with a start in the doctor's bed, and was horrified to see the soft flush of dawn light through his shutters.

Fear consumed her at once. The palace would be awake soon, and she could hardly expect to remain here. She would be missed by the other women when they rose to wash and dress, and how to explain such a lengthy absence? It was one thing to spend the night in a high-ranking nobleman's chamber, for such arrangements were tacitly accepted at court when the woman was not herself of noble blood. But if it was discovered that she had been with Master Elton rather than his lordship…

Even if she left now, the chances of being seen were high, and all she had to preserve her dignity was her night shift, lying crumpled on the floor after last night's passion.

She swung her legs out of bed, careful not to disturb the man sleeping next to her, and winced as she stood up. He had not forced her, but their lovemaking had been rough, especially later in the night, when she had thought he would go gentler. Instead Virgil had hammered at her with long, powerful strokes that had left her gasping and clawing at his chest and shoulders, desperate for release. Taking his own satisfaction first, he had then crawled between her legs, licking and sucking her to a violent, much-needed climax.

Her sleep afterward had been so heavy she had no memory of

anything beyond that last blinding moment of pleasure. But now her body ached in unfamiliar places, and Margerie was ashamed to remember how she had cried his name and clung to him, begging for more. What must Master Elton think of her now?

She sighed, wriggling into her night shift and dragging it down over her hips. That question was easily answered. Virgil thought her a whore, and why should he not? She had chosen not to give him an explanation for her precarious reputation at court, nor for her curious arrangement with Lord Munro. That was her business, not his. And she had hardly come to him a virgin, after all.

It had been a night of intense pleasure and all-too-brief pockets of rest, during which Virgil's strength had renewed itself almost miraculously. She had not thought any man could remain aroused for so long, nor return to full hardness with such speed. Even Wolf, at the height of his youth, had not shown such virility.

She glanced back at him. He lay in exhausted sleep, one strong forearm flung across his eyes, his body gloriously nude and male. He was so handsome. Margerie examined him through narrowed eyes, and felt an aching throb between her thighs that no amount of lovemaking could assuage.

Lean-flanked, his hips angular, his belly flat, thighs long and muscular, Virgil Elton seemed more like a Roman statue of manly prowess than a mere mortal. The thought terrified her. He was a man, that was all. No noble lord, it was true, but a man like Wolf all the same, and he would seek to own her too, to stamp his seal upon her. Though she could not blame him for that either, for at the height of their passion last night she had begged him more than once to control her, to possess and dominate her. And he had obliged, his hands rough, his kisses demanding.

She tried not to keep staring, but her gaze was drawn inexorably back to his cock, lying thick and relaxed against his thigh.

Her mouth grew dry. In all the long night, during which he had repeatedly teased her back to arousal with his tongue, she had never once tasted *him*.

Daringly, Margerie knelt on the bed.

She took his cock in one hand, trying not to rouse him from sleep, then bent her head slowly. She was breathing hard before he was even at her mouth, and gave a little moan when she found his broad crest too large to fit without her lips parting more widely.

Her tongue flicked out, tasting the moist slit, and again she moaned. Her legs trembled and her belly tightened with need. Then she wet her lips and sucked him inside. First the smooth head, then the full thick length of him.

Sleepily, Virgil groaned.

Suddenly he was awake, his body tensing beneath hers, and she thought he would push her away. But instead his hand tangled in her hair, tugging her down as he parted his thighs. Nothing loath, she lowered herself still further, her shoulders bowed, until she lay between his legs like a whore. He made a rough noise under his breath, then his shaft began to swell and fill her mouth, hardening as though in response to her obedience.

Instinctively tilting her throat, Margerie took in as much of him as she could manage.

Dear Lord, she had never tasted anything so delicious!

She let him slip out again before drawing his shaft back inside, working her tongue over him at the same time, loving the way his flesh hardened, learning the veins and sturdy length of his cock.

After a few moments of this lascivious treatment, she felt his hips arch upward, then heard him hiss out his breath. He tugged on her hair. "Suck on me hard, woman," Virgil said throatily. "Pleasure me."

Once she would have fought against such authority, hating any man who sought to enslave her. Yet now the note of command in his voice sent her wild. Margerie moaned in the back of her throat, her face aflame with a heady mix of excitement and humiliation. So she obeyed his command, not sure why but wanting to please him all the same, to show Virgil how eager she was to play the wanton.

The flesh between her thighs grew slippery with need, aching for him inside her. But she ignored the demands of her own body. This moment was for Virgil, she told herself sternly. Not for her.

She might be inexperienced in the ways of pleasuring a man but she was determined to learn swiftly. Listening to his every gasp and whisper, she responded to the subtle shifts and peaks of his body, guessing what pleased him most by the way he reacted to her touch. Virgil grew rigid under her ministrations, despite having already spent himself several times during the night. When Margerie glanced up, she saw his face tense and dark, his eyes fixed on her, his lips drawn back from his teeth as though silently growling.

"You…are so skilled," he muttered, his voice tortured. "I would not have believed…this possible…but I am almost ready again."

Master Virgil Elton.

She imagined him as a Roman lord in a British bathhouse and herself as his Celtic slave girl, performing her daily duty of pleasuring him. Perhaps she might even have been lightly whipped beforehand, to soften her spirit and make her more willing to obey her overlord…

Her inner core moistened and tautened at such a barbaric pretense. It was a seductive image, both exciting and dangerous. Yet she could not seem to shake it.

Her jaws ached as she served the man beneath her, acting the powerless slave girl because it aroused her to do so. Using only her mouth and hands, she closed her eyes, her head sliding up and down, urging him on to complete satisfaction. And she was rewarded for her hard work. After another moment of strong sucking, her lips clamped about his swollen shaft, Virgil exploded with a shout.

Gasping, he thrust hard and his shaft leaped in her mouth,

pulsing his creamy seed down her throat. "Margerie!" Virgil jerked her head against his groin, groaning, "Yes, take me with your mouth. Swallow it."

―⁓―

Afterward, they lay tangled and sweating together as the sun rose and she could hear the muffled sounds of servants moving about the palace.

She would have to borrow a hooded cloak, Margerie thought sleepily, arranging herself more comfortably against his body, and hurry back to the women's quarters before she was missed. Though if she discreetly let it be known that she had been in Lord Munro's company last night, no further questions would be asked.

That was the way of the court. A nobleman might take a mistress from amongst the lower ranks without exciting much interest. But the same woman, unmarried, could not disport herself with just any man. Or not without risking censure and punishment.

"What are you thinking, Margerie Croft?" he asked, stroking her hair as his heartbeat slowly subsided beneath her cheek.

"Of you in a toga and laurel wreath crown," she said at once, without considering how it might sound, "and me on my knees before you."

To her surprise, Virgil threw back his head with a short bark of laughter. "Well, getting hold of a Roman toga might be difficult. But I'll see what I can do."

Twelve

ALONE IN HIS CHAMBER, Virgil opened the small vellum-bound journal in which he kept a record of his various herbal mixtures and their effects. He studied the last few entries by candlelight, then dipped his sharpened quill in the inkwell and began to write out his most recent findings.

Third dosage: two drops in strong wine following first ejaculation. A second ejaculation achieved within thirty minutes of imbibement, followed by a third and fourth that night, and a fifth on waking at dawn.

Physical symptoms during intercourse: a raging pulse, coupled with strong physical stamina and desire. Recovery time between ejaculations ranged from thirty to sixty minutes.

Symptoms following cessation of intercourse: a dry mouth, general fatigue and aching limbs, but no abatement of desire. A dangerously elevated pulse at intervals, coupled with moments of extreme priapism, beginning to tail off circa twelve hours post-imbibement.

Virgil read carefully over his notes. He dipped his quill again, then underlined the words strong physical stamina, and dangerously elevated pulse, finally adding a postscript:

Conclusion: this mixture too stimulating for any man of middling years or ailing health. Adjust strength accordingly and repeat experiment.

Once the ink was dry, Virgil closed the journal and walked to the window. He had heard distant shouts and the sound of hooves clattering on cobblestones, but looking out could see nothing, only the palace gardens stretching out into the dusk.

Closing the shutters, he shifted uncomfortably, for he had become aroused again, recalling with what heat and frequency he and Margerie had coupled over the past few weeks. It was hard not to smile with satisfaction. Margerie Croft was magnificently passionate in her lust, and as eager and ready for each of their couplings as he was. He could not deny how perfect she was for his experiment: a beautiful, sensual woman, and sexually available without the need for a wedding ring. Plus she was intelligent enough to please him with her conversation and wit as well as her body. Quite a beguiling companion, indeed.

Yet he felt guilt.

Margerie had no knowledge of his experiment, nor the potential dangers of the new medicament he had invented, nor why it was necessary for him to test the mixture on himself. She would find the whole business distasteful, he had no doubt, and perhaps even feel herself betrayed if she discovered his true purpose in coupling with her so frequently.

But he could not administer such a powerful aphrodisiac to the king without being sure it would not kill him. He had a duty to the throne as well as to his trade as a physician. Besides which, his own death—and a violently bloody one at that—would swiftly follow *that* error.

A knock at the door made him turn, frowning. "Come."

It was his servant, Ned. "Master Elton, there is a message for you."

Virgil took the proffered letter and unrolled it. He disliked showing emotion in company, and especially before his servants. But he was so shaken by the message as he glanced through it, he could barely conceal his surprise.

"How and when did this arrive, Ned?"

"A page brought it in haste but two minutes ago. I carried it straight to you, sir."

"Thank you, Ned," he murmured, trying to look unconcerned. "That will be all."

His servant bowed and withdrew.

Virgil waited until the door was shut, then read the message again by the light of his candle, cursing softly when he reached the end.

Virgilio Christina salutem

Do not be shocked by this letter. I have just arrived at court and cannot wait to see you, my dearest friend. I have been given quarters near the privy gardens.

Dare I beg you to visit me tonight?

I know the hour is late but I complained of aches and fatigue throughout our long journey, so no one will question a visit from a court physician. Not with my precarious health.

I have missed you sorely this year, Virgil. Do not desert me now that I have finally left my prison.

Bene vale, C.

He was anxious, and a little angry too, that Christina had attempted such a difficult journey against his advice. But he had to admit that he was pleased that she had come to court. For Christina was indeed his "dearest friend," and much as he occasionally resented the imposition of their long engagement, he could not conceal that he would be glad to see her again.

He reached for his cloak and cap, for the palace corridors were chill now that autumn was approaching, and made his way to Christina's quarters.

He had intended to spend some hours with Margerie tonight.

But a note had arrived earlier, briefly advising him that she would be otherwise occupied, in Munro's bed.

Damn his eyes.

Virgil had intended to smile at his own jealousy, but the thin stretch of his lips felt like more of a grimace. He had tried to be philosophical about her affair with Lord Munro, even now it was an open secret at court. After all, he had known from the outset that he must share her body with other men. But knowing it and hearing it from the lips of amused courtiers were two separate things.

The current rumor went that the inexperienced youth was so besotted with Mistress Croft, he had kept her a prisoner in his rooms while she taught him every sexual act known to such a skilled courtesan. Virgil had laughed with everyone else when he first heard this tale, but inwardly he had been bleeding.

It was said some servant had stumbled in upon Margerie kneeling upon the bed, half-naked, while the embarrassed nobleman hid himself beneath the covers…

Even the king and queen knew of her shame. But to his surprise, Henry had merely laughed upon hearing the tale and said he wished the young nobleman well. It seemed odd when Margerie had refused to lie with King Henry himself.

Master Greene had taken him aside soon after, and explained that the king was once again taking the mild aphrodisiac he had prescribed for their wedding night, and had managed to enjoy intercourse with Her Majesty several times since their wedding.

So King Henry was in a generous mood.

"But he would still mount his queen more than once every few weeks," the king's physician had whispered lewdly in his ear. "He will not get an heir unless he can bed her more frequently, and His Majesty knows it. So tell me, is that new potion of yours finished yet? I told him you were working on a stronger aphrodisiac, and he is adamant that he will try it."

"The mixture is not ready, no." Virgil had refused to part with its secret ingredients. "It is far too dangerous for a man of his years."

"Then he can take a smaller dose."

"No, for once His Majesty has experienced the power of its effects, he will be tempted to take more and more. And to do so might kill him."

Master Greene had stared at him in horror. "But you have tested it on yourself, and still live."

"Thus far it works as intended, as I have documented in my journal. But even at small doses it makes the pulse race and the heart begin to falter. Which could be lethal for a man whose health is already ailing. Sir, I need more time to refine it."

To his relief, Master Greene had reluctantly agreed to wait until he had refined the concoction. "Do not take too long about it, Master Elton," the king's physician had warned. "I will give you until the approach of Christmastide, no longer. Then you must either give me the refined aphrodisiac for the king, or resign your position at court."

Virgil stopped before a large wooden door studded with iron. A guard in country livery half-slumbered there on his pike, his stubbled face pale, his helmet askew.

"Sirrah," he said, waking the man with a sharp tap on his helmet. "I am Master Elton, court physician. Your mistress is in need of my attention. Take me to her."

"Yes, sir," the guard said hurriedly, fumbling with the door. It was clear that he was accustomed to his young mistress requiring a physician at odd hours, for he showed no surprise whatsoever. "At once, sir."

He found Christina sitting up in bed, flanked and supported by pillows, and with fragrant oils burning at her bedside to keep her disease at bay. Her nurse was brushing her beautiful golden hair, long enough to fall to her waist, which framed a white face with high cheekbones. Christina's face and arms were thinner than he remembered, and she looked quite haggard from her journey. But when her eyes flew open at the sound of his approach, he saw the excitement in them and knew her will to be as indomitable as ever.

Christina struggled to sit up straight. "My dearest friend," she said breathlessly, then waved her nurse away with an impatient gesture as she fussed about her. "It has been so long since I last saw you, I thought you must have forgotten me."

Smiling at this naive speech, the nurse curtsied to Virgil, then drew discreetly away into a side chamber.

"Thank you for visiting me at such a late hour, Virgil." Christina held out her hands to him. "You cannot know what this means to me. Ethel swore you would not come, that it was not fitting for a gentleman to visit me at night. But I *knew* you would not fail me."

He took her hand and bowed over it, kissing the cool skin. "Christina," he murmured. "I would never fail you, you know that. But, my dear girl, you should be resting. I cannot believe your uncle permitted you to undertake such a foolhardy journey." He straightened, frowning as he glanced about the plainly furnished chamber. "Where is Sir Edmund? I must speak with him at once."

"Oh, Virgil, you must forgive me for not being more honest with you in my letter." Her vast blue eyes glowed luminously in her white face, a purity about her wasted form that tugged at his heart. "But my uncle is dead."

He stared. "*What?*"

"Ten days ago," she explained briefly. "A sudden fever. It took several of the villagers too. I stayed only to bury Sir Edmund and hear the terms of his will, then I set out for court."

There was a sharpness to her voice that surprised him. Had Christina been angry with her late uncle? She had every reason to be, of course. Sir Edmund had controlled her every movement since her father's death at an early age, and only allowed Virgil's visits because he was training to be a physician and often brought her healing drafts. But Virgil had never known Christina to speak angrily of anyone.

"My uncle kept me from you and the world long enough," Christina continued. Her thin mouth curved into a triumphant smile. "Now I am free to do whatever I wish. I have received a handsome allowance from my uncle's coffers, and the whole estate will be mine so long as I marry," she said, pausing significantly, "within a twelvemonth."

"Marry?" he repeated numbly.

Lightly, Christina touched the back of his hand. "This can be no surprise, my dear friend. Unless you have changed your mind?"

He could not reply, staring down at her.

"We must have joked about it a thousand times, I know, planning our wedding and how many children we would have, all the time aware that my uncle would never permit me to wed. But now I am a grown woman and free to marry whomever I choose."

Her smile was disturbingly seductive when compared to the innocent child he remembered from his youth, a girl who would rather discuss philosophy or Roman poetry than think of love and marriage.

"You and I have been betrothed forever, Virgil. The time has come for you to claim my hand."

"But your illness…"

"What better husband for a sick woman than a physician?" She released his hand, suddenly looking exhausted. "Oh, Virgil, I know I should be in mourning for my uncle. But he was so cruel, keeping me a prisoner in the country, never letting me come to court… He knew the estate would pass to my husband if ever I married, under the terms of my father's will, and so disinherit him. *That* is why he prevented us from marrying for so many years, not because I was too sick to be your wife."

She looked up at him searchingly. "But now Uncle Edmund is dead, we can be wed straightaway. If you still love me, that is?"

He met her forthright gaze and did not know what to say. Knowing how sick she was, he had thought she would never come of age, and had given his promise at a time when she was near to death. In truth, he was delighted to see Christina battling with such brave determination against her illness, and loved her more than ever. But as a dear friend, not a lover.

How to tell her though?

It was simply not possible to tell her. Any more than it had been possible to refuse her when Christina was feverish as a girl, and had seized his hand and begged him to marry her once she was grown and well enough to say her vows before God. She had been sick for so long. He would die rather than see this wonderful new light in her eyes extinguished.

Virgil forced a smile to his lips. "Of course I still love you. But you must be patient, Christina, and not overexcite yourself. You have only just arrived at court and seem very fatigued." He sat on the edge of her bed and placed two fingers on her throat, feeling for her pulse. "As I thought, your heart is racing. Let me recall your nurse so she may put you to bed. I will visit you again in the morning, as soon as I can be spared from my duties, and bring a tonic to calm your nerves."

"Dearest Virgil," she murmured, and stroked his cheek. "How I have missed you and your smelly potions."

"I have missed you too, Christina."

"Have you, Virgil?" she whispered, watching him intently. "Truly?"

His eyes lifted to hers, then he leaned forward on impulse, setting his mouth briefly against hers.

She was so cold to the touch, it was like kissing a marble statue. But he felt her lips tremble beneath his, and knew how powerfully the lust for life beat inside her wasted body. Her heart would not beat for much longer though; her illness was too seriously advanced, he could tell that without examining her. If Christina lived even another year, she would be fortunate indeed.

A tender wave of love flooded him, almost breaking his heart, and he closed his eyes. Christina was the closest he had to a sister. He could not bear the thought of losing her. He had lost enough in his life. This, at least, was within his control.

"Of course I have. And it is very good to see you at court, Christina," he whispered, close to her ear, then pulled back. "Until tomorrow."

"Until tomorrow, Virgilius."

—⁂—

The barge drew alongside the dock, bobbing on the dark swollen tide as the boatmen tied it up. In the distance she could see torchlight on the water, and knew they could not be far from the city of London itself.

Lord Munro jumped out, then turned, holding out a gloved hand. "Madam?"

But Margerie did not move. She stared up at the looming facade of the palace, suddenly uncertain that she was doing the right thing.

Every other time she had visited his lordship at night, he had left her in an antechamber for an hour or two before returning, flushed and smiling, to escort her back to her chamber unmolested. It had been a comfortable arrangement so far; silence about his lordship's true tastes in bed in return for a modest estate where she could live out her days without the need for either a husband or lover.

Yet now they had left Richmond, traveling by barge to this crumbling old palace on the banks of the River Thames. And she had no idea what would happen once he took her inside. Margerie was suddenly aware of how very alone she was, far removed from the familiar surroundings of court.

"Why here?"

"Some affairs are best conducted away from the royal court," Lord Munro said shortly, his hand still outstretched. "Come, the hour is growing late."

There was no turning back. Not now she had put her trust in his lordship. She only hoped she was not mistaken in his character, which she had discovered was both amiable and docile once he was away from the other noble youths at court. Setting her hand in his, Margerie followed him onto the rain-damp wooden dock, trying not to slip in her heeled court shoes.

"What is this place, my lord?" she asked, as she was led past guards into a riverside courtyard. She tilted her head back to study the high walls and turrets rising above them in the darkness. "It looks very fine."

"It belongs to my family," his lordship murmured, also gazing up at the carved stone facade, lit by torches that flared and dipped in the gusts blowing sharply off the Thames. "A rather too vast palace, once a famous duke's residence. It was a gift from the king's father, old King Henry, after the wars. I am not often in residence, but… Well, you must know how closely everyone is watched at court."

She nodded, glancing at him.

"When I wish to be completely private, I come here. Or visit one of my country seats." His smile was grim. "There are no spies here to carry tales back to the king. Or to my mother."

She knew what he meant, and felt easy in her mind for the first time since agreeing to become his "lover." It was impossible to live at court without being aware of observers at every step, unseen gazes that followed each person of note along labyrinthine corridors and up dark stairways.

Even she had been watched, nobody though she was. Perhaps by the queen's people, for she knew Queen Jane disliked her and no doubt wished to know if she was the king's concubine. Or by those in power who suspected Lord Munro of not being like other men, and were curious to know for sure if he was bedding her.

"This way," he said, gesturing her through a low gateway into the palace.

Two young guardsmen sprang to attention within, pretending not to watch as his lordship escorted her toward a flight of stairs, his arm snaked intimately about her waist.

"There is a chamber ready prepared with every possible comfort. I'm afraid the hour is so late, we shall not be returning to court until tomorrow. I trust that will not inconvenience you, madam?"

"No," she lied, and wondered how much trouble she would be in when she finally returned to her duties.

"Do not look so worried. Bribes have been allotted to the relevant people," he whispered in her ear. "Your absence will be noted tomorrow, I have no doubt, and the reason for it known. But you will escape a whipping."

"I thank you, my lord."

The high-ceilinged chamber they had entered was sumptuously furnished, with cloth-of-gold bed curtains and thick furs laid over the bedsheets. Near the window stood a delicately wrought table set with silver goblets and a flagon of wine, and behind it a shelf containing several vellum-bound books. The room was lit by more than a dozen candles, a generous fire roaring in the hearth, and a maidservant waiting silently by the bed to take her mantle.

After Margerie had been made comfortable, his lordship snapped his fingers to dismiss the maid.

"Now," Munro murmured once they were alone together, kissing her hand, "it is time for me to leave you. You must forgive me for abandoning you so abruptly, but because of the tide, I believe my…" He hesitated, then finished awkwardly, "My *friend* has been waiting several hours for me to arrive. Will you be happy here tonight?"

"Surely," she agreed.

"There is a book of French poetry for you to read, or the psalms if you prefer." He smiled a little nervously, she thought, indicating the wine. "And something to help you sleep. I know these long nights alone in a strange room must be difficult to bear."

Margerie laid a hand on his richly embroidered sleeve. "Go, my lord," she told him softly. "Enjoy yourself."

His frank gaze met hers. "I am grateful to you, madam." Then Lord Munro bowed and went straight to a little door cunningly concealed in a shadowy alcove, stepping through into what she assumed was an adjoining chamber. "Good night, Mistress Croft."

Left alone, she wandered to the bed and sat there awhile. It was soft and comfortable. She would sleep well, at least, whereas at the king's court she had been forced to slumber as best she could in a chair. Then she took herself to the table and poured a little red wine into a silver goblet, enjoying the momentary pretense of wealth, sipping at it delicately as any noblewoman.

Selecting the volume of French poetry, she settled on a chair by the fire and read for a while, sounding out the words where they were unfamiliar. It was a story of chivalry and romance from long ago, and someone had helpfully underlined a few phrases, translating them in the margin. But she did not know the poet's work, and the French was painfully old-fashioned, so that after a few pages she could hardly follow what was happening.

At some point she must have fallen asleep, for she woke quite suddenly, startled by a cry from the adjoining room.

Her book had fallen to the floor. "Damn," she muttered, picking it up. Hurriedly she got up and replaced the book on the shelf, hoping she had not damaged the expensive gilt binding with such rough treatment.

At that moment, she heard the cry again. It sounded deep and male, and strangely tortured. She turned, her stomach clenched in instinctive response. It was a sound she knew from her own nights with Master Elton, of pleasure dragged from the darkest depths of the human soul.

Margerie crept toward the narrow door through which his lordship had disappeared. She stood there awhile, not wishing to be caught peering through the keyhole like an insolent servant, yet curious to know what exactly the young nobleman did all night with his *friend*.

She heard a thud from within the secret room, then someone gasping as though in pain. Her eyes widened and her hands fell to her hips. What in God's name was going on in there? She listened hard and caught another ominous thud. Was his lordship in trouble?

Daringly, Margerie pressed a hand against the door, and it gave slightly, opening just a crack. Putting her eye to the crack, she held her breath. At first all she could see were shadows dancing on the walls of the chamber, and the deep red glow of the fire. But she heard harsh breathing, and recognized the now-familiar smell of male sweat and seed. Then her eyes adjusted to the low light, and she was able to make out their forms, two men sporting together on the floor, shockingly nude. Lord Munro was on hands and knees, facing away from her, being mounted from behind by a larger, much older man.

As she watched, this silver-haired man thrust hard, almost violently, driving deep into his partner. She clasped a hand to her mouth, convinced that such rough treatment must hurt. Yet if it did, the pain was surely welcome, for Munro threw back his head and moaned his pleasure.

"Oh, sweet Jesu!" she whispered, and spun away from the door before she could be discovered.

Hurrying to the bed, she threw back the fur coverlets and slipped beneath them. Then she closed her eyes tight and tried to sleep, ignoring the muffled sounds of pleasure from the next room. But it was no use. She could not deny it. The sight of their male lust had aroused her, her belly softening and aching, her breasts tingling with excitement, so that all she could think of was lying beneath Virgil's thrusting body.

Virgil was not there though, and the surreptitious stroking of her own fingers brought only short-lived relief. It could not replace the man himself.

Yet even if the doctor had been there to couple with her, it would not have assuaged the need she felt inside. For she wanted what Virgil could never give her—and she was only just beginning to recognize it.

Virgil felt nothing for her beyond the raw physical desire they both shared. Did she really want to risk a broken heart?

There could be only one end to an affair between a respectable man and an acknowledged courtesan, and it did not involve marriage.

Thirteen

VIRGIL SIGHED, STRETCHING OUT his aching back. His modifications to the king's cordial were too intricate to rush, yet the king was impatient for better results. This had meant many hours' work on the formula over the past few weeks, and it still lacked the required strength—or not without unfortunate effects like dry mouth and a racing pulse, which clearly could not be inflicted on His Majesty.

Virgil had finished noting up his improvements and was packing away his bottles and flasks when there was a soft knock at his door. He frowned, opening it to find Margerie looking back at him.

She was dressed in a dark green gown, her bodice high and tight according to the new fashion, a simple string of pearls about her neck, knotted and falling provocatively into shadow between her breasts. As soon as their eyes met, her generous lips parted, smiling, and her restricted chest rose and fell as though she were breathing quickly.

Her flickering smile hooked into him, refusing to let go, and Virgil could not help but smile in return, his heart suddenly beating faster too. His cock stiffened in his codpiece as he remembered her writhing naked beneath him, and he had trouble not letting the desire show on his face.

The effect Margerie Croft had on his male anatomy was more potent than any aphrodisiac in the world, however exotic. If only he could bottle *this*, he would be a wealthy man indeed.

"Mistress Croft," he murmured, bowing.

She curtsied, a slight flush in her cheeks. "Master Elton."

"You are unwell, madam?"

He hoped not, willing her to have a more pleasurable reason for visiting him. Certainly she had brought no female companion this time, as she ought to have done when calling on a doctor. But she was no respectable lady, he reminded himself, so such niceties hardly mattered.

Her green eyes met his. "Forgive my intrusion at this late hour, sir, but I am in need of further medicaments. The sleeping draft you gave me… My last bottle has run dry."

"You are fortunate indeed, then, to have caught me still in my workshop."

"I was passing and saw candlelight under the door."

He raised his eyebrows, for his workshop was quite remote from the women's quarters. "Passing?"

She looked into the room, her gaze darting about the small workshop as though ensuring he was alone. "Yes, I often pass this way after my duties are finished for the day." She ignored his quiet snort of laughter. "Are you alone?"

"I am," he agreed, and stepped politely aside. "Would you care to come in and wait, madam, while I prepare another flask of sleeping draft for you?"

"Thank you, sir, I would."

Her hands folded meekly before her, Margerie entered the workshop, passing close enough that he could smell her soft perfume, that now familiar scent of roses in the air, and he felt his hand clench into a fist, his desire was so powerful.

Quietly, he closed the door, checking first that no spy had been watching his workshop that evening. Not that it mattered if this meeting was witnessed or not. No one would care that he was bedding a courtesan like Margerie Croft, surely? Still, Virgil disliked the idea that this evening's visitor might be noted and speculated upon by spies. A man's bed was his own business, after all.

The door safely bolted, Virgil turned to her and cupped her face in his hands, not wasting any time on speech. Their mouths met and he groaned. His tongue pushed impatiently between her lips, and he tasted her at last. It seemed so long—too long—since they had learned the ways of each other's bodies in bed together, and he was hungry to touch her again, to remind himself of how strongly she could move him with just the flick of her tongue or the caress of one knowing fingertip.

To bed a courtesan this skilled was an honor, and he knew it. Already his cock was hard, eager for her without any need for potions. He reached down and began to pull up her skirts, not thinking of anything but his desire to drive into her softness and take his pleasure.

"Master Elton!" she gasped against his mouth.

He drew back a little, the heavy green taffeta of her court gown still bunched in his hands, and his mouth curved in a smile. "Virgil," he reminded her softly.

"Virgil," she said, her eyes wide on his face, "I only came here to… That is, I did not intend you to kiss me."

"Liar."

Her blush deepened. "Well, maybe I hoped. But we cannot do more than kiss. Not here."

Virgil dropped her skirts, seeing at once that she had been startled by his lust. "Forgive me, I was too hasty."

His grip slid to her waist instead, so narrow he could almost encompass it with both hands. Yet she was not dainty; quite the opposite. Trim though, for all her Amazonian height, and pleasing to bed.

"Yes," she agreed, her tone a little sharp, but her gaze did not waver and she did not push him away, still open to his advances.

This was about respect, then. She might be a courtesan, but she preferred to be wooed in a more conventional manner. Well, he would not always be happy to wait for his pleasure. But she did not belong to him, and he should remember that. He was not paying for her body, as he suspected Lord Munro must be. The first coupling between them had been mutually agreed, more like lovers than he was entirely comfortable with. But he owed Margerie Croft the proper respect due to a lady of the court, for all her wantonness.

"I lost my head," he admitted, and put his mouth more cautiously on hers, willing her to take the lead.

Margerie hesitated, as though poised to refuse him, then her lips parted. Her tongue slipped cautiously against his, exploring, teasing. A surge of heat flooded him as they kissed, and he was hard-pressed not to raise her skirts again. Much as he suspected she would submit, and indeed enjoy his dominance, he did not wish to force her. That surprised him, for her submissiveness was part of the reason he found Margerie Croft so attractive. Yet it seemed distasteful to think of this woman merely *enduring* his attentions, rather than welcoming them with pleasure.

He raised his head, determinedly reining in his lust. "First, I must examine you," he murmured.

She licked her lips, staring at him as though in a daze. "Sir?"

"Before I can allow you to continue taking the sleeping draft, I must ascertain that it has not been harmful to you. I must listen to your heart, madam. So if you could loosen your bodice somewhat…"

Her eyes widened, then her lips twitched into a smile. "Of course," she said, and her fingers went to her bodice at once, loosening the dark green material with difficulty. "Forgive me, it is…tight."

"Allow me, mistress."

Carefully, trying not to tear the fragile material, he tugged at her bodice, pulling it down another few inches to expose the creamy white mound of her breasts. As the flesh spilled out, her rosy nipples became lodged against the dark green taffeta, half peeping out, half hidden, shown off to perfection. He held his breath, finding it hard to look at her, the desire that had him in its grip was so powerful.

"Now hold still," he said thickly, and lowered his head until his ear lay against her breast.

Closing his eyes, he listened to the erratic thud of her heart. It sounded healthy enough, but fast. As fast as his own, he thought drily. He opened his eyes, not moving, breathing in the sweet feminine scent of her body, and examined at close quarters the rosy whorl of her nipple. He circled the saucy peeping flesh with one finger, then hooked underneath the offending bodice and jerked it down, just far enough to free her nipple.

She had been gripping the side of his workshop table but now one hand came up to touch his head. She pushed off his cap, then stroked her fingers down through his hair, lingering on the back of his neck.

"Kiss me there," she whispered daringly, leaving him in no doubt as to her meaning.

His cock turned to stone.

Slowly, not wanting to scare her off, he nuzzled across her breast until his mouth was almost touching her exposed nipple. Her flesh tautened at his approach, and when he breathed warmly, he watched her skin tighten yet further, drawing up in exquisite folds like a newly budded rose. Then his lips closed over her, and he sucked deep and hard, his cock aching in his codpiece. She hissed, and her fingers tangled in his hair, first dragging him away, then pushing on to suck harder.

"Sir," she cried, "sir."

He dragged on her bodice, and both her breasts were freed, spilling out from the rich green gown in luxurious decadence. He squeezed her other breast, flicking roughly across it with his thumb so that her nipple hardened, then transferred his mouth to that silken point, sucking hungrily on one nipple, then the other, and back again.

Christ, he had to have her. It was sheer agony, this holding back.

Seizing her by the waist, he lifted her easily onto the worktable, lay her back and pushed up her skirts. This time she did not protest, but moaned, watching in wordless submission as he parted her thighs—gently, so as not to offend her with his impatience. Her mons veneris looked so beautiful, her secret lips pouting as if in invitation, he knew he must taste her.

Lowering his head, he put his mouth between her legs and felt her jerk in shock at the unexpected intimacy. He had tasted her when they coupled before, but only after taking his own pleasure. No doubt she thought it strange that a man would perform such an act *before* his own satisfaction had been achieved. But he found Margerie Croft fascinating and exciting in her powerful sexual responses; it would only augment his pleasure to put his own needs aside while he assuaged hers instead.

"You are beautiful," he murmured, then slid his tongue over and around the slick dusky pearl above her gleaming slit.

She moaned, and closed her thighs about his head. "Virgil," she groaned, but with pleasure. "Oh, sweet Jesu."

He licked slowly down her secret lips, then pushed a little way inside that inviting darkness, tasting her juice on his tongue. Her breath came pantingly as he continued to lick, up and down, in and out, pleasuring her, pausing two or three times to tug on the sweet pearl, listening to her sighs and whimpers. Then his mouth came back, fastened his mouth on that taut bud, and sucked firmly at last, ignoring her ragged cries.

She reached her peak a few moments later, back arching off the table, buttocks tensing, her long shuddering moan suddenly stifled as though she had put a hand over her own mouth.

Virgil straightened as her climax subsided, ignoring the throbbing pulse at his own groin, and threw open one of the smaller chests on his worktable. The chest contained only a few objects, rare and unusual, and he quickly found what he wanted; he returned to her in two swift strides, though in truth he was more than ready to finish these games and take her himself.

But he wanted to give her pleasure first. The kind of pleasure a woman remembers for a very long time, he thought, looking down at her intently.

———

Dazed, her senses slowly returning to reality after floating in a heaven of physical delight, Margerie opened her eyes to see that Virgil had left her. She wondered what on earth he could be doing, for she had assumed he would enter her as soon as her climax was achieved. Instead, he was returning with…

"What is that?" she asked, a little shocked, staring at what appeared to be a black leather baton in his hand.

His smile was dark. "What does it look like, my sweet wanton?"

She had never seen anything like it before in her life. Yet she guessed its purpose at once. Its end was smoothly rounded, fatter than the long shaft, and the leather exterior had been carefully molded to give the appearance of a phallus.

Her eyes flew to his face. "No," she whispered.

"Trust me, you will enjoy this. It is meant for your pleasure, not mine."

"I cannot…"

"You will obey me in this, if in nothing else."

She shook her head, staring at the thick leather phallus and trying not to imagine it being introduced inside her.

"Lie back a little further," he ordered her abruptly, "and lift your feet onto the table. Keep them well apart. I need to stand between your legs."

To her horror, the way he had spoken—so terse, so dominating—aroused her. She was excited, both by his command and the instrument in his hand, and could not deny it. Aroused by a thing! It did not seem natural, and yet she could feel her arousal, the heat at her core.

"Obey me," he insisted, and she responded instinctively to his command, pushing herself back down the worktable and setting her bare feet on the carved wooden edge, for her shoes had fallen off while he was pleasuring her with his tongue. Her feet were so far apart, her thighs fell open, and he stepped between them, close up to the table.

There was no time to be afraid.

While she had been positioning herself, he had turned away to oil the leather phallus from a small bottle on the workshop shelf. Now he set the cool slick leather against her lips and looked her in the eyes as he pushed, breaching her entrance with the rounded tip, then invading her body inch by shocking inch.

Her belly clenched, and her hands tightened on the rim of the table, her nails digging into the wood. The well-oiled phallus pushed further, filling her more completely than anything had ever done before, so hard and long and thick, she thought she would die from its inexorable invasion.

All the while his dark eyes watched her, glittering in the candle-light, his hand working the phallus gently in until it could go no further, then withdrawing it until the rounded end was touching her lips.

"Stop fighting it, Margerie, and take your pleasure," he told her hoarsely.

She could not reply, but found herself almost panting as he pushed it back inside more forcefully, then withdrew again, beginning to pump in and out of her with a slow, steady, screwing motion.

Oh God, it felt so good!

She moaned, and her legs began to shake. But he had not finished, for even as she grew accustomed to the thick phallus inside her, Virgil bent and placed his mouth on her again.

"Virgil!" she gasped, shaking her head.

Paying her no heed, his mouth clamped over her already taut flesh and tormented her, sucking and licking between her legs while he thrust the phallus inside her.

She could not seem to catch her breath. Margerie strained, jerking against him, raising her hips and buttocks for more, for deeper thrusts. Heat pooled between her legs, her flesh so wet and open, sucking him into her, the heavy phallus taking her relentlessly to the top of a high mountain. His mouth refused to stop, suckling her, his tongue lashing the tiny spot that just for that moment seemed to control her entire body.

Margerie cried out, writhing as the most glorious pleasure wracked her, leaving her sobbing for breath. It was too much, her body was on fire, everything was falling apart, tumbling down, even her brain was feverish, for she could no longer tell if she was awake or dreaming…

"Virgil," she managed again, her voice high and unfamiliar, then gave herself up to the pleasure, twisting molten beneath him.

Swiftly he straightened, slipped the leather phallus from between her thighs and unfastened his codpiece. His eyes were intense, his mouth tight, a dark flush in his face as he spread her with expert fingers.

A moment later, Margerie felt the smooth head of his cock pressing inside, and groaned at the sensation of warm male flesh after the impersonal phallus.

"Yes," she told him, gripping his strong forearms as he pushed her skirts higher and began to thrust. "Take me."

His smile was more of a grimace. "I intend to."

Virgil bent his head and took her mouth too, drugging her with a long passionate kiss even as his hips worked against her. "Yes," he muttered too, closing his eyes, his face taut.

It did not take long, a testament to how aroused he must have been when he tensed and drove hard inside only a short while later, groaning out his pleasure. She felt the spreading warmth of his seed inside her, and knew a flicker of fear—once again she had risked the disgrace of a child out of wedlock!—but it was swept aside by the look on his face, still flushed but heavy-lidded now, smiling, a kiss planted softly on her forehead as he withdrew.

"You see, it pleases me when *you* are pleased," he told her, meeting her eyes.

"I should not have…"

She could not finish, the thought slipping away into a wonderful drowsiness. Though part of her knew it was too dangerous to be here, in his workshop, her skirts raised, quite clearly this man's mistress. Lord Munro would not be pleased if he knew of it, for he had taken her as a mistress, not a wanton who was intimate with other men, and he would not wish to look foolish.

He came back to stand between her thighs, a cup in his hand. He drank deeply, then set the cup down by her head. She smelled the dregs of strong wine, and looked at him, surprised.

"I was thirsty," he explained, then stroked between her thighs, playing the slick tender flesh there for several minutes until she moaned. "Do you wish for wine?"

She shook her head, staring at him, breathing hard again, still aroused, her body aflame.

"For love, then?" he asked, watching her with that disturbingly intent gaze.

Margerie whimpered, moving to the insistent rhythm of his fingers. "But surely…you have only just…"

His smile was dry, almost ironic. "Give me a few minutes more, my sweet mistress, and I swear I will surprise you."

Virgil studied her wanton figure, skirts around her waist, her thighs apart for him, then leaned forward, kissing her exposed breasts, pushed up by the tight bodice and aching for attention. She gasped at the realization that he was still partially hard, his thick length pressed against her inner thigh, and he gave a throaty laugh.

"I told you I would surprise you, did I not?" His lips met hers again, and his tongue slipped inside, tender and provocative at the same time. He raised his head, looking down at her. "We have hours ahead of us and more playthings to explore. We have barely started. Wait until I tie you down and make you take me in whatever way I choose. Then you will understand the meaning of pleasure."

"Virgil," she groaned, and lifted her hips in eager submission.

Fourteen

"LET ME SEE," HER Majesty said abruptly, and Margerie, who had been kneeling beside her with a mouth bristling with pins, scuttled backward, head bowed.

Queen Jane walked slowly about the dressing room, then turned to consider her reflection in the narrow glass. "The kirtle is too short," she pronounced after a moment's consideration. "Make it longer. I will not have the court gawping at my ankles in the dance."

"Yes, Your Majesty," Kate Langley said soothingly, then nodded to Margerie. "It shall be done exactly as you wish."

Margerie knelt again beside the restless queen, refixing the heavy swaying kirtle to a more decorous length. Her fingers worked nimbly over the dark green silk, and with pleasure, for this was her skill, almost her trade. Whatever in life she had done poorly, or failed to do, at least no one could condemn her skill with a needle.

"And the foreskirt to match," the queen insisted.

"Yes, Your Majesty," Margerie replied.

The queen watched in silence as she worked. It did not disturb Margerie, for she was confident in her business. Though she did wonder if her skills were being assessed for a darker purpose, for instance if she was about to be dismissed. The court was rife with gossip about her and Lord Munro—which was precisely what his lordship wanted, to distract attention from his other interests.

Though in truth, she might have visited Lord Munro several times now, and waited in his chamber while he busied himself with his lover, but it was quite another man she was bedding. And she was sore from his relentless passion—and hers.

She had not known a man could reach his peak and recover as quickly as Virgil Elton did. Yet he was not selfish with his powerful lusts, for he brought her to pleasure even more frequently than he came himself, and seemed aroused by her climaxes, seeking them out with his lips and fingers, and the curious playthings he liked to use on her body.

She blushed to remember the visits she had paid him, and the places where they had coupled these past weeks, shameless in their desire until afterward, when he would escort her back to the women's quarters without a word, his arm tight about her waist.

Her heart was becoming engaged, and she feared what lay ahead. Each time they met, she wondered when it would end. When Master Elton would cease to send her notes or appear out of the darkness to whisk her away… That day must come, for every man eventually tired of his mistress. And she was thankful for that, even as she dreaded it. For to grow so close to a man she could never have was dangerous and foolhardy.

By the window, Kate and the other ladies of the royal wardrobe were laying out a dozen bolts of material for the queen to examine, fresh come from the docks: rich luscious silk to make the mouth water, and stiff taffeta, their colors dark and somber, for the queen claimed to despise the bright yellows, golds, and dazzling silvers once so common at court.

Margerie thought she knew why. Queen Jane was busy distancing herself from her flirtatious predecessor in every way possible. One could never be too guarded with a jealous husband.

"Leave us, ladies," the queen said sharply, without warning. "I would speak privily with Mistress Croft."

Margerie looked up, taken by surprise, then glanced at Kate. Her friend curtsied low with the other women, then left the room, not daring to meet her eyes.

The door closed softly behind them. The sunlit dressing room was quiet. She was alone with the queen.

Margerie's heart began to thud with a sickly erratic beat. She remained on her knees, staring up into the queen's face, waiting to hear her fate with the forgotten hem still clutched in her hands.

Queen Jane indicated that she should rise. "The court is not a safe hiding place for a wanton, Mistress Croft," she said coolly, looking directly at her.

Heat blossomed in Margerie's cheeks. "Yes, Your Majesty."

"These past months, I have heard rumors of your association with several gentlemen of the court. Such lewd behavior does not please me."

Margerie did not bother to lie or dissemble. Where would be the point? The court was rife with spies. Any one of them would attest to the known fact of her wanton nature.

"No, Your Majesty," she whispered, and bent her head.

What was it to be? A public whipping and dismissal? She would not be the first lady of the court to suffer such cruel chastisement for her lack of chastity. If only it might not come to her grandfather's ears…

"Look at me." Queen Jane's thin eyebrows arched at the tears in her eyes. "Why do you weep?"

"I am ashamed, Your Majesty."

"Dry your eyes. You are not to be punished." Queen Jane's mouth twisted at Margerie's incredulous look. "My family has long been connected with that of Lord Munro, and his lady mother is not…not displeased. As long as you keep in mind that you are a royal servant, there can be little harm in it. Only I must warn you to be less forward in your dealings with his lordship. His Majesty found such sport entertaining at first. But his amusement will soon pall, and you would be well advised to learn discretion." There was contempt in her well-bred face. "If you are capable of it."

Margerie was tempted to deny the whole thing. But she had made an arrangement with Lord Munro, and she instinctively shied away from breaking her word. If she was not to be punished…

"However, as for your meetings with the physician, Elton," the queen continued, "these must stop."

Merciful heavens. How much else was known that she had so foolishly dreamed private?

The queen hesitated, frowning. "You are perhaps unaware of that gentleman's history. But…"

That gentleman's history.

She must mean Virgil's betrothal. What else? She had never thought his intentions anything but dishonorable. Nor cared, she told herself stubbornly, even as she acknowledged a secret pain in her heart. Marriage was not a state she would ever enjoy—nor be forced to suffer.

Queen Jane walked to the window, the gown dragging on the floorboards, and looked out in silence. Her fingers tapped restlessly on the sunlit sill.

"Well, his history is neither here nor there. Let it be sufficient that I have forbidden you from pursuing the association. Henceforth you will eschew Master Elton's company."

Margerie tried to respond. She was shocked by her own hesitation. The queen had given her a direct command. What was wrong with her? She had known their meetings must end. There was no conflict here, merely a resolution reached more abruptly than she had expected.

"Mistress Croft?" Jane turned, her expression suddenly haughty, a still-new queen on her dignity. "I have not heard you answer me. But perhaps you did not understand aright. You must no longer associate with Master Elton, or you will face my displeasure. Is that clear?"

"Perfectly, Your Majesty."

The queen studied her a moment longer.

Perhaps the unexpected pain showed in her eyes. With an effort, Margerie lowered her gaze to the level of the queen's lustrous pearls. She held her breath in the same way she had held the hem, unable to let go.

Queen Jane nodded, seemingly relieved that the problematic conversation was at an end.

"You may recall the other ladies now. I have changed my mind about the length of this gown. Leave it how it was. I do not think it lewd to be fashionable. I shall take care not to dance to any tune that is not a stately measure," she added naively, "that is all."

—⁓—

"Your move, my lord."

Munro frowned, leaning forward, his chin on his fist. Chess was not his lordship's natural game, Margerie thought, watching his deliberations. The relentless monotony of the black and white squares defeated him every time. Too harsh a simplicity.

She looked away. It was dark outside, but she had heard the bell toll eleven while considering her own move. Queen takes bishop. An unlikely pairing.

"Oh, I had forgotten... I have a gift for you."

Her head turned, and she found herself smiling at his lordship. "A gift, my lord? For me?"

"In the eyes of the court, you are my mistress. It would be strange indeed if I did not reward you for your services with a gift from time to time." Lord Munro rose and fetched a small package from the bedside. Returning, he handed it to her with a shy smile. "I hope you like my choice."

She unwrapped the package and gasped at the beautiful and costly gold necklace, a rose pendant dangling from a chain, the rose shining with a large single emerald. "Oh, but it is beautiful! I love it. Thank you so much, my lord."

"Here, allow me."

She raised her hair while he clasped the necklace about her throat. He stood back to admire the effect. "Yes, I was right. The emerald matches your eyes."

There were footsteps in the corridor. Munro stiffened, looking round, a sudden flush in his cheeks. Someone scratched at the door. He hurried to the door like a servant, then stopped just short of it.

His voice was cautious. "Who is there?"

"Quince."

A password.

Enthusiastically, Munro opened the door, and gestured the other man inside. "Hurry," he said, dismissing the impassive servant who had accompanied his visitor upstairs, then closed the door. "You were not seen? Not followed from court?"

It was the broad-chested, silver-haired gentlemen she had seen on her last visit here. She ought not to have peeked, she told herself. Then she would not now feel so uncomfortable.

The man shook his head, removing his rain-damp cap and cloak. "I stopped and changed my route several times to make sure."

"Good, that's good. Very…good."

The two men stood looking at each other, then Munro seemed to recall her presence.

"Do you know Mistress Croft?" he said, grimacing, aware how awkward this moment was for all three, yet persisting with the *politesse* of it. "Margerie, this is Sir Thomas Whitley."

Sir Thomas, who was older than Munro and better able to hide any embarrassment at this unorthodox meeting, came over to greet her. Margerie remained seated, though she felt her cheeks grow warm under his intelligent scrutiny. If only she could learn not to blush. But she supposed her face would soon cease to betray her if she spent enough nights pretending to be bedded by one or more of these gentlemen, and in truth reading or embroidering by the fire.

He smiled, gallantly bending to kiss her hand. "Mistress Croft."

"Sir Thomas."

His lady mother was *not displeased*, the queen had said. Margerie wondered what Munro's lady mother would think if she knew the truth. But perhaps she did know it, and would rather the court saw this face of her son, than the other more private one. And what harm did it do?

None, she thought, and smiled up at his lordship's lover. "Has the rain stopped yet, sir?"

"I fear not."

"It is as well we are not out in it, then. Perhaps it will have stopped by first light." She looked at Munro. "Shall we continue the game another night, my lord?"

Lord Munro was smiling too, not hiding his relief that their meeting had been a success. "Yes," he said promptly, then remembered his manners. "I thank you, yes. Did you…" He glanced about vaguely, and she could see he was already in the other room in his mind, loving and being loved. "Bring something to read? More poetry?"

"You enjoy poetry, Mistress Croft?" Sir Thomas asked politely.

"Some, yes," she agreed. "Not all. Though it helps if it is in English."

His eyes sparkled, amused. "And do you ever compose your own verses?"

"Sadly, that is not a talent I can claim, sir."

This was the strangest conversation, Margerie thought, given the circumstances. Yet she continued to smile.

"Versifying is a rare talent, Mistress Croft, so there can be no shame in admitting so. I am sure you possess many other talents."

She raised her brows.

"Forgive me," he said at once, "I did not intend…"

She laughed, and he grinned, looking a little embarrassed at last.

"I shall be quiet now. It seems best." Sir Thomas bowed as though she were a highborn lady of the court and not a disreputable courtesan. His gaze turned slowly, uncertainly, to Munro. "Shall we, my lord?"

"Gladly."

With one accord, the two men left her sitting alone in the glow of firelight and retired discreetly into the adjoining chamber.

She touched her gold and emerald necklace, deeply pleased by his lordship's gift, then settled back in her seat. She tried not to listen to what was going on next door, taking up her embroidery and attempting a few stitches. But it was impossible not to hear *some* sounds. And to grow aroused again, intolerably. She glanced at the fire as a damp log spat at her. What was Master Elton doing tonight? she wondered. The man she was not allowed to greet even as a stranger. The man whose bed had been forbidden to her by the queen.

She had written him a note by way of explanation.

We may no longer meet. M.

Five words which had taken as many hours to compose. Poetry, indeed. Like drawing a tooth.

Pretending not to notice the exquisite pain in her heart, she set another rose-red stitch into her embroidery and pulled the thread delicately through: a loop that would have snagged, snarled up, except she freed it in time.

That gentleman's history.

What was Virgil Elton's history? The more Margerie considered the queen's odd comment—and it was hard not to consider it—the more inclined she was to think it more than a veiled reference to his betrothal.

History sounded further back than a betrothal. Much further back.

———

Virgil saw Margerie Croft and Lord Munro from the king's window while the sacrosanct royal member was being discussed in whispers by the king's chief physicians.

She was laughing with Munro, dodging raindrops as they ran across the inner courtyard, his cloak held over her head.

It should mean nothing to him. She was a courtesan. They had spent some heady nights together, that was all, driven by the mutual lust of their bodies and aided by his aphrodisiac. Sweating, laboring for pleasure, and being rewarded by it. He had demanded complete submission, and her sweet body had yielded freely. Virgil could still recall the immeasurable joy and relief of releasing inside her, so piercing it had been almost painful…

His cock stiffened at the memory.

Virgil cursed, turning away. Let her run. Laugh. Smile at Munro as though she knew his secrets.

We may no longer meet. M.

Had he failed to please her in some way? But no, it had been good between them. Too damn good. This abrupt dismissal was over her affair with Lord Munro, he was sure. His lordship must have refused to share, and so he was cast out into the darkness.

His hands clenched into fists, and he struggled not to imagine her in bed with the young nobleman. Damn the bastard.

The experiment had been all but concluded anyway. He would soon have cut off from her himself—had indeed been seriously considering whether to give up their nights together—if she had not sent that note. Women! He thought fleetingly of Christina, then dismissed the idea. She was still too fragile, so pure and white. It would be like lying down in an immaculate bed of snow.

Perhaps once they were married Christina would prove to be as passionate as Margerie. But he doubted it. Christina's powerful intellect was her passion. She would rather tease a man's brain than his body, and while he found such intelligence and wit irresistible in a woman, he was also a man of strong physical needs. Needs that had not been assuaged for some days now, he thought grimly.

The possibility of breaking off his engagement winked at him for a moment like a jewel in the cold autumn sunshine. Then he imagined Christina's hurt, her look of betrayal. Her childish anger.

Not possible.

The king's examination was at an end. The whispered discussions behind him drew to some kind of conclusion, then the bed curtains were pulled back to reveal a tight-lipped monarch in his nightgown. His Majesty's fervent attempts to father an heir to the Tudor dynasty had still not borne fruit, and it seemed a miracle was required.

Master Greene turned, sounding nervous. "Master Elton. Your improved cordial, if you please."

He bowed, unstoppered the vial, and demonstrated for the irascible king and his attendants how many drops and in how much wine, and how long before the act…

Later that autumn, he was out walking the grounds of Richmond Palace with Christina, pleased at her progress—she had been invalided so long, it was a rare delight to see his friend on her feet—when he caught sight of Mistress Langley first, then Margerie, the two ladies strolling together in the walled rose garden.

The roses were almost all finished, of course, and the rose bushes had been tied back and tended, ready for the next season's growth. But it was a more peaceful garden now that no one came there anymore, and he had often found himself walking there himself in the early mornings, thinking of it as his own private sanctuary.

So it was a shock to glance through the iron gate and see Margerie there with her friend, pausing to examine a bare rose bush, her head bent. His pulse had quickened at the first glimpse of that demurely white-capped head, wild red hair escaping, refusing to be controlled. He hated his instinctive response and fought it, teeth gritted, trying to ignore the painful rush of emotion.

Christina had been talking comfortably of their wedding plans while he listened with half an ear, concealing the emptiness he felt at such discussions. She frowned when he stilled, looking at him with surprise. "Virgil, what is it?"

"Nothing." He smiled at his betrothed, determined not to look in Margerie's direction. "A sudden chill. This north wind bites when it blows." He studied her face, hoping his own did not reveal his feelings. "Are you not tired? You have walked further today than ever before."

A spark of pleasure lit in her blue eyes at this praise, lending her an unusually lively air. "Yes, I am a little fatigued. But I wish to be quite well for our wedding," she admitted.

"When… When is it, again?"

"Oh, Virgil!" she exclaimed, pinching his arm. "Have you not been listening at all? I have written to your mother, and she thinks early next spring is best. But I would prefer to be married by Christmastide at least. I do not wish us to delay any longer. Why should we, now that I am free of my uncle's interference?"

"Indeed," he agreed huskily, glancing back at the rose gardens.

They had passed the gate now, but he could hear Kate Langley's voice in the walled garden, and wondered what they were discussing. Not him, that was for sure.

"You have something on your mind, Virgil," Christina accused him. "Tell me what it is."

"No, I am merely concerned for your well-being. I am convinced you must be tired. Let me escort you back to your chamber."

"I am tired, but my maid can escort me," Christina said primly, for the girl had accompanied them on their walk about the palace grounds. "Your mother warned me in her letter not to be alone with you here, for a woman's reputation is very fragile. And I have heard certain whispers at court…"

He stared round at her. "What whispers?"

Christina's coy look left him in no doubt what this gossip had concerned.

"Forgive me, I have no wish to discuss it further," she said. "But rest assured I am not angry. You are a man, Virgil. And this may surprise you, but I find it pleasing that you are not…not chaste. I had wondered, you see. For in all these years of our betrothal, you have never once tried to seduce me."

"Christina!"

She met his gaze without flinching. "Well, you must admit it is strange."

He was shocked now, and deeply troubled. "I was merely too concerned for your honor to attempt such a thing. And my mother was right to warn you. Very little at court goes unnoticed."

"But once we are married, you will…" Christina hesitated, clearly embarrassed, her gloved hand tightening on his arm. "*Love* me?"

Her blush was startling. It was like seeing a statue come to life, he thought. Pygmalion's perfect woman. Only she was not his perfect woman. More was the pity, for he would soon be forced to marry her. It was either that or hurt her intolerably.

"Let me escort you inside, Christina," he muttered, not answering her disturbing question.

In truth, he did not know his own mind on that topic. She was a woman, and not unattractive. There would be no hardship involved in bedding her. But for life…

Christina said nothing more, to his relief, and Virgil was able to escort her in silence to the arched doorway into the palace.

Once he had seen her and her maidservant safely inside, he turned and retraced their steps to the walled rose garden. The gate was ajar, and he slipped silently inside, glancing up and down the narrow paths. They were still there, near the rose arch. Two women admiring the stillness of an autumn garden.

The beautiful Kate Langley saw him approaching, and turned with a cautious smile. "Master Elton," she said loudly, dropping a curtsy, and he noted how Margerie stiffened at the sound of his name, her face suddenly rigid.

God's blood, did she hate him so much? What had he done to offend her so severely?

His heart was thumping violently. Get yourself in hand, he told himself sternly.

"Mistress Langley," he murmured, bowing to both ladies, then straightened, looking at Margerie. "Mistress Croft."

She did not waste time on pleasantries. "What do you want?"

It was like a slap in the face.

Virgil was abruptly angry. "To discuss your note, madam."

"There is nothing to say, sir."

"I have one question."

"Ask it of God, then," she countered sharply, glaring at him with those captivating green eyes that still haunted his dreams. "For I have said my piece."

"By the rood!" he exclaimed, a sudden heat in his face. "Will you not at least tell me *why*?"

"I shall not, sir."

Virgil struggled against the urge to speak more plainly. They were strangers, it seemed. And must converse like strangers, with forced politeness and veiled references. Forgetting how they had once lain together in intimacy and trust, keeping each other's secrets.

Why was he even here? It was humiliating. He would be married soon, the arrangements were in hand. The banns would be read, the church decked with flowers. Christina would walk down the aisle as she had always dreamed of doing. He would have a wife; he would not need a mistress. Another man's mistress, in fact.

"Mistress Langley, of your goodness," he managed at last, tempering his tone with an effort, "would you allow me a moment to speak privily with this lady?"

Kate Langley bit her lip, looking from him to her friend in consternation.

"Stay where you are, Kate," Margerie insisted, but her friend had the grace to move away a few steps.

Margerie was turning too. She was leaving. He put a hand on her arm and she turned sharply. Was that pity in her face? Contempt?

His lips tightened. "Why have you refused to see me again? Tell me the truth. Do I not deserve to know?"

She shook her head, stubbornly mute.

He had thought himself indifferent to her rejection. But now, standing before her, he found himself remembering something he had long since buried in his heart. Something so painful he was suddenly lost, no longer sure which direction to take, the compass spinning wildly, his craft out of control.

"Margerie…" he began, his voice hoarse.

"My name is Mistress Croft," she reminded him, shrugging off his hand. "Now if you will excuse us, we must go about our duties. I suggest you do the same."

He said nothing. He stood there a long while after they had departed. The wind grew chill and the rose leaves shuddered, dark green against the bare soil.

Fifteen

Hampton Court Palace, New Year's Day 1537

NEW YEAR'S DAY CAME crisp and cold, snow lying in thin white patches over Hampton Court, muffling the festive comings and goings of folk about the palace. Virgil trod swiftly up the stairs, wrapped in a fur-lined cloak, and came to the chamber where his mother was now lodging with Christina. A mangy wolfhound lay asleep across the threshold, perhaps having lost its way to someone else's fireside. He shooed the animal away, then knocked and entered, trying to look friendly. Though he did not feel friendly. His mother had arrived before Christmastide, planning to stay a month at least before returning into Kent with Christina to make the final preparations for their nuptials.

"Mother," he said coolly as she half-rose to greet him, "stay by the fire, I can fetch my own wine."

His mother was slightly built, white-haired under the stiff black hood, her gown old-fashioned even to his eyes, country clogs peeping out beneath. She had passed almost every day of her life in Kent's green county, far from the royal court, and had no pretensions.

But he knew his mother, now Mistress Tulkey, was proud that her son's godfather had been one of the king's tutors, for such things mattered. Not only that, but Sir John Skelton had been a well-known poet and scholar, and a man of the church, being rector at Diss in Norfolk until his death. And her first husband, Virgil's father, had been a scholar too. Not a rough-tongued apple farmer like her second husband, though his large estate must have made up for his coarseness when they married.

Eight years old. It had been a tender age at which to lose his beloved father. And gain another, rather less beloved.

He bent to kiss Christina's hand, searching her face. She had passed a difficult few days since the snow began to fall, for the cold always crept to her heart.

"You are well this morning?"

"Better for seeing you," Christina replied, smiling.

He hesitated, having caught a hint of strain in her voice. "They say the snows will not last. You are worried about returning into Kent?"

"I will survive," Christina insisted, and gestured him to stand by the fire. "Take some warmth with your wine."

His mother looked at him as he poured himself a cup of the warm spiced wine, the flagon standing on the hearth to keep out the winter's chill. He felt her gaze on his face, but would not turn. Even now, he found it hard to forgive…

Something nudged at his memory. "I brought you this, Christina," he said suddenly, reaching inside his doublet for the small silk-wrapped parcel he had tucked there before leaving his room. He handed it to her wryly. "I remembered we always used to exchange gifts at New Year, but have missed several years since I came to court."

Her eyes wide, Christina unwrapped the parcel and gasped. "Gloves! And so finely wrought. I shall put them on at once." With genuine pleasure, she pulled on the kidskin gloves, handsomely tassled and with a gilt *C* embroidered on each wrist. "But how beautiful they are. They look very costly too. You know my taste so well. Thank you, Virgil."

"I am glad you approve."

Covered too snugly with a fleece to move, Christina pointed to the table. "I have a New Year's gift for you too," she admitted shyly.

He took up the book and studied it. "The Letters of St. Paul in the Common Greek," he read aloud, then bowed solemnly to his betrothed. "I thank you, and see I shall have to brush up my Greek."

"We could study together, perhaps."

He turned, smiling. He liked Christina the scholar, her eager and tireless pursuit of knowledge. It was a trait he understood and could appreciate. Women so rarely had the chance for a good education. Latin. Greek. Philosophy. Mathematics. The keys to a rigorous mind.

"It would be my pleasure."

"Though only after we are married, of course," she added softly, glancing at his mother as though that worthy matron had protested out loud at the thought of them sitting for long hours in the same room, thumbing together through St. Paul's letter to the faithful believers at Corinth.

He put down the book. He found his mother's presence at court unbearable. But she had been a useful chaperone since her unexpected arrival. Christina had noticed his relief that they were rarely alone anymore, seeming to think—or perhaps hope—that he did not wish to be tempted into molesting his betrothed before the priest could join them in holy matrimony.

The opposite was true.

With his watchful mother as chaperone over the pair of them, he no longer needed to pretend. Not sit beside Christina and kiss her cold lips, nor discuss how they would be intimate after the wedding, a matter about which she seemed most curious. But of course she was a virgin, and her own mother had died long ago, leaving her with no one to ask about the rituals of the wedding night.

He hoped his own mother would speak to her about what was expected of a wife. Though if not, he would happily put off the moment of consummation until Christina felt more at ease. In truth, he had tried, lying alone at night, and still could not work up any enthusiasm over the thought of bedding Christina.

Yet all he had to do was think of Margerie Croft without her gown, and his body raced into life, heart thudding sickly, his cock stiffening in his codpiece. There, now he had done it. And Christina would think this hard flush and glittering look were for her. Traitor, he told his cock.

His mother was speaking to him in her reed-thin voice. He forced himself to look in her direction, to be courteous at least. More talk of the wedding. God send it would be over soon, and then…a lifetime of lying beside Christina. Dreaming of another woman's sweet mouth and body.

His betrothed was wealthy, he reminded himself, and her health might improve. It was an excellent match, and would elevate him still further at court.

"Are you even listening to me, Virgil?" his mother asked, her look pained.

"Forgive me, I am not."

Christina's eyes stretched wide at this insult. "Virgil!" She shook her head. "Have you forgotten that this lady is your mother?"

"I have not forgotten," he said bluntly, and downed the last of his wine, not looking at either of them. "Would to God I could."

His mother stood in a rustle of skirts and left the chamber, straight-backed, ignoring Christina's protest. He felt a twinge of guilt but was determined not to run after her and apologize. His mother seemed to believe he had forgotten what she had done when he was a child. The cruelties enacted. The lies told. But he had not forgotten. Nor forgiven.

Christina stood up too and came to him at the fireside, the fleece slipping unheeded from her lap. She was wearing a woolen mantle against the cold, her skirts hanging heavy from slender hips, her body still thin. Fragile even. She looked as though she would break if he made love to her. Another reason not to.

"Why did you speak to her like that?" she asked quietly. "Your mother does not deserve such treatment."

He looked at her silently.

Christina frowned, touching a hand to his cheek. "I am not a fool, Virgil. I know you do not love your mother. But I have never understood why." She waited. "Will you tell me?"

"I think not," he said tightly, not trusting himself to say more.

"Perhaps when we are married?"

Someone knocked at the door. It was an interruption sent from heaven, and saved him from distressing his betrothed with anything too close to the truth. Distressing and offending, perhaps.

Christina called testily that the door was open, and turned to sit down again, folding her hands in her lap with feigned contentment. Her look said, we will talk of this another time. But they would not.

It was his servant, Ned.

"Master Elton, sir," he managed, panting hard, "I…I have been looking for you everywhere. You are needed urgently."

Virgil saw from his face that it was serious. "His Majesty?"

Ned nodded, backing into the corridor with Virgil following at once. The boy must have run up and down every staircase in the palace, by the way he was breathing. His cheeks were flushed, and there was still unmelted snow on his boots.

"Master Greene would have you come at once, sir."

He did not look back at Christina, but felt her disapproval like a weight on his shoulders.

The king was not sick. He had finished with the elaborate New Year ritual of giving and receiving gifts in the Great Hall and was grinning like a schoolboy when Virgil entered the chamber, finding his sovereign engaged in a game of thimblerig with several rowdy courtiers.

"Ah, Elton!" The king beckoned him forward, generous in his joviality. "The man himself."

"Your Majesty?"

Master Greene nodded for him to approach. "You have done

it," he muttered conspiratorially, and clapped him on the back. "The new cordial meets with approval."

"Good for the heart," King Henry muttered, hovering first over one cup, then another, trying to decide which to pick. "And the sinews."

"Try the one on the left, Your Majesty," Master Greene suggested.

Henry knocked over the cup on the right. He frowned. There was nothing beneath.

"But where…?"

The lord who had set up the cups smiled, though very carefully, as one would smile at a man with a dagger in his hand, and lifted up the middle cup.

There, gleaming beneath, was a gold ring.

"God's blood!" exploded the king.

"Again, Your Majesty?"

"Of course, again. I was not ready. Now, more slowly this time, and let me see your hands…"

Virgil looked at Master Greene, who took him aside again. "Sir?"

"His Majesty is pleased with your efforts. But he summoned me to ask for another bottle. It seems the one you gave him before has almost run dry."

He was surprised, though pleased. "Already?"

"The king has been…busy."

There was a shout of delighted laughter behind them as the king finally chose the correct cup and claimed his prize.

Master Greene smiled wryly, lowering his voice. "And His Majesty is in an excellent mood at last, for which small mercy let us thank God. Can you make up more before the last of it is gone?"

"I have another bottle in my room, ready prepared."

Master Greene looked relieved. "Then fetch it, sir. And at once. Though discreetly, as always. None but us must know of this business. But I believe there will be a fat purse in it for you," he added cheerfully. "That should take the sting out of your nuptials. Remind me, when are you to marry?"

Virgil managed a smile. "In the spring. His Majesty is very generous."

All the way back to his workshop for another bottle of his aphrodisiac, Virgil thought of the king's generosity and tried to be grateful. But his impending nuptials still stung, whichever way he looked at them.

—⁂—

Three nights later, Virgil was working late in his bedchamber, recording dosages taken and the exact amount of each ingredient in the king's new cordial, when he became aware of a draft at his ankles.

Someone had pushed wide his door and wandered inside, not speaking.

Seated at the table, quill in hand, he turned wearily, his eyes blurred from the row of neat figures in his journal, thinking it must be young Ned or perhaps one of his fellow doctors, Master Greene perhaps.

But it was Margerie Croft.

She drifted into his room in a pale shift, not looking to left or right but straight ahead. Her hair was unbound, a soft red cloud tumbling down her back to her waist. Her feet, clad in woolen stockings, glided across the floor almost without a sound. If he had not known Margerie Croft suffered from somnambulance and often walked in her sleep, he would have thought her a ghost and crossed himself.

Instead, Virgil rose instinctively to shut and bolt the open door, then stood with his back to it, watching as Margerie walked across the chamber to his bed.

She paused at the foot of the bed, and bent, catching the hem of her shift in both hands and raising it slowly up over her head. He stared at her rear view, taking in first her long legs, clad in stockings gartered just past the knee, then her white buttocks, full and round, exposed to his view. She stretched, dragging the shift over her head, and the red hair-cloud was released, concealing her slender back as it tumbled down. She dropped the shift to one side, dreamily, still not speaking, and went to lie down on the narrow cot that served as his bed.

Margerie lay on her back, naked but for her stockings, staring up at the ceiling as though she could see angels there. Her eyes were open, a soft green. Nothing stirred in their depths as he approached the bed and stood looking down at her. No recognition, no shame at her bareness, no sign that she was even aware of his presence.

The somnambulant, he thought, studying her: asleep, but with the appearance and actions of one waking.

Night wanderings. A disordered mind that cannot tell night from day. Treat with one to three drops of poppy juice at bed, and such restraints as may be required to keep the subject from wandering.

"Margerie," he tried.

No response.

Virgil studied her in dispassionate silence, from the gartered stockings up to the reddish curls between her thighs, then over the softly rounded belly to her breasts, the pink nipples almost dusky by candlelight. Her full lips were slightly parted, and he could see her chest rising and falling with each shallow breath.

His gaze returned to her mons veneris, the delectable mound of Venus which was now the property of one Lord Munro. The shock and strangeness of it were acute. A perfect dewy-skinned goddess, stretched out naked on his own bed. It was hard not to stare open-mouthed, ogling her like a schoolboy faced with his first whore.

Asleep or not, Munro's or not, Margerie Croft was all but

offering her body to him. His cock stiffened and grew long, and his breathing quickened. He considered how it would feel to unfasten his codpiece, part her thighs and roughly mount the wanton, her body only open to him again because her mind was asleep.

Good, he told himself fiercely, staring. It would feel good. Better than good. It would be a fine revenge for her rejection.

His hands moving slowly, his gaze fixed on her relaxed body, he began to undress.

She did not stir.

His cock was already partially erect when he released it from the confines of his leather codpiece. He stroked it swiftly to rigidity, breathing hard, thinking again of how she had entered his room as though entranced. How she had bent over and raised her shift over her head, exposing her deliciously rounded bottom, and lain down on his bed in open invitation.

Margerie wanted him. Even in the depths of sleep, she wanted him to lie with her. What other explanation could there be?

Virgil smiled, watching her breathe, her chest steadily rising and falling, a faint rosy blush in her cheeks. He climbed onto the cot beside her, the ropes that held the straw mattress on the frame creaking, and studied her face while he stroked himself. Then he blew gently onto her cheek. "I know you are awake, Margerie. So you can stop pretending."

Her head turned slowly, and she fixed him with an intense green stare. "What gave me away?"

"My luck is not this good."

Her lips trembled into a smile, then it vanished. "I should not be here. I cannot be here."

"Then go," he said savagely.

Her eyes gazed into his a moment longer, then her eyelids closed and she sighed. Her hand slipped between her thighs and he watched, his mouth dry, as she teased her red-glinting curls apart and stroked herself.

She was utterly shameless, he thought, watching as Margerie pleasured herself. A born wanton. He should tip the woman off his bed and march her to the door. He could not understand why Margerie had come here tonight, pretending to be walking in her sleep, to be guiltless of desire. Should she not be serving his lordship instead, taking her joy of him, perhaps a bellyful of seed too?

Damn her.

Nonetheless, he soon found himself aping the languorous movements of her hand, reaching down to touch himself in the same way. At first he only stroked his cock from root to tip, his fingertips light, watching with fascination as she moaned and writhed, drawing up her knees.

Then his hand closed about the eager shaft, squeezing, plumping out the enlarged head. His cock thickened and twitched with each slow pump of his fist. As his balls tightened, Virgil gave a harsh gasp, and had to restrain himself from rolling on top of her and riding out his pleasure.

Why banish him from her bed if she still wanted him?

He was angry and aroused at the same time, an unsettling mixture, the one bleeding into the other, a raw fury feeding his hunger for her body. "Margerie," he whispered, and kissed her warm shoulder, turning in toward her nakedness.

She did not respond. His hand still gently pumping his cock, he watched as her mouth opened on deep gasping breaths, her knees drawn up to her chest, her hand working between her thighs. Her belly and thighs were pure white, like alabaster, never touched by the sun. But her cheeks were flushed and her chest too, her breasts taut, tinted with rose, swaying as she shifted and moaned.

He was close to the edge himself, his cock full and hard, only holding back so he would not miss a moment of her lascivious self-pleasuring.

"Virgil," she gasped, then arched her back off the mattress, her mouth a wide O, her cry high and agonized. "Now, now sir... Mount me."

He came above her at once, pushing her thighs down and apart, staring down into her face.

"I am not your puppet, mistress." He was terse, wanting her to serve him, not the other way about. "You came to me, I did not summon you. If you want this mounting so badly, let me hear you beg for it."

She moaned, holding her damp lips apart for him. "Please, master." Her submission was unfeigned, her voice pleading for consummation. "Fill me, sir, I beg you. Ride me."

He drove into her, crying out as she stretched around him, her velvet-soft flesh wet and clinging. His head felt thick with pleasure, he could not seem to breathe properly, snatching at the air as he pumped, using her hard and fast, not wanting to feel anything for this woman, his thrusts almost cruel.

"Wanton," he muttered, wishing to punish her, and heard her moan his name in reply.

So she was able, after all, to tell him apart from Munro, he thought bitterly.

Virgil pinned her to the mattress, suddenly furious. But he kept fucking her. He grasped her wrists and dragged them above her head as far as the wall, stretching her out as though on the rack. She was long, pleasingly narrow at the waist, her pale breasts jutting out. He stared down at their lower bodies, working fiercely as one, moving together with heat and precision and unadulterated lust.

She should be his alone. No other man's plaything.

He shut his eyes, not wanting to see her anymore, almost hating her. "Give it to me," he muttered against her throat. He was in charge. Whatever he might demand, she was helpless to refuse him. He wanted her to understand that. "Hold nothing back, I want it all. Open yourself to me properly."

She understood.

Shuddering, she wrapped her legs around his back, urging him on. "Yes," she hissed in his ear, and rotated her hips slowly against his, driving him mad with lust.

He wanted to hear her lose that controlled facade, to cry out in helpless passion beneath him. But he knew there was a good chance he would buckle first.

Her nails dug into his shoulders, then raked down his back to his buttocks, and he gasped as he rode her, gritting his teeth. His scalp was prickling, every inch of his skin alive with sensation. She was so slick and hot inside, it was like plunging in and out of a furnace. Blood-hot, her body made his seed rise swiftly. She was tight too, tight beyond what he had expected, as though no man had used her since they last lay together.

And yet he knew she had been intimate with Lord Munro many times since. For it was no longer a secret at court that she was his mistress. Jealousy gripped him cruelly. His rhythm became harder and more determined, thrusting inside her again and again, an iron driven into the heart of a fire. He wanted this to be fiercer than any past coupling she might have enjoyed with Munro, to be more memorable, fixed forever as the best.

Suddenly she shook violently and climaxed again, her eyes wild, writhing under him like a deer struck by an arrow.

"*Virgil!*"

Taxed beyond human endurance, he stood the provocative movements of her hips for less than three more gasped breaths, then let go.

His cock grew thick and impossibly hard, then abruptly he was spending inside her, pumping long jets of seed with every jerk of his hips. The white-hot pleasure felt like it was being ripped out of him, the world falling away as he arched his back and drove deep, crying out as though *in extremis*.

Sixteen

She must be out of her mind, Margerie thought, waking in his arms some hours later, the candle burnt down, the fire burning low. Her bones felt deliciously liquid, and she was sore between her thighs as never before, he had mounted her so forcefully. But to be lying naked in this chamber again…

To speak with Virgil Elton would be dangerous in itself, after the queen's warning. For both of them. But to come here as though in her sleep, too ashamed to admit she needed him, and then to couple with the man so fiercely and without any thought for safety. The only conclusion was that she had lost her good wits.

Virgil stirred against her, his head resting on her shoulder, one arm thrown warmly about her waist. His voice murmured against her skin, "Why did you come here, Margerie? And in such a guise?" He hesitated. She could almost hear the frown in his voice. "Did you think I would believe you asleep and take you anyway?"

So she was not the only one to think this was madness. Yet whatever had driven her to act so wildly tonight, she was not ready to answer his questions.

When she said nothing, fearing where truth would lead them both, he continued more sharply, "That is not the kind of man I am."

"You know why I am here."

Virgil shifted, slowly removing the arm about her waist, then pushed up to a sitting position in the bed. She turned to look up at him in the dull flicker of firelight, but his face was in deep shadow, unreadable.

Without the warmth of his body, she felt oddly bereft.

"Munro not enough for you?" His voice cracked the silence, shocking her with its fury.

"*What?*"

"You are his mistress, are you not? Is he inadequate in some way?"

She swallowed, recalling her promise to young Lord Munro not to reveal his secret. He had kept his side of the bargain, even discussing with her how she would like her gift house furnished when their arrangement came to an end.

"No…no. His lordship is a man, like any other."

Not a natural liar, she was glad of the dark masking her blush.

"So your appetite demands more than one man, is that what you are telling me?"

Dear Lord, that was even worse.

"I…I needed your company tonight, that was all."

"My company?" he drawled. "Alas, what a disappointment you must have suffered. And I thought it was my cock that had drawn you here like a moth to the flame."

She could not reply at first, her cheeks hot, then said furiously, "Must you always be so uncouth?"

His voice was laconic. "Come now, I have heard all the unsavory tales of your whoring, you need not dissemble. Long hard nights sweated out in Munro's palatial quarters in London, or so they say, your slick *quicunque* shared between his lordship and another man, far from the queen's prim looks. A man whose identity nobody knows, for he appears by stealth and heavily cloaked."

She was not fooled by the lazy laughter. There was a hint of steel beneath his voice.

"You will not give me his name," he finished, "so I shall not waste my breath in demanding it. For all I know, it could be the king himself. It would not be the first time His Majesty has played at that game." His voice hardened. "But by God, woman, do not come to me with that air of innocence. I cannot stomach it."

Virgil swung out of bed, crossing with swift hard strides to the table. She followed him with her eyes, drawn to his naked form with fascinated admiration. His buttocks were neat and tight, his thighs ruggedly muscular. When he turned, fetching a fresh candle from the mantel, she stared at the broad expanse of his chest, accentuated by the narrow hips, his belly flat and strong. His powerful forearms were thick, veined, and dusted with dark hairs like his chest. She recalled their strength as he had supported his weight above her, with seeming effortlessness.

It was like looking at a god. A god who had just fucked her senseless.

Margerie sat up in his bed, drawing her knees to her chest and wrapping her arms about them, very aware of her own nudity. She could never be as confident as Virgil, moving on bare feet about the chamber without a stitch on his very male body. She watched, holding her breath as her lover bent to kindle a fresh candle from the remains of the fire, then carefully poured himself a cup of wine, turning to offer her a drink too.

"Wine?"

She averted her eyes from the thick length of his cock, swinging deliciously between his thighs, still hard despite their lovemaking. But her mouth was dry as she remembered suckling on him once, how his cock had tasted, and the noises he had made when she sucked on him greedily. Somehow she managed a husky, "I thank you, yes."

It seemed to her that his hand trembled as he passed her the wine cup, and she wondered if he was still angry with her. And no surprise if he was. She had told him no, never again, then come to his chamber in the night like the whore he believed her.

She was shocked and bemused by her own behavior too. Just the thought of being found out left her shivering. Yet how could she obey the queen and stay away from Virgil Elton? All these years of celibacy and she had finally found a man she desired. Even if she could never wed him, she could still enjoy these few snatched moments of pleasure before the coldness of life closed over her head again like the deep waters of the Thames.

He had seen her shiver, and brought his cloak, wrapping it about her bare shoulders.

Margerie met his gaze, and knew it was hopeless. She had fallen in love with Virgil Elton.

Her heart ached as she realized her error. It was hard to keep the despair out of her face. But what a foolhardy thing to have done. This man saw her as a wanton, and indeed she had been one tonight. He thought her capable of promiscuity. He was to be married soon; she had even seen the lady herself, walking with him in the palace gardens, a thin, frail creature, to be sure, and young, but with glowing eyes and a high forehead. Beautiful and no doubt worthy of his love.

She had heard his betrothed described as a lady of great learning as well as fortune, and of good blood. Beside such a paragon, Margerie was a mere convenience, a sop for his occasional lusts. And she knew it.

"So," Virgil began, sipping his wine while he watched her over the rim of his cup, "why did you come to me tonight?"

"I told you—"

"But not any other night," he elaborated, interrupting. "Why now, and not before? Why cut me off without a right of appeal, then lie with me as though starved of a man's touch? You have an attentive lover, and a younger man at that. Lord Munro is barely old enough to grow a beard. His stamina must be ten times mine."

From beneath her lashes she regarded him with a look of irony, a smile playing on her lips.

"God's blood," he exclaimed, half laughing, half grimacing, "what does that look signify?"

But she shook her head secretly. Her delight in his rigorous lovemaking was not something she could share. Not even with him.

His eyes flickered over her face in the candlelight, settled on her

mouth, becoming intent. She wished she knew what he was thinking, and set a hand on his forearm, lean but powerful, loving the feel
of veins beneath her fingers.

"I wanted you more tonight than I did before, that's all," she said,
and hesitated. If she was not careful, she would give herself away. She
could not risk giving away the wound spreading inside her. To blurt
out, "I love you." The thought of his mockery was too painful.

"You gave me what I...what I needed," she finished, then
looked away.

He was studying her closely, frowning. "Something Munro
can't give you?"

Where was the point in lying?

"Yes," she admitted.

His demeanor changed. He downed his wine abruptly and set
the cup on the floor.

"Margerie," he said huskily, taking her cup away and placing
it beside his own. Then he seized both her hands, looking at her
strangely. "Sweet Margerie."

"Yes, Virgil?"

"You remember that I am to be married soon?"

She tried to look unconcerned. "Yes."

"I would like to keep you as my mistress after I am married,"
he said, then held up a hand, silencing her when she would have
protested. "I cannot offer all that Munro does. I earn a small fee for
my work at court and cannot lavish gifts upon you. I have a modest
family holding in Kent. My mother lives in the main house, and it
is likely my wife will join her after we are wed. But there is a small
cottage on the other side of the estate. You... You could live there,
if you wished to leave court and become my mistress. I would visit
whenever I could."

She stared. "With your wife nearby? Do you have no care for
her feelings?"

"If we were discreet, she would have no need to know," he said defensively. "The cottage lies near the top of a steep hill overlooking the valley, on a track where few travelers venture."

She shivered again. "It sounds a lonely spot."

"But beautiful, I assure you, and out of sight of the main house." Virgil hesitated, frowning, and a slight flush entered his cheeks. "Forgive me, I have not made myself plain. My betrothed, Christina, has always suffered poor health and is mostly confined to her chamber. Some years ago I promised to marry her, thinking Christina about to die and wishing to ease her pain. She was in love with me, being a young girl of a romantic disposition." He did not look at her, but she could see guilt in his face. "I should have stopped it, of course. But I always thought... I assumed..."

"That she would die before it became necessary to tell her?"

He glanced at her gratefully. "Yes."

"But she did not die."

"No," Virgil agreed, his mouth twisting in a wry smile. "And for that, I thank God. Christina has been a good friend to me over the years, and I care for her deeply. I have no wish to see her hurt. But although I know she expects me to consummate the marriage, Christina is of a weak constitution. I will not be in any hurry to breed her, for that would be the surest way to bring about her death." His face was grim. "I am duty-bound to marry her, all the same. To break it off now would be dishonorable."

She expects me to consummate the marriage...

A dart of pain nearly stole her breath away at the thought of him lying in another woman's arms.

"Yet to marry her and keep a mistress nearby is not?"

He raised his head, meeting her gaze directly. "You think me a villain for trying to be happy? With you, I could at least hope for a child. The king had it right. Better a bastard son than none at all."

Virgil put out a finger, trailing it along her lips. The touch was light but nonetheless sent a thrill through her. She trembled, her mouth suddenly dry.

"Munro does not make you happy in bed, does he? Or you would not be here with me now, betraying him."

She held her breath. "I cannot…"

"Forgive me, I should not have asked such a question. But I can see the unhappiness in your eyes. And a desire that keeps you in my bed, and out of his." He bent and slanted his mouth across hers, kissing her deeply. By the time he pulled back, they were both breathing heavily, their faces flushed. "Say yes, and I can make the arrangements. I am high in the king's favor at the moment. He will agree to your removal from court, I am sure of it."

Margerie thought of the queen's anger, and the young bride's look of betrayal when she discovered the truth, and she closed her eyes.

"No," she whispered.

Virgil was silent, and when she opened her eyes again, she found him staring at her, a savage look in his eyes.

"Why?"

"Must I give a reason?"

His reply was flat. "Yes."

Her temper flared. "Then you will be waiting a long while to hear it, sir."

"You want me, I can feel it in your kiss. Yet you say no." He frowned heavily. "Are you afraid I will desert you if Christina bears me a legitimate son, or if I grow tired of your company? Do not fear it, Margerie. I can have papers drawn up to guard against such an event, ensure the cottage is endowed upon you forever. Whatever makes you feel safe."

If I grow tired of your company…

She hugged herself, looking away, tears pricking stupidly at her eyes.

"No need," she said, and heard her own voice with marvel, for it was calm and not clogged with tears. "You see, Lord Munro has made me a similar offer. Only he is giving me a fine country house in Sussex, and a small estate to go with it. Forgive me for having led you into error tonight. I was…lonely…and his lordship is not at court at present. That is why I sought you out."

He was silent at last, and she was thankful for that. Even if she found the courage to defy the queen, she could never continue as Virgil's mistress once he was married. It would not be fair to his young bride, however ill she might be and unable to fulfill her wifely duties. Besides which, it would hurt more than a thousand cuts to lie with Virgil in heat and intimacy, then watch him go home to another woman.

"I thank you for your kind offer, sir," she finished, straightening her back, "but I must refuse."

When the time came for them to leave court, in the first few days of February, Virgil took the unexpected decision to accompany Christina and his mother back to Kent.

He did not know why but something had urged him to leave court, to return home, even if only for a sennight. His duties at court would not spare him any longer than that. But it had been an age since he looked out from his own bedchamber at home on frosty fields, rough grazing land bordered by woodlands to the east, a sloping meadow beyond that where sheep grazed.

Applegate was not a large house, but had always been comfortable if somewhat ramshackle, a huddle of mud-dark buildings hedged about by farmland that inclined toward marsh in the wet season. It had supported the Elton family in a meager fashion for some hundred and fifty years, and now it was his. He had inherited the house at the age of eight when his father died, but allowed his new stepfather, Harry Tulkey, to run the place, frankly not caring for many years if it went to ruin.

Harry Tulkey.

Even now it was hard to think of the man without feeling sick or wishing to break something. His stepfather had not been a kind gentleman. He had been a man in whose veins had run wine, rather than blood. Tall and lanky, his gray hair unkempt, the thin figure of Master Tulkey had haunted his dreams for years. Even his mother, in the end, had learned to cower at the sound of his stick on the stairs.

Yet his mother must have loved Tulkey when she remarried. Why else inflict such a drunken bastard not only on herself, but on her young—and still grieving—son?

Virgil stood at the window of his musty old bedchamber, hands clasped behind his back, and pondered how his life—and indeed his nature—had changed since becoming attached to the court as physician.

That auspicious appointment had been Sir John Skelton's doing, of course, his godfather. On his father's side, their family had been little better than farmers, and he might well have expected to dig turnips and herd sheep for the rest of his life without his godfather's interference.

Sir John Skelton, a distant cousin of his mother's and a man who had always enjoyed the king's ear, had noted how much Harry Tulkey hated his new stepson. Even though in failing health at the time, Sir John had made it his business to extract Virgil from that life. He had handsomely arranged for Virgil to attend the university at Oxford, where he himself had studied as a youth, and then provided him with a court appointment, as apprentice to one of the king's chief physicians for his first year.

If he had known his godfather's reputation better, he might have been less inclined to honor him, Virgil thought drily. For the man might have been a rector and a scholar, but he was also known to have behaved scandalously in his younger days. Even his poetry had been shocking in its lewd coarseness, depicting women as whores and drunkards. No wonder he had warned Virgil to stay away from the houses of Venus.

But the years had passed, Sir John Skelton had died, and Virgil had finally thought himself safe at last. No longer prey to childish doubts, he had sported lustily with a number of eager widows and the occasional whore, and grown unassailable in his understanding of the properties of plants, and their effect on the human body. Indeed he had grown quite knowledgeable about the act of sexual intercourse, its curious pleasures and how to augment them, and had often been consulted by courtiers on that very matter.

Then he had met Margerie Croft.

He looked out of the window, sighing. The high walls of the manor house were just visible through trees across the valley. It was odd to think that Christina lived there all alone now that both her uncle and her father were dead. They had played together as children under those trees, until Christina's condition grew worse and his friend was forced to retreat indoors, thenceforth an invalid.

His friend.

He examined that thought, his mood bleak and uncompromising. Was Christina still his friend?

Could a wife ever be a friend? For a friend was not an inferior, but an equal. Yet a wife was a man's inferior both legally and in the eyes of God. A wife could not be the equal of her husband and yet his possession too. Owned by him, submissive to him, his chattel and slave. His slave.

"What are you thinking, Margerie Croft?"

"Of you in a toga and laurel wreath crown, and me on my knees before you."

His loins tightened in response to that enticing and very pagan image. She knew how to excite him, Margerie Croft. She understood his passions instinctively, his secret desires. Would his loins tighten so forcefully when it was Christina in his bed, clad in some demure nightgown and with eyes modestly downcast, like the good virgin that she was?

How would Christina respond if he took her as violently as he had taken Margerie that last time? With bewilderment and a resentful silence afterward, he suspected. Certainly not with equal lust, wild and untrammeled sexual desires spurring him to even greater pleasure with every thrust.

Master Hayes, the old retainer, knocked at his chamber door, grizzled and looking puzzled to see his master back home without warning, standing in the narrow chamber he had occupied as a child rather than the larger room that overlooked their small park and was now his proper place.

"Will you want supper tonight, master? Only Mistress Hayes is asking so she may set the ham on to boil."

"No need for your wife to prepare a big meal; I will be dining at the manor. With my mother too. Mistress Tulkey is already there; I left her at the door an hour ago with…with Mistress Christina."

The old man smiled, bowing. "Very good, Master Elton. And may I wish you very happy, master?" He looked at him slyly, sideways. "We heard about the wedding. May, they were saying in the village."

"Were they?" Virgil turned resolutely away from the window. He had seen enough. "Then May it must be. Fetch my horse round, would you? No, don't bother. I shall walk over to the manor. The snow has almost gone, and it's been too long since I walked the boundaries."

"Very good, sir."

~~~

Christina looked frail and exhausted. The journey back from court had left her weak and barely able to stand, but she managed to preside over the dinner table with a certain grim determination. Afterward his mother discreetly took up some embroidery by the corner window, her work illuminated by a costly branch of candles, while he sat beside the fire with Christina, warming his damp boots and listening to her talk of guests and church banns and his own attire at the wedding, subjects which left him pained and silent.

"Virgil," she said at last, her thin brows drawn together, "it seems your mind is on other matters. I asked if you wished your cousins to be invited to stay here at the manor or at Applegate?"

"Forgive me, Christina," he said, hearing the hoarseness in his voice, and suddenly clasped her hand. "Forgive me."

He had lowered his voice, aware that his mother might not be as deaf to their conversation as she pretended. He looked at Christina's surprised face, and told himself that he should wait until the morning, or another day, or some time when they could be properly private. But then the fear gripped him that he might put if off forever, and he had to speak, audience or not.

"There is something I need to ask and I cannot seem to…" He became aware that he was avoiding the question, so forced himself to ask rather abruptly, "Are you sure we are not rushing this wedding?"

She stared. "I have been planning for months. There is no rush."

"Spring, though. It seems very soon."

"We agreed upon May."

"But that was months ago," he pointed out. "And now…"

"Virgil, what are you saying?" Her eyes were very cool, but there was anger there. He knew her too well not to see it. "You do not wish to be wed in May?"

"No," he said stubbornly. "I do not."

Christina took a deep breath, then let it out slowly. A log collapsed in the fire, and she glanced at it blindly. Her fair hair was so neatly arranged about her simple black hood, he could not imagine her with it hanging to her waist, standing before him proud and naked.

What had put such a lewd thought in his head? His jaw clenched. Damn Margerie Croft. She had seemed to be everywhere at court. He did not want her here as well, standing between him and the stark truth, confusing him with her faint scent of roses and the softness of her red hair.

"Very well," Christina murmured, watching him, "when would suit, then? Midsummer? Or is that too soon as well?"

He fought the urge to drop her hand and stand up, to leave the room. Leave the manor house with its knowing servants and expensive candles, and walk back through the dark to the familiar tallow stink of Applegate. God's blood, he would walk all the way back to the royal court, if necessary, in this mood.

"Christina, I…" He lurched to his feet, restless and angry, and caught his mother's disapproving look. "I should have said this long ago. Back when you were still a child and the wound would have healed more readily. Forgive me now for hurting you, but I do not wish to marry you." He realized too late how rude that sounded, and tried to make recompense. "That is, I am not ready to wed. And I would make you a very poor husband."

His mother had stood up too, the forgotten embroidery falling to the floor. "Virgil! What are you saying? How can you treat Christina so cruelly?"

"This is none of your affair, Mother." Virgil looked at the cold disapproval in her face, and the anger he had been crushing inside his heart suddenly flamed out. "And how can you accuse me of cruelty, a woman who thought nothing of allowing her husband to beat and starve her child, and shut him up in the cellar for days on end? And all so I would stop visiting Christina and attend more to my lessons in swordplay."

Shocked, Christina stared from his face to his mother's. "What?"

"You heard me," he said flatly.

His mother said nothing in response to this revelation, but her lips had tightened and she seemed unrepentant. He did not know what he had expected from her, in truth. An apology, perhaps? He would be waiting a long time to hear that, he thought grimly.

Christina looked back at him, shaking her head, very pale. "Virgil, oh Virgil, I am sorry. I did not know any of this. Why did you never tell me?"

"You were too young for me to confide in, Christina. And later, where would have been the help in raking over old injuries? No, I locked it in my head, just as Master Tulkey locked me in the cellar."

He heard pain and bitterness ringing in his voice, and with a kind of horror discovered that he was close to tears. It was with a powerful effort that he got himself back in hand. "But all that is past. What matters now is our future."

"A future you are about to throw away," his mother said, her voice shaking as badly as his had been.

"You are mistaken, Mother. Much as I regret hurting Christina, I must be true to my own destiny. And my path does not lie with Christina."

"Destiny? Your path? None of this means anything, Virgil. You must marry. Or the Elton line will die."

"Then let it die," he said simply, and lifted his gaze to his mother's face, his voice steadier now, his control back. "Not every man can beget a child. And perhaps some men should not. Perhaps I am one of those men."

Christina had sat waiting during this exchange, not looking at either of them anymore, hands clasped in her lap. He could see her lips working as though she wished to speak but could not find the words.

"I cannot marry you," he said more gently, kneeling beside her and taking her pale hand. "I love you as a friend, my dearest Christina. I always have, and I believe you love me the same way. I have done you a most bitter and grievous wrong in not admitting this earlier, and if you hate me now, I will not be surprised, nor consider you to blame for it. It is entirely my fault. I allowed the deceit to go on far too long, when I should have said all this months past."

"Then why did you not?" Christina demanded.

"Because I am a coward."

"Yes," she agreed, then turned her head in cold dignity. "I am tired now. You had better return to Applegate."

"I do not wish to leave you alone."

"Your mother is here," she said icily.

He glanced at his mother, surprised to see that she had sat down again, the embroidery back in her lap, and was looking over at him with every indication of contempt.

"You are staying?" he asked her, taken aback.

"Christina may no longer be going to become my daughter," his mother pointed out, "but she is still and always will be my closest neighbor. We take care of each other."

Virgil knew himself despised.

He stood, then bowed low to both his mother and Christina. "Good night then, ladies," he muttered, and made his way out alone through the moonlit hallway without waiting for the servant to appear with a lantern.

He had lost his temper with his mother, he thought with regret, recalling what he had said in anger and how she had responded. He had not merely snapped at her but spoken to her of her violent dead husband, used his name, spoken directly of his crimes, then laid the blame at her door. Virgil was shocked, despite himself. He had never raised his voice to his mother, though he had sometimes spoken sharply when she was trying his patience.

Master Tulkey, like most men, had been lord and master in his own home, and most boys were beaten occasionally for bad behavior. It was the severity of those beatings though, for the mildest of offenses, and the long incarcerations without food, that had darkened his childhood. The little boy inside him argued that his mother should at least have made an attempt to stop her husband. Not turned away, mute.

He would never marry now, Virgil thought, gazing up at the moon on his way home across the icy fields. The years stretched ahead in his mind, empty of passion and the laughter of children. Margerie thought him a poor second to Lord Munro. Christina was not the woman for him. He had run out of lovers.

Seventeen

"With child?" Virgil turned from his dissection of a frog, his thin-bladed knife still in mid-air, unable to hide his shock. "Are you sure?"

"She is most definitely with child, I assure you. I examined her myself yesterday. These are early days yet, of course, but from the signs she described to me, and the date of cessation of her courses, I would estimate her being brought to bed sometime this autumn."

Virgil sat stunned and incredulous.

Master Greene grinned at his expression. "Come, sir," he said, nudging his arm as though it were a tremendous jest, "do not frown as though you do not understand the significance of this event. You are to be congratulated!"

Virgil was even more surprised by that. "How so?"

"Need you ask such a question? Lay down that knife, sir, and let me shake your hand."

When Virgil obeyed, still reeling from the news, Master Greene seized his hand and shook it with great enthusiasm, seeming not to care that he had just been prodding a frog's innards with it.

"My dear Virgil, the queen is with child, and there is no doubt in my mind that your special cordial, that mysterious Eastern aphrodisiac you labored over for so many months, is the cause."

"His Majesty is the sole cause of our queen's pregnancy," Virgil said drily. "After Anne Boleyn's fall from grace, you would do well to remember it."

"Quite so, of course. The king has performed admirably and his new wife is with child. Your involvement in that process is not something that has been spoken of openly about the court, you may be assured. But many know this is your doing, and you will be rewarded for it, albeit discreetly." His master sketched him an ironic little bow. "Soon you will be among those doctors summoned to attend His Majesty first, and I will trail behind like an apprentice, in awe at your skill and importance."

"You overstate the case," Virgil remarked calmly, yet he was pleased nonetheless.

Pleased for the king and queen, and greatly pleased for the success of his aphrodisiac. If that had indeed been the cause of Her Majesty's pregnancy.

"And if the child born of this triumph should turn out to be a son, and heir to the Tudor throne, your future will be assured."

Virgil covered the splayed remains of the frog with a cloth, hoping to return to it later in the day for further study, and wiped his hands.

"How is Her Majesty? Well, I trust?" He would be unlikely to be granted an opportunity to examine the royal lady herself, so knew he must rely on Master Greene's experienced observations for his news. "There is no fever, and no sign of sickness yet?"

"She has suffered a little nausea in the early mornings, but is otherwise in prime health."

"I thank God for it. Long may she continue so."

"Amen to that, sir. But what of your own nuptials?" Master Greene watched as Virgil closed the journal in which he meticulously recorded all his findings, and placed it back on his workshop shelf. "Has the date been set for this auspicious occasion, or is the noose still dangling empty?"

"There is to be no wedding."

Master Greene frowned. "But at New Year you said…"

"Christina no longer wishes to be my wife," Virgil said flatly, not keen to go into his reasons for dissolving the knot, and thinking it better that he preserved her honor with a lie. "She has changed her mind. So that's that."

Truth be told, he did not know his reasons for saying no to Christina. But that was not something he wished to divulge, even to one of the men he had known longest at court.

"I am sorry to hear that, Virgil."

"Do not be sorry, I pray you. It is for the best."

"If you say so." Master Greene bowed, looking embarrassed, and made his way to the door, no doubt wishing to leave Virgil to his grim humor.

Virgil shrugged, his arms folded across his chest, staring at the floor. "I do say so, yes," he said quietly, then glanced up at his friend and master. "I have thought long and hard on this matter since returning from Kent last month, and I have come to the conclusion that I should never marry. I would make a bad husband."

Master Greene turned at that, and his brows shot up. "With the secret of such a powerful aphrodisiac in your pocket? No, my friend, you would make a *good* husband." He gave Virgil a dry look as he left the workshop. "Though a demanding one, perhaps."

Virgil sat a moment longer in thought, then went swiftly after the physician, spurred by a sudden thought. "Master Greene?"

Master Greene turned in the corridor, frowning. "Yes?"

"If a young woman suffered from such shortness of breath that she could barely leave her bed, and was fatigued by ordinary tasks, plagued by a feeling of sickness, and constantly pale," he said, listing Christina's usual complaints, "how would you treat such a condition?"

The physician rubbed his chin. "Are the lips and fingertips sometimes tinged a faint blue?"

"I have seen that once or twice, yes."

"Well then, I would prescribe bleeding first," Master Greene said firmly, "to excite the flow of the blood which governs the heart's activities. And with every meal, a cup of strong coarse wine in which a bulb of fennel has been steeped overnight. To be repeated every three days over a month's duration, and the results noted."

Uncertain, Virgil hesitated. "When I was a scholar at Oxford, I recall a suggestion that a small amount of foxglove might strengthen a weakening heart."

"No, on no account should foxglove be introduced into the body!" Master Greene shook his head vigorously. "It is a poison, and even the smallest amount can kill, as well you know." He put his hand on Virgil's shoulder, his voice not unkind. "Remember your Hippocratic Oath, my friend. *Nec alicui medicamentum lethale propinabo.*"

"*Nor shall I administer any deadly drug…*"

Virgil nodded his agreement, and put that dangerous idea aside. He had thought perhaps to alleviate Christina's breathlessness with a mild infusion of foxglove, which in small doses had been rumored at university to hold undiscovered properties. But his master was right; the foxglove was a powerful poison, and he dared not risk killing her with too strong a dose.

"Thank you, Master Greene. Your advice is excellent, as always."

It was early March and the weather was no longer so chilly, much to everyone's relief, for it had been a bad winter. After the feast, the tables and long benches were pushed back to make room for dancing. The king led out the queen to a stately measure, and everyone applauded politely, though the king still limped after his jousting fall the year before, and the queen danced like a wooden puppet, both her face and her limbs stiff.

Margerie looked at the queen with new eyes. There had been rumors that she was with child, but no formal announcement had yet been made. The court waited eagerly for news, and wagers were being placed on the likely month of birth, many jesting that the especially cold winter they had suffered would bring a crop of swollen bellies that summer.

Nor would those ladies be alone, she thought grimly, resisting the urge to drop her hand to her own belly. There was no swelling yet to indicate her shame. But she had missed her monthly courses some weeks ago now, and had begun to feel sick and light-headed on rising.

At first she had refused to believe the signs, telling herself it was simply nerves or that she had miscounted. But the days had stretched on with no sign of blood, and eventually she had conceded the truth: she was with child by Virgil Elton.

She was ruined, of course. To act the wanton behind closed doors was one thing; quite another to flaunt a swollen belly about the royal court.

Ruined twice over. It was quite ironic.

But she would not drag the doctor down into her hellish disgrace. None need know the child was Virgil's, for everyone at the court believed her to be another man's mistress. It would be unfair to ask Munro to acknowledge the child as his bastard, when they both knew such a thing to be impossible. But perhaps his lordship would at least keep to their agreement and allow her to retire discreetly to the country for her confinement, even though a twelvemonth had not yet passed since the start of their "affair."

It would be a cold and lonely existence, returning to a life spent hiding and in disgrace. But at least she would have Virgil's babe to comfort her in her solitude.

How long before she must leave court? Another month, perhaps? Any longer and her shame would begin to show.

Queen Jane herself looked pale and somber in a high-necked gown of black velvet, and had barely picked at her food tonight at high table, while the king had feasted with his customary good appetite, laughing with gusto as they were entertained by a troupe of Cornish mummers.

As soon as the king and queen had taken their seats on the dais, the musicians struck up a more lively tune. The courtiers began to cavort instead, flirtatious, light on their toes, rich silken bodices brushing fine doublets, their feet keeping time to the lilting hautboys and the tabor.

Someone sidled up behind Margerie while she watched them dance, her mind possessed by dark imaginings…

"A penny for your thought," Kate Langley murmured in her ear, smiling when Margerie turned, startled out of her reverie. "You were far away then, my love. In the arms of one Master Elton, perhaps?"

"Don't!" Margerie looked back at the dancers, her face carefully blank. "He is not for me, and you know it."

"I know no such thing. But I do know you will not be Lord Munro's lover much longer."

Shaken, Margerie stared at her friend. "What do you mean?"

"I have heard whispers this past sennight about Lord Munro and a certain young Alice Holsworthy, new come to court to serve the queen as one of her maids of honor. A wealthy girl and of high birth, but too pious by half. In Queen Katherine's reign, she would have made an excellent nun."

Kate looked at her with satisfaction, nodding as she saw the realization dawn on Margerie's face. "Yes, their families are in agreement, and they are soon to be betrothed. His lordship will make the announcement any day now. He waits merely for the queen to give her permission."

"I did not know."

Kate looked at her closely, perhaps wondering if Margerie was hurt by this news, for she did not know that she had been Munro's mistress in name only. "I hope Munro offers you something in exchange for your good service to him," she whispered in her ear. "Something worth the loss of your last shred of reputation?"

She knew she ought to tell Kate the whole truth: not just about Munro, but the babe growing in her womb. And she would soon. For now she needed to hug that secret to herself, to dwell on her hurts in silence. And to own the truth, she dreaded seeing the inevitable look of dismay and condemnation on Kate's face.

Though she deserved to be condemned for this pregnancy. She had behaved foolishly, and she knew it.

"A home for life, Kate," she whispered back. "That is what Munro will give me. A goodly estate, and the wherewithal to keep myself alive there, without need of employment at the court." Her eyes sought her friend's face, looking for reassurance. "Does that make me a whore?"

"Aye, my love, but a very well-paid one." Kate slipped an arm about her waist, her feigned laughter light and amused. "Only do not look so stricken. Keep smiling. You do not want anyone to guess what we are saying."

Margerie stood straight, forcing a smile to her lips for the sake of pretense. So young Munro was soon to be married, which meant his need for pretense was at an end. But all might still be well. If Lord Munro kept his side of their bargain…

Her smile faded a moment later when she saw Munro himself, looking about with a bored air. She had thought him still in the country, visiting friends. He had not told her he would be back at court so soon. She tried not to let her dismay show. Did this mean she would be required to spend another night with him as his false mistress? Her heart was so fragile these days, she did not think she could bear much more pretense.

But to her relief Munro did not appear to have noticed her. Instead he hailed Thomas Wyatt, a bold courtier known for his verses and his penchant for the company of ladies, and the two men stood in conversation, only a few feet away.

"Thomas Wyatt is looking less gray-faced these days," Kate

whispered, looking in that direction too. "They say when he was released from the tower, he could barely walk, his torturers had gone at him so hard. Yet he swore throughout his questioning that he had never lain with Queen Anne. Nor so much as kissed her lips in jest."

"The others denied it too. That did not save them, God rest their souls." Margerie crossed herself, thinking of those dark, horrifying days the previous spring when Anne Boleyn had lost her head and the court had lived for weeks under the shadow of that terror. "I am surprised Master Wyatt did not go to the block."

"There was a letter sent to Thomas Cromwell, they say." Kate's lips were barely moving, her voice a thread of sound. "After that, they left Wyatt alone, except to insist he return home to his estranged wife after his release, and make all well between them."

"He is a skilled diplomat, of course," Margerie pointed out. "He would have been a loss to the throne if he had been executed with the rest of those accused."

"Such considerations have never stopped the king before." Kate shrugged. "I do not know from whom that letter came, nor what it contained. But I would wager some kind of promise was made in exchange for Wyatt's life."

"But that would have been a very dangerous thing to do. Why would anyone risk themselves for Wyatt, but not the others?"

"You might as well ask why does the sun shine or the rain fall? There is always someone powerful to champion a poet. For without poetry, what are we?"

The two men were wandering toward them now, still talking, Wyatt charming and handsome, broad-shouldered and narrow-waisted, his dark beard trimmed to a point in the latest fashion, and Munro splendidly attired as always, a gold chain about his neck shown off by a black velvet doublet, his own beard worn boyishly short.

Suddenly Munro looked up and saw her.

His eyes narrowed on her face and he frowned, as though

unhappy at this encounter. She felt a chill run through her and wondered what she could have done to offend her benefactor.

Munro hesitated before nodding his head in greeting. "Mistress Croft, Mistress Langley."

"Lord Munro," Margerie murmured, and both women curtsied low. "Master Wyatt."

Wyatt greeted Margerie again with cordial good humor, his eyes heavy-lidded as they lingered over her red hair, then he took Kate's hand and pressed it to his lips.

"Mistress Langley," Wyatt said smoothly, "it is good to see you again. You please a weary man's eyes." He glanced across at the dancers, watching one or two of the younger women with a melancholy air. "There are not enough beauties at court these days."

"That is perhaps as well, Master Wyatt, for a new queen should always be the fairest."

Kate was smiling, but there was a bite to her words. She had liked Queen Anne, Margerie remembered, and no doubt held it a fault that men like Wyatt had openly and recklessly flirted with the queen, leading in the end to her death.

"Indeed," Thomas Wyatt said softly.

"I heard you had returned from the country, though somewhat earlier than expected. Your wife, Elizabeth, is well?"

Wyatt's gaze hardened on Kate's face. "I thank you, yes," he said curtly, "my wife is well enough."

With a curtsy so brief as to be an insult, Kate abruptly excused herself. "It hurts me to leave you, Margerie, but I have duties to attend to," and with that, she vanished into the crowd of courtiers. Margerie watched her go, somewhat astonished at her friend's abrupt departure, and saw Wyatt's dark gaze turn to follow her too. Had there been some intimacy between those two in the past? That would explain Kate's hostility toward Wyatt after his involvement in Anne Boleyn's trial.

Munro had been looking about the room again, as though avoiding Margerie's eyes. Was he ashamed to be seen with his supposed mistress in public? she wondered.

Then his face changed, and he looked almost scared for a moment. "Mistress Holsworthy," he muttered under his breath, glancing at Margerie. "Forgive me, I must…"

Without further explanation, he dropped Wyatt's arm and turned away, bowing instead to Alice Holsworthy, a soberly dressed young woman with pale fair hair beneath her neat hood, accompanied by an older woman in black, no doubt her widowed mother.

Alice Holsworthy paused and curtsied to her new suitor, smiling shyly. "Good evening, my lord."

Their match must have been mutually agreed, Margerie thought, watching them with interest. For there was no animosity between the couple. Then Alice glanced curiously at Margerie and Wyatt, her mouth pursed, her small dark eyes almost black, and she curtsied to them as well.

"I know Master Wyatt," she said in a well-bred voice, "but not this lady. Do introduce us, my lord."

There was a hard color in Munro's face now. "Forgive me," he muttered, then steered his new lady hurriedly away to dance, leaving Margerie alone with the poet.

He is ashamed by our association, she realized, and felt ludicrously hurt, even though she had never been his lover. Was this how low she had sunk at court? To have become persona non grata?

Thomas Wyatt glanced at her shrewdly. "Permit me to fetch you a cup of wine, Mistress Croft. His lordship did not mean to offend you. He is a young man, and quite naturally loath for his mistress to meet his betrothed, that is all. I believe the match is important to his mother."

He looked her up and down with dark, intelligent eyes, his smile admiring. "Munro is not a fool. He will come back to you once the girl is safely wedded and bedded. Meanwhile, you have a comely face and a figure worthy of one of the Graces. You need not sleep alone, Mistress Croft," he said pointedly, offering her his arm, "not while this poet is still searching for his Muse."

Margerie ignored his outstretched arm, her brows raised at his impertinent suggestion. To her knowledge, Wyatt already had both a wife and a mistress. Perhaps several mistresses.

"Good Master Wyatt," she said softly, gathering her skirts, "I admire your stamina, but to speak truth, do you not already have your hands full with your wife, and all your other ladies? I would not wish you to muddle our names in bed, sir."

With that, she turned and left the hall, feeling his angry stare on her back all the way.

———

The narrow corridor was busy, courtiers spilling out from the dancing, rowdy in their drunkenness, safe here out of sight of the queen. She pushed her way through the crowd, then saw Sir Christopher ahead.

She took another step forward, meaning to pass the knave with her head held high. Sir Christopher was laughing with two younger gentlemen, the three sharing some loud debauched tale about "a whore and a bishop."

She realized he must be in his cups, and likely to accost her. Courage failed her, and she turned aside before Sir Christopher could notice her.

There was a chamber with its door standing open. Inside, a few elderly statesmen were standing about, drinking idly and talking in murmurs. They turned to stare as she hurried through, her face averted, her heart thudding. Beyond that room Margerie found a smaller chamber, cold and unlit, and halted there in the darkness, her face in her hands, teetering on the edge of control.

The room was thankfully quiet. It was a place to be alone, to strip off that other face and be herself, if only for the breathing space of a moment.

Too much. It was all too much.

Virgil.

Now where was the use in thinking about Master Elton? He was another woman's rightful possession. Besides, he thought her a whore.

God's blood, now she was crying.

She would go to Lord Munro in the morning and beg him on her knees to let her take the house he had promised her before the twelvemonth was complete. She would have to seek the queen's permission to leave court, of course, perhaps claiming to be sick and in need of rest in the country. But if Queen Jane took pity on her, she might be able to disappear within a month, always assuming the house was ready to receive her.

Though she would happily live in a cave if it meant she could escape this terrible place and never return.

"Margerie?"

She turned, her hands dropping from her face, and stood in shock, her heart suddenly picking up speed.

"Sir Christopher!"

The knight came into the darkened chamber, a young page walking behind him with a flaming torch. With him were the two young men she had seen in the corridor, one fair-haired, the other darker and well built, both staring at her in a lecherous, predatory way she recognized.

"Ah, Mistress Croft. How fortuitous to find you alone. I was just telling my cousins about you. They are most desirous to make your better acquaintance."

One of these young men took the torch and summarily dismissed the boy, kicking the door shut behind him.

She backed away. "What... What are you doing?"

"And I was told you have a fine mind," Sir Christopher drawled, dragging off his gloves. He looked her up and down, sneering. "Did you think I would not follow, madam, when you issued such a bold invitation, slipping away from the mob to this... Where are we, would you say?" he asked, turning to the young man to the right.

"I do not know, sir," the fair-haired young man said, his watery blue eyes on Margerie, "but it is private enough, to be sure."

The other young man had thrust the smoking torch into a high sconce on the wall. He came toward Margerie, grabbing her arm, and dragged her toward the other two. His bulging eyes were already undressing her. "Come, Cousin Christopher, let us waste no more time in talk. You promised us sport if we followed you."

Margerie tried to scream, but the fair-haired young man clamped his hand over her mouth. He dragged her hair loose from its net, laughing as it tumbled in wild disarray over her shoulders and down her back.

"Hold her for me," Sir Christopher told them, and reached calmly for her bodice, no doubt meaning to drag it down.

She dealt him a violent kick in the shin, then struggled hard against her captors while he staggered backward, swearing under his breath.

"The king was right," Sir Christopher snarled, recovering, his thin cheeks flushed, "you are a vixen. So we will use you like an animal. Down on your hands and knees!"

To her relief, the door was suddenly thrown open, and the chamber lit brightly by several men with flaming torches.

"There she is!"

Sir Christopher looked round sharply at this interruption.

The young man holding Margerie's arms behind her back loosened his grip, his voice faltering. "Who... Who's this?"

Margerie blinked at the newcomers, half-dazzled by their

torches. But she recognized the page in the doorway, his arm pointing at her. One of the men tossed the boy a coin, then ruffled his hair in passing.

"Good lad," he said, and she gasped as the man came clear of the shadows.

It was Lord Wolf.

Eighteen

VIRGIL KNEW IT WAS over between them. Margerie had made things plain last time they spoke. She was no longer his mistress and would not welcome any further communications. Not even the note he had struggled several times to write to her, eventually tearing it up and throwing the paper on the fire. A stronger backbone was what he needed, he had told himself, watching his confused words of need and anguish darken and curl up into ash. Not a mistress. Not, at least, if one beautiful but heartless wanton could reduce him to this constant state of pain.

Standing on the edge of the dancing after the feast in honor of the French ambassador, he glanced about the Great Hall and caught sight of Margerie in conversation with Lord Munro. Virgil stared, abruptly forgetting to be angry with her. Margerie was so tall and slender-hipped and unbearably perfect, her beauty cleared everything else from his mind.

He watched her head dip, and her smile—for another man, damn it—and watched how her pale, long-fingered hands clasped each other at her waist. He imagined those hands clasping Munro's smooth shoulders as she lay beneath the young nobleman in bed, and fury coursed through him.

It became hard to breathe. Virgil suddenly realized he would cause gossip if he kept staring at them like a madman. So he turned his head to watch the dancing, not wanting her to think he cared whom she bedded—though in truth, it was eating him alive.

Glancing back a moment later, unable to help himself, he

noticed at once that Margerie had vanished, and not with Munro, for the nobleman was now leading a pale-faced girl into the dance.

Some prickling sense warned him that all was not well. So he ignored the bitter voice inside telling him to leave well alone, and went in search of her.

Catching a glimpse of Margerie in one of the thronging corridors beyond the Great Hall, he stopped and grimaced, thinking she was going back to the women's quarters. He would only make a fool of himself by pursuing her. But then she turned inexplicably into a side room, and almost immediately he saw Sir Christopher, accompanied by two young men, follow her with a look of evil intent on his face.

Pushing urgently through the crowd of courtiers toward the spot where he had last seen her, Virgil knocked into someone.

He backed away, grinding his teeth in impatience when the man did not budge, but stood blocking his path ahead. Only then did he recognize Lord Wolf, a nobleman high in the king's favor, and the man who had famously taken Margerie's virginity as a youth, then been jilted by her before they could marry.

Lord Wolf arched a dark brow at the collision, cold blue eyes unsmiling, one hand resting lightly on his sword hilt as he surveyed Virgil.

"Forgive me, sir," the nobleman addressed him with a sardonic air, "am I in your way?"

Virgil knew Lord Wolf only very slightly, and given his history with Margerie Croft, at any other moment would have stepped aside with some insincere apology, then continued his search for Margerie.

But then he saw who was with Lord Wolf.

"Mistress Langley?"

Kate looked at him, frowning at his sharp tone. "Master Elton? What is the matter, sir?"

"Have you seen Mistress Croft?" Not waiting for an answer, he searched the faces around them, hoping to see Margerie again at any moment. His stomach clenched as he remembered the look on Sir Christopher's face. "I fear she may be in danger."

Wolf's blue eyes narrowed on his face, the frozen demeanor dropping away at once. "Margerie? Speak, man. What has happened to her?"

He looked cautiously at Wolf, but Kate Langley urged him to speak freely. "Lord Wolf is a friend, Master Elton. You can trust him." She nodded to the other man at his side, a tall and broad-shouldered man with fair hair and eyes almost as green as Margerie's, who shook his hand with reassuring strength. "And this is Hugh Beaufort."

So Virgil told them briefly what he had seen, and what manner of man Sir Christopher Dray was where women were concerned. He then waited in an agony of impatience while Wolf disappeared into one of the side rooms.

His lordship returned a few moments later with a young page, who told them in a stammering voice how he had seen a comely red-haired lady alone in one of the privy chambers with three gentlemen.

"Quick, lad, show me this private room. I thank you for your help, my lord Wolf, but it is perhaps better if…" Virgil glanced at the others, but it seemed they had no intention of letting him go alone, Hugh Beaufort already loosening his sword in its scabbard, Lord Wolf's face dark and intent. "Let us hope we are not too late, then."

———

Virgil followed Lord Wolf into the privy chamber, and stopped just inside the door, taking in the scene before him. Margerie Croft, her flame-red hair wild and loose about her shoulders, her face shining like a heretic about to face the bonfire, arms held behind her back by some young fool…

Standing before her, a vicious sneer on his face, was Sir Christopher Dray. His codpiece was swollen out with lust, and the man was fumbling with it, his eyes on Margerie.

It took maybe three seconds for Virgil to understand what they had interrupted, and to be sickened by it. Fury turned to relief that he was not too late, then instantly back to fury.

"Get away from her, you bastard!"

He ran straight at Sir Christopher, not thinking of the likely consequences of such an attack, and rammed the man to the floor. There were a few confused moments where he was aware of slamming his fist into Sir Christopher's face, but not of much else, except a few blows which landed on his own face and were shrugged off in the heat of his rage.

The chamber seemed to have erupted behind him too, men fighting around them, yelling and scuffling. Suddenly one of the other assailants collapsed across them, breaking Virgil's fixed determination.

Sir Christopher rolled free and jumped to his feet, red-faced and panting. "You'll hang for daring to touch me, you whoreson."

Virgil launched himself after him, but Sir Christopher darted away, surprisingly light on his feet. He turned abruptly, wrong-footing Virgil, and threw a punch that landed on his jaw, only slightly awry.

Virgil staggered back into Lord Wolf, who righted him and pushed him back toward his opponent.

"Not done yet, sir?" Wolf demanded, laughing, then ducked as one of the young men with Dray hit out at him.

Slowly circling Sir Christopher, whose nose was bleeding, his cheek a dull red, Virgil could not help noticing how Margerie had backed up against the wall as though to watch the fight, her cheeks flushed, her green eyes unreadable. But there was a wildness in her face that told him how badly she wanted him to win.

God forbid he should fail her now.

Sir Christopher was looking at him with disdain. The man lifted a sleeve to wipe away the blood trickling from his nose. "So, Master Elton comes to defend his whore. I should have known you were tupping her yourself, you damn leech. And you have struck me now," he said thickly, and drew his sword meaningfully, "so I must make an end of you. As a lesson to other upstart physicians tempted to forget their place."

So he was to die, was he?

Virgil looked at the sword, glinting in the torchlight with grim intent, and half-wanted the knight to make an end of him. Better a quick death now than a slow and more torturous one, growing old alone. He felt rage and misery in the same instance, and a creeping sense of futility that made it hard to focus on what was needful to stay alive.

"Here, catch!" Hugh Beaufort called out cheerfully, and threw his sword across to Virgil, hilt first.

To his own surprise, Virgil caught the sword hilt in a firm grasp and turned, prepared to fight.

He had trained to use a sword as a boy, of course, like everyone else. But this was nothing like slamming a wooden sword against his fellow's, knowing he risked nothing but a sore thumb. This was cold heavy steel in his hand, and an enraged and highly experienced knight as his opponent, plus the gnawing awareness that if Sir Christopher managed to break his guard, he was almost certainly going to die.

Would Margerie be sorry if he died here tonight? Or would she turn away with a shrug, barely remembering his name this time next year?

Sir Christopher lunged.

Purely by instinct, Virgil managed to counter his stroke, then attacked in return, beating the man back a few paces.

"Bravo," Lord Wolf said softly, away to his left.

Sir Christopher grinned, dancing lightly about and rolling his shoulders back as though getting comfortable. "So you know how to hold a sword, leech. But can you kill with it?" His taunting voice mocked Virgil. "You whose duty it is to heal the sick, do you have it in you to *take* a life?"

Kate Langley called out, "Fie on you, Sir Christopher. Put up your sword. This brings you no honor."

Margerie said nothing.

The door had been left open. Others had now gathered in the torchlit doorway to watch the fight. Virgil felt as though he were in a nightmare. There could be no hiding his interest in Margerie Croft now, nor their affair.

He felt sick, and furious too. And desperate.

Much as the king held him in favor at the moment, fighting in a royal palace without proper cause was an offense that carried the most stern punishment, and while Sir Christopher was likely to escape censure, due to his rank, he himself would be punished, then dismissed from court.

If, that is, he survived this night's work...

Virgil parried two swift passes, then a thrust that almost broke through his guard, finding himself pushed back against the wall. He was being pressed hard by his opponent. There was sweat on his forehead, and already the sword felt like lead in his hand.

"Have at you!" Sir Christopher snarled suddenly, lunging with fatal intent.

But it seemed chance was on his side. A second or two beforehand, he had caught a flicker in Sir Christopher's eyes and rightly interpreted what was coming. Parrying the death thrust to his heart, Virgil pushed on past it with a snarl of his own. Their swords clashed violently, slithering together, steel along steel, bringing the two men so close they were eyeball to eyeball.

Sir Christopher panted in his face. "I'm going to slice your belly open so she can watch your guts spill out!"

Virgil bared his teeth in response. "Not if I skewer you first, you bastard!"

"Put up your swords!" a voice cried from the doorway, ringing with authority. "In the king's name!"

Virgil held his stance regardless, his furious gaze locked with Sir Christopher's, neither one turning nor dropping his sword. He was unwilling to cede the ground he had taken, and besides, he was not sure he was in full control of himself any longer. Rage was in his blood, and for several minutes now he had known a very strong desire to make an end of the man in front of him. The knowledge that he was capable of such violent intent was not altogether comfortable.

Several pairs of hands plucked him away from the knight, and he stumbled backward, his sword point lowered to the floor.

Hugh Beaufort took the weapon from his hand and slid it back into the scabbard at his belt. "Well fought, man," he said, and clapped Virgil on the back.

Virgil recognized the courtier who had interrupted the fight as Thomas Wyatt. No doubt some observer had brought him here to prevent bloodshed, for Wyatt was known for his skills of diplomacy when negotiating between enemies.

Thomas Wyatt came forward now, his gaze assessing both men's condition, and spoke sharply to Sir Christopher—whose sword was still naked in his hand—demanding the nature of his quarrel with one of the court physicians.

Behind Wyatt, his face pained and uncertain in the torchlight, stood Lord Munro with several of the king's guards.

Virgil looked at them dully. Was he to be the one arrested, then? He was not of Sir Christopher's rank, after all. It would be on his shoulders that the blame for this night would fall, he did not doubt that.

"This leech," Sir Christopher was saying, pointing contemptuously at Virgil with his blade, "spoiled my sport with a courtesan."

Wyatt glanced at Margerie Croft, who was still standing motionless with Kate Langley, her expression unreadable.

"You mean this lady?"

"Lady?" Sir Christopher sneered. "She is a whore, sir. Let us not be delicate about the matter."

Munro muttered angrily, "God's blood, sir!" but to Virgil's surprise and contempt did nothing further to silence the man. Did the ungrateful, slick-haired youth not care what happened to his mistress? Virgil glared at him and wished he still had Beaufort's sword to hand.

"Forgive me, my lord Munro," Sir Christopher continued, "but my reputation is at stake. But if it makes Mistress Langley uncomfortable, I shall temper my words. As I was saying, my cousins and I were…conversing, let us say…with Mistress Croft, alone in this private chamber, when that oaf barged in and attacked me out of hand. I gave him no provocation, but the lunatic would make a fight of it, so out came the swords, and the rest you have seen for yourself."

Wyatt turned to him with cold eyes. "Master Elton, is it not? You are a doctor?"

Virgil nodded.

"Is this a true account of your quarrel, sir?" Wyatt looked him up and down as though the courtier had already made up his mind who was at fault here. "Did you attack Sir Christopher without provocation?"

Virgil looked again at Margerie, and found her watching him. There was a strange intensity in her face, her slanted green eyes alight with it. He wondered what it might mean. Was she angry that he had caused this rout and brought her reputation into question?

She had never looked more beautiful, he thought.

To explain himself would entail a disclosure before all these people that she had been his mistress as well as Munro's. To act as courtesan to a nobleman was acceptable at the royal court. But to lie with a man of lower rank would mark her out as a whore. He could not permit that to happen.

"I did, sir, yes," he heard himself say, and waited for his arrest.

There was a stir from the others watching, then Margerie stepped forward, dropping Kate Langley's hand. Her face was very pale, but he had seen that determined look in her face before.

"Master Wyatt," she said clearly, and a hush fell at once, all heads turning to listen, eager to hear the wicked courtesan's version of events.

"Mistress Croft? You need say nothing, madam, it is all resolved." Wyatt was plainly warning her to stay silent, shaking his head. Virgil felt a sense of relief, for it seemed he was not the only man there who wished to protect Margerie's reputation. "This is not your concern. You may leave, if you wish, though you may be required to give evidence later."

"I wish to give evidence now," she insisted.

Lord Wolf had been leaning against the wall through much of these exchanges but straightened now, coming forward into the torchlight. Those around him fell back in silent deference, for he was known to have the king's ear.

Wolf sounded almost angry. "Pray be silent, Mistress Croft and listen to this gentleman's advice. You can do no good here and may do great harm."

"Let the woman speak," one of the older men in the doorway called out, a star glinting on his chest, and several others with him agreed loudly. "She wishes to be heard; let us hear her."

"My lord, this is hardly the place for a testimonial..." Wyatt remonstrated with the elderly nobleman, but sighed, nodding to Margerie to continue. "Briefly then, madam. For I must discharge my duty and take this man prisoner."

"There was provocation," she stated calmly, looking directly at Virgil, her back very straight, her chin up as though unafraid.

But Virgil knew her too well to be fooled, and noticed what others would miss: the trepidation in her eyes, the slight tremor in her voice. He knew what courage it had taken for her to speak on his behalf, and raged inwardly as she publicly destroyed herself for him.

For him!

"This vile man," she said, and indicated Sir Christopher with a nod of her head, "and his cousins trapped me in this room and planned to rape me. They would have succeeded but for Master Elton, who came to my defense and attacked Sir Christopher in a fair fight."

Sir Christopher's face was mottled with fury. "Rape you? You jest, surely? No man can take what is so freely given. You were more than willing to sport with us tonight, and this man, Elton, was jealous. Because he is one of your many lovers at this court. Is that not so, Mistress Croft? But alas, the poor dupe thought himself the only one…and see how he suffers now for your whoring."

"You lying dog!"

This time it was Lord Wolf who attacked him, his face a mask of cold contempt, hands tight about the knight's throat, all but throttling him until he was pulled away by Wyatt and Beaufort.

"Enough, my lord!" Wyatt cried angrily, his face flushed, then signaled to the guards. "Take both Sir Christopher and Master Elton away for further questioning. There is more to this matter, and I will find out the truth. Mistress Langley, pray convey Mistress Croft back to her quarters, and stay with her tonight. She will be questioned separately tomorrow."

Nineteen

"SIT DOWN WITH ME, for pity's sake," Kate begged her from the cushioned fireside bench. "You will wear out the soles of your shoes."

Margerie stopped pacing the narrow chamber where she had been left until Master Wyatt was ready to question her, and looked wearily at her friend. She had spent the long wintry night and morning as she waited to be questioned thinking about her predicament. Stripping away the lies and self-deceit from the simple truth in her head. Now the time for thought was over and she yearned to act. Yet still nobody came.

"Forgive me, Kate. I cannot settle. Not until I know Master Elton's fate."

"Oh come, I have told you, the worst will be a whipping or a few weeks in the Fleet prison," Kate said with a shrug, no doubt thinking this prediction would reassure her.

"A whipping?" Margerie did not understand how Kate could seem so calm about that prospect. "On *my* behalf? For coming to *my* defense?" She shook her head. "It will hurt, Kate. Badly. And he will be disgraced, perhaps even dismissed from his post here. Can you not understand how wrong that would be?"

"No," Kate admitted, but looked at her pityingly. "Though I know you will be lucky to escape a whipping yourself. I thought you had finished with Master Elton, and very wisely too. Now this."

"I tried not to think of him." Margerie sat down at last beside her friend, suddenly exhausted. Her hands were trembling. She regarded them crossly, then pushed them into her lap. "I put Virgil Elton out of my mind, told myself it would not do. But he kept returning there. He would not be forgotten. I...I love him."

"You fool, Margerie."

She nodded, not denying it. "I know."

"A doctor."

Margerie's head rose and she regarded her friend sharply. "What of it? Yes, Virgil Elton is a doctor. He heals people, saves their lives. He does not spend his days clerking like your own husband, or trying to make up for the sins of his past like Thomas Wyatt. He is his own man and wends his own way."

Kate's mouth twisted in a wry smile. "You leave my husband out of it. He is chief clerk, anyway. He makes others clerk while he sits and grows fat on the court's bounty. And keeps me in fine gowns, so I will not leave him."

"Forgive me," Margerie said at once, squeezing Kate's hand. "That was very wrong of me, I should not have spoken to you like that. You have never deserted me, even though it might stand against you when my reputation is so besmirched. I am just on edge because... Oh, why does no one come?" She jumped up and walked restlessly to the door, then back again, staring at the floor. Her hands clenched into fists at her side, and she muttered, "I must go home. That is it. I will leave court as soon as the queen agrees to release me."

Kate Langley watched as she paced back and forth. Her eyes narrowed, then she asked, "Why must you go home? This business will not ruin you. Her Majesty knows you are Munro's mistress and has condoned it. Besides, you cannot return home yet. Did your grandfather not send you back to court to seek a husband?"

"Then old Master Croft must be disappointed. For I shall never marry now."

Margerie did not look at her friend. She was remembering how Virgil had fought for her honor so fiercely, though he was no trained fighter like Sir Christopher, had never borne arms in defense of his country, and must have known his very life was in danger with every cut and thrust.

She closed her eyes, there again, seeing his dark, familiar face, how his voice had struck through her like flint against stone, setting her body alight. Virgil could be suffering now because of her. If only he had not followed her. What had he been thinking? She was not worth his disgrace.

Sickness flared inside her and she winced, clutching her belly. Not again. Not now. She sat down again heavily, this time not pushing Kate away when her friend bent over her in sudden concern.

"Margerie, what is the matter?"

"Nothing. I will be well again in a moment. I am…I am overcome, that is all."

"You were never overcome in your life, Margerie Croft, you are made of sterner stuff than that," Kate said sharply, and took her by the shoulders, staring down into her face. "Tell me the truth. What ails you?"

Oh, what did it matter anymore?

She would be gone from court within a day or two, and Kate would never tell her secret abroad. She was too good a friend to betray her.

"I am with child," she admitted.

Kate released her, nodding with grim satisfaction. "I knew it," she said, then sat beside her, her look suddenly stricken. "But oh Lord, Margerie. This is a fine muddle you are in. If you are with child, which of them is the father?"

———

Lord Munro looked across at her in open disdain. Summoned to appear before Thomas Wyatt and Lord Wolf, by order of the king himself, he had come but reluctantly. Now Wyatt had put to him that she was with child, and would he acknowledge the babe as his own bastard, and provide for its welfare once born?

"Mistress Croft?" he queried, his brows raised.

She felt her cheeks grow warm under that look. But indeed this summons had been Kate's doing, not her own. She knew, and Munro knew, that it was not his child. That such a feat of parentage would be impossible. And yet neither could admit it without also disclosing their very unusual arrangement.

"Forgive me," she said.

Lord Wolf, standing with arms folded and legs apart, regarded the young nobleman with a cold stare. His voice was hard. "I take it you do not intend to acknowledge this bastard as your own, my lord?"

"I cannot acknowledge it," Munro replied, meeting his stare without flinching.

"How so?"

"Need you ask, Lord Wolf?" Munro turned and glared at her, his unspoken message one of malice. He clearly believed that she was doing this on purpose, to trap him into some greater reward than the house he had already promised her. "I am not the only man to have frequented Mistress Croft's bed. Therefore I cannot be sure this child is mine. If the wanton is with child, which I very much doubt."

"*Lady*," Wolf growled with soft emphasis, his eyes on Margerie's face. "Mistress Croft is a lady."

"And Master Greene examined her but an hour ago," Wyatt told Lord Munro warningly. "She is with child."

Munro examined her figure, frowning. "There is no sign."

"Nonetheless."

"Well," Munro said sulkily, his jaw set hard, "I am still resolved not to acknowledge any child she bears. And that is an end to the matter. You must bring in her other lovers and question them too. I freely admit that I have taken this...this *lady* as my mistress, but I was not alone in enjoying her favors. Ask her yourself if you do not believe me."

"Trust me, Munro, if it can be proved there are other men, I shall question them all," Wyatt said smoothly, placating his young friend.

He came to Margerie and studied her face, his gaze not unfriendly, but not warm either. "What say you to Lord Munro's accusation? Have you taken any other lover into your bed besides his lordship? We must know the truth, for it would put your child's parentage in doubt."

Margerie said nothing, her mouth tight. It had not been her idea to pretend to sleep with Lord Munro in the first place. And she understood his perfectly natural reluctance to assume responsibility for a predicament that was none of his making. But Munro did not have to incriminate others in order to avoid being saddled with a bastard that was none of his making.

A new fear crossed her mind. If Munro managed to avoid responsibility for this, would he also wriggle out of their arrangement? If she did not get the house he had promised her in exchange for her tarnished reputation, her only course of redress would be to admit in public that she had never lain with him. Only pretended to.

The thought of shaming Munro in public turned her stomach. They had come close to being friends over the months, even if he seemed to hate her now.

She could not do it.

"I need their names, Mistress Croft," Wyatt pressed her. "After last night, I can guess at least one name myself. But you must help me if I am to help you."

She turned to look out of the window. "I regret, I cannot help you, sir."

Wyatt sighed. He came closer, lowering his voice so only she would hear. "An unmarried woman with child... You may be whipped and turned out of court for this, as others have been. You have no wealth, nor a powerful man to protect you. You would end up destitute, begging on the streets. Do not do this to yourself. Or your unborn babe."

"My grandfather will take me back."

"Are you sure of that? Would you stake your life on it?" Wyatt met her eyes, his face somber. "Master Croft is a proud old bird, from what I recall. He will not want his family name linked to another scandal because of you. Not after what happened with Lord Wolf."

She winced, fearing he was probably right. Yet she could not relent. "I cannot give you a name," she said stubbornly. "Have me escorted to a cell, sir, or whatever it is you intend to do with me. I shall say nothing more."

Wyatt stepped back, shaking his head. "It is out of my hands then."

"Thomas," Lord Wolf suddenly said in his hard voice, "if I might beg your indulgence a little longer, I crave five minutes' speech alone with Mistress Croft."

"But I have nothing to say," she repeated, panicking. She felt forced into being rude. "And I do not wish to speak to you, Lord Wolf."

But to her dismay, Thomas Wyatt paid no attention to this discourteous remark. He bowed to the nobleman, then shepherded the others out of the room, including a bemused-looking Munro.

"Come friends, let us away." He turned in the doorway. "Lord Wolf, you have five minutes, no more. Then I must discharge my duty."

"Kate, do not leave me," Margerie exclaimed, but watched helpless as her friend grimaced, hesitating on the threshold, only to be steered from the chamber by Wyatt's firm hand.

The door closed.

She looked at Lord Wolf in trepidation. He returned her gaze steadily, but she saw an edge of temper in his face. "The truth now, if you please."

"Truth?"

His mouth twisted. "You and duplicity go hand in hand, is that it?"

"My lord?"

He stalked to the fire and stood there, holding out a damp boot to the steadily burning logs. "We were lovers once," he said. "That gives me some right to…"

"It gives you no right whatsoever," she replied tightly, her hands abruptly clenching into fists. "My father is dead. I am not married. I belong to no man. I answer to no man. Nor lord either. I have fought for my freedoms, Lord Wolf, and I will keep them even… even now I am with child."

Wolf raised his head and glanced round at her, his dark brow arched in silent query.

She remembered the brutally short cut of his thick black hair as a youth, the blue eyes that had cut so cruelly into her after their night together, that pierced her again now, determined to discover her secrets.

"You will answer to the king, I fear."

She let out her breath, and heard her voice tremble, giving her away. "As to that, I will face whatever punishment comes from His Majesty. His judgment is absolute. But you are not the king and cannot command me."

"Nor am I your enemy, Margerie," he reminded her softly. "But there are many at court who would happily take that part and seek to destroy you. A woman who dares to live free of the rules that bind the rest of us draws no love from those who are still prisoners. Let those of us who would be your friends shield you from this scandal, Margerie. Regardless of your desire to hate yourself, you are not without protectors."

"I do not hate myself!"

"Then what drives you to act so recklessly?"

She could not answer him, her hands twisting together in anger and confusion. "Did you beg five minutes with me so you could berate me for my wanton behavior, or to offer me counsel? For I desire neither and would rather await my fate alone."

"I do not know what game you have been playing with Munro," he said starkly, leaving the fire. "But you are not, and I would go so far as to say, have *never been*, his lordship's mistress."

She was shocked into silence.

His smile was grimly satisfied. "I thought as much. So how did it go? He paid you for saying you had lain in his bed, while in truth all you did was *lie*? Only now the trick has gone awry, for you lay with one man in earnest, and Munro will not pay for someone else's mistake, will he?"

"Th—that part was not my idea," she stammered.

"Busy Kate again?"

She nodded, not quite able to meet his eyes. "I would have kept quiet about the child. Only Kate would not be silenced. She fears for my future without a male protector."

He grinned. "She is right to do so, and I share her concern. Nor can I blame the lady, for Kate's good intentions have saved me on more than one occasion. As you would do well to remember."

She managed a smile. She and Kate had conspired last year to make the king lose interest in Wolf's beautiful bride, a pact which had brought her much peace after years of fearing and loathing Lord Wolf.

"How is Eloise? She… She was brought to bed with a child at Christmas, is that right?"

His smile was dry, and she knew he understood she was trying to turn his mind away from her dilemma.

"My wife is very well, I thank you. I will remember you to her on my return to Yorkshire. And the babe is in good health too. A boy."

"And… And her younger sister, Susannah?"

She frowned, struggling to recall the gossip that had surrounded that lady's scandalous affair with Hugh Beaufort. She had been so bound up with her own problems, she had paid little attention to the whispers. But she recalled speaking with Susannah around the time of Queen Anne's execution, and warning her not to throw away her reputation. Much good that warning had done.

"She too was with child, I think."

"And out of wedlock, yes." Suddenly Wolf gave a laugh of genuine amusement. "Though she and Hugh Beaufort were lately married. A quiet wedding, for he was only recently released from the Tower for her unlawful seduction. Since then, of course, my house has never known a moment's quiet. For after Eloise was brought to bed, she insisted Susannah must stay for her own confinement. So now we have one screaming infant just out of the womb, another knocking at its mother's ribs, and no talk at the dinner table except of babies and wet nurses. Small wonder Hugh asked to accompany me back to court for a sennight or two. He loves his new bride, but a husband can hear too much of such matters at table."

Tears pricked inexplicably at her eyes. It sounded idyllic. More than that. It sounded like heaven on earth. And an impossible dream of happiness for her.

"I am glad for you, Wolf," she said simply. "And for Eloise and her sister. I wish your family well."

"I thank you. But it means, you see, that I know a little more about women than when I bedded you as a callow youth," Wolf said bluntly, and took her hands in his, searching her face. "I know the look of a woman who is in love with a man. There was no passion in your eyes when you looked at Munro just now. Not even carnal knowledge."

"Perhaps I lie with the gentleman, but hate him."

"I do not think so." He continued steadily, "Yet when you watched Master Elton at his swordplay last night, you were in terror for his life."

She closed her eyes. "You...you know, then?"

"My dear Margerie, I have always known, and so has the world. There can be no secrets at this court. We live with our bedchamber doors wide open. And Lord Munro is no different, for all he tries to hide his private dealings with men. Some truths have a way of wriggling out, however tight they are restrained." His gaze dropped to her belly, his words significant, "As do their consequences."

"But he is to be married," she whispered, her heart hurting for the innocent-looking child she had seen with him last night.

"Oh, I daresay they will do well together, for Alice Holsworthy has no love for a man's touch and he no taste for women."

She stared. "Do you know everything?"

"Hardly." Wolf released her hands and stepped back, sighing as he looked her up and down. "Now, my proud lady, will you accept my arrogant male protection and advice? Or would you rather stumble about in the dark and call it freedom from tyranny? For if you do, I must warn you that you risk losing everything you have worked for since returning to court. This is a man's world, and a woman who insists on dashing herself against that hard truth is soon broken."

Margerie looked at him searchingly. Despite having forgiven him for ruining her life as a girl, she had considered Wolf unchanged in essentials, still brutal and distrustful of women, still cold at heart, for all his maturity and hard-won experience on the battlefield.

Yet indeed he had grown as a man since his marriage. More than that, he had become whole.

She had not missed his tender laughter as he spoke of his wife and her sister, nor the catch in his voice when he mentioned his newborn son. Wolf was not cold, nor controlling, but *controlled*. And her instincts told her that she could trust him.

"Very well, my lord," she whispered, and shivered as she put her life in his hands. "Tell me what I must do."

Twenty

"THE KING WILL SEE you now," Lord Wolf said curtly, and gestured him forward.

Summoned into the Royal Bedchamber while the king was being dressed, Virgil found all his carefully rehearsed words gone from his head when he dropped to his knees before his sovereign, King Henry.

To own the truth, he was still stunned by the news Wolf had brought him that morning while he was at his desk, hastily writing his will in case he should be committed to prison.

Lord Wolf. What was his part in all this? he wondered jealously. For his lordship seemed privy to things even Virgil had not known nor guessed about his mistress.

"Margerie Croft is with child," Wolf had told him softly, watching Virgil's face as though curious to know how he would react.

A child.

Virgil had stared at this unexpected news, struggling to hide his emotional response. But indeed he felt knocked off balance, not quite able at first to comprehend what it meant. His instinctive response was brilliant, unthinking joy. He was to be a father. He had to see Margerie at once. Speak with her privily, somehow persuade her to…

Then he saw Wolf watching him with those cold intelligent eyes, and reality intruded on his joy. Turned it inside-out like a sock so that all the knots and rough seams could be seen.

A child, he thought more logically, and groped his way toward sense. Perhaps his. But perhaps Lord Munro's.

"Does my lord Munro know?"

Wolf nodded. But his voice was curt, and Virgil sensed strong disapproval. "Munro insists he will not acknowledge the child as his bastard. His lordship says he will have nothing more to do with her."

"I will marry her," he said simply.

"You think it yours, then?"

Ah, that blade drove deep. But he survived it, almost with relief shouldering the burden that he had secretly known would always be his from the moment of their first kiss. To shelter Margerie from harm. No doubt she would rail at the thought of marriage to him, and try to escape the dreaded knot. She had made her feelings clear at New Year. But if she was with child and Munro had abandoned her…

"I will marry her," he repeated with cold determination, and met Wolf's gaze without flinching. "If she will have me."

Wolf's mouth twisted. "Oh, she'll have you. No question there, the queen will insist upon it."

"Her Majesty knows?" .

"Not yet, but soon. It cannot be hidden from either of Their Majesties. Indeed, it would be best coming from you. In the form of a frank confession of your guilt. Though you would thereby risk heavy punishment for her seduction, while Munro escapes his share of the blame." He paused. "Will you do it?"

"I will, my lord. And at once."

Wolf studied Virgil through narrowed eyes, then nodded, his look strange, almost admiring. "I thought… Well, no matter. If you are content to marry the lady, despite her association with Lord Munro—"

"I am content." Virgil had no doubt on that score. "I care for nothing but my own part in her shame and willingly make amends for it."

But now he was on his knees before the king, and all he could think was that he had failed her. He had seduced Margerie Croft, not once but many times, and now...

"Rise," King Henry said sharply, frowning down at him, his small dark eyes impatient.

The king was being dressed for hunting, his arms outstretched as his attendants labored to fit his paunch into a flattering black and green doublet.

"What is it, Master Elton? What is so important it cannot wait until after the hunt? If it is on the matter of your duel last night, you must know that it rests in Wyatt's hands." The king glanced at Lord Wolf. "But it is true that you have served me well of late, and his lordship has persuaded me to hear you out. So speak."

"Forgive me, sire. I...I have a confession to make."

"Then make it, and be quick."

"I have got Margerie Croft with child, Your Majesty," he said, "and request permission to set my fault to rights by marrying her."

The king's attendants froze, staring round at him, and even Henry himself looked startled.

"Margerie Croft? But is she not Lord Munro's mistress?"

Smoothly neutral, Wolf intervened before Virgil could think of a careful enough answer to that dangerous question. "Lord Munro has refused to acknowledge the child, sire. He is about to announce his betrothal to Alice Holsworthy, and I suspect he fears the marriage plans may be upset by such a revelation. The family is very...pious."

Henry snorted. "Aye," he said drily, "and stubborn too. They will need watching." His interested gaze flicked to Virgil. "So you would take on another man's bastard, Master Elton?"

Virgil nodded, his calm returning as he realized now how much he loved Margerie. Completely and without reservation, whatever her past sins.

"If she agrees to accept my name, Your Majesty, then willingly, yes."

"She would be a fool to refuse you, given her shameful condition. Though it would not be the first time she has refused an offer and soiled her reputation by it."

Wolf stepped forward to put his hand on Virgil's shoulder, a gesture which indicated more loudly than words his approval of the match.

"I suspect the lady will have fewer qualms about this match, Your Majesty," Wolf murmured, then changed the subject adroitly. "Might I suggest they be permitted to marry at once by special license, before her shame begins to show? Though I fear their wedding may yet be delayed, with this other business hanging over Master Elton's head…"

King Henry looked at him broodingly. "What do you suggest, my lord?"

"Order both men fined for brawling, and bind them over to keep the peace. It can be done in a day, then your physician here will be free to marry his lady and return to his duties at court."

The king nodded slowly. "Very well, let it be done as you have suggested." He looked at Virgil intently. "Your quarrel with Sir Christopher was over Mistress Croft too, was it not?"

"Yes, Your Majesty."

"Never draw sword against one of my Gentlemen of the Royal Chamber again, regardless of the provocation. Or you will face more than the whip for your impudence."

Virgil bowed his head, hearing the justified wrath in his sovereign's voice. "Forgive me, sire. I lost my head in the heat of our quarrel. It will never happen again."

"You will apologize to Sir Christopher."

He looked up sharply. "Yes, Your Majesty."

"But wait, there is something here I do not understand. Lord

Wolf has more right than you, Master Elton, to take offense at this attempted rape. For Margerie Croft was promised to Wolf once. And knew him intimately, by all accounts." The king was almost smiling. "It was the talk of the court that year. Is that not so, Lord Wolf?"

"As you say, Your Majesty."

"So it would appear I am alone in having been rebuffed by your chosen bride," Henry drawled, watching Virgil with cruel eyes.

For a moment there was a dangerous silence.

Virgil lowered his gaze with an effort, saying nothing, though his heart thudded with rage.

"Of course the queen must give her consent too," the king continued coldly, turning to finish being dressed. "Mistress Croft is one of her seamstresses. But since she is already with child, a swift marriage would seem a *fait accompli*. Perhaps now the lady will learn to restrict herself to one man's bed."

Virgil's hands tightened into fists, and it was only Wolf's hand on his shoulder that kept him steady.

"You have my thanks, Your Majesty," he managed, and bowed.

Safely out of sight of the royal apartments, Virgil leaned his forehead against the wall and breathed deep and slow, struggling to regain his composure. Throughout that nerve-wracking interview, he had felt as though he had been riding full-tilt toward the edge of a high cliff. His palms were damp with sweat, and his stomach was churning. It was all he could do not to vomit.

He had never broken the law in his life. Now he had faced judgment for unlawful actions twice in one day. And endured a reprimand from the king himself.

Wolf stood waiting patiently. "Better?"

"I may be sick."

"But the job is done. You did well. You will marry Margerie and take her into Kent. I will arrange it all. I will even pay your fine for you."

Virgil raised his head, staring. "My lord, I cannot accept such generosity," he began, falteringly, then stopped, frowning at the nobleman. "Why are you helping me? Forgive me, my lord, I have no wish to sound ungrateful. But I do not understand. I thought you and Margerie were enemies, to be frank."

"As the king said, I wronged the lady a long time ago," Wolf told him softly. "This should go some way toward redeeming my fault, I hope. Besides, I owe her a favor for her help with Eloise last year. And I do not like to leave my debts unpaid for long."

Virgil nodded, straightening. "What now, my lord? For you seem to have all the answers."

"Now you ask Margerie to marry you. And hope to God the stubborn wench does not refuse." Wolf grinned, and clapped him on the back. "That is one answer I cannot give you, alas."

He had always been hard on her. Too hard. Not merely demanding in bed, a trait due to his nature perhaps, which was earthy and physically needful, but demanding on her as a woman. To submit to him, to agree with him, to leave when he was tired of her company, to remain when he was aroused and bring him to pleasure. He had accepted that she was Munro's mistress too, and hated it at the same time as he shrugged it off, telling himself she was a wanton. For he had known all along that she was not. He knew the smile and simper of an experienced courtesan, and Margerie had neither. She was simply herself, in bed and out. And he loved her.

Yet standing before her later that evening, Virgil found himself unable to articulate a single one of those thoughts.

"You are with child," he stated bluntly upon entering the room where Wolf had arranged for them to meet.

No greeting for her or Mistress Langley, who was standing a little apart to give them privacy during this interview. No bow, no courteous asking after her health, or kissing her hand.

Instead, he directed a searching glance at her belly—no more rounded than he remembered it—then raised his gaze to her face, which was very pale. She looked, he thought, as though she had been crying.

For a moment his resolve faltered.

Then he remembered the difficult meeting with the king, and he felt resentment, blaming Margerie for the king's cruelties even though he knew with his rational mind that she was not at fault. The king was merely angry that she had not lain with him for the asking.

"Well, madam?"

She raised her chin, her eyes defiant. "Since you know my condition already, sir, my confirmation can hardly be required. Unless being a doctor, you wish to examine me yourself? To satisfy yourself that I am not…mistaken."

He ignored that last, knowing it to be mere goading on her part. Besides, he had already met with Master Greene and discussed her symptoms in detail. The dates were right. Both for himself and Munro.

"We will be wed tomorrow morning at ten," he informed her coldly. "It is all arranged. Lord Wolf and Hugh Beaufort have agreed to act as witnesses. Perhaps Mistress Langley will help you dress and accompany you to the chapel."

The slanted green eyes widened, and her lips parted in surprise. "But…you are already betrothed to another woman. Indeed, I thought you might even be married by now."

He said nothing for a moment, but felt a tell-tale muscle jerking in his cheek. Then he inclined his head stiffly. "Christina has released me from my obligation. Our betrothal is at an end."

"Good God, because of this?"

He looked at her then, bitingly angry. "What kind of man do you think me? You believe I would go to a lady I have long admired and respected and hurt her with a debauched tale like this?"

Margerie's face worked in silence, and he thought she might explode with wrath herself. He was almost disappointed when she seemed to get herself back in hand.

"I do not know," she said, her voice so quiet he strained to hear her. "But I will marry you, Master Elton, since that seems to be my only choice besides disgrace and destitution. And I owe my unborn child better than a short and brutal life on the streets."

He had expected more from her at his announcement of their impending nuptials. An argument perhaps. A shining forth of passion on her bright brow, he thought with a sudden uncharacteristic burst of poetry. Not a rather still, composed expression and downcast eyes, as though she had been asked to fold the laundry or preserve fruit.

"You are very calm," he remarked bitterly.

Her brows arched in delicate response, but she said nothing.

Virgil frowned and folded his arms across his chest, telling himself this was to discourage him from shaking a proper response from her. He was not protecting his heart. This was to do with his loins, and her womb. His heart had no connection with either.

"Is this what you hoped for all along, perhaps?" he demanded, goaded into discourtesy by her unexpected lack of rebellion. "That if Lord Munro failed to acknowledge any child from your union, you could at least fall back on Master Elton for a husband?"

"Don't be a fool," she said tartly, then screwed up her face in a quick grimace. Her voice became muted again. "Forgive me, sir. I am...I am grateful to you for your generous offer of marriage."

She shot a glance at Kate Langley, and he noticed a silent message pass between the two women. He had the impression this was an exchange she too had rehearsed carefully. "And I accept."

"Accept?" he tossed back at her. "Accept what? I have made you no offer. This is not something that can be negotiated. This is a demand. An expectation of obedience. You will wed me and yes, you will be grateful."

There was a growing flush in her cheeks.

He recognized that sign of female agitation and squared his shoulders, standing with his legs apart, planted like an oak before her. She would not budge him, however hard she pushed. He was an Elton.

That was what his drunken stepfather had said, of course, whenever he bent Virgil over his study table for chastisement. The rod always cut so deeply into his bare young legs and buttocks, Virgil would squirm and struggle against the thin whipping strokes, crying out in pain. "Keep still and take your beating like a man, you scurvy knave," his stepfather would roar. "You are an Elton, and not a Tulkey, or you would know not to dodge the rod."

This child would be an Elton too. Regardless of whose seed had put him in her belly. On that score he was determined.

"For all I know the child in your womb is his, not mine," he said belligerently, ignoring what he had just thought. "Or some other man's, perhaps."

Arrant nonsense, of course, to suggest she might have taken a third or fourth or even fifth lover beside him and Munro. He knew it, and Margerie knew it too, from the fulminating, dagger-under-the-rib look she threw him. But it made him feel better to insult her, to force her to understand the full humility of her position. She was being rescued from her own wanton nature. And he was the man having to sacrifice himself for her reputation.

Her reputation. That was a fine jest.

His skin prickled though at the way she stared back at him, not speaking.

"Tell me, Margerie," he demanded silkily, "would you ever have informed me about the child if his lordship had agreed to acknowledge it?"

It was an unfair question he had promised himself that he would never ask. But now, face to face with the woman who had spurned him, preferring a rich lord's company to his, he could not help himself.

"No," she snapped back.

Virgil clasped his hands behind his back, considering that response. He had not expected to feel wounded, yet he did. Wounded and furious. But there was the hard truth of it at last, and he had to face it. He had always been a poor second choice after Munro. No doubt the nobleman had bettered him in bed too. She might as well have slapped his face.

He struggled for control, but knew he was almost sneering, a dangerous thud to his heart. "I see," he said.

Had she ever cared for him at all? Or had he been merely a means to an end, an honorable man who would foolishly consent to marry her if Munro refused?

He remembered how passionately they had coupled. Had that been a pretense too?

He could not seem to breathe properly. He must not dwell on such thoughts, Virgil told himself. It no longer mattered what had been real and what had been false between them. The thing was decided. They were to marry. He tried to shut out the wounded voice in his head, hating its weakness, and when it would not be silenced, he let himself laugh at it instead, his smile mocking. But not in a pleasant way, and he could see she had noticed.

"Perhaps a word in private might be wise," Kate murmured uneasily, glancing sideways at Margerie.

"Oh, why bother?" Margerie said icily, and dropped him a curtsy. "You heard Master Elton, the wedding is all arranged. What need for further speech when there are so many preparations to be made?"

"Indeed," he managed.

Her color was high. "Until tomorrow, sir. I shall be at the chapel at ten."

"Remember to pack your things; we have been granted permission to leave court immediately after the ceremony," he told her shortly, then turned, heading for the door.

Virgil paused in the doorway, suddenly not wanting to leave her on that sour note. There must be more things to be said. He had imagined a longer meeting. More gratitude. Perhaps some soft words. On her part, of course. She was to be his wife, after all.

He opened his mouth, meaning to discuss the journey into Kent, where they would stop for the night on the road. But Margerie was no longer looking at him. She had turned away, her back very stiff, as though nothing he could say would interest her.

Kate Langley looked at him expectantly, her brows raised, her face disapproving.

He closed his mouth, and felt his jaw clench in frustration. Margerie was right. There was nothing more to be said. And let Mistress Langley stare if she wished. It was none of her affair how he spoke to his bride-to-be. *She* would not be asked to put up with his manners.

Virgil bowed, then left the room.

God's blood! He had not even kissed her.

—⁓—

Early the next morning, Margerie bathed before the fire, then reluctantly allowed Kate to dress her as though she were her maid, unable to rouse much interest in which gown she was to wear, though she paused a moment before the handglass to admire the fragile white silk rosebuds threaded through her red hair.

"Beautiful," Kate declared, pausing to tuck a stray red strand behind one ear, then stepped back to consider the full effect of the straight fall of green silk from hips to floor, flaring out from a pale jeweled bodice lent to her by one of the queen's own ladies-in-waiting. Her look was one of grim satisfaction. "Yes, the white roses are perfect. Master Elton will have eyes for no one but you today."

"Wait," Margerie said huskily. "My necklace. The one Lord Munro gave me."

"Yes, of course." Kate searched for the costly gold and emerald necklace among Margerie's possessions, then hurried back to clasp it about her throat, smiling. "Now you look perfect. A bride to make any man proud. Whatever else you may say of him, Munro has a good eye for beauty."

Margerie glanced at her in surprise. "Are you crying?"

"No!" her friend exclaimed at once, defensively, though her eyes were glassy. "Well, yes. Maybe a little. It is a wedding, after all."

"But not a love match."

"They never are, dearest." Kate smiled at her indulgently. "I am certain you could be happy with Master Elton though. If you allow yourself to be."

Margerie caught her wrist as Kate bent to tweak her skirts. "Kate, are you happy with Master Langley?"

"You have met my husband. He is a man in his middle years, balding and portly. But he knows who I am and does not hold me to account for my occasional indiscretions. And there is affection between us. We deal well enough together."

She kissed Margerie on the cheek. "Virgil will not be cruel forever. He is just angry, as men so often are when they feel trapped into marriage. And when you tell him the child is his—"

"What difference would it make to tell him the truth now? He would never believe me, and will only suspect me of trying to make a fool of him. No," Margerie insisted, choking slightly as emotion got the better of her, then collecting herself with an effort, "let Master Elton make of this marriage what he will. Better for him to think me only wanton, and not dishonest to boot."

"Very well then," Kate said, handing her the fur-trimmed mantle she had chosen to wear to the chapel, for the weather was still sharp despite signs of spring everywhere about the palace. "If you are ready, it is time for you to leave off your old name and become Mistress Elton."

Margerie shivered at the unfamiliar sound of her new title, but did not resist when Kate led her to the door. She had made her peace with this marriage overnight, after planning first how she would run away under cover of darkness…

But then Margerie had fallen asleep, wearied beyond thought, and when the light of dawn crept into her chamber, cold and gray, it had brought sense with it. She would marry Master Elton today, and her grandfather would be pleased enough with the match, for while Virgil was no great lord, he did attend upon the king. And there were still many at court who respected and were wary of him, despite this unwise marriage.

Virgil did not love her, that was clear. The cold and abrupt manner of his proposal had cut her to the heart, yet what had she expected? Rose petals strewn before her door and a passionate suitor down on his knees?

She was a wanton he had used from time to time, and now he was being forced to marry her. She had seen the icy sneer on his face, the glitter in his eyes, and understood at once.

How he must hate her!

She had meant nothing to Virgil Elton except a release for his sexual needs. She might as well have been his whore—except then he would have paid her to yield, and none would have questioned the transaction. As it was, she had gained nothing from their affair but this shameful disgrace—and forced marriage to a man who should have wed his childhood sweetheart instead.

She had a new life to consider now, growing within her. She must marry Virgil Elton for the child's sake. But that did not mean she must *feel* anything for the man who would soon be her master.

He felt nothing for her, so in that at least they would be equal.

Twenty-one

VIRGIL HAD AN AIR about him, she thought, glimpsing him in deep and earnest conversation with the priest as she and Kate entered the echoing palace chapel. An air of quiet determination and authority. And in bed it became…not forcefulness, exactly, but a pleasing sexuality that appealed to her own curious need to be dominated yet cosseted at the same time.

Nonetheless, the knowledge that Virgil did not love her and would forever resent this marriage haunted her as she made her obeisance at the threshold and entered the chapel.

Lord Wolf was there by the arched stone doorway, his friend Hugh Beaufort to his left.

"Mistress Croft," he greeted her formally, both men bowing while she curtsied, just as though she were a lady and not a wanton being forced to marry her lover.

Wolf was wearing a fine doublet and black velvet cap, no sword by his side today. His body was taut, muscular, powerful, barely concealed by his hose and codpiece, and it was hard not to think the nobleman rather attractive as he offered her his arm.

Lady Eloise was a very lucky woman, she realized, yet still could not find it in herself to feel any true desire for Wolf. Not with Virgil waiting only a few feet away, a thought which was sufficient to make her blush.

"I shall give you away, with your consent," Wolf said softly, meeting her surprised gaze. She guessed a little of her panic and trepidation must have shown on her face, for his brows drew sharply together.

"Unless this union is no longer what you want, Margerie. Give me the word, I can call a halt at any moment until your vows have been said and witnessed before God." He seemed genuinely troubled. "To state the matter plainly, you do not need to marry Master Elton if it will make you unhappy. Indeed, I myself would be glad to see you installed in some quiet country house for your confinement, if you prefer."

She shook her head. "I am content to marry Master Elton, my lord. And I fear your lady Eloise would never consent to such a scheme, lest it bring you censure at court. But I thank you. You have been very good to me. Both you and your friend," she added, glancing at Master Beaufort.

"Not good enough, by God. Or you would never have found yourself in this fix." His look was grim. "It was I who ruined you as a girl, Margerie, and did not stop to count the cost of your lost virginity."

"And it was I who refused your perfectly honorable offer of marriage," she reminded him, then took a deep breath. "No, this is how things must be. Lead on, Lord Wolf. I am keeping my husband waiting."

"He is not your husband yet. And besides," Wolf added with a sudden grin, "this is the last time you will be able to keep Master Elton waiting and not be chastised for it. So let the man sweat and fear you have changed your mind."

She almost laughed, but then remembered where she was. And now they were being watched. With a nod to the absurdly handsome Hugh Beaufort—could any man's shoulders truly be that broad?—she allowed Wolf to lead her toward Virgil.

Not all the ornate wooden pews were empty, as she had assumed. Several of the other ladies of the royal wardrobe were there, smiling in approval and whispering among themselves as she walked the length of the intolerably long aisle between door and rood screen. Virgil too appeared to have brought a number of groomsmen with him, some of whom she recognized as physicians—Master Greene, Master Bellamy—and loitering at the back, his servant, Ned, who winked at her.

Someone had dressed the end pews in white silk roses, like those in her hair, and trailed ivy in and out between the ornate fretwork of the pew gates. Kate, she guessed, but did not dare pause to admire the beauty and elegance of the floral decoration. She was too busy not catching anyone's eye, in case she lost her nerve and dashed from the chapel still unwed, and also remembering to breathe, which was harder than she could have imagined.

Her heart was thudding and she was astonished her legs carried her the last few feet without buckling. No doubt Wolf's steadying presence at her side had some influence over that, she thought, and was immensely grateful to him, his past sins against her suddenly insignificant compared to his great service to her these past dreadful days.

Kate Langley slipped into the pew beside Mistress Carew, who smiled and whispered, "You look so comely, Margerie!"

Wolf relinquished her with a bow, then stood to one side. Virgil Elton was already on his knees before the priest, very stiff, staring straight ahead.

He did not glance at her as she sank to her knees beside him. But it was not hard to read his mood, she thought wearily. Resentment burned in every line of his body. The king's physician had been forced into this marriage, instructed to marry a nobleman's mistress to conceal her shame, and he wanted everyone in the chapel to know it.

Margerie studied his rigid profile as the priest addressed them, looking hurriedly away when he turned as though sensing her gaze.

She felt sick, and swayed there on her hard little kneeler, horribly light-headed, the chapel darkening around them as though the sun had gone in. For what felt like hours, she fought against a very strong inclination to faint, and remained upright on her knees, listening to the priest droning on in Latin at times, and occasionally in English, and the congregation shifting uncomfortably on their buttocks, and even Virgil beside her as he muttered his responses, his voice deep and abrupt.

Her own voice sounded thin and breathless, like that of a young girl, barely audible even to those in the pews directly behind them, she was sure. But the priest, though he looked at her intently at one point, seemed satisfied that her vows were sincere.

Then they were standing, his hand helping her up after the long time spent on her knees, and they were married, it seemed.

He tipped her chin up and brushed his mouth against hers as though they were strangers.

"Now into Kent," Virgil muttered, and she said nothing.

He drew her along out of the chapel and into a rain of white blossom. The early spring had furnished the congregation with fresh petals, and they showered both bride and groom as they ducked under the archway, cheering lightly as Virgil lifted her in his arms like a true husband, carrying her across the cobbled yard to the horse-drawn litter that would take them to his home in Kent.

Her home too, now.

Kate gripped her cold hand as Margerie leaned down out of the litter, staring at her friend, suddenly desperate not to go. She did not even realize she was weeping until Kate tried to comfort her.

"Do not cry, dearest. I will see you when you are allowed to return to court," Kate promised her, smiling. "Or send for me when you are confined, whichever comes sooner. The queen may consent to release me for a few weeks."

Virgil had been talking to Lord Wolf, a little apart from the others. Now he climbed into the litter beside her, grim-faced, and signaled the driver to depart. The juddering cart swayed along the narrow path to the palace gates, and within a few minutes they had passed beyond the high palace walls and begun lumbering south.

She sat tensely, the litter curtains flapping loosely in the wind. Now they were safely on the open road, she half-expected him to kiss her properly, not just brush her lips with his own as he had done at the chapel.

The driver would not know if he kissed her, not with the curtains drawn about them. Besides, it was his right now, and she could not deny him under the law. Virgil Elton could do whatever he wished with her body, chastise her at his will, force her to serve him, to couple with him whenever he wished. For he was her husband now, and she belonged to him outright. It was her duty to obey him, and she knew his carnal appetite. He would enforce that duty with his hand if need be.

To be possessed without love, day after day, year after year, until death parted them, seemed the most terrible thing to her.

So why was she trembling in the hope that he would kiss her? Wanton fool!

Virgil did not even look at her though, settling back against the hard bench with his eyes closed and his cap drawn down to hide his face.

The space was narrow. She could feel the heat of his thigh against hers like a fire, scorching through the green gown she had worn for her wedding. There was still a scattering of white blossom on his shoulder, she noticed, and almost lifted her hand to brush it off. Then froze, stopping herself just in time.

She must not touch him. It was too bold for this confined space, too open to being misread as an invitation to intimacy.

Heat flooded her cheeks as she imagined them coupling passionately on this bench, their bodies swaying to the jerking rhythm of the litter. Of course, she would have to kneel and ride on top...

"Who gave you that necklace?" he suddenly demanded, interrupting her lewd and heated thoughts. His eyes narrowed on the blush in her cheeks. "Munro?"

She nodded, her mouth too dry to speak.

"Take it off."

She obeyed, her hands trembling, and he watched her without speaking.

"Get some sleep while you can," he said curtly. "We will stop for the night at the Green Man, just beyond Redhill, and should reach Applegate after noon tomorrow."

They were the first words he had spoken to her since leaving the chapel, she realized, quickly hiding the unwelcome necklace in the folds of her skirt. Judging by his refusal even to look at her, their wedding night at the Green Man would not be a joyous occasion. Yet she doubted he would spurn her body once night fell and they were in bed. They had not lain together in months, and he was too physical a man for abstinence, even when wielded as a punishment.

Applegate.

His home in Kent sounded like a goodly place, a vision of rich fertile greensward and long-established orchards, rather like the delightful estate in Sussex that Munro had promised her—and never delivered. It certainly did not sound like a prison. Yet it would become *her* prison.

She should never have agreed to marry him. Not when he so clearly resented having to abandon his betrothed for her. There had been no other choice though, not with his child inside her.

Once she had thought they might have a future together, that Virgil was beginning to feel something for her. Now the long years of their marriage stretched ahead without his love, cruel and barren as a desert. Oh, he would take her once he was ready. She knew that. He was her husband; he would not deny himself that pleasure. But without love, his cold possession would feel more like a rape than lovemaking.

Her womb might bring forth life with Virgil Elton by her side, but her heart would wither and harden to a stone.

—∿∿∿—

Margerie waited over two hours for her husband to return from downstairs in the Green Man, propped up against the generous bolsters in the inn's best chamber, the curtains drawn discreetly about the tester bed, a fire burning in the grate. She was wearing a beautifully embroidered silk nightgown, given to her as a wedding gift by Kate, and though it seemed a little loose about her breasts and hips, it felt luxurious against her skin. In a sudden moment of daring, she had dabbed a subtle rose scent against the back of each knee and behind her ears.

Everything was ready, everything was prepared for their wedding night. But the groom remained absent.

She thought of that narrow cot at Richmond Palace, with its creaking ropes and straw mattress, or his desk, neither of them comfortable for the lady, while the candlelight lit up her shamelessly naked body.

Tonight Virgil would bed her in this soft darkness, as a husband beds his wife on their wedding night, with clean and lawful propriety. It seemed bloodless.

Would he think it so as well?

Still she waited, listening to the sounds of men carousing drunkenly in the tavern below, and still her husband did not come. At last, overcome by the nervous trials of the past few days and her own physical exhaustion, she fell asleep.

She woke to the bed tipping gently as someone climbed in beside her. The candle was out, and the fire too. But she knew it was Virgil.

"Margerie?" he whispered.

She held her breath, not answering. She wanted him inside her, wanted him so badly her body trembled and the physical need was like a knife to her belly. Yet at the same time she could not bear the thought of him touching her, kissing her, making her cry out with pleasure under him—and all the while despising her for a wanton.

"I know you're awake," he said drily. "So stop hiding under the covers, little coward."

Virgil fumbled for her hand in the darkness, then drew it to him. She gasped, recoiling as she touched bare flesh and realized he was naked. But he would not let her go, his cruel fingers biting into her wrist.

"Touch me," he ordered her.

Her hand closed about his cock, already hard, erect. Her lips parted, and she found herself breathing lightly and quickly, her hand stroking him firmly, back and forth, up and down, pleasuring him just as she had been wont to do as his mistress. His cock was very long and thick tonight, throbbing in her hand, as though his lust had grown as strong as hers after her long absence from his bed.

Margerie longed to set her mouth there too, to moisten him for the ride, but it seemed he had other ideas. "Enough!" Virgil suddenly groaned, and pushed her roughly away. "Lie down."

She obeyed, and felt her husband reach down, lifting the heavy hem of her embroidered nightgown, raising the material to her waist. She lay exposed to him, wet and trembling, eager to be entered and stretched. She could not see his expression but heard his breathing quicken, and guessed he was already at a high pitch of excitement.

"Open your legs to me, Margerie."

Again she obeyed at once, thrilling to the dark authority in his tone, and he touched her between her legs, first cupping her mound, stroking the fine curls there, then slipping a finger experimentally inside her wet depths. Another finger joined it, then three, then four, pressing into her tightness as though exploring how ready she was to take his cock.

He did not stroke her with his fingers though, merely held them inside her, rotating his wrist until his thumb was trying to enter her too, stretching her moistening entrance until she could not bear it any longer…

She moaned, writhing with pleasure against his hand. "Oh yes, Virgil!"

Suddenly his fingers were withdrawn. "You are my wife now. Not my whore. You will be silent when we couple. I do not wish to hear such lewd sounds from you." He leaned close and she could smell wine on his breath. "Do I make myself plain, Margerie?"

She licked dry lips. "Yes," she managed to whisper, smarting from the unexpected reprimand.

"Yes, *sir*," he prompted her.

Her heart felt like it would burst, it was thudding so hard.

"Yes, sir," she repeated, and felt a hot gush of pleasure between her legs at the words, her power given up so submissively, so yieldingly, to the man who now owned her.

He positioned himself at her entrance, then pushed inside, filling her with one hard thrust. He felt impossibly large and she had to bite down on her lip to prevent herself uttering a cry, her whole body jerking in shock.

"Lie still while I take my pleasure," he commanded her.

He was forceful, coupling with intent, his breath rasping in the darkness. She lay still beneath him, and felt his strong lean body move against his, rising and falling, working inside her until she was wet and open, her body responding against his order, against her very will. But it was impossible not to respond.

She had always feared becoming any man's possession, had run terrified from Wolf when he showed her this force, and from the king when he would have used her too. Yet with Virgil, it was a natural pairing, male and female, earth and water, and his demand for submission was part of that, not a lessening of her self but a completing of it.

He shifted suddenly, breaking his own rhythm, and dragged

up her bare legs, bending them, pushing them back and open so he could lie between them. Anchored there, he took his weight on his hands and lowered into her again, driving deep, lying stomach to stomach.

Pumping into her with long hard strokes, he turned his head and sought her mouth in the darkness. She gasped against his mouth, for she had not expected a kiss. Not after his coldness. And it was not a brutal kiss but a subtle one, arousing her still further, showing her that even a kiss could make her womb ache with a sudden raw need.

He licked inside her mouth, not concealing his greed, playing games with her tongue. First he tasted her lips separately, light delicate brushwork that set her trembling. Then he teased her mouth wide and pushed his tongue between her lips, withdrawing slowly only to thrust back inside, each deep wet invasion aping the thrusts of his hips.

Her heart was racing with every thrust of his tongue. Not content to lie entirely passive beneath such a kiss, she fought back, molding her mouth to his so that their lips at least could move sensually together.

She felt his jerk of surprise and took advantage of it, her mouth following his, tasting him hungrily.

Abruptly she pulled away.

Now it was her turn to tease him, dragging hard on his lower lip until he growled. Then she kissed the corner of his mouth, his chin, his rough throat, the veins standing out along it like whipcord.

"Margerie," he hissed, and grasped her chin, holding her prisoner while he drew their mouths back together. This time the kiss took fire, her tongue mating fiercely with his, their bodies mating too.

Virgil cursed against her mouth. She guessed he must be near the edge. He rose up above her, thrusting deeply and urgently, forcing his thick length in to the hilt, and Margerie felt the sweet sharp pain of not quite being able to accommodate him. She clenched around him, panting now, urging him on, telling him without words that she needed it hard, that she welcomed his aggression.

Now only his lower body was moving, his cock slipping wetly in and out, his upper body almost still, every muscle in his chest and arms tensed to stone.

She wondered why Virgil did not simply take his pleasure, as he had said he would, but continued to prolong their fucking with this steely control.

Then it struck her. He was waiting for her to take her pleasure first.

The thought shook her to the core. For all his anger and his icy commands, Virgil had never intended this to be a rape.

The pleasure which had been tight-coiled inside her for some time now abruptly found its release, as though that realization alone had allowed it to rise and overwhelm her. Her walls clenched about him hard, then again, and again, and yet again, one dancing ripple of sweet pulsing joy that rose and fell, twisting inside her, the pleasure lashing like lightning straight up her spine to her brain, so that her scalp tingled with tiny shocks and she forgot everything, even her name, in a wondrous tide of physical release that drowned her entire being.

Margerie screamed, unable to bite the sound back, and felt his hand clamp down on her mouth, silencing her. His skin tasted of sweat, so heavy she struggled to breathe, her chest heaving for air.

You will be silent, he had commanded her, and she had disobeyed.

Shame at her own lack of discipline made her remain as still as possible, very rigidly not allowing her hips to move as pleasure burned through her, despite the temptation to grind her sweating body against his—and somehow the restraint of not being permitted to move intensified her pleasure a thousandfold.

His hand slipped from her mouth. "Wanton," he growled, his eyes glittering, watching her through the darkness.

He had been holding still inside her while she came, but now he plunged deep, his strokes driving hard and swift, pinning her to the soft mattress with the weight of his lean body. She did not resist, burying her hot face in his chest, her body limp with pleasure.

At last he gave a hoarse cry, his head thrown back, his whole body shuddering violently against hers, and a delicious liquid heat spread throughout her belly as he achieved his end inside her. Then he rolled off her almost immediately and collapsed beside her on the soft mattress, panting wildly.

She lay in sweaty torpor, exhausted and relieved in equal measure, sure now that the worst must be over. He was furious with her, thought the child in her belly was probably Munro's, but the fire was still there between them. It had not been doused by his anger.

And she was in love with him, her tenderness for him growing with every moment they were together.

This could still work, she found herself thinking sleepily, and was shocked when he suddenly swung out of the curtained bed and, to judge by the sounds of rustling, began to dress again in the darkness.

"Where…where are you going?" Margerie whispered after a few agonizing moments, unsure whether to remain submissively silent or challenge him.

It was their wedding night, after all.

"That is none of your concern," Virgil told her, and her heart sank. The curt anger was back in his voice, nagging at her, driving the chill deeper into her heart. "Go back to sleep. We make an early start in the morning."

And with that her husband left the chamber. Left her to sleep alone on her wedding night and went God knew where.

He had not forgiven her. However brilliantly their bodies might fit together, she was still—and always would be, she now realized—the wife Virgil had not wanted. The ice about his heart was too thick to admit her.

Twenty-two

VIRGIL SAT HIS GRAY gelding, staring across the muddy fields in the early spring sunshine. He was broodingly aware that his mood was dangerous and he ought to ride home. It had been almost a sennight since he had brought his new wife home to Applegate. And in all that time, he had not visited her bed again, having installed her in the master bedchamber and then chosen to sleep in his damp old room instead, as though pretending to be a boy again.

The strain of staying away from his bride was doing nothing for his temper though, and he knew it. But there was a greater danger in allowing himself to use her delectable body as he pleased. For every time they lay together, he came away feeling as though Margerie had peeled another bloody layer from his skin, and the wound was becoming more and more tender.

Wanton, he had called her. For having taken pleasure at his mounting.

Lie still while I take my pleasure...

What had possessed him to speak so coldly to his wife on their wedding night? To use her like a whore with no caresses or soft words of love, leaving her to sleep alone once his coupling was done?

"Why am I so angry with her?"

His horse shifted under him, not knowing the answer. Virgil did not know the answer either. He rubbed a gloved hand across his forehead, bewildered and more than a little guilty.

"I offered her marriage of my own free will, knowing the child was most likely not mine. I was not coerced into that offer. I was not even deceived."

Yet he knew himself furious and resentful, all the same. Margerie had the power to bring him to his knees, and he knew it. Yet this was a woman who might be carrying another man's child in her womb. Virgil would look at her and feel tender, and then come straight back to that truth, to the hard knowledge that he had been her second choice. That without this unfortunate pregnancy, she might still be warming Lord Munro's bed.

He had his pride. How could he allow Margerie to see the power she wielded over him? Better to show her coldness than risk revealing how weak he had become.

During that intense coupling on their wedding night, he had known a swift fierce joy, and then just as abruptly a terrible fear of being unmanned. Of losing his hard-won control and ending up on his knees.

Descending to the tavern's public rooms, he had found them empty but for the grizzled old landlord, and had drunk deep with the man for hours, then slept on the wooden settle until dawn, waking with a thumping head and a foul taste in his mouth from all the cheap wine he had consumed.

It had not been an ideal start to his marriage. But he was here now, married to his one-time mistress, and life must go on.

He had sent a note over to his mother at Christina's. Now Margerie had been given ample time to speak to his housekeeper, Mrs. Hayes, and formally assume control of the household keys, it seemed a good time for the two women to meet and be introduced.

He did not know why his mother was still staying with Christina, though he had been relieved not to find her at home when they arrived on that first day. But it was clear such a state of affairs could hardly be allowed to continue. Once he returned to court, Margerie would be left alone here at Applegate, apart from the servants. And his conscience nagged at him not to abandon his bride to a lonely existence in a strange household, but to provide her at the very least with female companionship while she awaited her confinement.

So he had penned a note to his mother, hesitating over the wording, for he knew Christina would of course read the note.

> *Mother, you may have heard by now, but I was lately wed to a lady of the court, one Margerie Croft, granddaughter of Thomas Croft, late of the king's service. My wife is now safely installed at Applegate and likely to remain here for some considerable time.*
>
> *I must leave to resume my duties at court within a few days, and therefore beg you to return and make my bride's acquaintance.*
>
> *Your dutiful son, V.*

He could not help wondering how Christina would take the news. Again his conscience pricked him. He should have told Christina himself, face to face. He owed her more than this furtive secondhand note. But he had to admit that he did not relish the task.

Likely to remain here for some considerable time.

Only a fool would not understand that to mean his bride was already with child. So he had waited for the inevitable explosion. Three days had passed, yet to his astonishment and irritation no reply had come to his note. Yet he knew from Master Hayes's testimony that both his mother and Christina were still in residence at the manor house, for they had been seen at church.

This morning he had taken his horse out, pretending to himself that he merely wished to ride the bounds of his property and check for any holes in the hedgerows and withy fences where errant sheep might slip either in or out, when in fact it was at the back of his mind all the time to ride over to the manor house, and confront both Christina and his mother.

He had wanted to ride out with Margerie for several days now, show her the grounds himself while the sun was shining and winter at last seemed to be retreating.

But Margerie had repeatedly refused. "I am still not quite well, I fear," she had told him, watching him with anxious eyes, her face pale. "Perhaps another time, if you do not mind."

He had not argued. He hated the wariness in her eyes, suspicious that she was afraid he might punish her for refusing. As though he were an ogre looking for any excuse to beat his wife. Besides, he was not assured of the wisdom of a woman in her condition sitting a horse.

Applegate was no grand estate of course. But although he had avoided returning for years, it was his home and his inheritance, the place where he had played—and suffered—as a boy. Despite the crueler memories, there were some happy ones too. Perhaps Margerie would eventually come to love it as he did. And perhaps one day his own son…

Carefully, as though unthinking that thought, Virgil gathered the reins in his gloved hands, and clucked his tongue at the horse.

"Come, Thunder," he commanded.

He spurred the gelding forward and over the low hedge between his property and Christina's. When he arrived at the front of the house, the place seemed deserted so he walked his horse round to the stables. Looping the gelding's reins over a post, he called for a groom, but none came.

He frowned. "Where is everyone?"

There was a sturdy unfamiliar cob standing saddled in the yard, also tied up, his hooves and hocks splashed with mud. He pondered it for a moment, wondering if Christina had a visitor, then his attention was caught by the sound of a sharp cry from one of the open stable doors.

It was a woman's voice. "Ah no!" she was crying in what sounded like acute fear and pain. "Oh God, no, please!"

His hand fell to his dagger hilt, and he strode to the door, then stood frozen at the sight of his beloved friend Christina, his fragile, delicate Christina, bent over a bale of last season's straw at the back of the stable. Her gown had been tossed up over her hips, displaying a shapely bottom and thighs, and a man in hose and leather jerkin was laboring between them.

"Yes, by Christ!" The man looked like a stablehand, and indeed sounded like one too, his language coarse as he thrust and jerked and swore at her.

His head thick with rage, Virgil ran across the stable, almost slipping in the horses' muck, and dragged the startled man from his pleasure.

"You'll die for this rape, sirrah!"

Virgil knelt on the man's chest, pressing his dagger to his straining windpipe, though in truth he would have liked to place that dagger somewhat lower on his person.

"Christina, are you... God's blood, are you hurt?" He had heard her cry out in shock at his intervention, but did not dare look round. "Fetch... Fetch help from the house. I will guard this villain. You need not fear, I am here to protect you now."

"Yes, Virgil," she bit out, "so I can see."

He turned his head then, surprised by her icy tone, and saw that Christina was not running to the house, but standing resolutely behind him. There was straw in her unbound fair hair, and she was smoothing down her skirts with an unsteady hand. There was a spot of red burning in each pale cheek, and he slowly realized it was sexual excitement, not fear, that had put that color there.

"This fellow was not...not raping you," he said slowly, as understanding dawned. "He is—"

"My lover," she finished for him succinctly.

The man was panting hard, staring up at him as though he were a madman. He was young, perhaps five and twenty, close to Christina's age. His black hair was cut straight across his forehead, and his eyes were dark too, rather like Virgil's own. But his build was short and muscular. He did not look afraid. Nor angry, surprisingly.

"Get off me, you bastard," he grunted, and Virgil obliged, though he kept his dagger in his hand in case the man decided to avenge the insult.

He looked at Christina, feeling indeed as if he were going mad. "Your lover?"

"And soon to be my husband," she said proudly, showing him a small silver ring on her finger. "He is Humphrey Delacour, a distant cousin of mine. He came on a visit a few weeks ago, to pay his respects, for he knew my uncle had lately died. He found me alone here with only your mother for company, and thought it wrong for two women to live unprotected." Her eyes flashed intimately to the man's face, and a lewd smile passed between them. "So he stayed."

And fucked his way into your fortune, Virgil thought, his lip curling.

"You must forgive my haste in assuming the worst," he said grudgingly to the man.

The fellow was after her money, of course. Humphrey Delacour did not look as though he had a pot to piss in, yet here the villain was, after a few bare weeks of acquaintance, treating her like a whore.

In the stables, for God's sake! Where any servant might have seen them. Or even his own mother. Had she no shame?

He glanced at her face, and guessed not. She was enjoying her transgressions too much, and would not yield easily to any argument against this interloper. He would have to tread carefully if he was to dislodge him.

"I have known Christina for many years," he explained to the newcomer, "and have only her well-being in mind. So you are her cousin, sir?"

"Distant," she insisted, watching them with sharp eyes and an over-bright smile. "Humphrey, this is my friend, Master Elton. The one I told you about."

Humphrey did not speak, but gave him a wary nod. He had dusted himself down, and was now fumbling with his codpiece, trying to make himself look respectable. But there was no shame in his face either.

A distant cousin. At least their coupling could not be seen as incest then, he thought grimly. But he was not happy. She would have been a virgin when Humphrey first took her. How long ago? A week? Two, at the most? Or had he moved even more swiftly than that?

It would not have been difficult for a personable young stranger like Humphrey to make her fall in love with him, he realized, eyeing the lusty glow in her face. Christina might be only a few years younger than he was, but she was so much more childlike in her mind than other women her age. She had spent most of her life in bed, a confirmed invalid, and had only recently left her house to visit court for the first time.

She was an innocent, by God.

And this rough fellow had taken advantage of her, treating Christina little better than a whore. Now he would wed her for her estate and the wealth in her family coffers, and probably kill her in the process.

It made him sick.

"Perhaps we should talk privately," he said, turning to Christina.

"And perhaps you should leave," she countered, her look defiant. "For I have nothing to say."

"Christina, please. Five minutes."

"Now, Christina," Humphrey intervened sharply, his clothes

restored to rights, "you have no father, nor even uncle now, to guide you. And no brother either. You told me yourself, Master Elton is as close to an older brother as you ever had. So let the man say his piece, he has the right."

"But, Humphrey—"

"When he finds it is a love match, I am sure Master Elton will give us his blessing. Now do as I bid you, girl, and don't argue."

She swallowed, then lowered her gaze to the floor. "Very well, Humphrey. Since you wish it."

For a second, Virgil was tempted to punch Humphrey Delacour in the mouth for speaking to her so roughly. But then guilt spurred him, and he remembered his own cruel commands to Margerie on their wedding night, eschewing tenderness and forcing her into submission instead.

Was he no better than this coarse ruffian, then? It was a cold and sobering thought.

Humphrey had a dagger on his own belt, Virgil noticed with interest, but had not reached for it once, not even when torn away from his lover and wrestled to the ground.

Not a fighter, then. But certainly a lover. And a cunning strategist.

"I will go for an hour's ride about the place, as I purposed before Christina distracted me," Humphrey said calmly, and they followed him out to the yard to watch him swing up onto the broad back of his cob. "I shall see you anon, Christina."

"Ride safely," she whispered after him, and watched her lover clatter out of the yard, her blue eyes smiling and a silly fluttering look on her face that made her look about twelve.

She turned to him and the smile on her face faded. "Don't judge me, Virgil," she said tartly. "Humphrey may say you have the right, but you do not. You and I could have been married by now, and doing what you…" At last she blushed, though her eyes did not leave his. "Enjoying such sport as you must have seen there in the stables."

"I would not have hurt you in the same vile way he did."

Her eyes flashed. "I enjoy that *vile way*, as you put it."

"God's death, woman. *That?*"

"Yes, *that!*"

"It looked little better than a forced debauch to me."

She raised her chin. "Yes, and at my request. Do my tastes shock you, my dear Virgil?"

His jaw clenched hard. Yes, she was trying to shock him, to send him on his way. But he had not yet made her see sense, so he refused to budge.

"Humphrey may call himself your 'cousin,'" he ground out, ignoring her question, "but I swear to you, that man is after your money, not your body. He is little better than a peasant. And he ruts like one too."

"I like the way he ruts!" she flung back at him. "And yes, his family is poor. But what care I for that?"

She pulled away from him when he would have caught her arm. "No, I shall not listen to your doubts. I am sick of being stuck here alone in the country, sewing my samplers and waiting to die. If I had known you would break our betrothal, I would have stayed at court and taken a gentleman as my lover. Or a lord. But instead all I have is Humphrey."

Her face turned scarlet and she began to raise her voice. "Do you still not understand, Virgil? I wanted a man. Not only to warm my bed at nights, but so I may inherit all my property according to the original terms of my father's will. And you were gone." Her mouth tightened. "Then Humphrey arrived. And it was not friendship. He *wanted* me. There was no courtship, he merely took me to his bed one night. Oh yes, he wants my money too. But he has a good, thick cock, and knows how to use it for my pleasure."

"*Enough!*"

"What, have I shamed you with my lewdness, Virgil? Do good

women not use words like 'cock'? Well, forgive me if my scholarship is at fault, but I seem to recall your favorite Roman poets using such obscenities in every other line of their filthy Latin verses! Verses I studied to please you, Virgil. To make you love me. But you never did."

This last plaintive cry almost broke his heart.

"Oh, Christina," he groaned, and took her in his arms, his own eyes damp, embracing her tightly. "My poor girl. My dearest friend. I thought… God's blood, I am a fool. Please forgive me. But, Christina, you cannot marry that oaf. He is beneath you."

"Not…not every time," she managed damply, then smiled up at him in a mischievous way, drying her tears. "Most times I am beneath him."

"You rogue," he exclaimed, amused despite himself, and kissed her lightly on the forehead. Then he frowned. "You are so hot, Christina." He laid a hand across her forehead. "You have a fever."

"I am merely hot from my…my exertions with Humphrey," she said unsteadily, and gazed up into his eyes. "I cannot let him go, Virgil. He may be rough and poor, and not fit to be a lady's husband, but he gives me what I want. He is a steady young man and looks after both me and your mother, and he makes me happy."

"And how does my lady mother like him?"

"She likes him very well. He compliments her and takes care of us both."

Virgil's hands curled into fists. So even his mother preferred that ruffian's company to his own? But then, Mistress Tulkey was no doubt impressed by his raw virility. He himself had always been too soft-spoken as a young man. He had heard her complain of it to his stepfather once, and had afterward striven to sound more curt and "manly" when speaking to women.

"I am not your keeper nor even close to it, whatever Master Delacour may say. I cannot forbid this union. Only you must beware of over-exerting yourself, Christina. You are still not well. Does he understand how fragile you are, this rough lover of yours?"

"He knows I have a condition which does not allow me to leave the house very often."

He looked at her assessingly. "And have you explained to him about children?"

"I have told him it may be...difficult."

"For pity's sake, Christina," he exploded, concern for her making him angry. "Difficult? You would not survive childbirth. Be sensible as to your weaknesses. This marriage could kill you. Why do you think I hesitated so long myself? Because I knew you were too frail to bear a child and live."

She pulled away from him. "Then my death will be God's will," she said harshly. "But at least I will have *tried* to live, instead of hiding away and fearing even to dance in case my weak heart gives out. Besides, that is not the only reason you hesitated to marry me, is it? I read the note you sent your mother."

"Oh," he muttered, staring at her, and waited for the inevitable.

In the shock of seeing Christina bent over for Humphrey Delacour in the straw, he had forgotten his errand.

Her look was scathing. "At least now I know the truth behind your decision to break off our betrothal. You preferred to marry your mistress rather than me. Oh yes, I knew of her existence. A red-haired wanton who has lain with half the men at court. Now I suppose she is with child."

"Yes," he admitted.

"And so you rescued her." Her brows rose insultingly. "Can you even be sure the child is yours?"

He looked away, but he was furious. Furious with her and with himself. And furious with Margerie yet again, for making him feel like a cuckold. Even now, here at home, safe away from court, where he had foolishly thought her reputation could not follow.

"That is one advantage Humphrey has over you then," she said softly, seeming to enjoy his discomfort. "For I was a virgin the first time with him, and he saw the proof with his own eyes. That is not true of your wife, is it? Though I imagine she must know a trick or two to keep you interested beyond the normal way."

He was almost glad when his mother threw open a casement overlooking the stable yard and called down coldly, "Oh, so you have come calling at last, Virgil. A *note* to inform me of your marriage to that infamous wanton… Sent with a servant, as though it were a request for eggs and butter." She stared down at him. "For shame, sir. I am your mother. Have you no better manners?"

"Clearly not, madam," he bit out, and bowed to her in an exaggerated way. "I learned mine from your example."

Twenty-three

Applegate, Kent, Spring 1537

THE FIRE WAS DYING in his study late one night in April when the door creaked open and Virgil looked up to see his wife on the threshold, a ghost in her white shift, just as when she had come to his chamber at court.

Was she walking in her sleep again? He had thought those episodes at an end now that Margerie was no longer at court, her mind tormented by the fear and despair that place had inflicted on her soul.

She shut the door, then trod silently toward him on bare feet. Her night shift floated about her, simply cut, falling from an embroidered bodice to her ankles. A vision of purity, he thought, and gripped his wine cup so hard his knuckles whitened.

He was no poet. And he was not in love. It would not do to wax lyrical, and dream himself another Catullus or Ovid.

For a moment Margerie said nothing, but stood looking down at him, sitting in his high-backed chair by the fire. Her head was on one side, her red hair gloriously free, and her eyes met his with a sharp intelligence.

Not asleep, then.

He looked back at her steadily. Her breasts swelled against the thin fabric, and he could see her nipples stiff with cold beneath. The shift hid the rest, but in his mind's eye he saw it all again, that cloud of red hair tumbling down her back, the snow-white nudity as she disrobed in his room at court, presenting herself to him.

A wanton beyond compare. Narrow-waisted, high-breasted, and with long lithe legs between which any red-blooded man would gladly bury himself...

He felt himself harden, and raised his cup to his lips in instinctive response. Better to drink than make love, he thought grimly.

"Are you drunk, Virgil?"

"Yes."

"I have made you angry somehow, and you cannot forgive me for it."

It was a strong wine, coarse on the tongue, and had helped soften the edge of his mood after dinner. But it could not mask the truth of her accusation. He hated himself, and seemed to enjoy wallowing in the feeling. He hated that too, loathed his own weakness. She must despise him, he thought, and wished she would go away.

"Why?" When he did not answer, Margerie came to kneel between his thighs, gazing up at him. It was an intimate position. "Why are you angry with me?"

His hand trembled a little as he raised the cup to his lips again. Alarmed by the symptom, he drained the cup, then set it down on the floor before she could notice, straightening with his head still turned away.

"I do not know why," he admitted, staring into the fire rather than at her, his jaw clenched hard against the ache behind his eyes.

Because I am hurting you with my coldness. Because I do not deserve you. Because it is easier to be angry with you than with myself.

Now, where the hell had that come from?

He turned his head and regarded her somberly. "You should be in bed," he managed accusingly.

"Willingly," she whispered. "Come with me, sir."

His cock twitched and stiffened inexorably as their eyes locked. God's death. The tinder was dry, so dry. And she was holding that flame so close.

"Wanton," he said deliberately.

"I am your wife," she countered. "Is it wanton for a wife to wish her husband to join her in bed? It is late, past midnight. Perhaps tomorrow we could—"

"I must return to court tomorrow," he told her harshly, and this time she flinched.

"So soon?"

"Master Greene has written to demand my return. I have been away from court nigh on a month and cannot tarry any longer. I stayed only to persuade my mother to move back to Applegate as your companion. I failed, which I suppose was predictable. Now Christina has married that ruffian, Delacour, and my mother is refusing to leave her side in case the oaf hurts her." He clenched his fist until his nails cut into his palm, knowing himself on the edge of some foolishness and needing the pain to steady him. "You know I do not wish to leave you alone for your confinement. But I cannot remain here any longer. Not when the queen is with child."

"I am with child too," she reminded him.

He looked into her beautiful face, scourging himself with self-hatred even as he insulted her again. "I have no proof of that. Only your word, and Master Greene's early examination. It does not show yet, does it?"

"A very little," she murmured.

His gaze caught on hers, and he drew a shaky breath, caught in the web now, struggling against temptation. How far could he let it go and still pull back from her? It was a challenge to his self-imposed discipline. That was what he told himself, at any rate.

"Show me."

His voice had been curt, almost cold, and for a moment he thought she would refuse. She *ought* to refuse, he told himself.

Her eyes had widened at the command, then Margerie rose to her feet, staring down at him, and slowly bent over. Grasping the hem of her white shift, she raised it slowly past her thighs and the reddish triangle of her sex, then to her white belly, holding it bunched below her breasts, the loose material falling at the back to cover her hips and buttocks.

"You see?" she whispered, and curled a hand about her lower belly, where a small bump could be seen protruding. "I am with child."

He stared at the exposed body of his wife. Her soft belly, so pale and smooth, and below it...

Heat flared along his cheeks in a flush of lust. He was painfully hard now, his cock pressing urgently against his codpiece, his balls heavy and taut. Could Margerie see his arousal? Did his wife know what she was doing to him with this shameless display?

It had been nearly four weeks since their wedding night, and his forceful consummation of their marriage. He had not dared go near her since, fearing a repeat of that dangerous rush of emotion...

"But whose?" he heard himself say coldly, and could not quite believe it was his own voice. Who cared whose child it was? It was Margerie's, and he would love the child regardless, provide for it regardless, as though it had been his own. Which it might yet be.

She dropped the shift, concealing herself again. Her face was very pale. "If I could assure you that it was your child," she began, stumbling over her words, "that it could not possibly be Lord Munro's—"

"A brave attempt," he sneered, and shook his head. "But a fantasy, all the same. Let it go: I do not wish to punish my wife for a lie. Come, sit on my lap and serve me."

She took a step backward to the door. Her lips moved soundlessly, then she managed the word, "No."

"I am your husband, Mistress Elton, or have you forgotten the vows you spoke but a bare month ago? You will obey me, or feel my displeasure."

"I would prefer you did punish me than buried your anger beneath your lust," she said frankly. "Let it out, rather. Let me see and feel your anger. Then it will be done, and we may start our marriage afresh."

Virgil stared at her, his eyes narrowed on her face, not understanding. "You *want* my anger? You *want* to be punished?"

Margerie hesitated. He laughed, not believing her.

His mockery seemed to snap something in her, for she gasped, a little color in her cheeks at last, and wrenched her white shift up again. Only this time she pulled it past her breasts, so that they bounced enticingly, then off her head, discarding her nightgown without a second glance.

He forced himself to look at her nakedness, though he could scarcely breathe. He wanted her so badly.

"You are angry, sir, though you say you do not know why. But your anger hurts me, whether you exercise it or not on my person. So I say, chastise me for whatever wrong I have done you, whether it be lying with Lord Munro, or not pleasing you enough as a wife, or bearing a child you cannot be sure is your own."

When he did not reply, Margerie licked her lips, watching him. "And when my punishment is done, it will be over. You may never again accuse me of those things. Do you agree?"

She was a beauty, his green-eyed, red-haired wife. And so passionate, her gaze searing and intense. He had dared to look, and now could not look away, the silence in his study suddenly unbearable, tense with expectation. So it must feel, he thought dizzily, to stand on the very edge of a cliff, looking down at the waves below…

"What kind of punishment?" he asked hoarsely.

She came toward him on bare feet, her skin all white and rose, curves and straight lines, nude and breathtakingly perfect. She bent, looking into his face where he sat in his high-backed chair, and slowly undid the fastenings of his codpiece.

He did not move to stop her but watched instead, his pulse

racing. She tugged at the codpiece, fumbling a little. Not as confident as she looks, he thought, almost with relief.

Then his cock was out, thick and rigid, veined with desire, and he was breathing hard, his eyes on her face. He should call a halt now. The cliff was crumbling beneath his feet. He must not, could not fall.

Dear God though, he could not stop now.

She had straightened. "Now, sir," she whispered, her own voice breathless, like a scared girl's, "you will chastise me with your hand. As long and as hard as you wish, sir."

He watched in frozen desire as she stepped round, then bent forward across his lap, carefully arranging herself facedown over his lap. She stretched out her hands to the floor and balanced herself on her fingertips, then straightened her long legs out behind, her rounded white arse presented like the most perfect gift of all.

He swallowed hard, still holding himself in check.

"You have done this before," he stated flatly. "For some other man."

She turned her head, her cheeks lightly flushed now, rose on white, her eyes bright. "Never, sir."

He did not believe her. He sat in agony, imagining Lord Munro chastising her like this, the young nobleman's hand on her bare flesh, branding her for his pleasure.

"Never," she repeated.

He moved then, unable to resist. His right hand cupped her buttock. It was so smooth and warm, living alabaster. He remembered stroking under her buttocks as they coupled at court, pulling her forward, plunging into her deep and hard, her cries of pleasure.

Pressed against her belly, his erection throbbed.

His hand relaxed, stroking her, first one buttock, then the other, listening to the catch of her breath, hearing his own heartbeat increase, thudding now in his ears.

"Spread your legs wider," he muttered, and she obeyed.

As long and as hard as you wish.

He did not want to hurt her. She was a woman, and his father—his true father, the good and gentle scholar who had given him the poetic name Virgil—had taught him that men should protect women from harm.

All except their wives, he thought drily. For a man could chastise his wife as he pleased and no other man would call him to account for it. Yet she was right. He was angry, though he could not be sure of the source, and his anger lay between them like a sword. Would it release something in both of them if he were to raise his hand to her?

Yes, his body told him, his cock aching fit to burst.

But how to control his anger? How to be sure he did not lose himself in the chastising of this woman, and do her some lasting harm? It was what he feared was at the heart of him, a cruelty and coldness inherited from his stepfather, the desire to hurt and brutalize that Master Tulkey had shown him in spadefuls, beating after beating, starvation and imprisonment. If he broke through that hardness, cut cleanly through it and pushed beyond, what would he find?

His heart.

He gritted his teeth and raised his hand, then brought it down sharply.

"Virgil!" she cried out in a high voice, her buttocks jerking, the shape of his hand showing red and cruel on her white skin.

"Silence," he ordered her. He struck her again, cleanly across her other buttock, and she remained silent this time, only her breath hissing out.

His cock had never been so thick and swollen, he realized, striking her again, the sound of the blow sweetly satisfying to his ears. She shook, her soft belly pressing into him. Yielding to his authority, pure woman, strong and yet pliable, surviving both his anger and his love.

He wanted to stop and plunge into her, his whole body trembling with the need for sex, only inwardly; outwardly he was upright and unmoved, a man. He suddenly thought that he had never known true sexual excitement until this moment. Everything before had been juvenile, shallow, incomplete in comparison with this raging heat in his blood.

God's death, what was he thinking? This was all poetry, it made no sense. She was his wife, his possession, his chattel, that was all, and he was chastising her.

But for what? For being his wife. For unmanning him with her beauty and softness and her fascinating green eyes, for the life in her belly that would make Applegate a home again at last, for the love that was building inside him with every blow…

He struck again and she moaned.

It was a sound he recognized. His cock twitched. He struck again, harder this time, sharper, and heard his beautiful bride moan again, deeper and more soulful.

"Yes," he muttered, as though she had spoken.

He struck again, then again, then again, her body writhing beneath him, his hand rising and falling in a rhythm all its own.

Virgil could no longer remember his anger, none of that foolishness or heartache. All he knew was how beautiful his wife was in her nakedness, how yielding and open and wet she was, the perfect offering, the ultimate submission.

Her buttocks were a bed of roses now, glowing red and white, shockingly scarlet in patches, as though scratched by thorns. Margerie was writhing against him, rubbing her rounded belly back and forth on his hard cock, panting and moaning freely, the sound bubbling up out of her throat as though she could no longer control it…

He spanked her again, and Margerie shook under his hand, hard and demanding, her face so hot she felt she might burst into flames.

He was ruthless. He was her husband. And his breathing was harsh, his cock superbly erect under her belly.

She had thought him broken and out of reach when she came to his study tonight. Virgil had been sitting alone in the dark, no candles lit, not reading or writing as he used to do at court, but staring into the fire. His shirt and doublet carelessly unfastened, a wine cup balanced on his thigh, his face grim, unreadable.

The way he had looked up as she came toward him…

No, he had been broken tonight. And drunk, taking solace in wine. A long way beyond her reach. The clever, charming physician she had grown to love at court was lost to her, buried somewhere in there under a sea of ice. These days, all he would ever let her see was the dismissive, unloving cruelty he had shown her on their wedding night.

He had stopped spanking her.

Now his hand rubbed over her burning skin, and she cried out, her nerves stretched raw, her body trembling and ready for his. His hand slipped lower, between her thighs. "Margerie," he growled. It was a demand. "Open for me."

She bent further forward and her legs parted naturally. She was wet, dripping for him, and he knew it now. Brazenly aroused by his spanking. She had known how it would be, that an act like this would be the only way to break through the ice he had erected around his heart. And all these nights, lying alone and longing for Virgil to kiss her, hold her…

All that pain would be at an end if the ice shattered.

He pushed a long finger inside her, and she writhed, her mouth open, panting for him. Wanton, indeed. But only for him. It had only ever been for him.

He raised his hand again, then brought it down on her bottom. Then his hand dipped between her legs again, cleverly stroking, driving her mad with desire.

"Yes," she gasped.

Virgil tumbled her off his lap and she lay on the hard floor, eyes closed, her knees drawn up, one hand between her legs, rubbing greedily at her wetness.

He stood above her, watching. "On your hands and knees," he ordered her, and the curt note was gone.

She opened her eyes, looking up at him.

He stood, legs apart, his erect cock in his hand. His dark eyes were heavy-lidded, his sensual lips parted, one hand stroking up and down his shaft with a lazy rhythm.

"Obey me," he insisted, his voice liquid.

She rolled over onto her hands and knees, parting her legs instinctively, bowing her forehead to the floor so that her bare arse was presented to him.

He dropped to his knees behind her. His fingers played the taut knot of pleasure at the entrance to her body, rubbing and teasing, his fingers stroking in and out. Then he paused, and she felt his mouth on her there, his tongue entering, pressing inside, then his lips sucking on her wet bud, squeezing, tormenting her. And as he sucked, his fingers twisted back inside, opening out to stretch her wide, then pumped, hard and fast, almost to the wrist.

Suddenly she was there, and falling hard. Margerie tensed, her mouth twisted in a grimace, then gave a high-pitched cry, almost a scream, rocking back against him as pleasure burst through her.

"I love you," she moaned. "Oh, Virgil, I love you."

A few seconds later he was kneeling up, pressing his hard thighs against hers, and she felt the blunt head of his cock enter her, stretching her further. He plunged deep and she groaned, dropping her forehead to the floor again, urging him deep.

He understood her need, slipping his long cock in to the hilt. He was so thick, so rigid, she could not bear it.

She scratched and tore at the floorboards, almost out of her mind with passion. "Harder, harder… God's blood, fuck me!"

He growled and dragged her hips against him, pinning her to

him while he fucked, thrusting with rapid, powerful strokes. She was nude, completely at his mercy.

"You are the most beautiful woman on this earth, Margerie. Fate favored me when it put such a precious jewel in my path."

She mewed at his praise, thinking it could never be more perfect than this moment, his cock deep inside her, so huge and demanding, and her body responding with instinctive submission, wet and open.

"Are you still angry, Virgil?" she asked, fearing that he might retreat behind that ice again, but needing to know. "Can you forgive me?"

"I am the one who needs forgiveness. I was never angry with you. Only with myself." His hand slipped beneath her belly, pausing to caress the smooth hard bulge of her baby, then finding her taut bud again. "Come for me, Margerie. Give me your pleasure. Give me that gift. Forgive me, I beg you…" His breath came in gasps now, his fingers still working her as he thrust raggedly. "Forgive me for hurting you… Forgive… Forgive…"

He gasped, suddenly slamming deep inside her, and she felt the wet heat of his release. Yet still his fingers rubbed, and his cock, not even soft, continued to thrust even after he had finished pumping his seed into her.

She moaned, lost in ecstasy, scarcely able to breathe for pleasure, and felt his other hand stroke her buttocks, still aching where he had spanked her, soothing the hot skin.

Being spanked tonight, bending for him, taking the strict chastisement of his hand, all that had stripped her of defenses. Removed her last shred of resistance to the love she had been harboring inside her heart. She did not want him to hurt her. No, she wanted to be bare before him, dignity lost, to kneel and serve, and know he would do the same for her.

Give me your pleasure. Give me that gift.

Listening to him again in her head, like a refrain of music

echoing on the air, she suddenly understood what he meant. His words were not merely those of a man urging his lover to climax, but deeply significant. The pleasure they felt with each other's bodies, the pleasure this beautiful intimacy gave them, it was a precious gift. Not to be shared with anyone else, but experienced together, tasted on each other's lips and skin.

This love was an elixir of their own mixing, and to drink it would heal them forever.

"Can you forgive *me*, Margerie?" he whispered, his voice tortured, leaning over her, his lips on her back. "I have treated you so badly this past month. I have hurt and neglected you, too bound up in my own personal hell to see what I was doing." He hesitated, and his words became bleak. "I will understand if you say you cannot forgive me. I have not been the husband you deserve."

"I forgive you, Virgil," she sobbed, and as his fingers rubbed between her legs, finally allowed herself to arch into pleasure. "I love you and forgive you."

She came repeatedly, her body rigid as climax after climax swept over her, clamping down on his organ inside her, her cries only fading to silence when his teasing fingers dropped away.

He held her tight then, kissing her, whispering her name, stroking the skin where his hand had fallen so firmly.

He had not said he loved her, Margerie only realized later, cradled in his arms before the fire. The ice about his heart was still in place. But she had distinctly heard it crack tonight. That was something.

With a man whose heart was so closely guarded, that might be the best she could hope for.

Twenty-four

MARGERIE WAS EXHAUSTED, SHIELDING her eyes against the brilliant August sunshine. The hill had been steep, but worth the climb. Now she could see right across the valley to where the road to London snaked between trees and vanished beyond the river bend. She sighed and rubbed a hand absentmindedly across her swollen belly. Her gown was tight again, and would need to be let out another few inches. Another month, the midwife had said, and clucked her tongue at the empty nursery, with so much still needing to be done.

There would be a crib made for the nursery. But the babe would sleep in her own bed for the first few months, Margerie was determined. And she would not employ a wet nurse, regardless of Mistress Hayes's disapproval. The housekeeper seemed to hold her in awe, perhaps for having lived at court so long, or being one whose grandfather had served the king with distinction.

"A lady should not feed her own babe," Mistress Hayes had insisted one morning after breakfast, then mentioned the names of several women in the village who would be proud to act as wet nurse to Mistress Elton.

But Margerie had refused. She cared nothing for the niceties of rank, only that she should not be separated from her child when he—or she—finally arrived. Not even for a few hours.

"I am no lady," she told Mistress Hayes firmly. "I shall do well enough without a wet nurse."

"And will Mistress Tulkey be returning to oversee your

confinement? For there must be someone to give me my orders while you are…indisposed."

Mistress Hayes looked at her with bright, insistent eyes. She was an inveterate meddler, who was clearly intent on bringing the two women together, despite Virgil's stern injunction that Margerie was not to visit his mother or Christina while he was at court.

"Perhaps you could invite her to supper one evening, mistress," Mistress Haynes pondered, clearing away the breakfast tray. "I have birthed no children myself, but Mistress Tulkey will know what is to be done."

"Mistress Hayes, I cannot go against my husband's wishes even in his absence. He is master in this house, or had you forgotten? When I am indisposed, you may order the household to your own satisfaction. The rest will take care of itself. And I do not need Mistress Tulkey to hold my hand." She had been adamant on that score. "Goodness, I am not the only woman who has had to face giving birth alone. My husband is at court and cannot be spared. That is an end to the matter."

But in truth Margerie was a little nervous about her impending confinement. Another month…

Soon she would have to restrict her movements to the house alone, then to her stuffy bedchamber with the shutters closed to keep out the light. It would be expected, and to flout tradition would bring down yet more censure on her head. She knew there had been whispers about her in the village, for she had heard Master Hayes telling his wife only the other day what the villagers were saying of their new mistress.

So no more playing in the gardens with Virgil's two dogs. No more climbing hills in the hot sunshine. No more wandering the grounds with one of Virgil's letters in her hand, whiling away the interminable days until the babe arrived.

But oh, this view! She loved the countryside, it was so restful on the eye. And although she missed the bustle and grandeur of the royal court, she was not afraid to live in this quiet spot. There were none here who would pursue and torment her for their sport, nor did she have to lie and conceal the truth at every turn. Here amongst Kent's green hills, she was able to live and speak freely, without fear of intrigue.

Virgil wrote to her every few weeks—long leisurely letters describing the antics and latest gossip at court, the progress of Queen Jane's pregnancy, which was almost keeping pace with her own, and always ending with a coded promise of what he would do to her once they were together again.

His latest letter had made her cry as she came to the end, wishing Virgil was there in person to hold and kiss her. For as her belly grew larger, so did her heart, swelling with emotion at the slightest thing.

I miss you more than words can say, my dearest wife, and would be with you at Applegate if I could. But duty keeps me here until autumn at least, when the queen should be brought to bed with her royal child. Master Greene has said he will give me leave to go if your own confinement comes early, but he cannot make a promise of it.

Be sure that when I do see you again, it will be with such passion, nothing on this earth could keep our lips from meeting.

Ever your servant, as much as your husband, V.

She had laughed at that, pressing the letter to her lips and wishing it was his mouth she kissed.

Her servant! He was her master rather, and her world.

And this was his child in her belly. If only he could be brought to believe that, she thought, and stared wistfully across the valley.

"Ho there!" a deep male voice greeted her cheerfully as she

began to descend the hill again, and she turned, staring at the rather swarthy-looking man who had emerged from the clump of trees at the top of the hill.

He was dragging a pale-skinned, fair-haired woman behind him, and Margerie realized with a shock that this must be Christina, Virgil's former betrothed.

Which meant that this young man…

He bowed before her, grinning. "I should not have yelled like that. But I did not want to miss speaking with you. You must be Mistress Elton. My name is Delacour, and this is my wife, Christina."

She curtsied. "I know who you are, sir," she said shyly. "I can see the manor house from the upper windows at Applegate. I am glad to meet you both at last."

"You must forgive me for never having ridden over to introduce myself, Mistress Elton. But my wife does not enjoy the best of health, and her care is my constant concern."

She liked his smile, both friendly and a little saucy at the same time. He was a straightforward young man, she thought, if somewhat rough around the edges, and not at all what she had expected from Virgil's description of Christina's lusty and uncouth suitor.

Christina did indeed look sick though. Her large eyes were red-rimmed as though she had not been sleeping, with dark bruise-like shadows beneath, and although her skin was delicately pale, she had a flush in each cheek, as though touched by the heat.

She glanced now at her husband, a flash of irritation in her face, then nodded reluctantly to Margerie. No doubt she thought it beneath her station to curtsy to a woman of Margerie's reputation, even if her husband had no complaint with her.

"Mistress *Elton*," Christina said with heavy emphasis, then lowered her gaze to Margerie's swollen belly. She was oddly breathless, though she did not appear to have been exerting herself. "I am surprised to see you out of doors, let alone up a hill. Your confinement must be due soon, surely?"

Margerie looked back at her steadily. Christina's gown was slightly soiled and askew, as though the young couple had been kissing and sporting together under cover of the trees. Though there was no reason why they should not play at lovebirds out of doors in this fine weather, Margerie thought, and ruefully considered what she would do with her own husband if he were at home.

"This will be my last walk until after my confinement, yes. You are right, it was foolish of me to walk so far from Applegate. And onto your land too." She bit her lip, suddenly realizing that this hill was on land belonging to the manor. "Please forgive me for trespassing. But it is such a fine day, and the house is so dark and cool, I did not want to miss coming out in the sunshine for the last time."

"Walk wherever you like, mistress. I shall be pleased to welcome you here as often as you like." Master Delacour winked at her; he had his arm about his wife's waist, and Christina seemed flushed and uncomfortable, even a little jealous of his attentions to her. "My wife is with child, and expects to be brought to bed early in the new year."

"But that is marvelous news." Margerie smiled, though in truth she was a little concerned by Christina's sick look. "Please accept my felicitations!"

"I thank you," he said, grinning broadly. "Would you care to dine with us tonight at the manor house? Your mother-in-law, Mistress Tulkey, will be there, for she is Christina's companion these days. It would be good to see all three ladies together at the same table."

Her smile faded. "Oh," she murmured, and looked away.

Virgil had strictly forbidden her to speak to his mother in his absence. She did not want to go against his express command, yet she did not wish to seem rude. What possible excuse could she give?

"What a generous invitation, sir. But I am afraid—"

"Master Elton would not like it?"

She met his eyes frankly then, biting her lip. "Forgive me, sir. You are very kind."

"Never mind. We can bring about a reconciliation between you all another time. Perhaps when the child is born."

She nodded with relief. "Perhaps."

One of the manor tenants called to him at that moment from across the field, a stocky man with a drooping hat pulled low over his head.

Delacour's face darkened. "That's Master Brookes. I wonder what he wants now. More complaints about the well running dry, I suppose. As though I control the rainfall." He bowed to Margerie. "Forgive me, I had better speak to the man. Though in truth I would rather turn him and his family out of their house, for they are always late with the rent."

"My father's oldest tenants," Christina muttered, tugging on his sleeve.

"Yes, yes, I shall be kind." He bent and kissed her on the mouth, despite Margerie's presence, and Christina's arms came up at once, clutching his dark head. He was breathing thickly when he straightened. "Can you walk back to the house alone?"

Christina nodded, though she was even more breathless now, and seemed too weak to walk another step. "Go, go."

"I will help Mistress Delacour down the hill," Margerie offered, and the young man turned, smiling and bowing in an extravagant manner.

"Thank you, mistress," Delacour said, and raked her with an openly admiring stare. "You are a good neighbor indeed."

And with that he was gone, vaulting a withy fence one-handed to speak to his tenant.

Christina watched him until he was out of sight, then turned to Margerie with an undisguised air of resentment. "Not content with stealing Virgil from me, now you would take my husband too? I thought the courtiers cruel when they called you wanton, but I see now how it is. Even now, heavy with child, you give that little smile and look unsure of yourself, and men fall over themselves to bed you."

"No, no indeed!"

"It is your…your red hair, I suppose." Christina looked her up and down. "The mark of a whore."

Margerie was shocked into silence.

"I do not need your help," Christina said coldly, and began to descend the hill clumsily. She did not seem steady on her feet though, and after a few hundred paces slipped and fell awkwardly, crying out in pain. Margerie hurried down to her, careful not to slip herself, for the babe was so large now, it was hard to move with any grace.

"Can you stand?" she asked, helping the woman to sit up.

"Leave me, leave me."

Yet when she put an arm about her shoulders, Christina did not push her away. She sat rocking back and forth, breathing harshly.

"What is the matter with you?" Margerie asked quietly. "It is not the baby, is it? You are sick."

"I have a…a condition. My heart. When I was younger, the doctors thought it was a wasting disease. I spent years in bed. They said I would die before I reached the age of twelve." Her voice broke. "Do you know what it's like to be…to be told you will die young and never live to marry, to love a man and bear his children?"

Margerie shook her head. "Poor child."

"Virgil loved me. We were friends, though he was much older than me. He was like an older brother at first, and then…I thought… When I was still a girl, he promised he would marry me." Christina looked at her blankly, her eyes wide. "And then you came along. And I knew then that I would never marry. Never do those things with a man…"

"But you have married a fine young man," Margerie tried to reassure her. "And when the child is born—"

"I am dying!" Christina burst out, then buried her face in her hands. "I will be dead before this child is born. It will die within me. There are still days when I can get out of bed, and…and be a good wife to my husband. But I can feel my heart like a fist in my chest. It hurts…it is squeezing the lifeblood out of me."

"Have you seen a doctor?"

Christina nodded, wiping her damp face with the back of her hand. "He tells me to rest. To stop…stop being intimate with my husband. But Humphrey says it is all nonsense. That I am pretending my heart hurts so I may have his pity, just as Virgil pitied me when I was young." She looked at Margerie, her chin raised. "But I do not want pity. I just want his love. I would rather die in his arms than have him pity me. For if he pitied me, he could never love me again. Not like he does now. Can you understand that?"

"Oh yes," Margerie replied. "I understand."

Margerie helped her to stand, and Christina began to hobble down the hill, resting on her arm. At the bottom was a wooden bridge over a stream, and Christina stopped there, waving her away.

"I can go on alone from here, I thank you." She hesitated, looking at Margerie's belly. "May I?"

Margerie nodded.

Tentatively, Christina laid a hand on Margerie's belly. Her hand jerked and she stared at Margerie in shock. "It… It kicked me."

"Yes, he does that often."

"He?"

"Or she." Margerie smiled shyly. "Though the kicks are some-times so hard, I feel sure it is a male."

Christina gave her a hard, uncompromising stare, leaving Margerie uncomfortable under her glare. "Was the child in your womb fathered by Virgil, or by some other man?" she demanded. "Or do you not know?"

"*What?*"

"We have all heard your reputation hereabouts, do not look at me like that. Come, tell the honest truth with God as your witness. I will tell no one your answer, I swear it on my life." Christina crossed herself. "See? Now the truth will go with me to the grave. But I must know before I die if this is Virgil's child or not."

"As God is my witness," Margerie told her, also crossing herself, "this child is Virgil's. I have only lain with one other man my whole life, and that was Lord Wolf, when I was only a little younger than you are now."

Christina's eyes widened, but she said nothing.

"What you have heard," Margerie insisted, afraid the other woman still thought her dishonest, "were mere lies and gossip. Virgil is the father of my child, believe me. There has been no other man, but only him."

"I do believe you," Christina whispered. "For Virgil is not a man to trust a woman easily. If he chose you as his bride, and brought you home to Applegate, it was for a special reason. Not merely that you were with child and in trouble."

Margerie bit her lip, then took a dangerous leap. "Mistress Delacour…Christina… What is wrong with Virgil? Why is he so…such a hard man to know? And why does he seem to hate his own mother?"

"If Virgil has not told you such things himself, it is not my place to do so."

"Please, I beg of you."

Christina sighed. "Virgil's father died when he was a young boy, about nine years of age. I was only a small child then myself, so I do not rightly know."

"Yes, he told me about his father's death. Then how his widowed mother married Master Tulkey."

"Master Tulkey was a brutal man and a cruel stepfather to Virgil. When Virgil was older, he tried to forbid us from playing together, even though we were close neighbors. He said it weakened a boy to have such a young girl as a friend." Christina sounded angry, her mouth trembling. "Virgil defied him and came to see me secretly. To read Latin with me, and teach me how to riddle it out. He knew how boring it was for me, you see, always in bed, always alone."

"And Master Tulkey found out?"

Christina nodded, staring away at nothing. "He beat Virgil. He beat him every night for a sennight. Thirty strokes of the rod every night. I knew he had been beaten, but Virgil did not tell me the extent of it until much later. Until quite recently, in fact." She swallowed, a look of horror on her face. "He made Virgil sleep in the cellar until he would promise never to visit me again. But Virgil refused. So he kept him there for days. Weeks, perhaps. I do not know all the details. But Master Tulkey would not let his wife take down anything to the boy but bread and water."

"God's blood!"

"At last, he let Virgil out. And Virgil came straight over to see me at the manor house. He would not allow his stepfather to choose his friends for him, he told me, as though such punishments meant nothing."

Christina shook her head, her voice very small. "But I knew better. Oh, his spirit was not broken. He would never have allowed Master Tulkey the satisfaction of *that*. But Virgil never smiled the same way again. It was as though the light had gone out of him, shut up in that dark place for so long."

"I had no idea." Margerie felt like crying herself. She wanted to draw that scared little boy into her and hold him tight. "Poor child."

Her look almost feverish, Christina suddenly squeezed her hand. "You will make him happy, won't you? Virgil is still my friend. And I miss him."

Margerie embraced her, agreeing, though she was not sure she could make Virgil happy.

She was not sure anything in this world could make Virgil truly happy after what he had suffered.

―⁓―

"Master Elton?"

A tall figure stepped out of the shadows, and Virgil stopped, his hand falling to his dagger hilt. It was late at night, a cool evening in early September, and the man had been waiting patiently outside his locked workshop instead of approaching him in the morning. Which meant the man knew he had been in attendance on the queen that evening, and would return here before bed.

Which also meant this was some court intrigue, Virgil thought, instantly on his guard against treachery.

"May I help you, sir?"

"A moment alone, if you please." The man stepped into the dim flicker of torchlight from further down the corridor, and Virgil recognized him at once. "We need to talk in private, Master Elton."

"My lord Munro," he muttered in some surprise, not having expected to find his wife's former lover waiting for him, but he recollected himself and bowed. "A pleasant surprise, my lord. Let me unlock the door and we may talk more privily within."

The workshop was dark and gloomy. Virgil kindled a lantern and set it on the table, illuminating the little space. "Now my lord, how may I be of assistance?"

Lord Munro studied him broodingly. "You take an oath, do you not, when first you enter in this profession of doctor?"

"Yes, my lord. The Hippocratic Oath, after the learned Greek physician Hippocrates."

"And this oath, it prevents you from speaking abroad any secret you may hear in the course of your work? Even if it does not closely concern a patient?"

"Indeed, my lord." Virgil quoted the relevant passage in Latin, "*Ea arcana esse ratus, silebo. Of those things which should be kept hidden, I shall be silent.* Whatever secrets I hear, whatever might prove shameful if repeated, whether about a patient or any other man, I must keep to myself. The oath is clear on that point."

Munro nodded slowly, seeming satisfied with this. The nobleman then withdrew from his doublet a bundle of folded papers, sealed in red wax, and threw this on the table between them.

"Well, then, master doctor," he said clearly. "With the contents of these papers, I hereby discharge my debt to your wife, Margerie Elton, formerly Margerie Croft, with whom I entered into secret business one year ago."

Twenty-five

Virgil held his breath. He looked from the folded bundle to the nobleman's face. "What secret business is this? What is in those sealed papers?"

"You will keep it hidden if I tell you? You will uphold the Hippocratic Oath?"

Virgil stared back at him, sick with jealousy. His hands clenched into fists as he imagined Margerie lying in bed beneath this wealthy young lord, pleasuring him as his mistress.

"As a physician, I am sworn to silence on such matters for the duration of my life, and here reconfirm it to you," he said flatly. "Now what is this debt you owe my wife?"

"I do not like your tone, Master Elton."

"And I do not like that you have been intimate with my wife." His voice thickened in rage. "Is it your child Margerie carries? Is this some provision you make for his upkeep and education? For I tell you now—"

"It is not my child she carries," Munro interrupted him sharply. "Would to God it were that simple. I would acknowledge the child as my bastard and be happy to do so. But I cannot, not in good conscience, and knowing I may yet beget a true heir on my wife."

"How can you be sure it is not your child, any more than I can be sure it is not mine?"

"Because I never lay with your wife!"

"*What?*"

"I have never lain with any woman in my life. Not even now I am married to Alice Holsworthy." He was breathing hard, staring at Virgil across the steady lantern flame. His voice broke. "Not even now."

Virgil felt as though he were going mad. "But… But my wife told me herself she *had* lain with you. There were stories about the court…"

"Lies, all lies. Most of the worst stories I put about myself, to ensure it was widely known I was bedding her. I knew the gossip would reach my mother, and please her. Which it did." He sounded bitter. "God knows I never pleased her before in my life."

"I do not understand, my lord."

"I have no taste for women," Lord Munro bit out, a sudden terrible anguish in his face.

For a moment there was silence, both men staring at each other as the dangerous admission sank in.

Then Munro turned away, pacing the room with his head down, muttering to himself, "I have tried, I swear it. But I cannot. I lack the… Oh Christ, must I explain it? Surely it is enough to know Margerie was never wanton with me, that the child she carries must be yours. For it is not mine. That is why I came here tonight, when I might merely have sent those papers with a letter," he said, jerking his head at the documents on the table, "because I knew you might harbor doubts of the child's parentage, and I could not have that on my conscience. You may think badly of me, Master Elton, and you are right to do so. I have been wary of speaking before now, for I could not be sure you would keep my secret. But I have heard whispers that disturbed me. And you are still here at court, rather than with your wife in her time of confinement."

The young man turned and came back to the table, his face earnest. "Master Elton, what if it is a boy? I would not see you leave your firstborn son unacknowledged when you could be assured of his parentage. It is not my way."

Virgil ran a hand over his face. His chest was tight as he thought through the implications of Munro's confession.

"Let me be sure I have this right. You besmirched Margerie Croft's reputation, made her a whore in the eyes of the court…all so you could hide your true nature?"

"For payment, yes," Munro said weakly, tapping the sealed papers on the table. "But only for payment. And I did not *make* your wife a whore, sir. Forgive me if this angers you, but Mistress Croft's reputation was already that of a wanton long before I entered into this agreement with her. She was Lord Wolf's mistress years ago, or some such, I forget which nobleman had the taking of her virginity. But she was no innocent."

Virgil picked up the papers, not deigning to answer that, but did not break the sealing wax. "What are these papers?"

"The deeds on a handsome estate of mine in Sussex. Thirty acres of land, orchards, grazing. A fine house. It is what was promised to your wife should she pretend to lie with me and conceal… Conceal what she knew for all eternity." Munro was pale. He wrenched at his collar, turning away, his face in shadow. "You will tell no one of it either. You must never speak of this business to any man. If any ask how you obtained the property, say you…you won it from me at dice."

"I have already sworn to keep your secret. You have my word on it. None but my wife will ever know what has passed between us tonight."

The young nobleman turned back to stare at him. "I had heard you were a formidable man, Master Elton. I did not believe it until now. I wish you and Margerie well. So then our business is concluded. The original agreement was for a twelvemonth, but since I released her early, I cannot fault her on that. The deeds to Blackthorn Hall are yours now, as her husband, to keep or sell as you prefer." He nodded his head. "I bid you good night."

"Wait."

His lordship halted at the door, his voice angry, clearly impatient at being recalled. "What is it?"

"Do you *want* to lie with your wife, my lord?"

His eyes flashed. "What manner of question is that?"

"Yes or no?"

"I have told you, I wish to get her with child, but cannot bring myself to the point," Munro replied sharply, watching with a frown as Virgil turned away to search among his high shelves. "God knows I have tried more than a dozen times to bed her since we wed. And she is willing enough, though I feared at first she would not be. I cannot fault Alice as a wife. But there is no..." He hesitated. "There is no lust in me to achieve the act."

Virgil put a small flask down on the table. "Take three drops of this in strong wine before bed, and there should be lust for a short while at least. Enough to accomplish the deed."

Lord Munro picked up the flask and examined it. "Three drops, you say?" His eyes narrowed on Virgil's face. "How can I be sure it is safe?"

"I have taken it myself. There may be a headache the next day, but otherwise a man of your youth and vigor should suffer no ill effects. Indeed, you would not be the first nobleman at court to have had recourse to this potent cordial." Virgil smiled drily at the young man's startled expression. "Though I cannot tell you who, of course, for that would break my oath. Now take it, and tell no one how you came by it."

When the door had closed behind Lord Munro, Virgil picked up the deeds again.

The child is mine, he thought, and felt almost numb with relief at this confirmation. For if Margerie had not lain with Lord Munro, then she had not lain with any other man but himself, he was sure of it.

"*It is my child*," he whispered, closing his eyes.

Then guilt hit him, and he recoiled from himself in a wave of remorse, sickened by his arrogance and lack of trust.

He had wronged her. How Margerie must have suffered, knowing herself innocent and yet unable to prove it, so keeping quiet and allowing him to think her a wanton.

And all the while, he had been taunting her with cruel names, calling her "whore" and "wanton" even after their marriage, taking her to bed in the most callous manner imaginable. He had drunk his own potion and coupled with her several times in a night, forcing her to perform acts on him that made his gorge rise to remember them.

And he had allowed a strange and bitter anger to take hold of him, and had beaten her over his knee, unable to help himself, then used her afterward for his pleasure.

He deserved to be horsewhipped. He had treated Margerie Croft as shoddily as though he had paid four shillings for her services in an alleyway. And she was his wife.

He broke the seal on the deeds and read swiftly through the document. It was all as Lord Munro had described, and there at the end was his lordship's thick black signature, sprawling across the page.

Blackthorn Hall, Sussex.

And he could do whatever he wished with it.

———

He was saddling his horse in the courtyard at Hampton Court Palace three days later when Ned came running, out of breath, waving a paper in the air. "Master Elton! Master Elton! Stay a moment, sir!"

His heart sank. It had taken him three days to persuade Master Greene to allow him a visit home. Surely the queen's pains had not begun early?

He raised his brows, turning to the boy. "What is it, Ned? Never say Master Greene has changed his mind and bid me stay at court?"

"A letter for you, master. Just arrived."

He took the paper and turned it over, seeing his name written across it in his mother's hand.

For a moment he could not bring himself to open it. Had Margerie been brought to bed with their child? But if so, why would she not have written herself to let him know if it was a boy or a girl?

Virgil was suddenly cold.

He broke the seal and opened it, his hands shaking. A few short lines. He read the note through twice, but only four words stood out to him.

She is near death.

"What is it, master?" Ned asked inquisitively, his head on one side. Then the boy seemed to notice Virgil's stillness, and the way the blood had drained from his face. "Are you unwell, master? Should I fetch someone?"

"Forgive me," Virgil muttered, more to himself than to the boy. "Forgive me."

He fumbled for the reins, led his gray gelding over to the mounting block, and swung himself up into the saddle. His mother's letter he had crumpled in his fist, and thrust now inside his doublet, next to his heart. He had to hurry, he could not risk coming too late…

She is near death.

"Master?" Ned was still looking up at him, concern on his young, dirt-smudged face. "What is it? Bad news?"

Virgil turned the horse's head south and toward home. "Yes, boy," he managed hoarsely, his throat tight with emotion. "It is bad news. I thought to go home to a birth. Instead I may be going home to a funeral."

"Not… Not your wife's, Master Elton?" Ned whispered fearfully, crossing himself.

"No, not my wife." He closed his eyes. "The woman I once thought to marry."

—✎—

A thin shaft of daylight was touching his face when Virgil finally stirred. His body felt heavy and aching, and he opened his eyes, not sure at first where he was. The room swam a moment before steadying. Wearily, he gazed at the tapestry-hung wall and the tester bed, hung with red and gold drapes, gradually realizing that he had fallen asleep again in the chair beside Christina's bed.

"Christina?"

He straightened, stumbling to his feet and leaning over the bed. Christina lay against her pillows, so still and pale, she did not look alive.

His heart squeezed in pain. "Oh God, Christina," he said hoarsely. "Please…"

He had sat at her bedside for a day and a night, nursing his friend through her sickness. A simple chill on the chest had turned to a feverish ague, and with Christina's heart so weak, they had all feared her body would not be strong enough to beat off the fever. Last night it had peaked and for several hours Christina had lain steeped in sweat, flushed and twisting on the pillows, while her pulse raced and her heart, never strong but now tried beyond endurance, stuttered as though at any moment it would break. He had ordered the maid to strip her mistress down to her shift, then thrown all the windows open despite the cold wind, for the fever would kill her sooner than the sickness itself.

Yet by midnight Christina was breathless, her lips pale blue, her hands clawing weakly at the bedsheets as she struggled for air. In desperation, Virgil had taken from his bag a small handful of dried foxglove leaves, and steeped these in a pan of hot water over the fire. When the infusion was ready, he had Humphrey Delacour steady his wife's head, then gave her a little of the potent drug. Humphrey had frowned, asking what it was, and Virgil had told him, explaining the dangers before allowing the cooled liquid to touch her lips. To his relief, her husband had merely nodded, seemingly aware this might be her only chance of survival.

Nonetheless, his own heart had been racing as she swallowed those few drops, for he knew himself to be administering poison that could kill not only Christina but her unborn child.

Now he looked at her closed eyes and the white stillness of her face, and felt like weeping. Had he killed his dearest friend in his arrogance and determination to be right?

Humphrey had been sleeping next to her on the bed, and stirred at his voice. "What is it?" he croaked, then sat up, his hair disheveled, his clothes creased. He turned and looked down at his wife, and his mouth trembled. "Is she… Is she gone?"

Virgil forced himself to place two fingers against the side of her pale slender neck, feeling for her pulse. Her skin was cool and a little clammy, but not cold as he had feared. To his amazement, he felt the quiet thud of her heartbeat. Not weak as it had been last night, nor strong either, but pleasingly steady…

"The fever is gone. She lives." He raised his eyes to her husband's face and smiled. "Christina lives."

"And the babe?"

"I fear only time will tell, my friend." Virgil leaned on the bed, breathing harshly, his head bowed as he realized that the crisis was over. "We must pray for both their lives, and keep administering a few drops of this foxglove tea every six hours, to strengthen her heart."

It was raining in the narrow lane as it reached eleven of the clock, the church bell tolling in the distance and a chill September rain falling that seemed to mark the end of summer. The hedgerows were still richly woven with flowers though, the tall white and purple spikes of foxgloves thrusting upward from their dark pendulous leaves, all the heavy-headed grasses bent over with seed. Above his head, starlings were already dancing in black swarms over the meadows and woodlands, ready to fly away to some warmer clime. His eyes followed them in silence.

Coming to the familiar ramshackle buildings at Applegate, Virgil climbed wearily over the damp stile in the rain, and jumped down into his grounds. He was so exhausted, he had no memory of stumbling through the garden and entering the house until he found himself swaying at the bottom of the stairs, hair curling wet and unkempt, cap in hand, half-asleep where he stood.

"Virgil?"

He opened his eyes. It was Margerie, swollen-bellied in a rich green gown, at the top of the stairs. She was in her time of confinement and could not leave the house, for fear the babe should come.

He looked up at her longingly. He had barely spoken with her since his return home, every nerve in his body bent toward making sure of Christina's return to health. Now he could think of nothing but burying himself in his wife's body, of forgetting the fear that had driven him here from court...

Vaguely, he became aware of others watching him too. His steward and housekeeper standing in the doorway to the kitchen, both staring. His mother standing beside him, a hand on his arm, tugging at his sleeve in distress.

"Speak to us, Virgil, please speak to us," his mother was sobbing, her face stained with tears. She crossed herself. "Is poor Christina dead?"

He wondered then how long he had been standing there, silent and unmoving, deaf to his mother's pleas.

"No, no," he managed hoarsely, and drew a hand across his own face, finding it wet—and not just with rain. "The fever broke. She will live. I came back because..."

But Virgil found he could not continue, staring up at his waiting wife. He handed his rain-damp jacket to his steward, Hayes, spoke a few words of comfort to his weeping mother, then took the stairs two at a time.

Margerie welcomed him into the darkened bedchamber and shut the door against the world. Her red hair had been plaited loosely and lay over one shoulder in a homely fashion, her green eyes searching his face anxiously.

"My love," she whispered, and then he was kissing her fiercely, pressing her toward the bed.

They lay together in the shadowy room, her vast rounded belly between them, kissing hotly, tongues playing against each other, his heart beginning to race.

"I want you," he muttered against her throat.

"The baby—"

"It will not harm the child," Virgil told her confidently, then found her mouth again, teasing along her lower lip with his tongue. She gasped and he smiled. "Indeed, I know several respected court physicians who swear by this method."

"Method?"

"Of bringing on a speedy birth."

Her eyes widened, then she was laughing. "Virgil Elton, you are making that up!"

"No, I promise you."

He raised her green skirts, his hand tracing up her thigh to the soft curls between them. Margerie whispered his name, so he pushed a finger inside her snug heat, then two fingers, stroking in and out, his mouth on hers, persuading her to sport. He ought to have been too fatigued to make love after nursing Christina back from the brink of death, yet something deep inside was urging him on toward this intimacy, this moment of ultimate closeness, as though to remind him that he too was alive.

Her hands were busy too, reaching for his codpiece. After a moment's play, he rolled onto his back and let her work unencumbered. He watched her with a smile. His heavily pregnant wife, his one-time mistress, infamous wanton of the court of Henry Tudor—and yet utterly innocent at this moment, wrestling with his codpiece, her reddened lip caught between white teeth.

"Let me," he said, and brushed her hands aside, freeing himself in an instant.

"Well, you cannot blame me if I have forgotten how," she said sotto voce, looking at him from under lowered lashes, "when you have not come to my bed for months."

"Master Greene refused to release me before now."

Her eyes darkened, and he realized belatedly that she thought he had only returned to attend Christina in her hour of need. Not for the birth of their child.

"Virgil," she whispered. "There is something I must tell you before—"

"Speak then."

"It is not her fault, for I pressed her, but Christina has told me of your childhood. How your stepfather beat you when you visited her house against his orders."

"Hush," he said, shutting his eyes against that painful memory. "I do not want to speak of that. Not now, in our bed. Those days are done, Margerie, they are in the past. Let old injustices lie there and be forgotten."

"Forgive me," she murmured, watching him.

"You have done nothing wrong. It is I who need to beg your forgiveness. I have not been a good husband."

Her smile did not deceive him. "Then perhaps you should make amends," she said teasingly, but he could see from the shadows in her eyes that she was still unsure of him, careful not to reveal her true thoughts and feelings.

"Margerie…"

But suddenly his wife was kissing him again, her tongue slipping into his mouth, and the moment was lost in a flood of desire.

He undid her plait, playing with her hair until it fell in a soft red cloud about her shoulders and down her back. He dragged down her gown until her breasts were exposed, bigger than ever before, white and swollen with tiny blue veins, her nipples soon stiff and erect in his mouth. She writhed beneath him, gasping and begging for more, and he smiled at her passion, taking her hand and placing it on his cock.

"Get me ready," he ordered her, and her green eyes widened at his command, hungry and intent, eager to be dominated even when she was heavy with child. Now his cock was freed from its trappings, her fingers moved there skillfully, stroking and squeezing, soon bringing him to full erection.

"Virgil," she murmured, staring down at him. There was a deep flush in her face. He thought she had never looked more beautiful, swollen with child and hot-cheeked, her lips glistening wetly from their kisses.

My wife, he thought deeply. My wife.

Then she knelt, smiling at him, bent her head to his groin, and drew him into his mouth.

His head fell back and he groaned at the wet slide of her mouth down his shaft. My wanton, he thought. God's blood, my sweet wanton.

He let her play him with her mouth awhile, then, panting, he pushed her away. "Mount me," he said curtly.

She knelt over him, hoisting her gown up, openmouthed, her eyes like green lightning. Then he felt her against him, wet and tight, sliding down his length, encasing him like a glove, unbearably snug.

His hands bunched the covers, and he arched his back, moving with her.

It was too much, he thought wildly. Too much. Margerie rode him, and he moaned low in his throat, taking her heat, the weight of her pregnant body. He remembered the starlings dancing in the sky, and the aching need built inside him, inexorably.

It had begun to rain more heavily outside. Pattering now, rattling the shutters. The earth in the pasture would be turning to mud soon. Sticky and wet. She cried out, a strangled noise, and his hands came to her hips, moving her faster, faster…

They were joined together in the shadows, riding together, rising and falling, gasping and crying, the light in the distance growing closer and closer. Suddenly the world was spinning faster. She snatched at the air, her strong thighs bunched, working hard on his cock.

Her back was sweating, her breasts taut and tingling, and still she rubbed back and forth, falling into the good rhythm, the one that kept her laboring because she could not stop, because even the ache of tired muscles was pleasurable.

Rain drove against the battered old shutters. Margerie hissed too, every inch of her skin alive to his touch, his male scent, throwing her head back, hair tumbling. He caught it in his hand, twisted red strands between his fingers. She was lost, pumping on his cock, so hungry and feral, she felt like a wild cat, caught in her oestrus. His cock caught the fever too: thickened and lengthened inside her, she could feel the broad head swelling out her lips.

She brought him to the wet edge, then sank back down, taking him all the way with her.

"Margerie," he growled.

Her fingers found the tiny moist bud just above where she was taking him inside. She rolled it, then pinched herself, crying out, enjoying how his thick organ stretched her walls.

Clearly impatient, Virgil groaned with frustration. His hands lifted her, then brought her down, a series of short hard thrusts, impaling her mercilessly, pumping to his own rhythm. "Christ," he bit out, blaspheming.

She knew what he was feeling because she was feeling it too. Her fingers pinched, rubbed at herself. She cried his name, "Virgil!" her body abruptly exploding with heat. Pleasure shot up her spine, and she shook with it, utterly taken over, still riding but only by instinct. Then she collapsed on top of him, suddenly no longer able to hold herself up, her legs weak and trembling.

There was a dark flush in his face, sweat on his brow. He forced her up again, taking her full weight, grunting as he continued to slam into her, his hips jerking up into hers. His lips were drawn back in a grimace, his hands tirelessly lifting her up and down as though his forearms were made of iron.

Suddenly he thrust deep and held her still against him. He gave a great cry, and came, pumping his seed into her body.

"Margerie, oh my love, my love," he gasped.

His hands slipped up her back, dragging her forward over him. He continued to cry out even after his climax was done, gripping her compulsively.

"Oh God," he sobbed, his whole body shaking, and she realized he was weeping. "I love you."

Margerie turned her head and kissed her husband, their mouths meeting warmly, tenderly.

She had not dared to hope he would ever admit it aloud.

"I love you too," she whispered, and her heart was singing like a bird.

—∽∾∽—

They woke some hours later, still tangled together in the darkness, loose-limbed and drowsy. The rain was falling more softly now, a low rhythmic sound that lulled them. Virgil forced himself to slip out of bed and kindle a fire, filling the chamber with flickering light, then he undressed properly. He joined her in bed again and helped her disrobe, his hands gentle and confident with her swollen body.

He could not quite believe he had wept as he climaxed. Him! Master Elton, always so controlled, the one in charge. He did not know the meaning behind it, but he had never experienced such joy and unutterable love as he had felt at that moment, joined with his wife in sweet release. Now he felt so close to Margerie, as though he could say anything to her, do anything with her, and still be loved.

It was a wonderful and yet unsettling feeling. He would have to make love to her like that many times, he thought drily, before he grew accustomed to it.

Lying beside her again, both of them comfortably naked, Virgil buried his face in her hair. "I am going to have to attend Christina while I am here. She is still weak, but I hope her health may improve now that I have found a possible medicament for her condition."

"She is with child, do you know?" Margerie whispered.

He nodded.

"She has been so happy this summer," she whispered. "But afraid too. She fears she may die before the child can be born."

"I will do my best to avert that tragedy," he said firmly.

She stroked a slow hand across her own large belly. "Sometimes I am afraid too, Virgil. He kicks so hard some nights. What if my body does not understand its task when the time comes? What if I am not strong enough to push him out?"

"Him?" He smiled wryly, then shifted down the bed, laying his cheek against her hard belly. "Or *her*. You need not be afraid, my love. You will not be alone at the birth. The midwife will instruct you what is to be done. And I shall be there too, and help you push."

"You?"

"Do not sound so shocked," he said drily. "I am a doctor, you know. And Master Greene has given me permission to stay until you have been brought to bed. The queen's own child is not due until next month, and I have a strong feeling our child will make its appearance long before October."

She lay very still. "*Our* child?"

"*Ours*, yes."

Virgil closed his eyes, enjoying the hard warmth of her belly against his cheek almost too much to stay awake. It was a while before he spoke again, for he was drowsy and content.

"I spoke with Lord Munro before I left court, my love. He told me some rather interesting things about my wife, the *wanton*."

"Oh."

He smiled at the catch in her breath.

"I wanted to tell you the truth, Virgil, but—"

"Hush," he interrupted, wrapping an arm about her comfortably broad girth. "It was entirely my fault. I sensed there was something you had not told me, but was so afraid it would be some confession of your love for Munro, I dared not let you voice it."

"You? Afraid?"

She had sounded incredulous.

"Margerie, I may be a man and find it hard to speak my heart. But that does not mean I do not *have* a heart, nor that my feelings are not as strong as yours." He sighed. "A man has fears just as a woman does, believe me."

"Well, you need not be afraid any longer. I love you, and care for no one else. You are my husband, and your child is inside me. Nothing more is needed to complete me."

"Now that is a shame," he said lightly.

She stilled, staring at him. Her voice was small, as though he had hurt her. "How so?"

He pressed his lips to her warm skin, drowning in the feminine scent of her, like roses, like full summer. "I have a belated wedding gift for you, my love. But if you need nothing else to complete you…"

"Don't tease," she said accusingly, pouting, then snuggled into him, one hand trailing down his spine, making him growl softly under his breath. "What is this gift?"

"Blackthorn Hall in Sussex. Thirty-odd acres and a large house fit for a fine lady and her entourage. Lord Munro's fee for your, erm, *services*." He laughed as she pinched him. "Ah, cruel. But I shall not hold that against you, any more than I shall ever chastise you again for your past. It was before you consented to be my bride. Besides, I like that you have thorns, my love. It would be dull for one's wife to be all soft petals and no sharpness."

She embraced him, and he took comfort in the generosity of her love, wrapped in her softly yielding warmth and power, the kind of strength only a woman could possess. "I accept your gift. A home of my own. Will you live with me there?"

"If you wish it. I do love this old place, but perhaps it is time for a change. And with such bounty, I would not need to remain at court unless the king insisted."

"What, I may keep my husband in my bed more than a sennight at a time? Now I am indeed complete." She sighed. "Well, maybe one thing more would make my life perfect."

He raised his brows. "Your life is not perfect, my love?"

Margerie raised her head and kissed him lingeringly. "I would like another babe after this one," she whispered, and set his hand on the top of her belly.

"Oh, I think we can probably manage…"

At that instant, Virgil felt a violent thump under his palm, almost strong enough to dislodge his hand, and stopped abruptly.

He sat up and stared at her belly. "That was… What was that…?"

"Your child."

"Good God," he said blankly. Then put his hand back on the top of her belly. "Again, please."

Epilogue

IT WAS A GLORIOUS spring day, and the breeze off the river was rippling the pennants on the towers of Hampton Court Palace. A bell was tolling somewhere, signaling the noon hour, and suddenly there was a lady in the palace gateway, beautiful and stately in soft blue silks. Margerie rose from wiping a smudge of dirt from Jack's chubby face, and waited for Kate to reach her, both women smiling, arms outstretched.

"Oh, Kate, how good it is to see you again, my dear friend. I have missed you!"

"It looks like it," Kate exclaimed, laughing and holding her out at arms' length. "But let me look at you. How long to go before this one is born?"

Margerie felt herself blush. "Another six months. We thought it best not to wait, for life is so uncertain, is it not? But look at Jack. He was only a tiny baby when you came into Kent for the christening. But see he can walk now." She bit her lip as her young son stumbled, ending up on his bottom in the grass, his blue smock not quite hiding his sturdy legs. "Well, he is learning."

Kate's eyes narrowed on the necklace about her throat. "That pretty bauble does become you well, Margerie. If only one of the wealthy lords who flatter me with such lavish attentions would offer me a gift as beautiful as that." Her gaze lifted to Margerie's face. "I am surprised your husband allows you to wear it though. Considering who gave it to you."

"Oh, that is all forgotten now." Margerie put a hand to the golden rose with its single emerald heart, and smiled. "Or forgiven, at least. We are none of us perfect."

"And where is your doting husband?"

"Virgil is with my grandfather," she said, pointing along the riverbank to where Virgil stood in conversation with her elderly grandfather, whose health had improved startlingly since their visit last year. Indeed old Thomas Croft looked almost ten years younger. "I don't know what medicaments Virgil has been giving him, but my grandfather looks well on it."

"The king has demanded his return to court. Has he told you?"

Margerie nodded. "They are saying King Henry will marry this foreigner, what was her name?"

"Anne of Cleves."

"*Another* Anne?" She sighed, remembering another queen of that name. Her cruel execution had darkened the court for months. Even now her name was never mentioned, as though to do so would be unlucky. "It does not seem very auspicious."

Kate met her eyes. "It has been quiet at court since Queen Jane's death. The king has been subdued, and not cast his eyes about much for a new bride."

"Poor Queen Jane. I was so horrified when I heard she had died. And her dear little son, left without a mother." She shivered. "I find it hard to believe that King Henry has mended his ways though. He is such a lustful man, he must always have someone to warm his royal bed, even if the lady is unwilling."

"I believe His Majesty did fix his attention on young Kat Howard, but Cromwell scotched that one. He will not stand to see a Howard rise too high at court. So Anne of Cleves is to be petitioned for her hand." She shrugged. "Besides, Kat Howard is far too young for a man of his age. She is barely out of the nursery."

"Hush, have a care what you say!"

Kate smiled, kissing her on the cheek. "Never fear for me. I have a charmed life. But it is so good to see you back at court. How long will you stay?"

"Not long, I fear, so we have little time together. Though I am content enough to go, I assure you. This life at court is no longer for me, not when I have found such happiness beyond it. The king has said he will do my grandfather some honor at the feast tonight for his long service, then in a few days I shall travel into Sussex with Jack and my grandfather." She sighed. "Virgil must stay on at court, alas. But he will come down for the summer, to see how I am refurnishing the place. Blackthorn Hall will look very fine when I have finished. You must come and visit too. And bring Master Langley."

"Bring my old husband? Must I?" Kate pretended to look pained, then laughed, holding out her hand as Virgil approached. "Master Elton, I am so glad you have brought your wife back to court. We have just been talking of old times."

"Have you indeed, Mistress Langley? Then I am glad to have interrupted you before too much mischief was done." Virgil bowed over her hand, then turned politely to Margerie's grandfather. "Master Croft, permit me to introduce Mistress Langley. This lady is wife to the king's chief clerk, and your granddaughter's dearest friend at court."

Her silver-haired grandfather, looking rather sprightly in his best black doublet, bowed and doffed his cap to both ladies. He took Kate's hand and kissed it gallantly, then winked. "I trust your husband will not mind if I lead you out in the dance tonight, Mistress Langley?"

She laughed merrily, glancing sideways at Margerie. "Oh call me Kate, sir. And I'm sure my husband will neither notice nor mind. But come, Master Croft, let us walk back inside together. For I believe your granddaughter wishes to speak alone with her husband."

Kate and Master Croft walked slowly through the narrow riverside gateway into the palace, and were soon lost to sight.

Virgil scooped up his dark-haired son in his arms, hoisting him to his shoulder so he might kiss the boy. "How now, Jack?"

"So tell me, my love," Margerie murmured tenderly, watching her son and husband together. Their two heads turned to look at her as one: the same dark ironic eyes, the same mobile brow, both raised as if in query. "What kind of treatment have you been giving my grandfather since he came to stay?"

Virgil's mouth twitched. "A tonic."

"This would not happen to be the same 'tonic' you administered to His Majesty King Henry when he was in need of a male heir? The same I suspect you gave to Lord Munro, now a proud father of twin daughters?"

"It might be something similar, yes," he admitted wryly, then dodged away when she came crossly toward him. "Come, it was only the odd drop in his wine. It will do your grandfather no harm. And see, he is already back on his feet. Dancing, no less!"

"I only pray he does not dance with Kate tonight and drop dead of an apoplexy!"

"She is a *very* beautiful lady," he conceded, then grinned at her expression. "*Pax*, my love. You are the only woman for me, and well you know it."

She smiled, then looked over his shoulder at the lonely figure further along the riverbank, her dark gown blowing in the breeze, head bent as she stared into the fast-flowing current.

"Perhaps there is another woman for you, Virgil."

He turned, understanding her at once. "Yes, my mother is ill at ease, I know, and has not been sleeping well. She is still haunted by her past mistakes, though I have told her what's done is done. The only pleasure she seems to take in life is looking after Jack, and Christina's newborn babe. Indeed, I fear she has been missing the younger Delacours and their noisy household ever since we left Kent. Are you sure it was wise to invite my mother on this visit to court?"

"She lives in our house, Virgil, and yet we hardly speak to each other: she is forever in Christina's company these days."

He shrugged. "My mother does dote on babies, as you have discovered, and Christina and Humphrey have produced two children rather quicker than us."

"I'm doing my best!" she protested.

"Pray do not hurry on my account. I must admit to preferring a little space between the arrival of our offspring," he said drily, kissing her hand. He raised his gaze to hers, then lowered it meaningfully to her mouth, then to the gold and emerald necklace about her throat. "I rather like it when the two of us can be private together, my love. I am privileged to know your skills in the bedchamber, you see, unlike other men."

Her cheeks warmed under that bold look, but she continued doggedly, "Well, this is a perfect time for us to bring your mother into the family. Your mother and my grandfather. For when we all move together to Blackthorn Hall, I will need her more than ever." He frowned at that, and she watched him with sudden compassion, knowing how difficult he still found it to talk to his mother about the past. "Someone must be there for little Jack when it is time for my confinement, to comfort him and play with him. You are so often at court, after all."

He put Jack down and watched the little boy toddle precariously toward his grandmother, calling out to her in his piping voice. Mistress Tulkey turned at once, her face breaking into a smile, and bent to speak to the child.

"I will be there for the birth, Margerie," Virgil promised her, "even if I have to drug the king to escape his royal demands." He took her in his arms. "I was there for Jack's birth, and I will be there for this child's too. I am your physician and I swear it."

Oh, but she loved him so much. Her heart ached with love, she was overflowing with it. "Then if you have sworn to it, I believe you *will* be there," she said simply.

He looked at her mouth, and hunger was there in his eyes, undiminished by time and her thickening waistline. His hands slipped up from her waist to rest just below her breasts, and she caught her breath, wanting him again. The silken threads of her bodice were so thin, she could feel the warmth of his fingers there, pressing into her.

"Do you think there might be time," Virgil murmured, smiling lazily into her eyes, "later this afternoon, for us to slip away together before the feast?"

She was breathing hard, her gaze locked with his. "If not, I shall have to make time."

"You make time as well as you make babies, my love," he commented idly. Cupping her full breasts through the silken bodice, he rubbed his thumbs over both nipples at once. Her nipples tautened, clearly visible through the silk, and his eyes narrowed on them, suddenly intent. "My beautiful Margerie. You are at your best when you are with child. But how I miss your old bouts of sleepwalking. If only you had not been cured of that strange disorder. How did I manage that, by the way?"

"By loving me," she whispered.

"That's it. An arduous task, but one I have embraced as my husbandly duty. Though some nights I wish you would wander in your sleep again. I did so love to play with your delectable body while you were dreaming and unaware—"

"Why, you...!"

Virgil grinned, catching her hand before she could slap him. "Rough play? Not while my mother is watching, dearest. Though if you wish to obey *me* later, I will be happy to oblige and play master."

She bit her lip, trying not to laugh. "Listen, you must speak to your mother properly, Virgil. This silence has gone on long enough. It is time."

She understood the wariness in his face. He feared reliving the horrors of his childhood, and what demons that might bring back into his heart. Demons they had chased away together with love. But his mother was growing old, and Virgil would regret it forever if she died before he could steel himself to open his heart to her. She could not allow that to happen.

"Must I?" His eyes were dark with pain, but he bent and kissed her mouth passionately, then rested his cheek against hers. "I have not yet forgotten, you see," he whispered into her ear.

"You never will, my love, I assure you. But perhaps…you may be able to forgive?"

With an effort, Virgil nodded.

"Come then, sir, and let us both be healed." Margerie linked her hand with Virgil's, lacing their fingers tight, and smiled at her doctor husband. "Together."

About the Author

Elizabeth Moss was born into a literary family in Essex, and currently lives in the southwest of England with her husband and young family. She also writes commercial fiction as Victoria Lamb, Beth Good, and Jane Holland. For more information about her, visit her blog at www.elizabethmossfiction.com.

Wolf Bride

Lust in the Tudor Court

by Elizabeth Moss

Bound to him against her will...

Lord Wolf, hardened soldier and expert lover, has come to King Henry VIII's court to claim his new bride: a girl who has intrigued him since he first saw her riding across the Yorkshire moors.

Eloise Tyrell, now lady-in-waiting to Queen Anne Boleyn, has other ideas. She has no desire to submit to a man she barely knows and who—though she is loath to admit it—frightens her more than a little.

Their first kiss awakens in both a fierce desire that bares them to the soul. But as the court erupts into scandal around the ill-fated queen, Eloise sees first-hand what happens when powerful men tire of their wives...

"Fifty Shades of Tudor sex!" —*The Sunday Times*

"Full of sexual tension and political intrigue...a terrific historical romance." —*RT Book Reviews*

For more Elizabeth Moss, visit:

www.sourcebooks.com

Rebel Bride

Lust in the Tudor Court

by Elizabeth Moss

He is under her spell...

Hugh Beaufort, favored courtier of King Henry VIII, likes his women quiet and biddable. But Susannah Tyrell is neither of these things. She is feisty, beautiful, opinionated, and brave. And Hugh is fascinated by her—despite himself.

When Susannah pulls an outrageous stunt and finds herself lost in the wilds of England, Hugh must go to her rescue. Neither of them is prepared for the dangers that lie in wait. But most deadly of all is their forbidden desire for one another. Hugh has long held himself in check, but even his iron will has its limits as they remain alone together in the forest, far from the restraints of court...

"Descriptive, sensuous, and romantic." —*RT Book Reviews*, 4 Stars

For more Elizabeth Moss, visit:

www.sourcebooks.com

Playing Doctor

Meeting Men

by Kate Allure

Three sizzling-hot stories to make your heart race

In *The Intern*, the temperature of Dr. Lauren Marks's office quickly rises when her new medical intern Courtney turns out to be a passionate and sexy young man.

Valerie realizes all of her fantasies when her sexy surgeon and her loving husband team up to offer her some extra-special treatment in *My Doctor, My Husband, and Me*.

Nikki gets more than she bargained for in *Seize the Doctor* when the hot guy she recently met at a bar walks into her exam room wearing a white coat. Good thing she wore her sexiest lingerie.

The doctor will see you now...

"This trio of hot and steamy tales is escapism of the richest, most decadent variety." —*RT Book Reviews*

"Three sensational reads that will have readers panting..." —*The Book Enthusiast*

For more Kate Allure, visit:

www.sourcebooks.com

Lawyer Up

Meeting Men

by Kate Allure

Three sizzling stories so steamy they should be illegal

Wrongly accused in *Attorney-Client Privileges*, sexy but innocent Beth has nowhere to turn but straight into the arms of her hotshot LA lawyer, Jon. Can this attorney manage to get her off in time?

Liza reaches a meeting of the minds—and more—when she unleashes her inhibitions and gives herself over to the primal allure of Main Street lawyer Hawk in *Of Unsound Mind and Body*.

In *Of Writs and Writhing*, fearless defense attorney Pat gets more than she bargained for when she goes toe-to-toe with New Orleans's infamous Playboy Judge. When things get heated both in and out of the courtroom, more than temperatures rise.

Praise for *Lawyer Up*:

"The sensuality and sexuality are palpable."
—*RT Book Reviews*, 4 Stars

"Intense chemistry, great characterization, and a…page-singeing ending will have readers clamoring for more." —*Publishers Weekly*

For more Kate Allure, visit:

www.sourcebooks.com